Joshua's
MISSION

Books by Vannetta Chapman

PLAIN AND SIMPLE MIRACLES

Brian's Choice
(ebook-only novella prequel)

Anna's Healing

Joshua's Mission

THE PEBBLE CREEK AMISH SERIES

A Promise for Miriam

A Home for Lydia

A Wedding for Julia

"Home to Pebble Creek"
(free short story e-romance)

"Christmas at Pebble Creek"
(free short story e-romance)

Joshua's MISSION

VANNETTA CHAPMAN

HARVEST HOUSE PUBLISHERS
EUGENE, OREGON

Cover by Koechel Peterson & Associates, Minneapolis, Minnesota

Cover photos © Shutterstock; Wikimedia; KsC Photography

This is a work of fiction. Names, characters, places, and incidents are products of the author's imagination or are used fictitiously. Any resemblance to actual persons, living or dead, is entirely coincidental.

JOSHUA'S MISSION
Copyright © 2016 by Vannetta Chapman
Published by Harvest House Publishers
Eugene, Oregon 97402
www.harvesthousepublishers.com

Library of Congress Cataloging-in-Publication Data
Chapman, Vannetta.
Joshua's mission / Vannetta Chapman.
    pages ; cm.—(Plain and simple miracles series ; Book 2)
ISBN 978-0-7369-5605-5 (pbk.)
ISBN 978-0-7369-5606-2 (eBook)
I. Title.
PS3603.H3744J67 2016
813'.6—dc23
                                                                                                    2015021165

Printed in the United States of America

        15 16 17 18 19 20 21 22 23 24 / LB-CD / 10 9 8 7 6 5 4 3 2 1

For my friends,
Janet and Ed Murphy

Acknowledgments

This book is dedicated to Janet and Ed Murphy. They graciously provided us with a place to stay on Mustang Island and readily answered my questions regarding the area. Janet and Ed possess an obvious love for the area and a gracious, giving spirit. On top of all of that, they love my dog. They have been a true blessing to me, and they helped to make this novel a better piece of writing than it otherwise would have been.

I'd also like to thank the folks at Mennonite Disaster Services who answered my questions. Although I made every effort to remain true to the way they conduct mission work, I allowed myself literary license where it was necessary for the progression of the story. Cameron Pratt with the Port Aransas Museum was very helpful. Charles Crawford also took the time to meet with me, and he was the inspiration for the character Charlie Everman. Thank you to Bill and Connie Voight for the use of their dog, Quitz. And thanks to Bill and Ann Rogers for the use of their names.

My prereaders Kristy and Janet rock. True friendship is always a gift, and I appreciate both of these ladies and their commitment to quality fiction. I owe a debt of gratitude to my family and friends who encourage me as I work to share God's grace through stories. Two agents were instrumental in the release of this book—Mary Sue Seymour, who helped me to place the project, and Steve Laube, who has been with me through its production and release. The wonderful staff at Harvest House deserve an acknowledgment page all their own.

I again would like to express my gratitude to the Amish communities in Oklahoma who were kind and welcoming and showed graciousness to me. If you find yourself near Tulsa, drive east on US-412 for forty minutes until you find the small community of Chouteau—my inspiration for Cody's Creek. And if you're ever in south Texas, stop by Mustang Island and enjoy one of God's places of respite and peace.

And finally…always giving thanks to God the Father for everything, in the name of our Lord Jesus Christ (Ephesians 5:20).

Truly I tell you, whatever you did for one of the least of these brothers and sisters of mine, you did for me.

~MATTHEW 25:40

If you can't feed a hundred people, then feed just one.

~MOTHER TERESA

CHAPTER 1

Port Aransas, Texas
October 5

Charlie Everman walked along the beach, his heart heavy with the memory of the things he'd lost. Waves crashed against the sand, causing his black Labrador to jump back and then dart forward. Seagulls cried overhead. The last of the day's light lingered on the horizon as the night nudged the final rays from the beach. The beaches of Mustang Island stretched eighteen miles, from Port Aransas at the northeastern tip to Padre Island via a roadway at the southwest. That end of the island also connected to Corpus Christi via the John F. Kennedy Memorial Causeway Bridge. Charlie preferred the solitude and quiet of Mustang Island. He always had.

"Fetch, girl." Charlie threw the stick, and Quitz plunged into the water. For a moment she looked like the pup she had been when Charlie had found her eleven years ago—found her under an abandoned shack on the bay side. Quitz was back at Charlie's side in seconds. Over the years, he'd bought the dog all manner of toys, but Quitz preferred a simple piece of driftwood. Go figure.

"Good, girl."

He patted the lab on her head, which was all the reward that Quitz needed. They continued down the beach, side by side, neither feeling the need to break the evening's quiet. The dog would slow occasionally to sniff some fish or shell or garbage washed ashore. Charlie would pause now and again to study a ship in the distance.

The waves continued their march inland as they had since the beginning of time, but Charlie could only testify to the last forty-five years. He'd moved to the town of Port Aransas when he was twenty-two and newly married to his high school sweetheart, Madelyn. His younger self had been impossibly naive, still expecting each day to bring a miracle. And many of them had, but then there had also been days black with pain.

Saltwater splashed across his foot, drawing him back to the present. The smell of ocean spray filled the air. A breeze tickled the hair at his neck. Moonlight bounced off water.

Somewhere close by, a crane cried out before plunging into the water, searching for fish.

It was easy enough to love Port Aransas—Port A, as the locals called it. Charlie was now considered among that group. And love it he did when he looked toward the gulf, but his feelings were harder to define when he turned inland. Behind him buildings rose daily, or so it seemed. Monstrosities. Condos that cost upward of three hundred and fifty thousand dollars, and homes that easily sold for more than a million. Structures that looked to him like great shipwrecks. The development along the beachfront bothered him, but Charlie understood that the condominiums provided much-needed jobs for many of the people in Port Aransas, and the additional tax base helped the local economy.

The truth was that the world had moved on, as his wife Madelyn had often reminded him. At sixty-five, Charlie was feeling the difference—the gulf between himself and others. This area, the very town where he had become a man, now felt like a foreign land. And most of his neighbors were strangers. Maybe that was true everywhere.

Did people even know one another anymore? He watched them at the diner—eyes glued to their cell phones, not bothering to speak to the person sitting across from them. Often not bothering to raise their eyes to the gulf waters outside the window. Folks said the new generation of teens was disconnected from one another, but to Charlie it seemed they were merely following the example of their parents. The whole world had come apart, and each person was a little island floating in a sea of technology.

These things bothered Charlie. They pricked at his soul like a splinter that was too deep to be removed. Suddenly he thought of Alice, a waitress who worked at the Shack. She was old enough to be his daughter, or nearly so. There was a span of seventeen years between them. Though he and Madelyn had no children, he often found himself thinking of Alice that way and viewed her grandkids as his own. He liked to think that if he and Madelyn had raised a daughter she would have turned out like Alice—hardworking and honest.

Charlie ate at the Shack regularly. Usually Alice patted him on the shoulder as she scooped up the money he'd left on the table, including a generous tip because—well, because he knew how hard she worked and that the tips in a small way helped with the raising of her grandchildren. She'd provided those grandkids a home for the last several years. Some families managed to squeeze three generations into the period usually occupied by two. Alice's family had done just that. When her daughter visited the island and announced she was taking a job overseas, one where she could "find herself," Alice stepped into the role of parent without hesitation.

Charlie wished he could help more, but he couldn't—retired teachers made very little. So he left the tips and made sure to eat at the diner at least three times a week. That's what friends did. They watched out for one another.

The beaches were open to horse riding, bicycling, and even street vehicles. A car filled with college-aged kids passed him, driving slowly down the hard-packed sand. Music and laughter spilled out into the night. They didn't honk or acknowledge him in any way. For all Charlie knew, he'd become invisible.

"Don't sulk," Madelyn would have said. She'd peer over her glasses and point whatever was in her hand his way—usually a crochet hook or a pen or maybe a bookmark. "The world doesn't stand still, Charlie. And you wouldn't want it to."

A cloud drifted in front of the moon. When it had passed, Charlie stopped to study the sky. Hurricane Orion was out there, churning, gathering strength from the warm waters of the gulf. There was only a forty-percent chance it would head their way—or so the computer models said. Charlie looked for signs in the surf and the sand, but he wasn't a weatherman. He couldn't tell what would happen in the next six hours or six days.

Quitz pressed against his side, no doubt wondering why they had stopped.

Most of the time Madelyn was right, but not always. Would he wish for time to stand still?

He might. Given a choice, he could easily opt for the world to stop turning, for life to simply freeze on a moment, for nothing at all to ever change.

He wouldn't pick this day, but they'd had a fair supply of good ones. He wouldn't have any trouble choosing one—perhaps ten years earlier before they had ever heard the diagnosis of breast cancer. When Quitz was still a young pup and less of the coastline was covered in condos. Arthritis wouldn't cause his knee to ache, Quitz wouldn't have trouble standing in the morning, and Madelyn—well, Madelyn would still be by his side.

A child's wish.

He understood too well that the world would keep moving, keep trudging forward. God had His reasons, and who was Charlie to question the Almighty? As to the fate of Port Aransas, the hurricane either would come or it wouldn't. He supposed there wasn't much he could do either way. The little community had blossomed into a vacationer's paradise. It wasn't his idea of a perfect place, not anymore, but then no one had asked him.

His mind drifted back over his memories of 1970, Hurricane Celia, and the aftermath of that beastly storm. They had suffered through it together—as a town, as a community. Each family's loss had affected others, and they had done their best to help one another rebuild. Out of that terrible storm had come some of the worst memories and best friendships of Charlie's life.

And though many of those fine people had remained his friends, most had moved away now—to golf course homes and senior communities. They had sold out, and Charlie didn't blame them one bit. Perhaps he should consider doing the same. There wasn't a month that went by when someone didn't offer him an enormous amount of money for the three acres of ocean frontage he'd bought all those years ago.

Quitz whined as they turned toward home. The old dog would continue down the beach until she could no longer walk if Charlie let her.

"Maybe I'm the one who's tired," Charlie said, and then he reached down and scratched behind the dog's black floppy ears.

Glancing at the sky once more, he peered into the darkness but could see little. The steady roll of waves crashing provided a background to his world, his life, that he couldn't imagine living without. Move? Not likely. He would stay as long as God saw fit to allow him a home there.

His thoughts turned back to Hurricane Orion as he trudged through the sand. Where did the meteorologists get these names? Orion, indeed. He'd looked it up. The name meant *fiery hunter*. How could a hurricane be that? He'd been an English teacher for forty years, but if that was some weatherman's idea of symbolism, it made no sense.

Madelyn had enjoyed astronomy. She'd loved quoting verses out of the Book of Job from the Old Testament. She especially liked the parts that mentioned the stars and nature and God's omnipotence.

Orion. Charlie supposed a hurricane could look beautiful when seen from a satellite—those great white swirls that covered miles upon miles of sea and sometimes land. Perhaps a hurricane could be a hunter, though it seemed to him more like a beast.

He thought of *Beowulf*, a text his high school seniors had

sometimes struggled with, but ultimately they had enjoyed the tale of the hero, the monster, and the tragic aftermath. It had appealed to their teenage sensibilities. Charlie hadn't been in a classroom in three years, but he still missed it.

Hurricane Orion sounded ominous. If tragedy were to strike, Charlie didn't think the community would withstand it. Oh, maybe the insurance companies would pay and the people would rebuild, but it wouldn't be Port A anymore. The people wouldn't grow closer because of it. Those days were gone now. The world had, indeed, moved on.

As he walked back toward home, the clouds parted and the moon again cast its spotlight on the water.

CHAPTER 2

Cody's Creek, Oklahoma

Joshua Kline heard the pebbles hitting the window near his bed, but he ignored them. At twenty-seven he might be in the prime of his life, but farming was hard work and he longed for more sleep. He turned over, covered his head with the pillow, and attempted to fall back into his dreams. The onslaught continued. Finally, he sat up and glanced at his brother's bed—empty. No surprise there.

Groaning, he pushed away the covers and walked to the window, heaving it open at the same time he warned, "Hit me with one of those pebbles, Alton, and you'll be doing extra chores for a week."

"You're not my *dat*, you know."

"Then why are you waking me?"

Moonlight spread shadows across the front yard of their parents' two-story house. Like most Amish homes, it was a rambling structure, having been added to as needed. All of the bedrooms were upstairs. Joshua and Alton shared the room at the front of the house. His parents slept at the back. Four sisters occupied the two rooms in between.

Alton ducked his head, a familiar gesture when he was about to confess to something. "I need your help. Can't you just come down?"

His words slurred slightly, and he stumbled when he craned his neck back to look up at Joshua. Had he been drinking again? Or was he merely sleep deprived? His brother had recently turned seventeen, and he appeared intent on fully embracing his *rumspringa*. Joshua thought that time of testing, of trying *Englisch* ways, was merely an excuse for bad behavior, but then he'd always been the more serious of the two boys—the more responsible. He'd heard it all his life, and he'd come to believe it.

So was Alton sleepy or drunk? Either way, it was best Joshua dealt with the problem. His father had enough on his agenda the next day with the harvest and the cranky tractor that required constant tending. It would be selfish to wake him if it was something Joshua could handle. He dressed quickly and crept quietly down the stairs.

As soon as Joshua joined him on the front lawn, Alton wrapped an arm around his neck. The smell of wine caused Joshua to step back. He didn't reprimand his brother. That would have been a waste of words. Instead he growled, "What's the problem this time?"

"A little spell, I mean spill, with the truck. I was hoping you could bring the tractor. Help a brother out."

Joshua escaped his brother's drunken embrace and walked three steps away. Then he turned and studied him in the moonlight. "You want help?"

"Pull me from the ditch with the tractor."

"You could have done that yourself."

"It's a bit more complicated than that."

"Why am I not surprised?" Joshua shook his head and weighed his options. If he didn't help Alton, his parents would have to do so and the coming day would be busy enough. They had fifteen acres of corn to be harvested, followed the next week by twenty-two acres of soybeans. The sorghum, their largest crop at sixty-two acres, would be harvested last. Then the planting of winter wheat would begin. It was a busy time for farmers, and his father didn't need this latest situation with Alton complicating things.

"The tractor will wake everyone. Best to take Blaze." Of the two workhorses, he was the easiest to control. Percherons in general did well behind a plow but were less predictable in strange situations. He could count on Blaze to remain calm and follow instructions. Plus, the gelding could use the exercise.

Too much of their work was being done by the tractor now. He'd even heard his parents talk of selling the two workhorses, but Joshua was fairly certain they wouldn't do it. Selling Blaze and Milo would be akin to selling the family pets. Everyone knew their blue heeler, imaginatively named Blue, wasn't going anywhere. Joshua's gut told him neither were the Percherons.

"Splash some water on your face while I get Blaze. Maybe it will help you sober up."

"*Gut* idea." Alton said, but instead of walking toward the barn, he sprawled onto the porch stairs. "I just need to close my eyes for a minute—"

"Oh, no you don't, little *bruder*." Joshua had him by the shirt collar before Alton realized what was happening. He yanked him to his feet and gave him a shove in the direction of the barn. "You created this mess, whatever it is. You are not sleeping through it."

"All right. All right. You don't have to be so pushy."

But Alton was grinning, which in Joshua's opinion was part of the problem. His brother didn't take the trouble he fell into seriously. Why should he? They were constantly bailing him out. If he didn't straighten up soon, he'd find himself knee-deep in something he couldn't get out of. If he didn't change his ways, Bishop Levi was bound to become involved. The man was patient but not stupid. He was looking the other way because an Amish teen's *rumspringa* was ignored whenever possible, but when someone could get hurt, or when the *Englisch* police became involved, Levi was quick to intercede.

To Joshua's way of thinking, they were past the point where Levi should become involved. Perhaps he would talk to the bishop. Was it his place to do so? He wasn't perfect, and he'd had his share of rebellion—though it focused mainly on fishing and a little travel. He'd never owned a car, though he had driven a truck for a time—a job he was glad he no longer needed. He'd tried alcohol only once and hated the taste of the stuff. He certainly didn't step out with any *Englisch* girls.

"What's so funny, *bruder*?"

They were walking the horse down the dirt lane. Rather, Joshua was walking. Alton was stumbling. The moon cast enough of a glow for them to see their way. The light allowed Joshua to make out his brother's silhouette. Alton was still gangly. His hands and feet often seemed too large, causing him to be clumsy. The same height as Joshua, just shy of six feet, his frame was a bit too thin. His too-long blond hair flopped constantly into his eyes. Just the day before their mother had reminded him to come home early so she could cut it, but apparently other activities had kept Alton occupied until the wee hours of the morning.

"I can practicing, I mean practically, hear the gears in your brain turning."

"I was thinking about how different we are."

"You are half as good looking but twice as bright. Isn't that what *Mammi* used to say?"

Their grandmother had passed the previous spring, and Joshua missed her still. They turned onto the two-lane blacktop road fronting their property.

When he didn't answer, Alton said, "You might as well lecture me now. I know you're going to do it sooner or slater—I mean later." He covered his mouth as the laughter threatened to bubble out.

"And what *gut* would that do?"

Alton stumbled, but regained his balance before falling. "None at all! But it's your duty as the oldest son."

"Hardly."

Alton made a gagging sound, covered his mouth with his hand, and ran to the side of the road, vomiting into the ditch. Joshua didn't bother waiting on him. Five minutes later his brother had caught up and resumed their conversation as if nothing had happened.

"I was only seven when you were my age. I barely remember your *rumspringa*."

"That's because there's nothing to remember."

"*Ya?* The older boys still tell stories about the fishing boat and your attempt to pull it to Samuel Schwartz's pond."

"I did pull it to Samuel's pond, and I shared the catch with him too."

"But you wrecked the tractor in the progress." Alton hiccupped. "I mean process."

To Joshua, those times seemed so far in the distant past as to be ancient history.

"You wrecked it coming home when the boat—" He put his hands together in front of him and mimicked a fish swimming through water. "Swerved off the road."

"I did."

"How long did it take you to earn enough to pay for the repairs?"

"All of my extra money for two years. I got off light. Someone could have been hurt. I should have never attempted to drive back in the dark."

"So you're not perfect."

"Never claimed to be." They had reached the place where the two-lane met the larger four-lane road. The moon was quickly setting, but Joshua could see well enough. His brother's truck sat nose down in the water that filled the ditch.

"It'll be dawn soon. Best do this as quickly as possible."

He made sure that Alton was the one standing in the water and hooking up the chain they had brought. He attached it to the rear bumper of the Ford. Joshua had fitted the horse collar harness on to Blaze before leaving the barn. With it, the horse could pull a sleigh filled with people or a truck from a ditch. Joshua stood by the horse, murmuring to him, promising him a nice bucket of oats when they returned.

"Easy, Blaze. Forward, now. Forward. That's *gut.*"

Some would be surprised that the horse could pull the truck, but Blaze weighed in at nineteen hundred pounds and stood seventeen hands high. He was a beauty all right, and the truck was no problem for him.

A splash and groan told Joshua that his brother had slipped and fallen. He resisted the urge to laugh, but the sight of Alton climbing out of the ditch, trailing water and mud, filled his heart with hope. Perhaps the bishop wouldn't be needed. It was possible that God would see to his brother's training.

CHAPTER 3

*B*ecca Troyer stepped out onto the front porch of her parents' home. Her grandfather was the local bishop, and her father was the only ferrier for their small community. The property he'd purchased on moving to Cody's Creek was shallow but wide—resembling a rectangle with the longer side fronting the two-lane road. Less than ten acres, it provided ample space to corral the horses that were left in his care and still enough land remained for the family garden, which was large by *Englisch* standards but small compared to many Amish plots. Because they only had three to feed—Becca was a rare only child in an Amish community—the small garden was perfect.

She'd stepped outside to watch the sun come up. It was something she usually did with her *mamm*, but this morning her mother was busy in the kitchen, preparing both breakfast and lunch for her father. A sew-in was scheduled for later in the day, and her father had declared he'd rather eat in the barn than fall into a bevy of chattering women. Suzie had laughed at that, reminding him that they worked while they chattered.

Becca's parents were like that—easily teasing one another, smiling, even occasionally kissing when they thought Becca wouldn't see. She liked that they liked one another. It gave her a sense of solidness, as if the foundation of their home was something that couldn't be shaken. She didn't know if she'd ever find love like that, but at twenty she realized it was ridiculous to worry about such things. Though in an Amish community, twenty was no spring chicken.

Becca laughed at that idea as she watched the sun slowly rise over their little farm. Two mares stood at the fence, watching her, no doubt wondering if she was going to bring them a treat. The old tabby barn cat made its way slowly across the drive and wound between her legs. Yes, the day looked nearly perfect, and the morning sew-in would be a welcome break from their regular chores. She found herself looking forward to the chance to visit with the other women.

But she needed this time of peace and reflection. The quiet mornings watching the sun rise seemed like a way to ground herself for whatever the day might hold. She'd been watching the sun come up from their front porch since she was a small child, cuddled against her mother's side. Her mother had shaped her life with a wise hand. Her father had provided the love and guidance she'd needed. Yes, Becca counted herself blessed. So why was she sometimes restless? Why couldn't she be satisfied with the life she had?

The sun peeked over the horizon, dispersing a virtual palette of colors—tangerine, rose, magenta, and lilac. Becca's mother was an artist—a painter, to be exact. Becca had grown up asking for the slate crayon from her box instead of the blue-gray one. She'd absorbed her mother's love of color, although she had no artistic ability herself unless you counted the flower garden bordering the front of her parents' house or the quilting she did only marginally well.

Now she sat on the front porch steps, enjoying the warmth of the coffee mug in her hands, the smell of the roses near the steps, and the miracle of another sunrise in front of her. And that was when she saw Joshua Kline leading a workhorse down the lane, followed by someone driving a battered Ford pickup. The sight might appear incongruous to someone not from their area. For Becca it was typical of what she'd come to expect of Cody's Creek. She could suddenly envision how her mother would paint it, and she had to press her fingers to her lips to stifle her laughter.

At that moment, Joshua's horse headed toward the side of the road, having apparently spied something that looked eatable.

"Whoa, Blaze. Let's go, boy. This way."

The large horse ignored Joshua and began cropping at the roadside weeds. Becca set her coffee on the porch and popped into the house.

"Something wrong?" her *mamm* asked.

"*Nein*. Well, I don't have a problem, but it seems Joshua does."

Her mother had been at the table making sandwiches for her father's lunch. Suzie stood and walked to the window, a wistful sigh coming from her lips. "That would make a wonderful picture, wouldn't it, dear? With the dawn splashing across the road…" She shook her head and returned to the table. "Some pictures are meant to be remembered but not actually painted. On the other hand, your father will need lunch while we're busy sewing."

"It's a fine-looking horse."

"Indeed, but I'm not sure boys today know how to handle them, especially our boys, who are more used to tractors. And why is a pickup idling behind him?"

"I have no idea, but hopefully this will help to move the horse." Becca chose a green apple from the fruit bowl.

"Your *dat* is in the back pasture feeding the guest horses."

The term *guest horses* always struck Becca as funny, as if they ran a bed-and-breakfast for the four-legged creatures.

"Would you like me to call him?"

"I don't think so." Becca walked out of the kitchen wishing she had taken the time to comb her hair properly when she'd first awoke. Too often, that was the last thing Becca thought of. She snagged a prayer *kapp* from her room, hastily tucked her brown curls up into it, and hurried out the front door. Her heart was racing and her palms were sweaty, but neither slowed her down.

Joshua was still trying to coax the horse away from the fence, and now he was joined by his brother, Alton, who apparently had been driving the truck.

"Problem?"

"The night has been full of them." Joshua shot a displeased look at his brother.

"Morning, Becca." Alton forgot the horse and walked over to join her. "You're looking awfully pretty this morning."

Becca didn't respond to that. She had no idea what to say. She was a mess and knew it. However, she did notice that Joshua was watching the two of them closely, as if to see how she would answer his brother's teasing. His expression cemented into a frown as he continued murmuring to the horse.

"A horse and a truck. You two must have big plans for the day."

"No plans, Becca. Unless you'd be interested in going to town with me—"

"Actually, we're helping *Dat* harvest the corn crop today."

"I don't know how much help I'll be with that." Alton scratched his jaw. "I haven't slept a wink all night. Had a little too much to drink, but I'm okay to drive. My *bruder* saw that I was sobered up good and proper before he allowed me to climb behind the wheel."

"Falling into a creek can do that for a person," Becca said, eyeing his wet clothes and dirty hair. Even covered in mud, Alton Kline was a good-looking young man. He was also still a child at heart. At least that was how she thought of him.

"If you're tired, we both know whose fault that is."

"I'll admit to that."

"Well, that's big of you."

"Excuse my *bruder*'s bad temperament."

"My temperament is bad because of you."

"He tends toward cranky in the morning."

"Maybe I am, which is understandable since you woke me up in the middle of the night."

Listening to the conversation between the two, it wasn't difficult for Becca to figure out what had happened. Mud was splattered across the front of the truck, the horse was wearing a pulling collar, and there was a muddy ditch a quarter mile down the road. As for Alton, it was well known that he was indulging his *rumspringa*.

Joshua? Well, he was the responsible one, or at least he had been as long as Becca had known him, which was all of her life. He had finished his last year of school when Becca was enjoying her first. Their paths only crossed at church and social gatherings. When they did, it seemed that Joshua had very little to say. Did he think of her as a child? Maybe as a younger sibling? How could she change his opinion of her? What did she need to do so that he would notice her?

"Perhaps this will help you with the horse." She pulled the apple from her apron pocket, walked to Joshua, and dropped it in his hand.

"*Ya*. Maybe so," he said, glancing away from her as if he were confused.

The horse was a beautiful black gelding—a Percheron with a splash of white between his eyes in the shape of a lightning rod. Blaze. That was his name. Her *dat* had reshod him a few months ago.

Joshua placed the shiny apple under the horse's nose, and then he jerked it away when the beast showed interest. The game was on, Joshua walking quickly away with the apple in his pocket, Blaze following eagerly.

"*Gut* thinking," Joshua called out.

"What my *bruder* meant to say was *danki*." Alton walked around to the idling truck, but before he slipped inside he said, "If you change your mind about going to town with me, give me a call. You have my cell number, right?"

Instead of answering, Becca waved goodbye. She didn't have Alton's number, and she wouldn't be calling him even if she did. For one thing, it would necessitate a walk to the phone shack because she didn't have a cell phone of her own. Second, it seemed rather a forward thing to do. So instead of answering, she walked back toward the house.

The Kline brothers had stolen her quiet morning and interrupted her moments of reflection, but she didn't mind so much. It wasn't every day that she saw two eligible Amish bachelors stalled in front of her home with a Ford pickup and a giant Percheron. Perhaps her mother would paint it after all. No doubt it was a scene the *Englischers* who purchased her art would enjoy.

As she walked back into the kitchen, she wondered if her mother guessed that Becca felt a thrill of excitement whenever her path crossed with that of the Kline brothers. Probably. Her mother knew her well and seemed to understand even those things they didn't talk about. Chances were that her mother had even been able to guess which boy had caught Becca's eye and captured her heart.

CHAPTER 4

*C*harlie slipped into his usual booth at the diner, one near the front windows that allowed him a view of the water. A crack in the vinyl seat had been covered with duct tape, but the table was clean, the coffee hot, and the food delicious. The walls were adorned with fishing pictures. Several were of students he had taught over the years. Some stood beside giant tarpon, others with large catches of trout and flounder. A girl posed next to an eighty-pound redfish, and a boy— one who had written an excellent paper on Shakespeare—had landed a good-sized shark.

Word had it that Orion was churning up the waters in the gulf, bringing in even bigger fish in unheard of numbers.

"Chances are up to fifty percent." Alice filled his coffee mug, worry marking a *v* between her eyes.

She was nearing fifty, which showed in the wrinkles around her eyes and the gray in her short, dark brown hair. Tending toward the heavy side, she always wore a freshly ironed apron over jeans and a T-shirt, bringing with her the smell of laundry detergent and good food. She didn't seem to mind standing on her feet for her entire shift and carrying armloads of plates laden with food. Alice had the energy of someone much younger and a pleasant attitude to boot.

He glanced at her before turning his gaze back out the window. "Looks the same."

"Sort of like heartbreak. You can't see it coming until it hits you." Alice laughed, a sound incongruous with her statement. She'd been dating one of the oil rig workers but had recently found out he had one girl in Corpus Christi and another in Rockport, plus the time he spent with her. Though she laughed at herself for acting like a "love-sick pup"—her words, not his—Charlie had the feeling the betrayal had hurt her more than she was admitting.

"We'll have plenty of warning if it does head this way." Charlie sipped his coffee and nodded toward her order pad. "The usual is fine."

"You got it." She touched his shoulder before she walked away. Because she needed to drop the grandkids off at school, her shift at the diner didn't start until eight. Charlie usually had coffee and a granola bar when he first got up. By the time he reached the diner at 8:30, he felt as if he were eating an early lunch.

As he savored the coffee, he listened to the conversations around him, most of which centered around the approaching storm. The men in the booth behind him discussed whether corporations would be pulling employees off the oil rigs. There were more than seven hundred active platforms in the gulf. British Petroleum alone employed more than two thousand men. The decision to shut them down and pull everyone in wouldn't be made lightly. It also wouldn't be made until the last possible moment.

As he was finishing his breakfast of eggs, bacon, and toast, Dirk Baker stopped by his table. "We're headed out for some fishing. Interested in tagging along, Mr. Everman?"

Dirk had been one of Charlie's students more than ten years ago. He was a man now, with a family and a job on the rigs. At six feet two inches, he was a hard worker, evidenced by the calluses across his palms when they shook hands and the fact that the years hadn't added much weight to his lanky frame.

"Guess I'll pass. How long are you on the island?"

"Another ten days, unless Orion hits." A smile tugged at the corner of Dirk's lips. "The boys and I have a pot started on *if* or *when* the storm will hit. Five dollars for a half hour slot."

Charlie wasn't surprised. Dirk had been suspended more than once for running similar betting brackets. The kid would gamble on anything, not bothering to limit himself to sports events. He'd once convinced more than fifty students to bet on when the health education teacher would deliver her baby.

"How would I collect my winnings if I choose the exact half hour when the hurricane hits?"

Dirk pulled down on his ball cap. "We'll all be over at Corpus in that case. You can find me at the Rusty Hinge."

The Rusty Hinge was one of the oldest and best burger joints on the mainland. The food was great, but the name spoke to the decor, which was in dire need of updating.

"And if I bet it's going to miss us and it does miss us?"

"We'll split the pot between all the naysayers."

"Which is everyone," one of his buddies called from the door.

"Think on it, Mr. Everman. You always were good with predicting stuff."

Alice stopped to refill his coffee cup as the group trooped out to their trucks. "Those fellas make me nervous. You shouldn't bet on tragedy."

"Don't worry about them. They're still boys at heart, and sometimes it shows."

Alice's gaze traveled up and down the booths in the diner—most were either empty or held folks nursing a mug of coffee after consuming the typical egg-and-bacon fare. Alice glanced at the clock, and then she decided to take advantage of the usual lull before the midmorning crowd arrived. With a sigh she scooted into the booth across from Charlie, dropping the rag she always carried onto the table top and setting the pot of coffee on it.

"I've never experienced a hurricane before. The mere thought of it terrifies me."

"And yet you live on a barrier island."

"Yes, and I realized when I moved here that hurricanes were a possibility. But you never believe it will happen."

Charlie didn't know what to say to that, so he sipped his coffee and studied his friend. She was worried about more than the storm or herself. He had no doubt that her grandchildren, C.J. and Shelley, were on her mind.

"The kids will be fine, Alice. If the hurricane does head this way, we'll have them off the island before it gets close."

"Yeah, but the thing is...they've finally settled down." She turned the pot of coffee left and then right. "They're both beginning to think of the island as home. Shelley doesn't cry herself to sleep anymore with that old teddy bear—"

The little girl tugged at Charlie's heart strings. At eight years old, her every emotion played across her face like a movie at a drive-in. She was young and vulnerable, and her life had been a bit rocky up to this point.

"And C.J." Alice busied herself straightening the sugar packets. "He's growing up faster than I can process."

That was an understatement. C.J. was ten going on twenty-one. Somewhere along the way he had decided to step up and become the man of the family. If anything, it seemed to Charlie that the boy was a bit too serious. He needed to learn to play, to be a child, and to leave the heavy stuff of life to the adults.

"How are they doing at school?"

"Better. Shelley still chews on her nails something fierce, but her teacher told me that she's started participating in class more." Alice's eyes sparkled when she bragged on her grandkids. "Mrs. Bradford says she shows a real aptitude for language arts."

"And C.J.?"

"There haven't been any fights this year. I guess word spread that if you were going to pick on Shelley, you were going to have to deal with her older brother."

"So what are you worried about?"

"That the storm..." She studied the clear blue sky outside the diner's window. "That Orion will disrupt their lives so much that it will push them back to the way they were when Georgia first left."

Charlie had offered his opinion of Georgia and her decisions more than once. He didn't think Alice needed to hear from him on that point.

"You can't control what happens in those kids' lives, not totally. At some point you have to trust them to the Lord."

"Yeah, I know. I've been reading the devotional book you gave me. But the thing is, Charlie, I've also been looking up past hurricanes on the Internet."

"Normally I'd say knowledge is a good thing."

"The pictures are terrible."

"Sometimes you can learn too much."

"There are even videos."

"Alice, there's no point in filling your mind with those images."

"Eight major storms in the last hundred years, Charlie. *Eight*."

"A hundred years is a long time."

"That's one every thirteen years. The last one was in 1980. We're overdue! And each time there was massive devastation and folks were killed."

"I was here for Celia—"

"That was in 1970."

"And Allen."

"Yeah, 1980." Alice drummed her fingers against the table. "Which was worse, in your opinion? I know what the weather site says."

"Allen was a bigger storm—a Category 5, but we took a more direct hit from Celia, which was only a Cat 3."

When Alice glanced again at him, her brown eyes flooded with fear. Charlie wanted to say something, say anything, to erase that look. "Things have changed, for the better actually, since those storms. We have stricter building codes and more accurate weather forecasting."

Alice sighed and slid out of the booth as a group of fishermen came through the front door.

Charlie stood and tossed some money on the table—enough for the bill and a nice tip. "I can't promise you that Orion won't hit, Alice, but I can promise you that I'll be there to help you and the kids. You won't have to go through this alone."

That seemed to be exactly what she needed to hear because she leaned forward, kissed his cheek, and picked up the pot of coffee. "You're a peach, Charlie. A real peach."

Coming from her, that was high praise indeed, and it was enough to put a smile on Charlie's face and banish for a moment his own fears about the coming storm.

As he walked outside, it seemed to him that the air felt different— as if there was an expectancy, a zing almost. Certainly, barometric pressure did change with a hurricane, but that wasn't what he was noticing. No, it was more the anticipation of folks walking past him.

People were keyed up. Danger was on their radar, and it was setting them on edge.

He'd go home and make a packing list for Alice. He'd also call some friends and find her a place to stay farther inland so she wouldn't have to pay the hyped-up prices for a hotel room. And he'd pray. If Orion had its sight on Port A, Charlie would pray that all of the good people in their small community would find a way to safety well before the hurricane made land.

CHAPTER 5

*J*oshua worked beside his father in the field to the south of their house. They had harvested the corn the day before, a process that would have looked strange to any Old Order Amish. Joshua had grown up in Cody's Creek, and they had been using tractors since he was a small child. Though his parents never spoke of any dissension among their community, he vaguely remembered quite a few of his classmates moving away when he had just begun school. No one ever explained why, but looking back he understood that it was because they didn't agree with the changes.

In Joshua's opinion, the tractors were a necessary tool. Early in the morning, they had hooked the corn picker behind the old Ford tractor. The stalks were pulled into the machine, which separated the ears from the stalk and husk. The ears then went through a shoot and were tossed into a wagon pulled behind the picker. They had nearly finished harvesting the field when the machine sputtered to a stop.

"More than one man has lost his fingers trying to clear these jams," his father had muttered as he stared into the bowels of the machine.

In the end they had been able to clear the obstruction, but then the tractor had stalled and refused to start. So they had harnessed the corn picker up to the Percherons, who had finished the job with no mishap. The horses still came in handy for harvesting, though the soil held too much clay for them to be much help during planting.

That was the reason their community had decided to allow tractors in the first place.

Over the years since, the community had continued to grow with like-minded individuals, and they were again numbering four districts, or nearly six hundred people. The people who had stayed had grown used to the tractors, though some, like Joshua's father, insisted on keeping the horses—just in case.

Today the corn needed to be transported to the crib where it could air-dry.

Alton had helped the day before in spite of his hangover and lack of sleep. He was a hard worker when he set his mind to it. But at lunch Joshua had noticed him standing in the shadow of the back of the barn, smoking a cigarette and thumbing through texts on his smart phone.

"I can't believe you waste money on that thing."

"You have no idea what you're missing, *bruder*." Alton didn't look up as he continued to stare at the small screen. Laughing at something he read, he held the phone at arm's length, smiled at the thing, and a small flash of light went off.

"Taking pictures of yourself?" Joshua thought of the gizmo as a child's toy, and he knew it was long past time his brother outgrew his fascination with such things. Most of the Amish he knew who indulged their *rumspringa* did so for less than a year. Alton was seventeen. Like all Amish, he'd left school after the eighth grade at the age of fourteen, but he had only begun to step outside the rules of their *Ordnung* during the last six months. Joshua hoped his flirtations with *Englisch* gadgets would be short lived.

Some days he worried that Alton's attitude indicated a more serious underlying problem. Perhaps he was considering leaving their community and fully embracing the *Englisch* life. Joshua prayed it wasn't so. While that road was understandable for some people, he fervently believed his brother was better off remaining with his friends, his family, and a simple faith.

"It's called a *selfie*, and a cute girl in Clarita asked for it." In response to Joshua's grunt of disapproval, he added, "No worries. She's Amish."

Alton continued to help with the harvest the rest of the day, but the next morning when Joshua woke, he was gone. He'd slipped out sometime during the night. No doubt he'd taken the pickup, which he kept hidden on the far side of their property. How had he managed to purchase the rust trap? And where did he plan to go in it? Perhaps he'd gone to visit the girl in Clarita. It was nearly a three-hour drive between the two communities—in other words, another day wasted.

Joshua didn't know how long his parents would put up with such foolishness. He did know he was tired of pulling his brother's weight as well as his own.

He spent the day transferring the corn to the crib, while his father repaired the tractor. They needed to plant the east field with winter wheat, and they needed to do so while the good weather held. Joshua finished storing the corn, and then he went to the barn to care for the Percherons and both of their buggy horses.

Work on a farm was never completed. It repeated itself from day to day and season to season. Joshua enjoyed that rhythm, though he was grateful they no longer had cattle. The beasts constantly bumped into things, broke things, and generally caused extra work. Instead, his mother now kept chickens and traded eggs with their neighbor for fresh milk.

Alton still hadn't returned by dinner, and his parents didn't bring up the topic, probably because his four sisters were all ears when it came to any tidbits about their brother. Betsy, Janet, Karen, and Katherine were twelve, eleven, and ten-year-old twins, respectively. To Joshua they looked like ducks in a row—all slim, blond, and brown-eyed. When he stopped to think about it, there was a ten-year span between him and Alton, and then a five-year span between Alton and Betsy. No wonder their family only had six siblings when most families had ten or more. His mother, Abigail, had gone through two periods when she must have wondered if her childbearing years were over.

Mamm was short and round. She was perpetually busy and somewhat outspoken for an Amish woman. Her tongue had a sarcastic edge Joshua never wanted to be on the receiving end of, but for all of her hustle and bustle she loved her family dearly and would do anything for them. She brokered little nonsense and was often quick to share her opinion, which explained the sharp tone with which she broached the subject of Alton once the girls had been sent upstairs to bed.

"I don't suppose your *bruder* bothered to tell you where he was going."

Joshua was reading the *Budget*. Though many of the contributing letters were about family matters, quite a few of them mentioned weather and harvest results. He scanned each column for any indication of what people were planting in the coming year. He was always trying to get his father to consider a new crop, but Daniel Kline was not one to make a change without a very good reason.

His father had recently turned forty-six; in fact, his mother and father were the same age. Neither looked particularly old to Joshua. His mother looked as she always had, though perhaps her hair had more streaks of gray in it. His father looked like most other Amish farmers—tall, with a slight build, calloused hands, and dark hair. His hair had receded over the years until it was a ring around the back of his head. His thick beard was steadily becoming more gray than black.

"Joshua, either tell me or tell me you don't want to tell me."

It took him a few moments to realize she was waiting for an answer about Alton.

"*Nein, Mamm*. He didn't say anything to me."

"Took that old truck I suppose. He thinks we don't know about it, but this farm isn't that big. We're not so old we can't hear an *Englisch* automobile that could use a new muffler."

What did his mother know about mufflers? And how long had she known about the truck?

"You need to talk to that boy, Daniel."

His father had been working on carving a design into a turkey call. He glanced up at his wife, shrugged, and returned his attention to the woodwork. The turkey calls sold at Bylers' Dry Goods and brought in a nice bit of extra money. Joshua thought that his father did it more because he liked the intricate work than because he wished for the additional funds.

"Shrugging at me won't make this problem go away."

Joshua stood and stretched. He knew when his mother's tone turned from sarcastic to cross it meant she was worried. Who could blame her? He was worried too. He walked into the kitchen and brought back the plate of cookies she had set back on the stove.

"Offering me sweets isn't the answer either."

"Would you like some coffee?"

"Milk would be good. *Danki.*"

Joshua was walking back into the kitchen when his father called out, "I'll take coffee."

He knew some men his age thought it was women's work to carry in snacks and drinks, but his mother had raised him differently—it was the work of whoever had the time and ability. Joshua appreciated how hard his parents worked, and it never would have occurred to him to ask his mother to bring him a treat. The thought of such a thing caused him to laugh. It would probably be as painful as tussling with the barn cat, who had razor sharp claws.

He'd grown used to having a snack before bed, and he was quite willing to fetch it himself. When he'd settled again on the couch, his mother returned to her interrogation.

"You really have no idea where he is? I know he snuck out this morning just after four."

Joshua stuffed an oatmeal cookie into his mouth.

"I heard the stair squeak. You boys never remember that. Your *dat* offered to fix it once, but I told him it was like an early warning system." She knitted another row of the blanket she was working on, and then added, "Alton worries me. He thinks he's grown, but he still acts like a child."

"No need to worry, Abigail." Daniel didn't look up as he spoke. "He's a grown man and is finding his place in the world."

"Does his place in the world have to include smoking those nasty cigarettes?"

"I remember you smoking a few yourself when we were enjoying our *rumpsringa*."

Abigail knitted even faster. "We didn't know how bad they were for your health. No one knew then. We thought it was a harmless thing, and it made us feel so much older—"

"Alton is a smart young man. He'll figure it out."

"So you say." She turned her attention back to Joshua, who was still trying to process that his parents had once smoked. "I wouldn't worry so if it were a Sunday evening."

"You know about the overnights?"

Abigail dropped the knitting on her lap and reached for her glass of milk. "Of course we do. Everyone knows."

Joshua shrugged. He'd found the entire *rumspringa* scene lame and couldn't understand his brother's fascination with it.

"It's not a Sunday, though. There's too much work to do for *youngies* to take off whenever they choose. I can't understand what he was thinking or where he might have gone."

"He was on his phone yesterday, that's all I know." When she continued staring at him, he added, "Maybe he went to see a girl in Clarita."

"Lord have mercy on my soul." Abigail resumed her knitting. She didn't bring the subject up again until Joshua said good night and headed for the stairs.

"Maybe this girl will have a *schweschder*, Joshua. None of the girls here seem to catch your fancy."

It was an old refrain she returned to time and again.

"Good night, *Mamm*."

"Smile at me all you want. Youth doesn't last forever, and you're no spring chicken."

Which was how he fell asleep, picturing himself, his brother, and even his sisters as a brood of chicks gathered under their mother's wing.

CHAPTER 6

Charlie was once again walking Quitz down the beach when he noticed a group of people a few yards ahead. Something was wrong there. No one was laughing. No one played in the sand or looked toward the waves. It was as if they were huddled around something.

"We better check it out," he murmured to Quitz.

By the time he reached them, the size of the group had grown. He heard the announcer's voice before he saw the radio.

"Again, Orion is strengthening in the gulf's warm coastal waters. Data from hurricane hunters indicate that the pressure continues to drop even as the storm has turned toward the barrier islands of Matagorda, San José, Mustang, and Padre. The entire southern coastal region of Texas is now in the bull's-eye."

Everyone started talking at once, and Charlie missed what the announcer said next, but then the *beep, beep, beep* started and a prerecorded voice announced, "This is an emergency announcement from the National Weather Service. This is not a drill. I repeat, this is not a drill. At sixteen minutes past seven, Central Standard Time, the national weather service determined that Hurricane Orion had turned and is now headed toward the Texas coast. If you are in the path of this storm, it is critical that you leave the area. Projections indicate Orion will hit land within the next twenty-four to thirty hours. Mandatory evacuations have been ordered for all of the barrier islands as well as the towns of Port Lavaca, Rockport, Aransas Pass, and Corpus Christi. If you are in the affected area…"

Charlie never heard the rest. Everyone gathered around the young man holding the radio started talking at once. Overall they appeared to remain calm. Some of the teenaged boys were laughing and talking about the waves, but it seemed like bravado on their part. Charlie had worked with young adults long enough to tell the difference between fear and amusement. Fear had a smell to it, and folks' eyes often told a story unlike the one professed by their words. He sensed some real anxiety in the people gathered around the radio.

He clipped Quitz's leash to her collar and hurried toward his home, but when he reached there he didn't go inside. Instead, he pulled out his keys, climbed into his truck, and headed into town. Alice would have heard by now, and he didn't want her to be afraid.

While he was driving toward her home, he turned on the radio long enough to find out that stage one evacuation was to begin immediately. Already he could see RVs pulling out onto Highway 361. Larger rigs were headed toward the JFK Causeway Bridge. Smaller campers would take the ferry across and were traveling in the opposite direction. The traffic was still relatively light, but Charlie guessed that within a few hours that wouldn't be the case.

When he pulled up in front of Alice's house, all of the lights were on—in fact, all of the lights seemed to be on in all of the houses. The neighborhood was one of Port A's poorer areas. Housing for the blue-collar class had been a problem on the island for years. There were the luxury condos and then there were homes that had been built fifty years ago and were now in various stages of disrepair. The real estate crash of 1983 had stopped most construction until recently, when the cost for new homes had skyrocketed from two dollars a square foot to two hundred.

The rising cost had attracted more tourists and oil-rich folks who wanted a place on the beach. In the last few years, a record two hundred to three hundred home and commercial permits were being issued, but they weren't for two-thousand-foot homes. They were for the six- to ten-thousand-foot monstrosities on Charlie's beach. Folks like Alice had two options: Buy or rent an older home on the island or live on the mainland and commute.

Alice opened the door as soon as he knocked.

"Did you hear?" Her hand fluttered toward the television. "They're saying Orion will hit Port A, and now there's a mandatory evacuation. I'm trying to pack—"

"Slow down, Alice."

"But—"

"I could use a cup of coffee. Do you have any decaf in the house?"

"Yeah. Of course."

She turned toward the kitchen and then seemed at a loss over what to do. C.J. and Shelley were sitting on the couch, staring at the television. Shelley clutched her tattered bear with one hand, and C.J. held the television remote.

"Could you mute that, son? I doubt they're going to say anything new."

"Sure, Charlie."

As Alice set the coffee to brew, her movements became calmer, her hands stopped shaking, and she pulled in a deep breath. By the time she'd filled both of their mugs, the panic had left her eyes. "Guess I let that announcer spook me."

"Don't be embarrassed." Charlie reached for the sugar bowl and added a spoonful to his coffee. Normally he liked it black, but he had a feeling he'd need the extra fuel tonight. "It's your first hurricane. It's normal to be frightened."

"I'm scared too, Charlie." Shelley scooted into the chair beside him.

"Well, don't be. We have a plan, remember?"

"The evacuation plan. You made us a folder." C.J. stood in the doorway.

"Can you fetch it for us?" Charlie asked.

The boy nodded and darted back into the living room.

"We keep it beside the television. I pick the thing up at least once a week to dust around it, but did I remember to pull it out when I needed it?"

"It's only been thirty minutes, Alice. You would have remembered the folder."

Quitz collapsed on the floor beside Charlie's chair. Shelley flopped down next to the Labrador, laying her head on the dog's chest and playing with her floppy ears.

"Here it is, Charlie." C.J. came into the room, dropping the red folder on the kitchen table. "Nana, can I have something to eat? I know it's late, but all this drama is making me hungry."

"We could all use something. Bring the Tupperware container of cookies over here and get yourself a glass of milk."

Shelley claimed she wasn't hungry. Charlie noticed her yawn and rub her eyes. She'd be asleep before they finished their first cup of coffee.

"Stage one began tonight." Charlie opened the folder and pulled out the Port Aransas evacuation plan. "I passed some of the RV folk on my way here. They're already moving off the island."

Alice was reading the page upside down. "Stage two—that's non-residents and tourists."

"Right. Because it's October, we have fewer tourists on the island, and most of them come on weekends."

"The thing across the bottom of the television screen said that stage two would begin at first light." C.J. reached for a chocolate chip cookie.

It did Charlie's heart good to see the boy handling the emergency so well, but then C.J. was mature for his age.

"Did it mention stage three?" Alice asked.

"No, but I can go and watch. Do you care if I take this in there?" He held up his glass of milk and a napkin with four cookies stacked on it. "I'm not supposed to eat in the living room, but—"

"We'll make an exception this once," Alice said. "But only during hurricane evacuations."

C.J. smiled at her before heading into the living room.

Charlie looked down to see Shelley asleep. "I'll take this one to her room, and then we can go over your plans."

By the time he'd tucked her in, Alice was already pulling out her emergency bags and ticking items off the list.

"Is your car full of gas?" he asked.

"Yes. I filled it this morning." Alice glanced up and smiled at him. "You taught me well, Charlie. When there's even a chance of a storm—"

"Keep the tank topped off." He sipped his coffee, calculating the miles and the extra hours she would spend on the road due to traffic and detours. "All right. That will be enough to get you a safe distance inland."

"I'm worried about getting caught up in one of those infamous evacuation traffic jams. I'd hate to run out of gas on the highway."

"I brought an extra five gallons of gas. You can carry that with you, but I don't think you'll have a problem. Evacuation plans have improved dramatically over the last few years."

"I remember watching the news and seeing miles of stopped vehicles trying to evacuate from the Houston area…"

"Houston has a population of well over five million. The entire Corpus area is half a million."

"Are they evacuating Houston too?" C.J. asked.

Charlie hadn't heard him return. He was standing in the doorway, eating a cookie and wearing a milk mustache.

"From what I heard on the radio, they're under voluntary evacuation. The most southerly computer model predictions put Orion coming ashore here."

He touched the map at the very southern tip of Texas, practically on top of Matamoros, "And the northern point of the zone is here." He touched Port Lavaca.

"We're in the middle," Alice said.

"Which is why our evacuation is mandatory. Port A will sustain a hit. The question is when and how big the hurricane will be at that point."

"The news guy says that resident evacuation will begin at ten a.m."

"Thank you, C.J."

"Maybe you should get to bed, honey. We're going to be up early in the morning."

The boy shrugged and walked off to his bedroom.

"They'll be fine, Alice. Now, let's go through this list."

They spent the next hour deciding what she should take and making a schedule for the morning. She needed to turn off her electricity, gas, and water at the street, but he didn't want her to do so until the last minute.

"I'll be here early to board up your windows."

"I don't even know where to go, Charlie. Do I just drive north and look for a hotel?"

He mentally thumped himself on the forehead. "I should have told you earlier. I called some friends in Bandera. They're happy to have you and the kids."

"I couldn't…"

"The hotels are going to be full, and you don't want to go to a public shelter if you don't have to. Shelley and C.J. will be better off staying in someone's home, and it's best to save the evacuation space for someone who needs it."

"You'll come too?"

"I will. I may be a couple of hours behind you, but I'll be there." He waited until she nodded before he continued. "The roads will be crowded, but the state will have set up contraflow lanes all the way up 37 to San Antonio."

"All lanes will go north?"

"Correct. Both sides of the freeway. You're not going into San Antonio, though. I want you to get off here and take 173 to Bandera."

"Looks like the middle of nowhere."

"Exactly. Bill and Ann Rogers will meet you downtown at the Episcopal church's parking lot." He pulled a scrap of paper from his shirt pocket. "Here's their phone number. Call them when you take the turnoff onto 173."

Alice had tears in her eyes when she glanced at him and nodded. He thought it was fear, maybe adrenaline, but when they reached the front door she put her hand on his arm. "Charlie, I don't have flood insurance on this place."

"Yes, you do. We took it out last year—"

"I know what we did, but I couldn't…I couldn't afford the payment when they cut my hours at the diner this fall. I've only missed two, maybe three payments." She pressed her fingertips to her lips. "I had to stop paying something, and there was nothing else…"

When her tears began to fall, he pulled her into a hug. "We'll think of something, Alice. Let's not worry about rebuilding your house while it's still standing."

She nodded and took a step back.

Quitz followed Charlie out the door. Alice went back inside to begin packing. Before climbing into his truck, Charlie glanced up at the sky. A million points of light and a quarter moon shone down on them. There wasn't a cloud in the great expanse of sky that he could see—only starlight and moonlight. But he knew, he could actually feel, Orion barreling toward them. The only question was how much destruction he would unleash on the town and the people he loved.

CHAPTER 7

*C*harlie was amazed at how quickly a situation could deteriorate. The night before he'd stayed up making his own lists and boarding over his windows, though doing so in the dark was no easy matter. There was now a seventy percent chance that Orion would hit Mustang Island as a Category 4 or even possibly a Category 5 hurricane.

"What does Cat 4 mean, Charlie?" Shelley walked with him as he unloaded the plywood he'd brought over from his place. Stores always ran out of plywood—he'd learned that when he first came to the island. He kept a supply at his house and rarely had to replace it. Usually it was only a matter of refastening it over his windows, and then pulling it back down when the storm never materialized. Two years ago, he'd purchased extra, knowing that Alice would need help should an evacuation be ordered.

Quitz walked between them, nose to the ground, sniffing for any sign of who had walked there before them. She seemed blissfully oblivious to the worries of men and girls.

"Well, now. It means that stuff will blow over."

"Blow over?" Shelley wore her hair in two pigtails, high if she was in a bright and happy mood and low if she was feeling worried. Today, the pigtails covered her ears and were pulled to the front. They sported bright purple ribbons that Alice had probably suggested to match her blouse. Charlie could tell from the way she worried her top lip that Shelley was afraid about what might happen next.

He carried the boards to the front porch of Alice's house, leaned them against the porch railing, and then he sat down. When he did, Shelley sat beside him, swinging her feet because they didn't come close to touching the ground.

"Hurricanes bring a lot of rain and a lot of wind. That's why we put the plywood over the windows. It protects the glass from stuff that is flying around. It keeps the windows from breaking."

"Mrs. Bradford always carries around a coffee cup with her, even when we're on the playground. The boys were playing ball and one ran into her." Shelley scrunched up her face. "It was terrible. The coffee cup busted and there were pieces of it everywhere. Then Stanley—he's the boy who broke it—cut his finger when he tried to help pick the pieces up."

"Things like that happen sometimes."

"He had to go to the nurse and get a Band-Aid. And Mrs. Bradford had to get a new mug. Now it's plastic."

"Sounds like a good solution."

Shelley reached up and pulled her pony tails tighter within their holder.

"What if our house blows over?" Instead of looking at him, she reached out and ran her hand gently over Quitz's head.

Quitz closed her eyes, basking in Shelley's affection. The dog was dedicated to Charlie, but she would protect Alice's two grandkids from anything that threatened them. She seemed to know that they needed an extra player in their court.

"Would our house break if Orion knocks it over?"

"Hopefully that won't happen, Shelley. But it's why we're all going to stay a few days on the mainland."

"The evac...umm, evacuation."

"Exactly, evacuation. We go inland because it will be safer there."

"But it probably won't happen. Our house won't..." She wiggled her head back and forth. "It won't just fall over."

"Probably not."

"What if it does happen?" She persisted.

"When the rain stops, we'll put it up again."

She looked up at him, her brown eyes wide with fear and surprise and hope. "Do you promise, Charlie? Do you promise you'll put our house back up again?"

He'd learned over the years not to make promises that he couldn't fulfill, but he vowed to himself in that moment that no matter what happened on the island, he would find a way to reconstruct Shelley's home. A child needed at least that much. Every child, from the very young to teenaged, needed to know that they would have a place to come back to, no matter what happened. Usually their parents were able to provide that security, but Georgia hadn't even returned Alice's call. Maybe she didn't realize how serious the storm was. Maybe her cell phone was lost and she hadn't received the message. Maybe where she lived there were no national news channels. Or maybe she didn't care.

Either way, Shelley and C.J. were depending on their grandmother, and Alice was depending on Charlie.

"Do you promise?" Shelley asked again.

"Yeah, I promise. Now I'd better get busy putting up this plywood."

"But there aren't even any clouds in the sky."

He glanced up and out toward the gulf—something he found himself doing every few minutes. If there was impending doom headed their way, it seemed as though he would be able to see it.

"Not yet. So let's get busy."

Shelley and Quitz both followed him around for another ten minutes, and then Shelley hurried off when she saw her grandmother loading boxes in the car. "Did you remember Bear? We have to take him."

Alice squatted down and said something to the little girl, who nodded once before running back into the house. The diner had closed until the storm passed, as had the schools. Mustang Island officials were assuring everyone that the mandatory evacuation was proceeding smoothly. They also reiterated that every single person had been ordered off the island.

Charlie had turned the news channel on as soon as he'd risen, well before first light. Though the evacuation route was crowded, the traffic was getting through and there were no reports of price gouging as far as gasoline.

Folks needed to go farther inland than Corpus Christi, so they traveled northwest—an hour to Mathis or two and a half hours to San Antonio. Charlie had contacted Bill and Ann days ago when the possibility of a Port A hurricane landing was still slim. Bill had said they would be happy to provide a place for Alice and the kids. Ann was already freshening up the guesthouse that was a finished part of their barn.

Staying in Bandera would keep them out of the city, where hotel prices were bound to be at a premium. More importantly, Charlie knew that Bill and Ann would provide the kind of peaceful refuge the kids would need. There would be no twenty-four-hour news channels blaring in the living room. No, they would keep the kids busy with odd chores on the little ranch and entertain them with the few horses Bill kept.

"Promise me you're right behind them, Charlie." Ann's voice was stern. He could hear the worry in it.

"I promise. There are a few folks I need to check on, but I'll get off the island in plenty of time."

Quitz plopped on the ground as Charlie adjusted his ladder and boarded over another window.

C.J. had been picking up everything out of the backyard and storing it in the garage that wasn't big enough to hold their car. The house was not well constructed, and paint was peeling off one of its sides. The neighborhood irked Charlie. Why hadn't they done more to minister to it? His church was always sending mission groups to other countries. Why didn't they send them down the road? Why was Alice living here, anyway? She deserved better, and so did the kids.

When he and Madelyn had bought their place forty years ago, the price of land and of houses had been reasonable. Now, an ordinary family couldn't afford anything but the ramshackle two-bedroom wooden structures like the one Alice lived in. It wouldn't take a Category 4 to demolish this neighborhood—a solid Cat 3 would have the same effect.

He continued working his way around the house, grateful that he was able to help in some small way. If the island suffered a direct hit, the boards would do little to protect the house. But seeing the plywood go up over their windows somehow made Alice and Shelley and C.J. feel better about leaving their things behind, and that made his labors worthwhile.

C.J. appeared at his side as he was covering the last window. His brown hair was just a little too long, obscuring his vision and curling at the collar of his shirt. When he glanced up, Charlie noticed the freckles across his nose. Still a kid in spite of the big feet that hinted at the man he would soon become.

"The guys at school were all talking about the storm."

"Were they?"

"Most of what they said made no sense. I think they were mainly trying to scare the younger kids."

"Huh."

"But some of the guys were pulling up pictures on their phones of Hurricane Allen."

Charlie wondered about that, fourth grade kids walking around able to access any information they wanted, whether they needed to see such things or not. "That one hit in August of 1980."

"You were here."

"I was."

"Was it...was it as bad as those pictures looked?"

Charlie stowed the hammer in his toolbox, handed the box to C.J., and picked up his ladder. He couldn't imagine what it would be like to grow up not knowing your father and having your mother dump you at Nana's. He tried not to judge others. Folks had their reasons, and he couldn't pretend to understand what today's young people dealt with. But he did recognize a scared kid when he saw one.

Quitz jumped up and walked with them back toward his truck.

"Allen was bad," Charlie admitted. "Mostly because of the wind."

"Over one hundred?"

"Yes. If I remember right, closer to one hundred thirty down in Port Mansfield."

"What about here?"

"Corpus withstood a lot of wind damage." He didn't mention the tornadoes that Allen had spawned. They had traveled north and done extensive damage in Austin. C.J. didn't need to know that. He had enough to worry about.

Charlie lowered the tailgate on his truck, and C.J hoisted up the toolbox, pushing it deep into the truck bed. Charlie added the ladder and Quitz began to whine. "Front seat, girl." The dog readily jumped in when Charlie opened the passenger door.

"The pictures they showed had trees blown over, and roofs...roofs completely gone, and some houses wiped away."

"I imagine those photos were taken in Port Mansfield. The storm surge...do you know what a storm surge is?"

"Waves, wind, and tide. Our teacher talked about it in school."

"All right. Well, the storm surge in Port Mansfield was more than twelve feet high."

"Twelve feet?"

"Yup. That would be..." Charlie glanced toward the front of the house where Alice and Shelley were coming out the front door. "Almost to your roofline."

"Holy cow."

"Which is why it's important for you and Shelley and your grandmother to get off the island."

"What about you?"

"I have a few things left to do. I'll be a couple of hours behind you."

They walked over to the little car Alice drove. The trunk barely closed, it was so full. Bags of clothing, a box of family pictures and important documents, and an emergency supply kit filled the back seat. The supply kit held things like food, water, flashlights, and extra batteries, plus a weather radio that could be recharged via a hand crank on the side. Charlie had bought them many of the items in that box over the years, with the fervent prayer that they would never need to use them. A small spot behind Alice's seat had been left empty for Shelley. C.J. would ride up front beside his grandmother.

"I appreciate your doing this, Charlie." Alice swiped at her hair, trying to keep it from blowing in her face. She also glanced continually out toward the gulf.

"Not a problem. Neighbors take care of neighbors." He helped Shelley into the car, carefully buckling her and Bear into the backseat.

When C.J. had settled into the front seat, Alice walked with him back to the truck.

"Get them off the island, Alice. Get to Bandera. Don't stop if you don't have to. Just keep driving."

"What about you?" She swiped again at her hair. The winds had increased considerably in the last hour, and Charlie expected the clouds would begin to build up any minute.

"I'll make the last ferry out."

"I just hate to…" She waved at the small frame house tucked in a row of small frame houses. Charlie could tell by the look in her eyes that she realized it would not survive even an indirect hit by Orion.

"I hate to leave everything."

"You're not." He put a hand on each of her shoulders. Though only forty-eight, Alice looked older. The last few years had taken their toll, as had the shifts at the diner. "You have the kids."

"You promise you're coming, Uncle Charlie?" C.J. had rolled down his window and was half hanging out of it.

"Yeah, kid. I'm coming." He squinted at his old truck. Quitz was leaning against the passenger door, her head stuck out the window. She and C.J. looked comically alike. "I want to check on a couple more people, and then I'll be out of here."

"Thank you, Charlie." Alice threw her arms around his neck, hugged him tightly, and then abruptly turned away. He watched as she hurried to the little Dodge Neon and climbed into the driver's seat. Once she was buckled, she started the engine. They all waved at Charlie.

He waved back and stood waiting, watching them until he was satisfied they had joined the queue of cars on the main road. The ferries were working overtime, taking folks over to the mainland. It was still a faster route than the bridge on the south end of the island. Also, by taking the ferry she would come out to the north and east of Corpus, bypassing a portion of the scores of folks who were leaving.

The evacuation had been orderly as far as Charlie had been able to tell. They would get off the island just fine, and if Alice drove straight through they would be in Bandera before dark. What was normally a three-hour drive would probably take them five or six, but it was still early morning. They would make it just fine.

He started his truck and turned on the radio. The announcer was saying that Orion remained on a direct path for the southern part of the Texas coastline. It was expected to make landfall within fifteen hours. There was now a ninety percent chance that Mustang Island would receive a direct hit.

CHAPTER 8

*B*ecca walked with her mother down the side of the two-lane road toward her grandfather's house. They could have taken the tractor or hooked up the buggy, but the fall day was nice, and a walk seemed more in order. Her mother was working on a new line of notecards with autumn scenes. They would stop occasionally so she could sketch the outline of a tree or flower or even Joshua Kline and his father planting what was probably winter wheat.

"Joshua's a nice boy." Her mother tucked the notepad back into her purse. "Don't you think?"

"*Ya, Mamm.* He is. So is Alton." Becca nearly laughed when her mother's eyes widened. "I thought you wanted to marry me off. Are you saying Alton would be a bad choice?"

"No…" She drew out the word as she hooked her arm through Becca's. "It's only that Alton isn't quite settled yet, but Joshua…well, Joshua seems steady."

"And steady is a *gut* thing?"

"It is indeed." Her mother squeezed her arm and then wandered toward the fence line where the Klines' Percherons were standing and looking hopeful.

"This one's name is Blaze." Becca rubbed the horse between the ears, scratching the white spot that no doubt had resulted in his name. "They were using him to pull Alton's truck out of the ditch two days ago. Do you remember?"

54

"I do. You nabbed one of my apples to feed the beast." Her mother reached into her pocket and pulled out two small carrots.

"How did you know you'd be needing treats for the horses?"

"Daniel and Abigail Kline are one of the few families left with workhorses. They bring them to your *dat* for shoeing when necessary. I always hope to see them when I'm walking to your *daddi*'s, but often they are in the back pasture."

"Funny the things you learn about your own mother."

"We've been neighbors with the Klines since you were born, Becca. I would think you would know how familiar we are with one another."

Becca shrugged and they continued toward her grandparents'. "I suppose I didn't pay that much attention when I was in school. Joshua was so much older than me."

"Age makes less of a difference when we're adults."

"And Alton was younger, so I certainly didn't pay much attention to him."

Her mother laughed at that.

"You know, *Mamm*…spending this past summer with *Aentie*'s family has caused me to view things differently. Sometimes it feels as if I'm seeing everything for the first time."

"A time away is often *gut* for us, especially for young women your age."

"Life is certainly different in Wisconsin."

"*Ya*. I've been to my *schweschder*'s many times over the years. Different is a *gut* word for it."

"I'll admit I like our bathrooms better."

Her mother nodded but didn't comment on the value of indoor bathrooms over outhouses.

"It's not only that we are more progressive." Becca said the last word carefully, unsure whether she liked it or not. "But outhouses and iceboxes? Unnecessary hardship makes no sense to me."

"The communities in Pebble Creek don't see it that way. And if I remember right, they have both an Old Order and a New Order group."

"They do, and they get along quite well. I just don't understand why there are differences."

"Because people see things differently." Her mother stopped and pointed toward a stand of trees in a pasture across the road. "Tell me what you see."

"Several trees. Bright fall colors—bronze and crimson and mulberry. And weeds growing at the base."

"*Gut.* But what I see when I look at the same scene are crunchy leaves—"

"You can't see crunchy."

"A bird's nest in the limbs."

"Too far away. You might guess, but—"

"And someone's initials carved into the tree trunk."

"You can't possibly have seen that!"

They both laughed and began walking again.

"True. Some things I didn't see, but still I know they are there."

Becca was quiet for a moment, trying to guess at her mother's point. Finally, she shook her head. All the talk about leaves and bird's nests… "What does that have to do with the vast differences in Amish communities?"

"We both looked at the same thing, but we saw slightly different details." Her mother's voice was gentle and patient, reminding Becca of the light breeze dancing through the trees. "The same is true with Plain communities. We read the same Bible and share the same faith, but the details we perceive vary somewhat."

"So neither is right or wrong?"

"How would I know?"

They had turned down the lane to her grandparents' home and waved at her grandmother, who was standing outside beating a rug she'd draped over the porch railing.

"But, *Mamm*—"

"I only bring it up to remind you that differences are never simple to understand."

Becca thought of those words later as she walked with her

grandfather to check on the boys who were planting his back field. Levi walked with a limp. He even used a cane. But he never complained about his left leg if it pained him. He still managed to run a small farm, though he accepted any offer of help that came his way. He'd once told her that it was important to be humble, and perhaps that was why God had allowed his leg to heal improperly after his accident. She couldn't imagine her grandfather being anything but humble. He was the bishop. He understood the Bible and its teachings better than anyone she knew.

"*Ya*, but understanding is different from doing. Isn't it, Becca Lynn?" No one else used her middle name, and in her *aenti's* community in Wisconsin, folks didn't even have middle names—opting for a middle initial instead. Her mother told her that practice was actually quite common. Funny the things you learned when you traveled away from home.

This conversation about understanding and pride had been several years before when she'd been struggling with vanity, owing mostly to the fact that she was a good twenty pounds heavier than the other girls her age. Somehow, when she was around her grandfather, those details she disliked about herself never mattered. Now when they visited, she thought back on those conversations. She appreciated her family more than any other thing in her life. Her mother, father, and grandparents all made her feel normal.

After they checked on the planting, Levi suggested they help her grandmother by picking what was left of her fall harvest. Most of the plants had been cut to the ground and the soil turned over, but there were still a few lingering bell peppers, cucumbers, winter squash, and even cherry tomatoes.

"We'll have our first hard freeze any day. Best to bring these in before we do."

Becca had gone up and down the rows, collecting a surprisingly large quantity of vegetables. When she'd finished, she joined her grandfather on the bench in the afternoon sunshine.

"Have you given any more thought to joining a winter mission?"

"I talked to *Mamm* and *Dat* about it. They were hesitant because I've only been back home two months."

"But—"

"But I think I would enjoy it."

"Any job prospects in sight?"

Becca sighed. "I could work at the Cheese House in town."

"A fine establishment."

"It would be a part-time position, and I'm not sure being around all the cheese and breads and sweets would be a good idea." Becca stared down at her hands. She'd always thought they were pretty, like fresh cookies rising in the oven. Then she'd heard one of the boys proclaim her "doughy," and suddenly she found herself sticking her hands in her apron pockets or behind her back whenever she was with a group.

Levi didn't respond to that, so she continued. "I think I'd rather help the Bylers in the dry goods store. They are very busy from Thanksgiving until Christmas. That would also allow me to spend the time between now and Thanksgiving helping *Mamm* with the canning."

"A *gut* idea." Levi patted her knee, and then he pointed his cane at the field. "The Lord gives us a time of planting and a time for the land to lay fallow. It is the same with people, but perhaps...in your case...your best use of some of those long winter days would be to visit a new place."

"*Mamm* is trying to marry me off, and you're trying to get rid of me." Becca shook her head in mock despair.

"*Nein*, Becca Lynn, but many communities are larger than ours. It's hard for one your age to have too few prospects."

Becca laughed. "That's a nice word for it. Is it so necessary for a woman to marry, *Daddi*? Is it a sin to remain single?"

"Of course not." Levi tapped his cane against the ground for emphasis. "Some are called to the single life. Remember, the apostle Paul tells us in the first letter to the Corinthians that it is better to remain single."

"So why is everyone concerned that I'm not dating?"

"In my experience, few are called to the single life."

He said no more, and they remained there, watching the occasional bird land in the garden's rows and peck the ground for worms.

When they stood and walked back toward the house, Becca asked, "How do I know which life I'm called to?"

"*Gotte* will make that plain to you."

"I rather like the idea of going on a mission trip. How do we know there will be a need for volunteers this winter?"

"There's always a need, both in Amish communities and in *Englisch* ones. Our brethren in the Mennonite church send out a monthly letter, requesting help for certain weeks in certain places. We will go over the next letter I receive together."

And so it was decided. Becca didn't expect that a trip to some far-flung community would bring clarity to her own life, but neither did she want to sit around the house through the long snow-filled months, quilting and cleaning and waiting for spring. A mission trip would at least provide her with a distraction.

Distractions weren't always a bad thing.

And perhaps when she returned home, she'd have a clearer idea of who she was and what she wanted her future to include.

CHAPTER 9

*J*oshua could tell before he took his first bite of stew that it was going to be one of those dinners.

Karen and Katherine were arguing over a homework assignment they had received at school that day.

"Brian said to write half a page first and then read the story." Karen reached up and rubbed at the braids under her *kapp*.

"That's stupid. How can you write about something before you read it?" Katherine ignored a look of reprimand from her mother. "That doesn't make any sense."

"Does too if you'd been listening—"

"That's enough girls." Abigail added a plate of warm corn bread to the table. "You can each do what you think is right, and we'll find out tomorrow who is correct. Until then, stop arguing about it."

Katherine rolled her eyes at Karen, who frowned into her stew. No doubt she was now wondering if she'd remembered correctly. Both girls were fiercely competitive. Joshua understood that as Amish they weren't supposed to worry about who was first in the class or who had the best grade, but he also knew his sisters. They had been trying to outdo each other since the day they were born—or so it seemed to him.

"If you two would stop passing notes during class, you'd know what Brian said." Betsy was only two years older, but at the age of twelve she was also only two years away from being out of school. She'd once confessed to Joshua that she didn't even like being around younger children and was convinced she would make a terrible mom.

"How would you know? You're busy making eyes at Caleb Stutzman." Janet was the tomboy of the group, and she couldn't understand why anyone would waste time flirting, dating, or courting.

"Boys seem hopelessly boring to me," she'd declared the night before at dinner, throwing an apologetic look at Joshua. Now she dug into her stew and said, "Betsy has a terrible crush on Caleb. She turns beet red if he even looks her way."

Betsy stared into her stew as if she might find a way to disappear there. Joshua felt bad for her, but he also wished his sisters would stop arguing. They were beginning to give him a headache.

His father must have been thinking the same thing. "Perhaps we should spend the meal in silence."

But silence was not to be.

Before Joshua was halfway through his dinner, the clatter of horse hooves was heard outside.

"Can only be Levi." His father wiped his mouth and stood. "Anyone else would be on a tractor."

Joshua followed him out onto the front porch. Possibly they would need his help. He knew the minute he looked at Levi's face that the news wasn't good. Their dog, Blue, followed Levi onto the porch and then sat with his head cocked, as if he were curious.

"It's Alton," Levi said. "I'm afraid he's in trouble."

"What kind of trouble?"

Joshua hadn't heard his mother follow them from the kitchen, but now she stood at the front door, clutching her apron in both fists. At that moment, Joshua found himself glad that he'd not married. If having children produced the kind of heartbreak he was seeing on his mother's face, he wasn't sure he was man enough to bear it.

"I had a call from the bishop in Clarita." Levi leaned on his cane, paused, and then he said, "Perhaps we should go inside."

The girls were hurried up to their rooms, though Joshua stood facing the stairs and could see that they had stopped at the landing. They were standing close together, eyes wide, waiting as intently as Joshua's parents were. He noticed that Katherine and Karen were now holding hands, all animosity over the school assignment forgotten.

"Alton apparently arrived in Clarita yesterday."

"He was gone when we woke. Actually, I think I heard his truck start sometime around four." Abigail was sitting on a chair, perched on the edge. "He left no note explaining where he went."

"Apparently this is about a girl," Levi said.

She looked at Joshua, as if for an explanation, but he only shrugged. He hadn't seen the photo of the girl Alton was looking at on the phone. He didn't even hear her name.

"The parents noticed that the girl wasn't around at lunch. She'd been manning a produce stand near the road. They thought she was off with some friends, but she didn't come home last night."

Joshua's father paced back and forth in front of the window. Then he turned toward Levi. "Are we sure she was with Alton?"

"Clarita is a small community. Smaller even than ours. Several folks saw them walking together, and then she got into his truck."

"Alton isn't the only Amish boy to own a truck." His mother shook her head. "It could have been anyone—"

"He introduced himself to one of the farmers when he first stopped at the produce stand. Didn't give a last name, just Alton. The bishop there figured he must be from here because we're the closest Plain community."

"It's a good distance from here to Clarita." His father ran his fingers through his beard.

"It is. Almost three hours by car." Levi hesitated, sighed, and continued. "That's not the worst of it. Last night they stopped to eat at an *Englisch* restaurant. Apparently Alton had a few beers—"

"He's not old enough to buy them," Joshua's mother protested.

"He used a fake ID. They aren't that hard to come by, unfortunately."

No one spoke for a few moments as they processed all that Levi had said. It was obvious by the way he was sitting—leaning slightly forward with both hands on top of his cane—that he wasn't through yet.

He continued. "The highway patrol in McAlester had stopped into the same restaurant—"

"What was he doing in McAlester?" Joshua's mom shook her head as if she was having trouble processing the stops along the course of her son's rebellion.

"Apparently, he started in Clarita, but he was driving back this direction for some reason. McAlester is more or less halfway. Regardless, the highway patrol noticed the boy weaving toward his truck and stopped him as he was leaving."

"Tell me my son is not in jail."

His mother's complexion turned from pale to red.

Joshua understood that meant she was quickly moving from shock to anger. What followed would not be good. His mother had a terrible temper, one they didn't see often.

He seriously doubted his brother had any idea just how much trouble he was in. Probably he hadn't even thought of home or what it would be like when he returned, if he returned. Joshua had the urge to walk out of the house—go to the barn and spend the next hour brushing down the horses. Somehow, he was certain the bishop had saved the worst for last.

"He is in jail, Abigail." The bishop's voice was soft, calming, even matter-of-fact.

Joshua wondered just how often he had dealt with this sort of thing before.

"Fortunately, the officers only issued a warning for the fake ID and the minor under the influence because both were his first offense. I believe their leniency was owing to the fact that he wasn't beyond the legal limit, but it is of course still illegal for him to purchase and consume alcohol in a public establishment."

When no one spoke, Levi added, "Alton wouldn't tell the authorities his real name. Apparently, the girl became upset and asked one of the officers to call her bishop, and the story unwound from there."

"So what now?" Daniel asked.

"He's a minor with a fake ID and no valid driver's license. You need to go and fetch him."

Daniel sat down heavily in the remaining chair, across from the bishop. He leaned forward, elbows on knees, and ran his right hand up and down his jaw. Finally, he said, "I just started planting my winter wheat, Levi. I will go and get the boy, but I don't see how I can do it tonight or tomorrow—"

"Send Joshua."

"Me? Why me?" Joshua had no interest in traipsing after his little brother. In his opinion, a week in the *Englisch* jail might do him good.

"You still have your driver's license, don't you? If I remember correctly, the church leadership allowed you to apply for one the winter you worked delivering supplies for the mill."

"*Ya*, but I haven't driven since then. I've had no need or inclination to be behind the wheel of an *Englisch* vehicle."

"Take the bus down first thing tomorrow morning. Pick up your *bruder* and drive him back."

When his father and mother shared a look, Joshua knew his fate was sealed. All that remained was to work out the details.

CHAPTER 10

Charlie realized he should already have left Port A. Though it was an hour until sunset, a strange darkness was creeping across the island. To the west, the sun was making a valiant attempt to overcome the shadow of Orion. To the east, the clouds were now filling the sky, reminding Charlie of a big, black runaway train intent on producing massive destruction.

The surf was up and the ferries had stopped thirty minutes earlier, according to the news bulletins he was listening to on the radio. Closing the ferries wasn't done until it was absolutely necessary. When the tide rose to the point where the ramps met the boat, they shut down. The ferries then went to the Corpus Christi harbor to ride out the storm.

Charlie could still leave by the bridge, though he didn't look forward to driving over it in gale force winds. As a last resort, he could catch a ride with the Coast Guard, who were dedicated to manning rescue boats as long as possible. But at some point they too would have to take shelter in Corpus—a fact that was being replayed over the radio every few minutes.

Would Orion be worse than Carla or Celia or Allen? No one could say, but unless it changed directions at the last minute, they could expect widespread devastation. Charlie didn't need a degree in meteorological science to understand that.

The wind rocked his truck as he turned toward the southern end of the island. He'd intended to check on Moose as soon as he'd left Alice's, but then he'd remembered two other old-timers who might be hesitant to leave. He'd gone to their house and helped them pack a few items. Then he'd taken them into town and left them at the Coast Guard drop site. They would be off the island within the hour.

By then it was early afternoon, and he knew he needed to attend to his own evacuation plan. Charlie had never considered himself a hero, but neither could he walk away from people who needed help. He couldn't just drive past the couple who were frantically packing their car while a baby cried from the backseat. The young parents were running back and forth, throwing trash bags full of who-knew-what into the car. He helped them with the last few items, which included a cat in a carrier, and sent them on their way.

Another car down the road had a flat tire. He pulled over and assisted the young man in putting on the spare—he was reading the car manual trying to figure out how to use the jack. At least the spare had air in it. Together they had changed the tire in just under forty-five minutes—and most of that time had been unloading and reloading the luggage. Once he was sure the young man was headed in the right direction, he'd driven toward the main drag and turned south.

He had to detour to his own place and pick up his bag that was already packed and a box of food and treats he had for Quitz. Neither was that important, and he probably shouldn't have taken the time, but he'd wanted—no he'd needed—to see his place one last time.

The house, like most of those positioned near the beach, was built with all of the living area on the second floor. Downstairs was a place to park two cars, a sheltered picnic area, and a large supply room. Outside stairs led up to the main area of the house—three bedrooms, a spacious living room, a kitchen that Madelyn had dubbed Paradise, two bathrooms, and a large family room.

Large plate glass windows normally provided a view of the ocean, but Charlie had fitted the plywood over the glass the evening before.

He had known all day that the situation was worsening. He'd been listening to the radio throughout the afternoon, and it was plain enough by the way the tide was churning and the sky was darkening that they were not going to dodge this storm.

He understood all of this in his mind, but his heart didn't accept the full scope of the situation until he'd driven to his house, parked, and climbed the stairs.

His pulse beat faster, as if he was being chased. He could barely hear over the roar of his blood rushing as adrenaline filled his veins. Why had he delayed so long? Why hadn't he left with Alice? Had he thought himself ready to leave this life? To join Madelyn? Thinking it and understanding he was in mortal danger were two very different things. As he stood at the top of the stairs on the little landing that led to his front door, he found himself praying for God's hand to protect him. He hesitated there, staring out where the beach should be—but it had disappeared under the swelling tide. Raising his gaze, he tried to take in the breadth and depth of Orion.

Quitz whined and pressed against his side.

The surf churned, pushing its way to the top of the dunes that separated his home from the beach. It pushed angrily at the sand, determined to find a way over or through.

The actual storm surge was going to be massive. If it reached fifteen to twenty feet, there wouldn't be much left standing in Port A. If it reached twenty-two feet, large portions of Corpus would be under water. He imagined he could see the outer band of Orion, though the news alerts said the actual hurricane was still several hours away yet. The waves, though, they had a restless, violent nature that was all too familiar.

He'd seen it before.

Suddenly all his memories from Celia—memories he'd been fighting to suppress since he'd heard the name Orion—flooded his mind, causing his heart to ache. He'd been so afraid then, so terrified of losing Madelyn. He would have gladly given away everything else they owned if only someone could guarantee her safety. But no one could, and that was when Charlie had first found his faith. When he'd needed it most.

Foxhole religion? Perhaps. But he'd accepted long ago that any path to God was a good path. In that moment, he'd lost all illusions of being in charge of his life. He'd literally fallen to his knees, wept, and prayed that God would hear his cry.

He wasn't alone. As the sky blackened and the water rose, he and Madelyn had clung to their faith and to one another in a darkened room, sitting among strangers who would become their lifelong friends.

Strangers like Moose.

Charlie came back to the present with a start.

Memories were fine, but he needed to get moving. Unlocking his front door, he saw the bag and box in the entry hall. Why had he left them there? He should have put them in the truck when he left that morning. He should have understood how quickly the situation could deteriorate.

Small beams of light slipped through the spaces where the plywood met.

Rain drops tapped a beat of urgency against the roof.

Quitz barked and snagged her favorite toy from the box of supplies. Standing in the doorway, her tail beating a rhythm of urgency, she waited for Charlie.

There was something he was forgetting, though. Something he needed to take with him. All of his important papers were in the suitcase, plus what little valuables he kept at the house—mainly some of Madelyn's jewelry and a book of old coins that had belonged to his father.

Quitz barked again, and the wind bounced and ricocheted off the boarded windows.

Charlie looked one last time around the room, and then he walked over to the fireplace mantle. He picked up a photograph, stuffed it into his bag, and then he followed Quitz out the door.

He'd purchased flood insurance long ago, and unlike Alice, he'd been careful to keep his payments up to date. Whether his house stood or not didn't matter. Not now.

What mattered most was being certain his friends were safe—all of his friends, including Alice and Moose. Alice was well on her way out of the danger zone. He'd drive out to find Moose, force him into the truck, and get off the island.

Only it wasn't as simple as that. "It hardly ever is," he muttered.

Debris had blown onto the main road, blocking his path. Emergency personnel were clearing the trees, timbers from a busted wharf, and even someone's boat as rain continued to spatter against the pavement.

"You're going to have to turn around and go the other way, Charlie." Officer Gage had to yell to be heard over the roar of the wind. Nicholas Gage was closing in on sixty if Charlie remembered right. Probably he was nearing retirement, an idea that would appeal to any sensible man trying to facilitate an evacuation while a Cat 4 storm barreled toward him. Gage had gained a fair bit of weight in the last ten years, but he managed to look solid even wearing the rain slicker. He was also as obstinate as an old mule.

The rain began to fall in sheets, obscuring everything beyond Charlie's windshield.

"I can't leave just yet, Nick. Moose is still out there. I have to go and get him."

"I'll call the Coast Guard. They can attempt a rescue—"

"Even if they made it to his place, I doubt he'd go with them. I need to talk to him. You know how unreasonable he can be."

"So let him stay—"

"We can't just leave him out there!"

"We can and we will." Gage didn't look happy about it, but he did look determined.

"I'm going to check on him one way or the other. If you make me go around by the back roads—"

"They're washed out."

"If you make me go around, it will take me that much longer."

Gage looked as if he'd like to argue, but in the end he halted the line of cars north bound long enough for Charlie to slip through and head south. He was surprised to see that the line heading away from him, heading toward Corpus, was actually quite short. It appeared most people had heeded the warnings and left the island early.

As he passed the state park, he noted the entire area was basically deserted. No cars at the condos. Gas stations were closed. No lights shone from the convenience store windows. The place looked abandoned, but Charlie knew a few of the old-timers had sworn they wouldn't leave. They had various reasons, all of them lame in light of the hurricane pressing toward them. Perhaps in the end it came down to fear. Their fear of leaving outweighed their fear of facing the storm. Whatever the reason, they were the diehards and no one could force them to evacuate—mandatory was that in name only. It meant that if you chose to stay, you were on your own, at least until the storm abated and rescue teams could be deployed.

Charlie prayed as he drove, that the men who came to his mind, nearly all widowers, would have seen the severity of the situation and left. He prayed for wisdom in speaking to Moose.

The man had lived a more difficult life than most, and perhaps that was part of the reason for his obstinate nature. But he'd also been a good friend to Charlie, visiting every day when Madelyn was sick, and before that helping them to rebuild after Hurricane Celia. No, he wouldn't be leaving Moose Davis on the island.

Charlie knew better than to panic. He still had plenty of time to make the bridge, so he kept his speed well below the limit. The rain had eased a little, but the winds buffeted his truck. The occasional canopy or trashcan blew across Highway 361. The road he turned west on led to one of the most sparsely populated parts of the island. Moose's neighborhood was isolated on the best of days. Charlie didn't see a single person. Quitz sat staring out the window, and Charlie's gaze turned again and again to the rearview window and the menacing, black clouds as day gave way to night. The last of the sun's light bled into the horizon.

It would be easy to be mesmerized by the wall of clouds churning out over the water. He tore his gaze away and focused on the road. He was looking at the bay side, and he could see that it was rising as well. They would have to hurry, but he vowed they would make the bridge before hurricane force winds hit.

He reached over and patted Quitz. "Don't worry, girl. We're going to check on Moose, and then we're headed for the mainland. We'll watch Orion deliver its worst from the safety of Corpus."

CHAPTER 11

*B*ecca sat at the kitchen table, separating pinto beans. She put the good ones into the pot of water beside her. They would soak overnight and be ready to cook in the morning.

Her mother worked at the end of the table. In front of her were various pencils, a sharpener, and an open sketchbook.

"Working on the fall postcards?"

"I am. A few sets are finished, and if I can put the final touches on these, you could take them all to the dry goods store for me tomorrow."

"Sure."

"Are you looking forward to helping Rebecca Byler?"

"I suppose. I've never done inventory before, but I'm glad she asked me. She says it will be *gut* practice and that I'll be able to tell if I want to work there during the holidays."

There wasn't a lot to do in Cody's Creek, and Becca always enjoyed visiting the store and walking up and down the aisles. She also liked the idea of earning a little extra money. Actually, she rather liked going into town for any reason, so she was looking forward to everything about the day—other than worrying whether she could do the job well.

"You and *Daddi* looked to be having a nice visit this afternoon."

"*Ya.*" Becca finished with the beans. She scraped the bad ones into the trash can and then carried the pot over to the stove, covering it with its lid.

She picked up her bag of crochet work from the sitting room and brought it back to the table. She wasn't particularly good at knitting, but even she could crochet—and crocheting a rectangle was no problem at all. The blanket was meant to be a baby gift.

"Nice colors."

"*Danki.*" Becca stared down at the soft pastel yarn—a variegated pink, blue, yellow, and white. She liked it. Even though she hadn't decided whom she would give the blanket to, she knew that someone would be needing it. So many babies were born in their community each winter that it was hard for her to keep up.

"About your *daddi*…"

"How did he hurt his leg, *Mamm*? I don't remember him ever telling me."

"It happened when I was young, before we moved here. *Dat* was working a team of horses and one spooked—a snake in the field, I think. Anyway, the horse reared and then the other panicked. They tossed him off and the harvester he was pulling ran over his leg."

"Rather like what happened last year to Anna Schwartz."

Anna used to live on the other side of Cody's Creek. She'd been rendered a paraplegic after being thrown by horses.

"I suppose. Your *daddi*'s leg healed, but he was left with a limp."

"That's terrible."

"*Ya*, it was bad. This was before *Dat* was called to be a bishop. Sometimes I think maybe it was the way that he handled that period of his life, or perhaps the work that *Gotte* did in his heart during that time, that caused the community to put his name down for nominees."

"And then he pulled the Bible with the marker in it."

"Indeed."

Becca thought about that as she crocheted. There had never been the need to choose a new bishop in their community, at least not that she could remember. Bishops were chosen for life. The only reason to elect a new one was if the bishop died or maybe the bishop moved to a different community.

For as long as she could remember, their bishop had always been her grandfather. But she'd heard about the process of electing a new one. Bibles were placed near the back of the schoolroom. Each man walked in whose name had been placed in a hat as a candidate. Each man picked up a Bible.

When all were assembled, the current bishop, or deacon if the bishop had passed, led the group in prayer. Then the men opened their Bible. The one with a marker in their Bible was chosen as the new bishop. In this way, they believed that God picked the man He wanted to lead them, and the man that God picked He would equip. No special training was required.

"I think *Daddi* is a *gut* bishop."

"I agree." Her mother laughed. "Your *mammi*, though, she wasn't sure she was cut out of the right fabric to be a bishop's wife."

"Really?"

"She was afraid everyone would judge her by a harsher standard, and she didn't want the extra attention."

Becca considered her mother's words as she crocheted another row of the baby blanket. She didn't like attention either. Maybe she was more like her grandmother than she'd realized.

Her father walked into the mudroom, knocking the dirt off his shoes and hanging his jacket on the hook on the wall. They each had two hooks—for jackets or scarves, hats or *kapps*. And under those hooks ran a shelf for shoes.

"An afternoon snack would be *gut*." Her mother glanced up from the postcard she was working on. "Would you fetch that cranberry bread I baked?"

"*Ya*." Becca put away her yarn and hook before retrieving the bread from the back of the stove where it had been cooling.

"I smell something *wunderbaar*." Her dad collapsed into a chair beside her mother.

"That you do, dear."

"Has Becca been baking?"

They all laughed. It was a joke between the three of them, because several of Becca's attempts had turned into disaster.

"Becca will try again next week," her mother assured him. "I baked this cranberry bread."

She set aside her drawing supplies and stood to gather glasses and the pitcher of milk. Becca sliced the bread and carried it to the table. She thought about resisting the urge to eat a slice, but then she noticed that her mother had added walnuts. Who could resist walnuts and cranberry? Who would want to?

Becca had eaten one slice and was considering another when she remembered her mother's question she hadn't answered.

"*Daddi* talked to me about going on a mission trip with the Mennonite Disaster Service group."

Her parents exchanged a knowing look, but neither spoke.

"I don't even understand the MDS program. And why are you two smiling at each other like that?"

"Your mother and I met on a mission trip."

"I never knew that."

Her mom shrugged and sipped her milk.

Her father sat forward, arms crossed on the table, and smiled at her. He had always seemed like a pillar of strength to Becca. More than anything, she appreciated the way he always spoke to her honestly—as an adult, not as a child. She liked that she could trust him to be truthful even when it hurt her feelings or she didn't agree. Like the time she'd thought that going on a liquid diet would change her appearance, maybe even change her life.

He'd gently reminded her, "We dress plainly because we do not want to promote pride. It is *gut* to be healthy and to take care of the body *Gotte* has given you. But comparing yourself—physically or any other way—to other girls will only bring anxiety and strife into your life."

She'd given up the liquid diet that night. One of the other girls, Sarah Yoder, had continued it for several weeks and actually fainted at church. It was later discovered that she had an eating disorder. Folks thought the Amish didn't have those sorts of problems, but they did. And if it hadn't been for the candid words of her father, Becca could have fallen into the same trap.

"I know that part of what we contribute in our tithe offering funds MDS," Becca said. "I suppose I've known that for years. Is it only Amish who volunteer?"

"*Nein*. Mennonites participate as well." Her father helped himself to another piece of bread.

Her mom ran the tip of her finger around the rim of her glass. "Brethren in Christ too, even some Christian groups who are not associated directly with our Anabaptist tradition."

That sounded like a lot of people to Becca.

"Who coordinates it all?"

"Each site has a crew manager," her father explained. "That person may vary from week to week or may stay through the entire length of the project. While there, they oversee volunteers as well as construction materials and the like."

"So it's not a lot of *youngies* running around on their own."

"It isn't. MDS does serious work, Becca. We assist people who don't have the means to recover from various disasters."

She thought about that a moment, while her finger traced the bread crumbs on her plate. "Like what kind of disasters?"

"Floods, hurricanes, fires. Pretty much any type of disaster where we can provide relief."

"I don't remember you two participating. Did you only go that once? The time you met?"

"We went on three different trips," her mother said.

"Three?"

"Two before we were married and one after."

"And then?"

"Then you came along, and we both felt we needed to stay home."

What did that mean? Would they resume going on mission trips once she had married or moved away? She'd never thought about her parents' life after she moved on—if she moved on. This conversation was opening up an entire new bundle of questions she wasn't sure she wanted to address.

"Would you like to go on a mission trip?" her *dat* asked.

"I don't know. It sounded like something fun to do. Well, maybe not fun exactly, but you know…different."

"Except…" Her mother studied her as she waited for Becca to finish her thought.

"Except I'm not sure I want to be responsible for someone else's recovery. I don't know anything about that."

Her father smiled and slapped the kitchen table. "We will pray on this. All of us. You will know, Becca. If *Gotte* wants you to serve somewhere, you will know it is the right thing to do. *Gotte* will provide for you and equip you."

Her father tromped back outside to finish his afternoon work.

Her mother continued adding final touches to the postcards.

And Becca crocheted. As she did so, her father's words continued to ring through her heart. "*Gotte* will provide for you and equip you." She'd never thought of herself that way before—as a tool in the hand of God, something He could use to help others. The idea was rather exciting and frightening at the same time. It was with those emotions stirring in her heart that she stored her crochet work, checked on the chicken dish cooking in the oven, and began to cut up vegetables for a salad. Even she couldn't mess up a salad. If she did go on a mission trip, she hoped that they wouldn't ask her to cook.

CHAPTER 12

Charlie knew that when the outer rim of a hurricane made land the weather would change instantly. He'd experienced it before, and still he was stunned by the wind that pushed his truck like a giant hand and the rain that obscured everything around him.

Quitz whined and hopped down into the floor area in front of her seat.

"I don't blame you, girl. We must have been crazy to stay this late." He should have left like Gage told him too. He thought of the picture in his bag, of the promises he had made to Madelyn. He prayed he would be able to keep those promises.

Though he'd slowed the truck's progress to a crawl, Charlie somehow managed to miss the turn into Moose's place. He reversed the transmission, prayed he would stay on the road, and backed up until he could just make out the lane leading to his friend's bay front home. It was a secluded community, and houses to the right and left were spaced a good distance apart. On any other day, Charlie would be able to see them, but not now. He saw nothing except a deluge of rain falling outside his windshield.

Like Charlie's house, the living portions of Moose's home were built upstairs. After Hurricane Celia, nearly all houses and condos were built this way. Any new construction in downtown Port Aransas was required to be built at a minimum of nine feet above sea level, which usually necessitated that fill dirt be brought in to raise the floor of the building to the minimum height. All new home construction had the same requirement—it was mandatory if you wanted to purchase FEMA flood insurance. If you had a loan to fund the construction, flood insurance was required.

Being on the bay side of the island helped a little as far as weathering the severity of your average storms, but it would make no difference during a Category 3, 4, or 5 hurricane. The waters of the gulf and the bay would simply meet—and most everything in between would wash away.

Moose had boarded up the main windows in his living area, but the smaller windows near the top of the rooms that usually allowed in the gulf sunshine remained uncovered. As Charlie drew closer he saw light peeking through these top windows and through the seam where two pieces of plywood met over the front windows.

Moose was in there all right, just as Charlie had feared he would be.

Should he take Quitz or leave her in the car? The dog practically clambered into his lap when he turned off the truck's engine. "All right, but we're both getting soaked. As long as you realize that."

His memory didn't prepare him for the physical violence of the storm. He struggled to push the door open, and then had to hold it with all his strength so that the wind didn't tear it from his hands. Quitz jumped out, splashed through the downpour, and bounded up the front steps. Charlie glanced once at his bags in the backseat. Best to leave them where they were. He was not riding out Orion here at Moose's place. The question was, how was he going to convince his friend to leave?

He leaned into the truck door and managed to close it. Then he dashed for the porch. The wind pushed him left, pushed him forward, and threatened to send him into the bay. Charlie fought it, head down and shoulders hunched. He lunged for the porch railing and pulled himself around and then up the stairs. Quitz was baying as if tomorrow wouldn't come when Moose opened the door.

"What are you doing here?" Moose stared at them as if he couldn't believe his eyes. "Never mind. Get in. Get in."

Charlie and Quitz dashed into the house. Moose closed and bolted the door, as if a lock could keep the storm outside.

"I heard Quitz and thought my senses had left me completely."

Perhaps they had. Charlie shook off the water that had soaked his clothes, and Quitz did the same. Moose handed him a towel from a stack he had placed on a bench near the front door.

"What gives, Moose? Why are you still here?"

"Come into the living room. Power's out, so I'm using my battery lamp, but I have some hot coffee in a Thermos."

Moose shuffled across the room. When had he started shuffling? And why was he wearing pajama bottoms and a camouflage coat? Moose was a small man, probably not more than five and a half feet tall. Charlie had always thought of him as strong, though. Having grown up in Montana, there seemed to be nothing Moose Davis couldn't or wouldn't do. He had a rancher's attitude about life, and he certainly wasn't afraid of hard work. He also believed in lending a hand to his neighbor—something he had done for Charlie on more than one occasion.

Stubborn—yes, but not crazy.

And yet Charlie had suspected the man would still be here. Why was that? What had nudged him to check on Moose? Regardless, he was grateful that he had. He'd lost enough to hurricanes in the past and would no doubt lose more to the one hammering at the door. He didn't plan on losing one of his oldest friends.

Charlie realized as he accepted the coffee poured into the Thermos's cup that something was wrong. Moose gazed around as if he were somewhat confused, and then he dropped onto his couch and motioned for Quitz to join him. The dog didn't need to be asked twice.

"We have to go, Moose. You can't ride out this storm here."

Moose seemed not to hear him. Instead, he focused on Quitz, rubbing behind the dog's ears and using another towel to dry the the excess water from the Lab's coat.

"Do you know what it's like out there? Have you been listening to the emergency reports?"

Moose waved Charlie's concerns away.

"I'm not kidding. It's worse than Celia."

"That was a storm, wasn't it?" Moose still didn't look up.

"The ferries have stopped, and I'm beginning to doubt we can make it over the bridge in this wind." A giant thunderous crash interrupted Charlie. Something had hit the plywood covering the windows.

Quitz whined, but Moose seemed unconcerned.

Charlie rubbed his hand up and over the top of his head. "Maybe the Coast Guard will be shuttling folks across—though I doubt there's anyone left on the island but us. We need to go—now. We have to try to make it to one of the Coast Guard evacuation sites."

"I can't go." Moose finally glanced up, and when he did Charlie's heart dropped like a stone to the bottom of the bay. "I can't leave Paula."

Charlie had been pacing in front of the couch, but now he stopped and stared at his friend.

"She'll be back soon. Don't look so worried. It's just a…just a storm."

But it wasn't just a storm, and Paula most certainly would not be back soon. She'd died a year earlier in a car crash—a driver in the oncoming lane had fallen asleep at the wheel and crossed the line. The police had assured Moose she'd never felt a thing. She apparently didn't see it coming because there were no brake marks. She was there one day and gone the next. When Charlie thought of that, he was thankful for the final days he'd had with Madelyn. Yes, she'd shrunk before his eyes, and the meds had caused her to sleep a lot. But they'd also shared precious moments, special memories, and promises—promises to see each other again on the other side.

Moose had taken Paula's death like a mortal wound, but he'd accepted it. So what was going on? Why was he waiting for her to come home? Could Moose be suffering from dementia, possibly

Alzheimer's? He was only ten years older than Charlie—only seventy-five, which increasingly seemed not so old to Charlie.

As Moose stared at Quitz, once again completely focused on reassuring the dog, Charlie thought back over an online quiz he'd taken a few weeks before. He considered such things silly and a downright waste of time, and he'd almost passed it up. But then he'd remembered his mother's struggle with dementia, and he'd clicked on the quiz. Fortunately, most of his own actions that had worried him were considered normal by the quiz makers—misplacing his keys, occasionally forgetting what day of the week it was, even having to look up the phone number for his pharmacy. He'd been on his home phone at the time. If he'd looked on his cell, it was plainly listed under *Pharmacy*. The quiz had reassured him that his forgetfulness fell in the "normal range."

Studying Moose, he remembered some of the more serious symptoms of Alzheimer's—confusion with time or place, poor judgment, even withdrawal from social activities. He had noticed that Moose attended church less, and he rarely agreed to a game of dominoes—something he and Paula had once loved. He had also given a fairly large sum of money to a telephone solicitor, something he'd been embarrassed to admit. Charlie had convinced him to file a complaint with the police. Scums who preyed on the elderly needed to be met with the full force of the law. The entire episode had been a costly mistake, though one that a good number of folks fell prey to.

But thinking that his wife was still alive? In Charlie's mind, that pushed Moose from the *maybe* column to the *probably* column in the dementia quiz. The question was—how could Charlie convince him to leave?

"She'll be home soon," Moose mumbled. "Paula hates driving in the rain."

"I know she does." Charlie sat down on the edge of the recliner. "Remember that night she stayed in Corpus because she didn't want to drive over the bridge during the storm?"

Tension drained from Moose's face as a smile replaced the worry lines around his mouth. "Spring of '97. We fought about that hotel bill. She called me a miser...and could be she was right. I was terribly tight with money back then."

Lightning flashed and wind continued to buffet the window coverings. Charlie felt an intense need to get out of the house, to get anywhere safer. "Say, Moose. I'm thinking that Paula's fine, but we need to get out of here."

The wind continued to pound the house. Though it was sturdily built, it wouldn't withstand a Category 4 storm. There wasn't much that would.

"Think she stayed over on the mainland?"

"Makes sense." Charlie stared at his friend, willing him to agree to leave. He didn't think he could force the old coot out of his house. No, his best option was to reason with him.

"Like in '97." Moose's voice grew stronger, more sure, and then his face fell. "But she would have called. She always calls if she's going to be late."

"Phones are out, Moose. Landlines and cell service."

"Oh." Moose gave Quitz one last scratch behind the ears. "We should go then and get over to her."

"Yeah. That's a good idea."

Charlie stood and walked to the front door. A suitcase was waiting there. A part of Moose's mind was still working on a functioning level. Then Charlie picked it up, and all of his doubts came rushing back.

"What's in here, Moose? This weighs a ton."

"Books. I packed Paula's favorites when I first heard the storm warnings."

"What about your legal papers, jewelry, photos...anything important that's not in your safety deposit box?"

"Nah. I can come back for that stuff."

"Well, you have to change clothes. You can't go in that." He pointed at Moose's pajama bottoms.

"Right." Moose hustled back into his bedroom and returned in old blue jeans and work boots.

Something crashed into the window near the front door. The panes rattled, but the plywood held. Lightning flashed and the higher window exploded, raining shards of glass down on them. The sound of the wind increased, and the roar of the rain made it nearly impossible to hear one another.

Charlie brushed glass off Moose's shoulders. A small spot was bleeding on his left ear.

"Is Quitz okay?"

"I think so."

"What about you?"

"Yeah. I am." In truth his heart was racing so fast he could hear his pulse pounding in his eardrums. He pushed the glass over into a corner with his foot. Wouldn't do for the dog to cut her feet before they got out of the house.

Was it smart to go back out into the truck? How would they ever get down the stairs?

But if they stayed…Charlie sensed that if they stayed they wouldn't survive. He knew they needed to go, and they needed to do it right that minute.

"I parked directly in front of your porch," he hollered over the storm's roar. "My bumper is practically touching your railing."

Moose nodded once. Quitz pushed herself against Charlie's legs. He could feel the dog trembling, and then Moose unbolted the door. The fury of the storm tore it from his hands, but Moose never hesitated. He stepped out into Orion, with Charlie and Quitz close on his heels.

What he saw stopped him in his tracks. Water was sloshing midway up the staircase. How had it risen so quickly? Charlie had walked into Moose's house no more then twenty minutes earlier. Logs and unidentifiable wreckage floated around the house or rammed into the porch. One of the seaside cabins that had been on the gulf side now sat in Moose's front yard, snagged by a backlog of debris.

And Charlie's truck?

It was gone.

CHAPTER 13

*J*oshua tried to sleep but succeeded only in tossing and turning. His bedcovers became a tangle of sheets, blankets, and quilt. He finally surrendered, threw on the pair of pants and a shirt he had folded and placed across the chair near his bed, and crept downstairs—careful to avoid the squeaking step.

He needn't have worried about waking someone up. His father had never gone to bed. He was sitting at the kitchen table, applying a glossy finish to three turkey calls.

"Kind of late to be working on that," Joshua said as he opened the refrigerator and reached for the milk.

"Kind of late to be snacking." His father cocked his head and studied him for a moment. When he turned his attention back to his woodwork, he said, "Grab me a glass too, and those cookies your *mamm* set back on the stove."

They ate in silence—savoring the taste of oatmeal, molasses, and raisins. His dad continued rubbing the oil into the wood between bites. It had always amazed Joshua that his father—a man who deftly handled their team of large Percheron horses and could still toss fifty pound bags of feed into the barn—could also work on something so delicate.

"You're a *gut* craftsman, *Dat*."

"Well, thank you, son." Daniel capped the bottle of oil and sat back. "But I suspect you didn't get up at one in the morning to compliment my woodwork."

"Couldn't sleep." Joshua popped another cookie into his mouth. "What about you? Why are you up so late?"

"Same reason."

Neither seemed to want to broach the subject of Alton. What was left to say? There were no easy answers, and the questions only continued to loom larger.

"Do you remember the time you ran away?"

"*Nein.*"

"I'm not surprised. You were a little thing—five going on twenty if I remember right."

"Guess I didn't get very far."

"Nope. Didn't even make it to the road. Your *mamm* and I were following at a discreet distance, watching to be sure you didn't get lost."

His father wiggled his eyebrows, causing Joshua to laugh. It felt good to relax. To forget the burden of his brother if only for a little while.

"Turned around, did I?"

"Yup. You trudged down the lane and stopped right beside that old maple tree."

"Where the lane curves."

"You sat down and stared back the way you had come."

"Can't see the house from there."

"And maybe that's why you turned back." His father ran his thumb across the grain of the table, another piece of his handiwork. "Your *mamm* and I, we beat a path back to the house and were sitting on the front porch when you climbed the steps and plopped down beside us."

Joshua shook his head. "I don't remember any of that."

"*Ya.* You'd even packed a change of clothes and a baseball that you'd taken to carrying with you everywhere. Put it all in one of your *mamm*'s grocery sacks, asked for cookies to take with you, and started off down the lane."

"I guess most kids run away at some point."

"Maybe so." His father finished off the glass of milk. "Know what you said after you sat down?"

Joshua shook his head, but something—perhaps a vague memory in the back of his mind—stirred.

"In a very matter-of-fact tone you said, 'I see you still have Blaze and Milo.'" His father grinned at the memory. "The horses were grazing in the near pasture, and you seemed real tickled that they were still there—that things were as you had left them."

"An hour before…"

"Something like that."

Joshua stood, picked up their dishes, and washed them off in the sink before placing them in the drainer.

Maybe he could sleep after all. Tomorrow was going to be a long day, starting out with a walk to the bus station in town.

"I suppose I should be off to bed."

"Joshua…" His father had returned to working the oil into the wood. He stared down at it as he spoke. "When I think of Alton, of how lost he is sometimes…I think of you, sitting down next to that old maple tree. That near about broke your mother's heart. She couldn't understand why her son would want to run away."

"I was a child. Young and stupid."

"We all have those days of questioning. For your brother, those days came a little later and lasted a bit longer. But to your *mamm* and me—it's the same. We're still watching and waiting for him to turn around and head back home." He glanced up, and the look of hope and worry pierced Joshua's heart through and through. "Bring Alton home to us."

Joshua nodded and started out of the kitchen, but he turned back and asked, "Why have you never told me that story before?"

"You didn't need to hear it before."

Joshua waited for his father to say more. He didn't, though, and finally Joshua turned and trudged back through the sitting room and up the stairs. When he'd burrowed down deep under the covers, his mind was filled with images—his father's expression, raisin oatmeal cookies on a plate, fresh milk poured from a pitcher.

His brother, Alton, as they pulled the truck out of the ditch.

Becca Troyer, offering an apple to him for Blaze.

And then, just before sleep claimed him, an older memory rose. It was of their two horses, standing beside the pasture fence—and his joy in finding that nothing had changed, that everything was exactly the same as when he'd left.

CHAPTER 14

Charlie realized it had been a mistake to open the front door. He pushed Moose back into the house, nearly tripped over the dog, and then both men had to lean into the door to shut it against the wind.

Staying in the house was not a good decision, but leaving the house—at this point that wasn't even a possibility.

The floor was now slick from the rain coming through the broken window. Charlie stepped back toward the corner and heard the glass crunch beneath his feet.

Moose calmed Quitz, who sat huddled and shivering. But Charlie was staring at the floor. The sheer volume of rain was causing water to push through under the door, and the pieces of glass were floating toward the back of the house.

"The door is not going to hold. We need to get up to your attic."

"What if the whole thing goes?"

"We'll worry about that later. Right now, we have to get out of this room and up to someplace higher."

Moose led the way to the hall, reached up, and pulled down a ladder.

"How are you going to get the dog up there?"

It was a good question.

"You go first, and I'll hand her up to you."

Quitz was a good sixty pounds, and it was all Charlie could do to climb the steep ladder with her in his arms.

Though he continued to question Moose's mental clarity, there was no doubt that the man was still physically strong. Moose reached down and heaved Quitz into the attic. Charlie followed them.

They both stared down through the opening as the force of the water busted the front door off its hinges. The surge had reached more than nineteen feet. The water rushed in and through the house, snatching furniture and carrying debris through the rooms. The last thing Charlie saw was a bathtub wedged in the hallway beneath them. It wasn't even Moose's bathtub. It was part of some other house that had been swept away.

Fortunately, the attic had a wood floor all the way across it. On one side, storage boxes were neatly labeled and stacked. Charlie walked across the large room to a small window that overlooked the front of the house. At first he saw nothing, but then lightning flashed, and he was able to make out the scene below.

"See your truck?"

"No, but I think the big crash we heard earlier was a boat. It's hung up on the corner of your property, stuck in those salt cedars."

"What kind of a boat?"

Charlie shrugged, "Not too big. Looks like a shrimp boat."

"How did it move from the gulf side of the marina to here?"

"I don't know, Moose. There's no telling what's out there. You remember Celia..."

"Yeah. Yeah, I do."

Charlie walked to each side of the attic, staring out through the small windows until lightning flashed again. He could see the trees Moose had planted on the south side of his house. They were bent to the ground. Toward the gulf side he only saw gray. Oppostite that there seemed to be no demarcation between the bay and the sky. Lightning flashed again, and he was able to see the house next door. It appeared to be faring even worse than Moose's. As he watched, a large part of the roof simply flew off.

He staggered backward, nearly tripping over Quitz again.

"Find your truck?"

"No, but your neighbor just lost his roof."

Moose sat down on the top of one of the boxes and stared at his hands. "You're sure Paula's okay?"

"I am, and she would want you to worry about yourself." Charlie was thinking the truck was no great loss. After all, it was insured, and he had always been careful to maintain adequate coverage. But what about the things that were irreplaceable? What about the bag he'd placed behind his seat? He would have liked to have kept that.

His heart hardened toward the storm. It could take his possessions, but it couldn't steal his memories. It could take his life, but this life wasn't all there was. He was certain of that. Not that he was ready to go just yet.

Which took his thoughts back to the truck. As far as a means of escape, the vehicle was useless. They wouldn't be driving to safety.

"We can't stay here." Moose sounded calm—disconnected, even.

"Going back outside seems foolish."

Moose glanced up, stared at Charlie, and shook his head.

A loud screeching sound permeated the noise of the rain and wind. They both hurried across the room to stare out in the direction of the neighbor's house. At first they saw only darkness. Then lightning flashed and revealed more than a missing roof. The entire structure listed to the far side. As lightning pulsed again and again, they watched the structure begin to teeter. Darkness shrouded the night, and then lightning struck one last time. The house was gone.

Charlie's heart raced as his mind combed through their options. Problem was, he couldn't come up with any. He walked across the attic space and glanced down through the hole. An eerie glow emanated from the battery lantern Moose had set on a shelf near the front door. The water inside the house was now four, maybe five feet deep. If they didn't get out of the building soon, they wouldn't be able to. If they did get out, where would they go?

"God help us," he whispered. As precious seconds ticked by, he prayed, wondering if God could even hear him above the sound of the storm, wondering what it would feel like to die.

To Charlie, it seemed as if his entire life was shifting. He sat on the floor, his back against the boxes, and Quitz plopped down next to him. Moose sat across from them, resting his back against one of the roof supports. They stayed there for what seemed like an hour. At one point, Charlie looked at his watch and realized the time had crept past midnight. The next day had arrived, and with it more danger.

Water swirled beneath them, and the rain continued to fall in a deluge that Charlie thought would never end. Quitz had stopped whining and finally closed her eyes, her head resting across his feet. Occasionally she would open one eye and stare up at Charlie, as if she trusted him to find a way out. As if she believed in him.

"Seems to be letting up," Moose said. "Think we're in the eye?"

"Depends on how fast Orion is moving. If it sped up, I suppose yes—maybe. But if it slowed down..."

"If it slowed down, that was an outer band, and there's not even a chance this house will withstand the full force."

"Same is true if we're nearing the eye," Charlie reminded him. "The back side is always worse."

"But it is letting up."

"I don't know what difference it makes. The water's chest high below—and that's in the house. I couldn't drive through what's outside if I did find the truck, and the truck is gone."

"We'll walk."

"Walk?"

"Yeah, walk. Or swim."

"Where?"

"Over to the bay front community center. It's built of cinderblock and just might still be standing."

Moose nodded in the direction of the bay. The community center he spoke of had always been a thorn in his side. More than once he had called it a waste of their home owner association dues, and he'd actively spoken out against the elaborate design structure. The price had been quite high, but if Charlie remembered correctly the architect had claimed it was built to Category 5 specifications—something they had all laughed at.

But maybe Orion wasn't a Cat 5, and maybe—just possibly—they could make it there. The distance was less than a ten-minute walk in fair weather. In this storm? Charlie didn't know. He was staring at the wall across from him, trying to calculate the distance to the center, when he suddenly realized the wall had moved.

Charlie jumped to his feet. "We have to go."

"Right this minute?"

"Yes, now. This place is breaking apart."

"Down the stairs?"

Charlie didn't like that idea. There was too much junk jammed up in the floor below. But there was no way out of the small attic windows.

"I'll carry Quitz. Do you have any rope up here?"

Moose hurried over to one of the boxes and tore it open. He pulled out a hammer, a tarp, and a roll of duct tape, dumping them on the floor. The house was now beginning to creak, and there was no doubt it was coming apart at the seams. Finally, he pulled out a long length of rope.

Without speaking he began to tie it around his waist. Charlie looped his end through Quitz's collar, and then tied the remaining portion around his own waist.

"Die together or live together, my friend." Moose's voice had grown stronger, and his eyes looked clear.

Charlie prayed that whatever form of dementia Moose was suffering from would relent until they found a safe place to hunker down.

There was a three-foot length of rope between each man and the dog, who sat staring from one to the other. Moose walked toward the ladder. "Let's do this now before I lose my nerve."

But Charlie was barely listening. The rain had lightened, but suddenly the wind increased, shaking the house and causing Charlie to press his hands against his ears. He felt as if his eardrums would surely burst. He felt as if his entire head might explode.

And then the roof was gone, and he was staring up into a sky that showed patches of starlight.

"God protect us, keep us safe, and guide our way." Moose's words sounded like a prayer—a desperate plea for divine intervention. He walked to the corner of the attic, pulling Charlie and Quitz with him.

"Wrong way. It's going to come apart!" Charlie struggled to be heard over the wind, and then he saw what Moose was aiming for.

The boogie boards probably hadn't been used in the past decade. Moose handed one to Charlie, and then he grabbed one for himself.

A great ripping sound confirmed Charlie's worst fear. They hustled back to the middle of the room, and Charlie glanced down in time to see the stairs pulled away from the attic. Then the north wall of the attic was gone. Charlie's exhaustion fell away as adrenaline pumped through his veins.

The house was shaking, moving actually—to the west, toward the gulf. Charlie fought the urge to grab onto the roof beams. The house was not going to make it through the next gust of wind. It held only false hope.

Moose must have figured the same. His head down, he walked toward where the north wall had been. Looking out, they both saw that the house had moved and was now past the neighbor's property line. When Charlie leaned forward to get an idea of what lay in their path, he could see they were about to collide with another structure. When he looked down, he saw that the storm surge had risen even higher.

"Are you ready?" Moose called.

"No! No, I'm not!" But his words slipped away into the night as he clutched the boogie board with one arm and Quitz with his other. Then he stepped forward, and they were falling into the cold, turbulent water.

CHAPTER 15

It was a miracle that Moose, Charlie, and Quitz were alive and moving in the right direction. The hurricane had weakened, and an eerie calm had settled over Port A. Charlie knew that wouldn't last. It was a pause, not a stop. They were in the eye of the storm. The temperature had risen, and the winds were almost nonexistent. Then there were the stars—thousands of pinpoints of light. They blazed brighter than normal, probably due to the power outage.

Quitz trembled, perched on top of the boogie board while Charlie clung to the side. Moose was next to them, holding onto his board with one arm and trying to direct their course with the other. Which was pretty much like trying to maneuver across the ocean with a Ping-Pong paddle.

A scream pierced the night, but Charlie couldn't see who or where it came from. He'd thought they were alone, but apparently not. It seemed that others had made the same costly mistake they had. The rain stopped completely, and Charlie noticed that his hands were shaking. At one point he lost contact with the board, but Quitz yipped and snagged his shirt sleeve, pulling backward and nearly falling off. It was enough of a tug for Charlie to grab hold again of the fiberglass board as he reached for Quitz. The dog licked his hand, whined, and then she sat as if she were riding in the front seat of the truck.

Just when he thought they were lost, that they'd been pushing in the wrong direction, the community center loomed out of the darkness to the side of them. A dim light shone from one of the upstairs windows. All of the electricity was out. That had to be a flashlight or emergency lantern. Could someone be in there?

"We're going to miss it!" Moose yelled.

And they almost did. There was no way to slow their progress. Though the rain had stopped, the current itself was quite strong, which explained how they had covered the distance from Moose's house to the center in such a short time. Moose snatched a piece of lumber floating by, and then he lunged to the right, still holding on to his boogie board. The lumber came in contact with a power pole that was still standing, and they spun, twisted, and turned backward, finally colliding with the east wall of the community center.

Pain shot up and through Charlie's shoulder—the arm he'd slung over the top of the boogie board. Quitz tumbled off, and with his good hand Charlie reached out and snatched her collar, dragging her first under the water before he managed to push her up and back on to the board.

Moose was still beside him. They were basically pinned against the facade of the building—which had indeed held through the first affront by Orion. But at least they hadn't floated by it. If they had...

Charlie shivered. He didn't want to think about spending the entire night floating in the bay. He didn't want to think about being out in the elements when the back side of Orion hit.

"How are we going to get in?" Moose asked.

Charlie looked for the doors. Finding none, he realized they were level with the second floor windows, and the water was still rising.

"Hand me that plank you used to turn us."

With the plank in his right hand, he pushed them north, along the wall until they were even with one of the windows. The pain in his left shoulder was excruciating, but he managed to hold on. What choice did he have? When they reached the first set of windows, he took the piece of lumber and attempted to smash it through the glass.

No luck.

He couldn't hold on to his board and still gain enough traction to slam the board with any amount of force. And the time he tried letting go to ram the wood into the window with both hands, he sunk under the water. Quitz yelped. Moose grabbed the collar at the back of Charlie's shirt and yanked him up and back over his board.

Charlie could no longer feel his left shoulder and his teeth were chattering. How long had they been in the water? How long would the eye of the storm hover over them? Panic rushed through his veins, and he began to holler, "Help! Someone help!" as together they futilely attempted to smash the window.

A voice from above hollered, "Stay where you are! We're sending someone down."

Charlie craned his neck back and saw a black man around thirty years old calling down to them.

"We're upstairs, but we'll get you in. Just hang on!"

Before Charlie could answer, the voice and the man disappeared.

Would they be rescued? Tears stung Charlie's eyes, and he looked away from Moose, suddenly embarrassed. But his friend only reached over and patted him clumsily on the back. Charlie was glad that words weren't necessary, because he didn't know how to voice all the thoughts running through his mind and emotions filling his heart.

Suddenly the window they'd been trying to smash opened. Kurt Jameson reached out and grabbed Quitz, lifting the dog up and into the room. A younger man, Charlie suddenly remembered his name was Dale, grabbed Moose's arm and pulled him in. Finally, Kurt reached for Charlie.

"I can't…it's my shoulder." Charlie had switched to holding onto the board with his right arm. "Left arm's no good. If I let go with my right, I'll sink."

Dale and Kurt filled the window, both leaning out.

"I'll get the board," Dale said.

"Charlie, I'll grab your right arm."

When Charlie nodded, Kurt said, "On three—"

For a moment it seemed that Kurt might pull his arm out of the socket, but then he was standing beside the man, and Dale was holding on to the boogie board, grinning. Kurt and Dale helped untie the rope that had kept Charlie, Moose, and Quitz together.

When they moved away from the window, Charlie's legs began to shake.

"Can you make it upstairs?" Kurt asked. "We have some blankets and dry clothes. Even some food, but not much, and there's bottled water."

Kurt was a round man with a bald head and a large, prominent nose. He was not in the best physical shape despite being twenty years younger than Charlie. But he was as honest as the day was long. He owned the lube and oil place in town, and he'd been working on Charlie's vehicle the last ten years.

Dale shook hands with Moose and then Charlie. "Boogie boards. Good idea. How'd you think of that?"

"Desperation," Moose said. "Happened to be close at hand when my house blew over."

Charlie suddenly remembered where he'd seen Dale before. It had been a few years earlier. They had been on the city planning board together. Dale Northcut had a tendency to dance on the progressive side of things, a stark contrast to Charlie's usual conservative stance. He'd dressed then as he did now—jeans and a plain T-shirt. His hair was always a tad too long and his voice a mite too loud. In other words, he'd grated on Charlie's nerves, and still Charlie was glad to see him.

"What are you two doing here? Why didn't you get off the island?"

"Let's talk about that upstairs." Kurt had pushed the window shut, but already water was creeping across the room, coming in through the window seals and possibly rising from the lower floor.

They started across the room, and that was when Charlie noticed Quitz limping. Looking closer, he saw a trail of bloody paw prints on the wet floor.

"Come here, girl." Charlie attempted to pick the dog up, momentarily forgetting that his left arm wasn't working.

"I got her," Dale said. He picked up the dog as if she weighed nothing.

Charlie started to argue, but he realized that would be foolish. His legs were still shaking, his shoulder had begun to ache again, and his throat felt as though it had practically closed up. He'd be lucky to make it up the stairs himself.

Five minutes later they were standing in the middle of the activity room on the third floor, and Dale had thrust bottles of water into their hands. He uncapped another bottle and poured half of it into a paper cup for Quitz. The dog immediately lapped it up, and Charlie's estimation of Dale rose another notch.

It seemed odd to Charlie that he was so thirsty. He'd nearly drowned! And before that he'd nearly been swept away. But thirsty he was, and he had to force himself to drink the water slowly. As he did, he studied the room they were sheltering in.

This floor of the community center had been planned for all ages, so it contained everything from Lego bins to Ping-Pong tables to reading chairs. Someone had moved one of the Ping-Pong tables to the middle of the room and placed supplies on it. The chairs had been positioned around the table. A woman and child sat on one side. Limping across the room toward them was the black man who had leaned out the window and called out to them to hold on.

"Lamar Johnson." He shook Charlie's hand and then Moose's. "What's it like out there?"

"As bad as it looks," Charlie said.

Moose sank into one of the chairs, and Charlie did the same. It felt good to be inside, and to be with other people. Some of the panic that had threatened to overwhelm him faded.

"My house is gone." Moose sounded as if he were describing an everyday event, his voice devoid of emotion. "Broke apart and then floated away."

"Sorry to hear that." Dale squatted down in front of Charlie. "Want to let me look at that shoulder?"

"Nah…it'll be fine."

"Charlie, you need to let me look at it. It could be twenty-four hours or longer before anyone comes to rescue us."

"You know first aid?" Moose asked.

"He fixed me up." Lamar pointed down to one of his legs, which had been splinted with a board from one of the shelves. "It's broken, but I can walk now without doubling over from the pain."

Charlie tried to remove his shirt and found he couldn't.

"Here are scissors." The woman holding the child picked them up from a box on the table and handed them to Dale.

"Charlie and Moose, this is Angela, my wife." Dale proceeded to cut away Charlie's shirt as he introduced his family. "And that pretty little girl is Sophia Claire."

Sophia hid her head in her mother's lap. Charlie figured her to be about three years old. Both Sophia and Angela had long dark hair. The mother's face was scrunched in an expression of concern. The little girl peeked out at Charlie from the safety of her mom's arms.

"How did you all end up here?" Charlie asked. "And what happened to your leg, Lamar?"

"I very unwisely decided to be the last person off the island." He laughed when Charlie and Moose gawked at him. "Maybe that wasn't my intent, but I realized too late that might happen. Made the mistake of thinking I had a little extra time."

Lamar was a large man—easily over six feet.

"I have a little fishing enterprise over on the docks, and no—I do not have FEMA insurance. Most small businessmen can't afford it. My idea was to move as much material as possible into town and stash it in one of the motel parking lots. I even rented a room and filled it with equipment." Lamar laughed at his own folly. "What I didn't plan on was Orion speeding up. Hit land a full two hours earlier than expected."

So that was what had happened. Charlie felt as though he hadn't heard any real news in days.

"I sure hope Paula is okay." Moose jumped up and began to pace. "I hope she didn't try to drive back on to the island."

"She's fine, Moose." Charlie saw that Kurt was about to ask a question. He shook his head once, quickly. Kurt had also worked on Moose's car and, more importantly, on Paula's. He'd even attended her funeral. "Authorities wouldn't have let anyone back on the island."

Moose considered that for a moment, and then he sat back down, leaning forward—his elbows on his knees, his head buried in his hands.

"Your shoulder seems to be dislocated, Charlie." Dale helped Charlie into a dry T-shirt and camouflage jacket that he'd pulled from another supply box. Then he grabbed a pillow from one of the chairs and placed it between Charlie's arm and his chest. Finally he took strips of a sheet, also from the box, and wrapped them around Charlie, binding his left arm to his upper body.

"You can't pull it back into place?"

Dale grinned but shook his head. "I've seen that in the movies too, but I don't know how to do it. This will keep you from making the injury any worse, and immobilizing it should help with the pain. I'm afraid all we have in the way of medication is a tube of antibiotic ointment and some aspirin."

"I'll take the aspirin then, but could you put some of that ointment on my dog's foot?"

"Sure, and I'll check to be sure there's nothing in the wound."

Kurt had pulled sweat pants from a box of clothing. He handed one pair to Charlie and another to Moose. He also found Moose a sweatshirt with a Corpus Christi slogan across the front. He pointed in the directions of the bathrooms. "Best change before you catch pneumonia."

By the time they returned, Dale was nearly finished working on Quitz. She lay patiently as he wrapped a bandage around her paw. Lamar picked up his story where he'd stopped.

"When I was driving back with my second load, I realized the storm was coming in quicker than expected. So I skipped the hotel, and cut across town through my neighborhood—nothing much left there. I headed straight for the ferry, but even as I drove in that direction I knew I was too late."

"Good thing you were," Dale said. "Otherwise Angela, Sophia, and I would still be out there."

"Our car broke down," Angela explained. "Lamar was headed back toward the south—"

"Hoped to make the bridge," Lamar said.

"But instead he stopped and picked us up." Angela pushed her hair out of her face. Her dark eyes took in each of them, but settled on Lamar. "You saved our lives. There's no doubt about that, and you risked your own doing it."

"I never would have made it onto, let alone across, the bridge. By then, I could barely keep my truck on the road. If my making the biggest mistake of my life saved you folks, I suppose God used my stupidity for some good."

"Are you sure your neighborhood is gone?" Charlie asked. "You live over by Alice, don't you?"

"Alice Givens? She's a couple blocks over from me, but yeah the same area. And yes, I'm sure it's gone. If houses out here are being swept away, I can't imagine anything surviving where I live…where I lived."

"I cleaned the wound and applied ointment to her paw," Dale said.

They all glanced down at the dog. She had a shiny black coat, a bandage halfway up one leg, and trusting eyes.

Dale stood, his hands on his hips, and looked around. "We got here and found Kurt moving supplies to the top floor."

Kurt finally sat, and the chair groaned beneath his weight. Charlie hoped he didn't have a heart attack while they were waiting out Orion. The big guy looked pale, and there was sweat beading on his forehead.

"My story's short," Kurt said. "Stupid. Just plain stupid. I thought I couldn't leave my stuff. And you know where it is? In the bay. Everything I own is in the bay."

"Sorry to hear that, Kurt." Charlie glanced from face to face. They were a pitiful lot, the seven of them, but he was glad to have found other survivors. He was grateful to God Almighty that he wasn't still floating in the water holding on to a boogie board.

He tried to think of what else to say, but his mind was blank, overwhelmed by all that had happened and what lay ahead. Suddenly rain began to crash into the building and the wind moaned as if it wanted to break free. The back side of Orion had arrived in a state of fury. There was nothing left to do but stay together and pray that they survived the night.

CHAPTER 16

Charlie stood at the window, watching the sun turn the sky first violet, then lavender, and finally a rosy pink. Sunlight bounced off the water, off the sea of debris, and off the destruction that had once been Port Aransas. It was a surreal beauty, and Charlie wasn't immune to it. He once again thought of Madelyn reminding him that the world had moved on, which was easy enough to believe looking out of that third-floor window of the community center.

In the distance he saw smoke from several different fires. Images from his past, from Celia, collided with what he was seeing now. It had surprised him then that fire could exist in the midst of a flood, but now he knew it could and did. Some of the smoke he saw rising was across the bay in the direction of Corpus Christi. As he walked from the west side of the room to the north, he also saw evidence of fires on the Port Aransas side of the island.

He suspected emergency crews couldn't get through the flooded streets, though they had no doubt begun crossing the bay at first light. What he was seeing had probably been burning for many hours. He'd read, after Celia, that the winds from hurricanes increased the fire danger. Once emergency personnel were able to make it to the site of a blaze, they still couldn't access fire hydrants that were under water or buried in debris.

No, the fires didn't surprise him, and they were only the first of the problems he saw. The water level had dropped but left in its wake pockets of water where there shouldn't be and mountains of debris—everything from telephone poles to pieces of houses to parts of boats and docks. Roads were completely obstructed in every direction.

What Charlie was looking at was enough to make a grown man cry, but he felt oddly serene. They had survived. The devastation was widespread, but he realized in that moment that most things could be set right with enough time and money.

Structures could be rebuilt. Boats could be repurchased. Infrastructure could be restored.

It was what he couldn't see that tore at Charlie's heart—the lives lost, the memories carried away in the ocean's tide, and folks injured who were waiting to be rescued.

Their small group had spent most of the night on the floor, sitting under the Ping-Pong table, with the chairs tilted to provide protection from debris. The water had not reached the third level where they sheltered, and the building had held. The first floor was certainly still under water, and the second floor had been severely damaged, if what Charlie had seen last night was any indication. On their level, several of the windows had blown out, and much of the floor was a wet mess of glass, water, and even pieces of rubble. He didn't know if Orion had topped out as a Category 5. Regardless, the architect of the community center deserved an award. And there were seven people and one dog who would gladly hand it to him or her.

"Rough night," Moose said. His mental state seemed better in the morning light, and he hadn't asked about Paula since waking. Perhaps his dementia was worse in the evenings. However, physically he sounded terrible. Sometime during the night he had developed a cough which had grown worse, and even in the warmth of the morning sun he shivered. "How's the arm?"

Charlie tried to shrug and then winced. "I'll survive."

In truth, he suspected the injury was worse than a dislocation. He now had trouble using his hand, and when he'd attempted to look at his shoulder in the bathroom mirror he'd seen that it had turned a dark purple and was terribly swollen and felt hot to the touch.

"And Quitz's paw?"

"Seems better. She's hardly limping this morning." Quitz sat beside Charlie, looking out the window. "I need to find her a place to relieve herself."

"We'll figure it out," Moose assured him, before turning his head and coughing into his fist.

They stood there for several moments, watching the sun rise over their town.

"I always thought the rainbow was God's promise of mercy to us, but perhaps it's the sunrise."

"His mercies are new every morning." Moose scratched at the stubble on his cheek. "It seems strange to see sunshine and blue sky."

Charlie sipped from the bottle of water he'd been nursing the last few hours. Their supplies were limited and might have to last them for some time to come. Based on what he was seeing out the window, it might take hours or even days before they were rescued.

"There are still quite a few of those strips of sheet in the supply box Kurt had put together. I suggest we go up on the roof to see if we can erect a flag of sorts."

Charlie had been thinking the same thing. "Better leave at least half of them in case we come across anyone else who is hurt."

When first looking out the window before the sky had significantly lightened, Charlie had thought maybe he'd seen people floating to the west of the building. Just as he was about to call out to Moose and Kurt and Dale, the light had shifted and doubt had crept in. Perhaps it had only been debris. He couldn't tell.

However the moment had served to remind him of the possibility of other survivors. If there was any way they could reach them, the bedding might be needed for bandages. But Moose was correct. The first thing they needed to do was call for help, and the way to do that was from the roof.

"I snooped around in the art supply closet and found some cans of paint." Charlie looked down at the box of supplies at his feet.

"Any brushes?"

"A couple. We don't have enough of the red, but if we use everything here we may be able to make something big enough to be seen by air."

"Good idea. Let's see what we can do."

Charlie picked up the container at his feet with his good arm, and Moose returned to the table to fetch the strips of sheets.

Angela was beginning to stir, but Sophia was still sound asleep in her mother's lap. Dale was out—he'd had the last shift, watching in the darkness in case they needed to leave the building. He'd passed out as soon as Charlie had taken over his watch. Lamar was awake, and attempting to hobble around with his hurt leg still splinted. It was obvious, by the grimace on his face, that the pain was worse than it had been the night before.

"That leg probably started swelling," Charlie said. "You need to try to keep it elevated."

"I need to help us get out of here."

"Nowhere to go, my friend. Not right now, unless you have a boat in your back pocket." Charlie explained what he and Moose were going to do, and Lamar stood there, holding onto the back of the nearest chair and nodding his approval.

Then Charlie remembered what he might have seen earlier. "I have an idea of something you can do."

Charlie set down the box of art supplies, grabbed one of the chairs, and carried it over to the westward facing window.

"I thought I saw someone out there this morning, but then I wasn't so sure. Keep an eye out. If you see anyone, holler for Kurt or Dale." As an afterthought he added, "We shouldn't be gone long."

Kurt was beginning to wake. The big guy looked marginally better than he had the night before, but Charlie didn't want him exerting himself and going up onto the roof. If Kurt broke a leg or stressed his heart, they would be in much worse shape than they were. Charlie was beginning to think the man needed a good week in the hospital to set things right.

"See if you can find any more rags or anything we can use as flags and hang out the windows."

"I could go downstairs—"

"I'd rather you wait until we get back. Many injuries happen after a hurricane because of all the debris. We need to operate off a buddy system. No one goes anywhere alone."

"How about the bathroom?" Kurt asked sarcastically, though there was no bitterness behind the question. The situation they found themselves in—well, it was something that none of them could have imagined.

"Feel free to take care of that by yourself," Moose said.

The night before they had found trash sacks and lined the toilets with them. The plumbing might not start working for weeks. This way, they could pull out the bag every few hours, tie it off, double bag the waste and set it in one of the large pails used for mopping. It should work for a few days and would keep the toilets from overflowing.

Moose and Charlie took the stairway to the roof, Quitz at their heels. They pushed through the door, careful to prop a trashcan in the opening to keep the door from closing. The last thing they needed was to get trapped on the roof. While Quitz trotted off to a corner and took care of her business, Charlie and Moose stepped out into bright sunshine and a cool October morning. Both men stood completely still, trying to comprehend what they were seeing.

"I knew it was bad…"

"But not this bad." Charlie walked toward the south side of the building, the side he hadn't been able to see from their room. The south side of the island was less populated than other areas, but this…

"It's all gone," Charlie said.

"Washed clean, so to speak."

"This must be ground zero where Orion came ashore."

"We're fortunate that we made it to this building, Charlie." A coughing spell hit him, lasting more than a few moments. When Moose was done and trying to pull in a good breath he added, "Anywhere else, and I don't think we'd be standing here today."

Charlie nodded, but he didn't speak. Suddenly his throat felt closed up, and his eyes had begun to sting. After Madelyn died, there had been days that he'd prayed for God to take him home. He couldn't envision living without her. He didn't want to imagine such a life. He convinced himself that he wouldn't much mind leaving this old world behind. Looking out over what was left of Mustang Island, he realized he wasn't ready to go yet. He was grateful for another day, thankful that he'd sheltered with these people, and looked forward to being united with others like Alice and the kids.

Charlie Everman understood, in the very depth of his soul, that God's mercies were new each morning, and he was grateful.

CHAPTER 17

*B*ecca was driving the tractor to town when she passed Joshua walking down the road.

She pulled to the side and waited for him to catch up with her. "Want a ride?"

He took off his hat, patted down his hair, and then replaced the hat. "*Ya*. I suppose I do."

Becca's dad had left the pickup bed attached to the back of the tractor, which was pretty standard in their community. The truck beds provided a good place to put sacks of groceries or extra passengers. Joshua climbed into the back and sat down. It wasn't very conducive to talking. Becca focused on driving instead. The last thing she needed to do was stall the tractor in front of Joshua Kline. He would think she was nervous because he was riding back there, which she was, but she didn't want him to know that.

When they stopped at the first light in town, she turned around in the seat to holler, "Somewhere you want me to take you?"

"Where are you going?"

"Dry goods store."

"Good enough."

She shrugged, turned back toward the front, and promptly popped the clutch as she attempted to move forward. The tractor lurched, coughed, and finally smoothed out. Her face flamed red.

She was twenty years old, and still she had trouble with the old tractor. She'd been driving it since she was twelve, though never often and never far. Perhaps she needed someone to give her lessons.

She pulled into the parking area beside the dry goods store, set the brake, and forgot to let out the clutch. The tractor jerked forward before it died. Becca closed her eyes for a second, prayed that she would not see Joshua laughing at her, and then she gathered up her purse.

When she turned to climb down, Joshua was there, waiting to help her.

"Tractors can be more stubborn than horses," he said.

"And harder to drive."

"My *dat* would agree with you. He prefers a Percheron to a Ford or a John Deere." He glanced at the front of the Bylers' store, which still sported a "CLOSED" sign, and then looked back at Becca. "It's a little early for shopping."

"Oh, no. I'm not here to purchase anything. I agreed to help Rebecca with inventory. That's why I came so early. I've been helping *Mamm* with canning, but she had nothing to do today, and Rebecca needs to order more stock for the holidays, so I said…"

She stumbled to a stop and stared right and left and finally at a spot over Joshua's shoulder. Why was she rambling so? And what was she supposed to do with her hands? They felt awkward hanging at her side, but when she crossed them over her front, she felt like a moody schoolgirl. Finally, she settled for clutching her purse with her right arm, and resting the left at her side.

Joshua stood with one arm propped on the front of her father's tractor and looked completely at ease. She envied him that. What she would give to feel at home in her own skin. Which sounded so funny in her mind that she actually laughed out loud.

Instead of asking what the joke was, Joshua raised an eyebrow and waited. He didn't hurry off, which she thought was odd. Maybe he was ahead of schedule the way she was. She hadn't wanted to be late on her first official day of work, even though she wouldn't be working in the shop regularly until mid-November.

"So, um, where are you headed so early?"

"Bus station."

"Oh?" For some reason the thought of Joshua leaving caused her emotions to dip. No doubt his life was much more exciting than hers.

"Headed to McAlester." He leaned forward and lowered his voice. "Alton's in trouble again, so they're sending me to fetch him."

"Oh." She realized she'd already said that and worried that she must sound like a simpleton. "I'm sorry. I didn't know."

"No one knows yet. But soon he will be the talk of the community."

Becca knew what that felt like, or she imagined she knew. Actually, she'd never done anything startling enough to draw much attention, but she used to think that people looked at her and talked about her size. Why was she thinking about that? She was healthy and reasonably happy and her weight was not a topic for discussion with Joshua Kline.

He seemed to be waiting for a response.

"We may have a few gossips, but they're kindhearted enough. It's only that they think they can...well, fix everyone's problems."

"If you hear of a *gut* solution, let me know." Joshua sighed and switched a paper sack from his left hand to his right. She hadn't even noticed he was carrying one.

"Long trip?" she asked, nodding to the sack.

"*Nein*. Under two hours. *Mamm* is always worried I'll get hungry, though."

Becca didn't know what to say to that, so she changed the subject. "I hear we may be getting some rain."

"From the hurricane in Texas. I heard about that too."

"I hate to think of what those poor people are going through."

"Most everyone would have been evacuated. The *Englisch* are good about such things. The Amish? We might just say that it's *Gotte's wille* and sit in our house until we float away." Joshua's grin indicated he was teasing.

Many Amish weren't able to laugh at their culture and its eccentricities. She was a little surprised to find that Joshua could, but then lots of things about him surprised her—including the fact that he was still standing there talking to her.

"The rain, though, it will be *gut* for the winter crops if it comes," he said.

They stood there for another minute, but Joshua seemed to be out of things to say and Becca didn't dare voice any of the questions running through her mind. Why wasn't he married? How old was he? And why couldn't she get him out of her mind? She'd been thinking about him since the day she'd seen him and his brother in the road, but she had tried to attribute it to boredom. Did she have a crush on Joshua Kline? And if she did, what could she do about it? Her shyness usually caused her to want to avoid people.

"Guess I should head toward the bus station. Wouldn't want to be late."

"Well, I hope you have a *gut* trip."

"And you have a fine day counting things."

That made her laugh. She'd worried for the last week that the job might be too hard for her, but Joshua had a point. Inventory was basically counting things, and she'd learned to count long ago.

"*Danki* for the ride." He tapped the hood of the tractor and started off.

Becca slowly climbed the stairs and waited for someone to open the door. While she waited, she prayed that Joshua would have a safe trip, and that he would find his brother and bring him home without any trouble.

CHAPTER 18

*J*oshua took a seat at the back of the bus, hoping no one would talk to him. In general he didn't enjoy chatting with strangers, though he'd had no trouble speaking to Becca Troyer. What had come over him? Usually when he was around a woman, the proverbial cat claimed his tongue. Around Becca, he'd sounded like a woman at a sew-in…chatter, chatter, chatter.

He sank down onto his seat and tipped his hat over his eyes. Perhaps he could catch a nap before he arrived in McAlester. But instead he kept remembering Becca's laugh and the way she fidgeted with her arms before clasping her purse to her side as if it might fall off her shoulder if she didn't. She was a pretty woman and should have married long ago, but Joshua knew only too well that some of the men in his community wanted the perfect wife.

Some thought the ideal woman had a small waist and an outgoing personality. And perhaps for some of his friends that was the case. He didn't know, though.

Take himself, for example. He was rather big and not especially good looking. His chin was not quite right, and his nose was too large. That's what one girl had told him as she peered up into his eyes. "Joshua Kline, your nose is rather large. And you're taller than any boy in our class. Are you going to keep growing?"

He hadn't known how to answer that, so he'd only shrugged. What could he do about the size of his nose or his height? Nothing.

She had giggled and run off to chat with her friends, pausing once to turn and look over her shoulder at him. He had the uncomfortable feeling that they were talking about him, and suddenly he'd wished he could be in the fields working.

That had happened in his last year of school, his eighth year, but he still thought about it occasionally. Alton enjoyed asking a different girl to singing every week and pushing the boundaries of their *Ordnung* because he could, because he was in his *rumpsringa*.

Now Joshua was twenty-seven years old, and girls rarely bothered to comment on his size or his nose. He'd become somewhat invisible in their community. A good worker. Someone who could be counted on to help move the church benches or set up the makeshift tables. He supposed folks had assumed he was happy living as a single man, but the truth was that Joshua had no idea how to go about pursuing a girl.

And he knew he wasn't the perfect catch.

Who was?

He shook his head and tried to scatter the thoughts about girls and marrying and Becca. He should be focusing on his brother and what he would say to him when he reached McAlester.

But he had no idea what to say to Alton. He didn't quite know how to explain the pain he'd seen in his father's eyes or the fear in his mother's. Those were things one either chose to see or chose to ignore. It was possible that a night in an *Englisch* jail had changed Alton's perspective, but Joshua doubted it.

Instead of worrying over his brother, he opened the newspaper he had purchased from the stand next to the ticket booth.

Across the top fold of the paper was a picture of Hurricane Orion as seen from space—a giant swirl of white that reminded Joshua of whipped cream on top of coffee, a treat that his oldest sister loved. He grunted at the idea of taking a photograph from space and sending it down to a newsman's desk. Then he realized the sound was one his father would have made. Beneath the photograph was the heading "Orion Battles Texas Coast."

Hurricane Orion made land at 11:21 last night as a Category 4 storm. With sustained winds of 140 miles per hour, Texas officials are expecting massive damage to the areas of Corpus Christi, Port Aransas, Mustang Island, Rockport, and Matagorda Island. The eye of the hurricane passed over the area at approximately 2:04 this morning.

Governor Aubrey Benton released the following statement. "Government officials will assess the situation as soon as it's safe to send personnel into the devastated areas." When asked if they were receiving any information directly from the affected areas, Benton replied, "Official evacuations began two days ago, and we are confident that everyone who wanted to leave has been relocated farther inland. However, there are always a few individuals who insist on staying. We have received intermittent updates from ham radio operators in the area, indicating that many structures have been destroyed and that there is extensive flooding."

A spokesman for the National Hurricane Center confirmed that the storm surge was over twenty feet. Widespread power outages continue throughout the area, and officials are working to reestablish cell phone service.

"If anyone is riding this out in the affected areas, God help them." Justin Sapp, the mayor for Port Aransas, said that they would rebuild. Port A, as it's known to locals, is the only established town on Mustang Island, with a population of approximately 4,000. "We'll be in there, as soon as Orion allows us in. Folks can donate to the Red Cross and specify that their funds be directed to Gulf Coast communities affected by Hurricane Orion."

Orion is already weakening as it passes to the northeast, though the danger of tornadoes spurred by the hurricane may hamper first responder teams. "We will deploy the Texas National Guard as well as Red Cross teams as fast as humanly possible," Governor Benton promised. "We have a crisis plan for this sort of thing, and rest assured that engineers, fire fighters, and medical personnel have been preparing throughout the night. We're not on our time clock, though. We're on Orion's. Until it's safe, we wait. In the meantime, I suggest people pray for the safety of anyone who was caught in Orion's path."

Joshua set the paper aside and stared out the window as the bus sped south on Highway 69. He thought it unusual that a governor would ask folks to pray, especially in this day and age. But then again, he understood that in times of crisis people often fell back on their faith.

Wasn't that true for their family as well? He recalled the last words his mother had said, as she handed him his lunch. "Pray for your *bruder. Gotte* will guide your path, Joshua. He will help you to bring Alton home."

CHAPTER 19

When Joshua asked the bus driver directions to the McAlester jail, the man didn't even blink. "Corner of Washington and First." He pointed to the right, never looking up from his clipboard.

It was a short walk from where the bus dropped him off. He'd finished off the apple, cookies, and sliced cheese his mother had packed, so he tossed the paper sack into a trash bin and walked into the McAlester Police Station.

The building was redbrick, single story. Joshua noticed a flyer for neighborhood watch groups taped to the counter. A woman in police uniform stood behind the desk. She looked to be about Joshua's age.

"Can I help you?"

"I'm Joshua Kline. I'm here to pick up my brother, Alton."

"If you'll wait over there, someone will be with you in a minute." She nodded toward an empty waiting area.

Joshua thanked her and walked over to the area she'd indicated. A television was on but the volume was muted. A coffee table held stacks of old magazines, and a dozen chairs surrounded the perimeter of the room. After two hours on the bus he didn't feel much like sitting, so he stood instead, studying the activity around the police desk.

An older man was on the telephone.

A couple was filing some sort of report, standing at the counter and consulting one another before writing on the form.

Posters with the heading *FBI Most Wanted* were pinned to a bulletin board.

Joshua shook his head, trying to clear it. The situation was all too surreal. He was standing in an *Englisch* jail, waiting to retrieve his younger brother. How had his life come to this?

A door opened and a middle-aged man motioned toward him. "Come on back, Mr. Kline."

The man was probably in his forties, had neatly trimmed dark hair, and a fatherly look. He took Joshua to a desk, where he began searching through stacks of paperwork. When he'd found what he wanted, he turned his attention to Joshua. "I'm Officer Straley. Thank you for coming down to fetch your brother."

"Is he all right?" Joshua didn't realize until that moment that he had been worried about Alton. Mostly he'd spent his time being angry, but under that was the emotion that seemed to color their relationship. He'd been worrying about Alton since they were children. Even then, his brother had managed to find trouble.

"He's fine. We would have released him by five o'clock today whether you made it or not. But we wouldn't have released the truck to him because he has no driver's license and the truck is registered in your name."

Joshua shifted in his seat, unsure what to say.

"I'll need to see some identification to release the truck to you."

Joshua pulled out his wallet and retrieved his driver's license.

Straley checked it and then pushed the license back across the desk, studying him the entire time. "Although your brother wasn't charged with anything, I want to stress to you that this is a serious situation. Driving without a license is against the law. He's fortunate that the truck was insured—otherwise we would have charged him. As it is…well, he's a kid who was drinking and about to drive. He could have hurt someone. I just want to make sure you understand that."

"*Ya*, we know that what he did was wrong."

With a sigh, Straley leaned back in his chair. "We see a lot of this, to tell you the truth. It can go one of two ways. Your brother may be testing his limits. If that's true of Alton, a night in our jail could have been a wake-up call."

"I hope that is the case."

"Same here. But I've also seen plenty of young men who start out this way and end up in real trouble. That happens all too often." He sat forward and opened the file. "I'll need you to sign some papers."

Once that was done, the officer stood to retrieve Alton. Before he turned away, he said, "We were all young once, and most of us did stupid things. But I will not be lenient with this young man if he shows up in my district again, drinking and driving illegally. Is that understood?"

"Perfectly."

A dozen questions circled Joshua's mind as he waited for Alton to appear. When he did, when Joshua first saw him, Alton looked much like the little kid who used to follow him around—hopeful, fearful, and defiant all at once. They said very little, though Joshua thanked the officer. Once outside, they walked two blocks over to the impound lot. Joshua showed the attendant the piece of paper from the officer, and they were given the keys and directed to Alton's truck.

Or was it Joshua's?

"I want you to tell me why this truck is in my name. Why the insurance is in my name." He started the vehicle and pulled out of the lot.

"I couldn't put it in mine. I don't have a driver's license." Alton stretched and then rolled down the window. The day was warm, and he seemed content to enjoy it.

"Explain it to me, from the beginning."

"What's to explain? I couldn't buy the truck unless I had a license, which we both know I don't have. Maybe I should have got one…" He looked puzzled for a moment. "Not in our town. *Mamm* and *Dat* would have heard about it before I got home."

"As if they didn't hear about the truck."

Alton shrugged. "So I borrowed your license. We look enough alike when it's just a headshot."

"You *borrowed* it?"

"I put it back, didn't I?"

"You took it without asking."

"Because you would have said no."

Joshua felt as if his head might explode. He saw the street in front of him through a red haze. "So you pretended to be me?"

"I guess."

"You guess? You either did or you didn't."

"Okay. I did. What is the big deal?"

"It's illegal! That's the big deal."

They were about to turn north onto Highway 69. Alton motioned toward a McDonald's. "Mind stopping? They don't feed you much in jail—nothing like *Mamm*'s cooking. Also they took away my cigarettes."

Joshua gripped the wheel and accelerated onto the highway.

"I guess that's a no."

"How do you afford it? A truck, registration, auto insurance, cigarettes, trips to Clarita, and alcohol. How do you afford it all, Alton?"

"One pays for the other." Alton glanced at his phone, which Joshua could see was dead. The screen remained black. With a disgusted look, he stuck the phone back in his pocket.

"How does one pay for the other?"

"I give folks rides. It's no big deal. After the singings most of the kids want to go somewhere. They give me a couple of bucks each, and I take them. The money adds up real quick."

"That doesn't explain how you paid for the truck."

Alton squirmed in his seat. Finally he admitted, "I borrowed the money from Myron Ferguson."

It was worse than Joshua had imagined. Myron was an *Englischer* who worked on cars and occasionally sold old jalopies. He had a terrible reputation among the Amish, mainly for things like this— enabling Amish teens to get in trouble. Rumor was that Myron would drive the older teens to the casinos in Tulsa and even provide them with fake IDs so they could get in and gamble. Maybe he wasn't an evil person, but he would do anything to make a buck.

They didn't speak for the next twenty minutes. Joshua tried to focus on the words his father had said—something about running away from home and everyone being lost. He tried to tamp down his anger, but he couldn't stop remembering. His mother's eyes as the bishop told them Alton was in jail. His sisters huddled at the top of the stairs. His father in the glow of the lantern light, unable to sleep.

All because of Alton.

By the time they had crossed Interstate 40, he couldn't hold his anger in any longer.

"You have no idea the hurt you cause other people with your irresponsible behavior."

Alton remained crouched down, his ball cap pulled over his eyes.

"Sit up when I'm talking to you." Joshua fairly spat the words at his brother. "You will not borrow my license or my name ever again. I will sell this truck, since apparently I own it, and you will take the money to Myron and pay him off."

"I doubt it would be enough. There's the cost of the truck plus interest, and I spent most of what I made from offering rides."

"Then you'll have to work off the balance. Maybe you'll even have to get rid of your phone."

For the first time, anger sparked in Alton's eyes. "You're not my father."

"And you are not my son." Joshua forced his hands to relax on the wheel. He flexed his fingers, attempting to restore the circulation. "As long as you live in our house, you will respect the people there. You will not cause *Mamm* any more heartache. You won't keep *Dat* up at night, worrying about whether you are on your *rumspringa* or falling completely away from the faith."

Alton was staring straight ahead now, refusing to meet Joshua's gaze.

"And you will not cause me to miss days working so that I can come behind you and clean up your mess. It's time to grow up *bruder*, and it starts today."

Joshua fully realized that he couldn't make his brother grow up, but neither did he have to enable him. The next few months would show which way Alton was determined to turn. Until then, Joshua planned to do everything he could to protect the rest of their family from his careless ways.

CHAPTER 20

*T*he Coast Guard helicopter arrived midafternoon.

They had been taking turns standing on the roof and watching for help. Charlie was there with Dale when the copter appeared crossing the bay.

Jumping up and down and waving with the flags they had made, at first it seemed the pilot hadn't seen them. But then the copter turned, and Charlie was overwhelmed by a sense of relief. He wanted to fall on his knees and thank his Creator. Instead, he allowed himself to be pulled into Dale's embrace.

"We made it, Charlie! I wasn't sure we would, but we made it." Tears streamed down the young man's face, and then Charlie realized that he, too, was crying.

Those who sow with tears will reap with songs of joy.

The psalm was one of Madelyn's favorites. He hadn't thought of it in quite some time, but now those words pierced his heart.

The pilot indicated to them that he would have to land on the roof. They backed away, waiting.

And then paramedics were leaping out, carrying first aid kits and following their direction to the others who were waiting inside the building.

Within minutes they were all boarding the helicopter. One of the paramedics explained that they usually only took on an additional six people, but because Sophia was so small, everyone could leave at once—even Quitz.

Dale held Sophia in one arm and clasped his wife's hand with his other. The paramedics wanted to load Lamar on a stretcher, but he insisted on hobbling under his own strength. He couldn't possibly climb into the copter, but two of the paramedics helped him into a sling, which lifted him up and inside. Of the seven who had spent the night in the community center, Kurt seemed to be fairing the worst. The paramedics had put a blood pressure cuff on him. Charlie heard one of the team ask Kurt if he took nitroglycerin for chest pains.

"Yeah, but I left the bottle in my truck, and it washed away."

They pulled a dose from one of the first aid kits. When they were confident he was stable to ride, they helped him into the copter.

Charlie was the last to climb aboard, waiting until they had loaded Quitz. It wouldn't have been a problem for him to wait for the next pass, but the paramedics insisted the Jayhawk could handle the weight.

As he climbed inside, he thought that he understood the severity of the destruction to his town, but then the copter rose, turned, and flew out over the bay.

Charlie pressed his forehead to the window. His mind didn't want to accept what his eyes were seeing—or rather what he wasn't seeing. Where the town of Port Aransas had been was now a new beach. He could only count half a dozen buildings still standing, one of them the Tarpon Inn. As they turned toward Corpus Christi, he saw that it hadn't been spared either. The bay was a jumble of boats, houses, and wreckage.

Water had swept several miles inland. Sea vessels lay in yards. Power poles were scattered like so many pixie sticks.

They flew past a building with all of the windows blown out. In fact, most of the downtown buildings were without glass.

And yet, already the tenacious spirit of the Texas people was evident.

Painted across one building were the words, "Orion came and went. We're still here."

Across another, "God bless Texas."

And a third proclaimed, "Still open." As they flew past, Charlie noted a queue of people lined up for food that was being cooked on giant outdoor grills.

Where the surge had receded, there were pockets of water that shouldn't be there—encompassing neighborhoods and business districts. Several fires still burned. Even as he watched, a helicopter with the words *Texas National Guard* dropped water onto a fire and then flew away.

Charlie was surprised when the copter he was in set down on the roof of the Corpus Christi Regional Medical Center.

Then he realized they were a ragtag group, most in need of medical assistance. Besides, where else could they go?

Kurt was loaded onto a stretcher and whisked away. His color looked better, but it was impossible to tell how he was feeling with an oxygen mask over his face. He did manage to give them a thumbs-up.

The ER personnel insisted that Lamar sit in a wheelchair. Though he grumbled, Charlie supposed the leg was hurting more than he'd admitted. An expression of relief washed over his face once he took his weight off the leg.

Moose was quarrelling with a doctor, which didn't surprise Charlie much.

"But I don't need an X-ray."

"Sir. You have a temperature over one hundred. That combined with your cough is a sure indication of pneumonia."

Moose continued to argue, but he allowed himself to be led away.

Sophie, Angela, and Dale stood beside Charlie. They were now in the emergency room waiting area, which was full of people. No one seemed to notice Quitz, who remained pressed at his side.

"Better get that shoulder checked, Charlie."

"Yeah. I will. After…these folks." His hand shook when he waved toward the crowd.

"This is only the first round. Better to get in and out of the way before people start lining up out the door." Dale turned and thrust out his hand. "I'm glad you bumped into our building."

"And I'm glad you pulled us inside." Charlie shook Dale's hand and realized that what they had in common now far exceeded the differences in their politics. "I'd like to stay in touch."

"Of course. We'll call and let you know where we settle. I still have your number from when we were on the council committee together."

Charlie nodded, his throat suddenly too tight to speak.

Angela, who had been markedly quiet through the night, reached up and kissed Charlie's cheek. Sophia waved as they walked away.

His group dispersed, Charlie stopped fighting the pain from his shoulder, allowed it to wash over him, and knew that he would have to get it looked after sooner rather than later. Before he did, he needed to do one thing.

"Come on, girl."

Quitz padded beside him as they walked toward the visitor area of the building. Cell phones were still not working, but the hospital had a bank of landlines. Charlie knew he'd found them when he spotted the line of people waiting to make a call.

He got in line, and then he realized that he didn't have any change. He didn't have anything—no wallet, no money. He'd even managed to lose his cell phone, though he supposed that could be replaced easily enough.

He needn't have worried. When he reached the front of the line, he saw that someone had left a stack of quarters. Placing one in the coin slot, his hand again began to shake as he dialed Bill and Ann's number.

His eyes closed in thanksgiving when C.J. answered the phone. "Everyone's outside. We're feeding the horses. Are you okay?"

It was in that moment that Charlie knew everything was going to be fine. He began to count the blessings in his life—Quitz, his friends, the Coast Guard, Bill and Ann, Alice and her grandchildren.

"Charlie?"

"Yeah, C.J. I'm here."

"You're okay, then?"

"I'm better than okay."

"And Quitz?"

Charlie glanced down at the dog, curled up next to him, trusting and waiting.

"Quitz is good. We have a few things to take care of here, and then we'll drive on up."

As he hung up, he realized he'd kept his promise to Madelyn—even in the midst of Orion's destruction, he genuinely treasured the many blessings of his life.

CHAPTER 21

Seven months later

May arrived, dark and stormy. The rain would be good for the crops, but Joshua wasn't worried about the crops.

He stood next to the tractor, watching Alton work in the fields. The sky was completely overcast, and the weathermen promised rain before evening. The weather matched Joshua's mood.

The winter wheat was coming along nicely and would be ready to harvest in another month. They were nearly finished planting, having increased the size of the corn crop and reduced the soybean crop. Which was where the problem lay.

"You are certainly frowning at that crop, Joshua." Bishop Levi limped over to stand beside him.

"Sorry, Levi. I didn't hear you arrive."

The older man waved away his concern. "I was in the area." He paused and then asked, "Problem with the crop?"

"*Nein*, and that's my problem."

"I don't understand." Levi nodded toward a picnic table Joshua's father had placed beneath a stand of maple trees years ago. "Can you spare a few minutes?"

"*Ya*." Joshua swiped at the sweat and dirt on his brow, and snatched up his jug of water.

They settled at the picnic table, side by side, both of them studying the fields. Joshua didn't know how to begin, something Levi seemed to sense. Finally he said, "Just tell me what's on your heart, Joshua."

"Alton."

"I see." Levi scratched at his right eyebrow. "Boy seems to be doing fine. There's been no more trouble since that bit in McAlester, and your father says he's attending to his share of work around here."

"He is."

"And yet you're worried."

Joshua shook his head, as if he could clear his thoughts. "As you say, Alton hasn't been in even a spot of trouble since that trip. If you could have seen him walking out of that jail cell, Levi. He looked like the little *bruder* who used to follow me around the schoolyard— all hopeful and worried at the same time. Like a pup afraid of being kicked."

Instead of interrupting, Levi pulled a pack of gum from his pocket. After offering a piece to Joshua, he pulled out a stick, popped it in his mouth, and then he made a motion for Joshua to continue.

"But I know my *bruder* very well. He's being more careful, is all. For sure and for certain he doesn't want to get caught again." Joshua sighed and darted a glance toward the bishop. "I don't know exactly what he's involved in, but I fear it's even worse than before. And now with the coming weeks of rainy weather? The last thing we need is Alton with time on his hands. He reminds me of my *mamm's* pot of soup on the stove, just waiting to boil over."

"I won't even ask you if you're sure. I can tell this is weighing heavily on you."

"My parents' hands are full with running this place and raising the girls. The last thing they expected at their age was to be dealing with a renegade son."

Levi tapped his cane against the ground. "It seems to me that Alton is trying to do the right thing. He completes his work each day according to your *dat*, helps around the house according to your *mamm*, and he attends church regularly."

"Though he still hasn't joined." Joshua wanted to tell Levi

more—about the nights he woke to find that Alton had fled their room. About the smell of cigarettes that clung to him. Even about the lipstick his mother struggled to wash out of his shirts. The pickup had been sold and the debt to Myron paid in full, but Joshua wasn't fooled. Alton was not satisfied with their plain and simple life.

"True. However, the time for one to commit his life to Christ, our faith, and this community differs with each individual. We cannot set the day when it should happen by looking at a calendar and counting forward from birth."

Joshua sighed. He knew the bishop was right, but he couldn't shake the feeling that Alton was slipping away from them, sliding toward an uncertain future and doing so right before their eyes.

"Sometimes when a person has trouble finding his way…" Levi popped his gum before continuing. "Sometimes a person needs to see his life from a different perspective."

"And how can one do that?"

Levi stood, leaning heavily on his cane. At times it was easy to forget the man's handicap. And then some days, like today, it seemed painfully obvious. No doubt the approaching weather made his injury hurt all the more, though Levi never complained about it. He'd once told Joshua that fretting over a thing didn't change it, so why bother?

Was that what Joshua was doing? Fretting over Alton?

"Sometimes time and distance both can help our perspective. Other times, it takes something more drastic—such as immersing yourself in another's problems."

"Whose problems?" Joshua had also stood and now he studied Levi closely. The bishop had something in mind, had probably been mulling it over even as he drove up their lane. Joshua had not been alone in his worries over his brother. Did that mean Alton had been in more trouble? Were there things Levi knew that Joshua didn't? Before he could ask, Levi began limping toward his buggy.

"My granddaughter Becca…you know Becca."

"I do." Joshua struggled not to blush. He'd managed to sit beside Becca on several occasions—at church luncheons and such—but he hadn't yet had the courage to actually ask her to go anywhere with him. They were too old for the singings, and he wasn't completely sure what else was appropriate.

"I thought, back in the winter, that I saw you look at Becca with a certain…interest. I thought maybe you cared for her." Levi stopped and turned an amused gaze on Joshua.

"*Ya*, I did. I mean, I do. It's only that I've been waiting on the right time to…well, to tell her."

"If you keep waiting for the right time, you may never begin."

Joshua smiled for the first time that day. "My *mamm* quotes that one too. The proverbs make things sound simple."

"Sometimes they are." Levi continued walking. "I bring up Becca because she leaves this week on a mission trip."

"To Texas. She mentioned it to me." Joshua had wanted to talk her out of it, but he couldn't think of one good reason that she shouldn't go.

"Becca had hoped to go earlier, but then her mother broke her foot and she was needed at home."

"Suzie's better now. I noticed at church meeting that she no longer wore the large black boot."

"She is better. Doc gave her the all clear last week. So Becca will go to Texas and work with MDS. Perhaps it would be *gut* if Alton also went on the mission trip."

"We can't trust him!" The words spilled from Joshua's heart before he could rein them in. "Alton at the Texas coast? Can you imagine how much trouble he will get into?"

"Perhaps, or perhaps it will provide him the perspective he needs to appreciate his family and home here. Such an experience may give him the courage to answer the call *Gotte* has on his life."

Courage wasn't what Alton seemed to be missing. Common sense, possibly, but he remained overeager to try anything—especially *Englisch* things.

"My sister-in-law will be traveling with Becca as a chaperone. Sarah Yoder will also go. It would be *gut* if you could travel with Alton."

"Me? Go to Texas?"

"I'm glad you like the idea."

"I didn't say I liked it, Levi. How can I leave? There's too much work here for *Dat*—"

"Yes, your father needs you here, usually. But in the next few weeks, especially given the rainy forecast, there won't be that much to do. By the first of June, when it's time to harvest the winter wheat, you'll both be back."

Dawning broke over Joshua. "You've already spoken to them about this."

"Your parents? They think it's a fine idea."

Joshua may have resisted a suggestion from the bishop, but not if his mother and father were fully behind it. Three against one was not a fair fight. "Does Alton know?"

"*Nein.* I thought you could tell him about it."

"Tell him about it?"

"Yes! Today is Tuesday. The bus leaves Thursday morning."

Joshua's head was literally spinning. He was to leave in two days? To the Texas coast? On a mission trip to help those who had survived Hurricane Orion? Perhaps he was sleeping and he'd wake to find this was all a crazy dream, one he could laugh about over his morning coffee.

But as Levi pulled himself up into his buggy and turned to look at him, Joshua knew he wasn't dreaming. The bishop's expression was suddenly serious. "It's a wonderful thing to be able to minister to others in the name of Christ. A wonderful thing. Your mission, Joshua, may be to minister to your *bruder* as much as it is to minister to the displaced folks in Texas. We will pray that you are successful in both endeavors."

Then Levi released the brake on his buggy, clucked once to his horse, and drove away.

CHAPTER 22

*B*ecca's father had harnessed the horse to the buggy for her trip into town. Her mother and father sat in the front. Becca and her two bags sat in the back. One was a small suitcase—with two changes of clothes and toiletries. The other was a backpack that she was carrying instead of a purse. She was able to put a book, her journal, her Bible, and her lunch inside the pack.

It was six thirty in the morning, and though the sun hadn't yet crossed the horizon, the sky was beginning to lighten.

Her mother turned to smile at her. "Did you remember your MDS forms?"

"*Ya*. They're right here." Becca patted the backpack.

"Did you remember the kitchen sink?" Her father asked.

"*Dat*. I didn't pack that much."

"I saw you sitting on the suitcase to close it, though." The laughter in her father's voice eased the feeling of anxiety that threatened to overwhelm her.

Her stomach had been in an upheaval since Sunday when her grandfather had asked the congregation to pray for their mission trip. That was when it had struck her as real. She was going to Texas! She would help to rebuild houses. What did she know about that? How would she be any use at all? And what if she got terribly homesick? She was thinking this was a bad idea, but her *aenti* would be waiting at the bus stop. She couldn't change her mind now.

"Nancy knows how to get in touch with your *grossdaddi* if you need anything."

What did her mother think she would need? Courage? Did someone have an extra spoonful of that they would be willing to give her?

Becca's pulse raced. She looked out the window of the buggy at house after house from their community that she knew well and had visited often. She took deep breaths and willed herself to calm down. She'd been away from home before. Certainly this was no different. It was only that she'd pushed it from her mind for weeks and now the day was here. It had all happened incredibly fast. How was it that winter had passed since her grandfather had first mentioned a mission to her?

And yet much of the winter had been depressing for Becca. There was her mother's injury, which reminded Becca that her parents were only human. What if something happened to them while she was gone? She'd hovered so close to her mother the last few months that her parents had taken to calling her "*Mammi*."

Some days she felt like a grandmother. Two more of her friends had married in March, making a total of four girls her age who were already married and now were expecting babies. It seemed to her that life had passed her by, and she wasn't sure what to do about it. So she did her chores, found extra work, volunteered whenever possible, and when she couldn't sleep she pulled out one of the books from their public library and read it by the glow of her flashlight.

In those books girls were always excited about adventures, even the ugly ducklings, but life wasn't always like a storybook. Maybe she should write a tale about a girl whose feet became cemented to her parents' land. Whenever she tried to step away, her feet refused to cooperate. In fact, the community had to hold church at her family's home every week, because this girl could not walk past the gate at the end of the lane.

"Becca, are you listening to me?" Her mother turned around so that they were nearly face-to-face.

"Sure, *Mamm*. Yes."

"What did I say?"

Becca's mind froze. She had been listening. Hadn't she?

"I said that we love you and we're proud of you. This is a *gut* thing to do."

"Are you sure I should be going though? Your foot—"

"My foot is completely healed. You were there when the doctor said so."

"But—"

"I promise you that I am fine. Today is about you, dear. You're about to make memories that will stay with you for a lifetime, times you will remember even when you're old and gray like your father and me."

Becca nodded, and then she turned to again stare out the window. They were pulling up to the bus loading area. Her grandmother and grandfather were there, as was *Aenti* Nancy. Standing beside Nancy was Sarah Yoder, who had agreed to go on the mission trip in order to escape the watchful eye of her parents. She'd told Becca at the last church service that if one more person reminded her to eat everything on her plate, she might run from the room screaming. Although she was supposedly over the eating disorder that she'd battled so desperately in school, she still seemed quite thin to Becca.

Several other people were also waiting to board the bus, which was just pulling into the parking area.

She craned her head to see better, and then her heart dropped—fell clean into her toes. She feared it would stop beating, but then her pulse began to race.

"Why are the Klines here?" she asked, her voice a mere squeak.

"I'm not sure," her father said. "They must be going on a trip."

Joshua and Alton stood beside Becca's grandfather, and she saw that both had a single suitcase, the same as hers. Joshua glanced up, caught her eye, and nodded.

Surely he wasn't going on the same bus. Surely he wasn't going to Texas!

Becca had been avoiding Joshua for several weeks. At first she had dared to hope that he liked her, that he might be *interested* in her. She often thought back to the day she'd given him the ride into town, but that memory held no new information for her. She'd played it over and over in her mind too many times.

Some part of her mind, or heart, had thought that Joshua would return from McAlester, with his younger brother in tow, and begin to court her. This is what came of reading too many books. Joshua had done absolutely nothing to give her that impression—other than be polite and charming and friendly.

In the following weeks, it became clear that he was not interested in pursuing a relationship. In fact, he'd acted quite distracted around her.

"Best not to dawdle, Becca." Her father wrapped the reins of their horse around the hitching post and reached for her suitcase as she tumbled out of the buggy.

She smoothed down the gray apron she was wearing over her blue dress. Both fit a little snugly.

Soon she was being embraced by her grandmother and grandfather, as well as her mother and dad. Her grandmother reminded her to eat right, say her prayers, and get plenty of rest. "Mission trips are exciting, but they can be exhausting too. Take care of yourself, Becca."

Nancy Troyer stood to the side, allowing them their goodbyes. Next to her, Sarah Yoder chewed on a thumbnail and glanced around furtively. Meeting Becca's eyes, she attempted a smile, but she didn't look exactly thrilled about the trip.

Nancy stepped forward. "Are you ready, dear?"

"Of course. I think so."

Joshua and Alton had already climbed up the bus steps. She could see Alton looking out the window next to where she stood. He waved hello, and she waved back.

"*Mamm...*" She pulled her mother away from the others. "Are Joshua and Alton going on the mission trip?"

"They are, but I didn't know until now. Your grandfather just told me. It seems it was a last-minute decision."

"But—"

Suzie pressed a finger to her daughter's lips, and then she pulled her a bit farther from the group. "I suspect I know how you feel about Joshua. Don't look so surprised. You blush or leave the room if his name is ever brought up."

"I do?"

"*Ya*. Now, Becca, I know you are startled by the fact that they will be on this trip with you."

Becca nodded dumbly. Startled didn't begin to describe the emotions tumbling through her heart.

"But this is *Gotte*'s doing, not ours. Perhaps you will return with three closer friends—four if we count *Aenti* Nancy. Perhaps one of those friendships will blossom into something more. Don't worry about whether it does or not. Focus on the mission."

"All right. I can do that."

"*Gut* girl. Now kiss me goodbye."

Becca again hugged her mother, father, grandmother, and grandfather one more time. Nancy was waiting for her, and Sarah had already climbed aboard the bus. Becca slung her backpack over her shoulder and hurried up the steps.

CHAPTER 23

The bus wasn't nearly full. Alton and Joshua had settled into seats halfway down the aisle, and Sarah had moved into the seats in front of them. Becca would have been more comfortable hiding in the back of the bus, but she remembered her mother's words: "Focus on the mission."

"You take the window, Becca. I get carsick."

"Um...okay."

Nancy settled into the seat across the aisle from them, no doubt so she could keep a better eye on the girls and the boys—actually, women and men. They weren't children any longer.

"I believe you'll enjoy the window seat, Becca." Nancy settled a shawl around her shoulders. "You'll be able to watch the *wunderbaar* Oklahoma countryside as it slips by."

Becca busied herself with pushing her backpack under the seat in front of her as the bus pulled out onto the two-lane road. She glanced out the window and saw her family waving. The sight caused tears to prick her eyes. She ducked back down, pretending to look for something else in her bag as she swiped her cheeks dry. Crying over a three-week trip! Her emotions were beyond ridiculous. When she sat up again, she found that Alton had poked his head in between their seats.

"It's our first time on a mission trip. How about you, Becca?"

"*Ya.*"

"Sarah?"

"*Ya*, mine too."

"I have been doing this once a year for the last five years," Nancy said, although Alton hadn't specifically asked her. "Since Walter died, and once the children were all married, it seemed like a *gut* way for me to give back. Even when we have limited resources to contribute, we can donate our time and our talents."

Nancy pulled some knitting out of her bag, as if she'd said enough on the subject.

Becca's aunt had recently turned fifty. She had a matronly figure, and much of her brown hair was gray, a good inch of it showing in front of her kapp. Many of the older women pulled their *kapps* forward until it looked as if they had no hair at all. Nancy didn't. There were other ways about her that lent a younger air to the woman—like the shawl or the paisley-patterned handbag she carried. She'd substituted in the classroom when the teacher was out ill, not often but a few times when Becca was growing up. Although she could be serious to the point of severe, she also was fair and even pleasant to be with most of the time.

In fact, she reminded Becca of a schoolteacher she'd had in the fourth grade. The woman had been quite strict, and it wasn't until the end of the year when Becca had fallen and scraped a knee rather badly that she'd learned the teacher had a compassionate side. After that, she'd been teacher's helper extraordinaire.

Nancy also had a very no-nonsense way about her, but she hadn't grown negative or grumpy as she'd aged. Even after the death of her husband, she'd managed to maintain a positive outlook on life.

"I've never considered a mission trip," Alton admitted. "But my family—especially my *bruder*—thinks it may be a *gut* idea."

"My family wasn't sure if I should go or not," Sarah said. "But Bishop Levi thought it was a *gut* idea. He convinced them."

Sarah didn't appear to be at all tongue-tied around boys. Becca envied her that.

"It seems the bishop has been looking out for all of us," Alton said, laughing as he sat back.

Becca glanced from him to Joshua, who still hadn't said a word. "*Gudemariye*, Joshua."

"And to you, Becca."

Sarah turned around in her seat and faced the two brothers. "Are you here because you wanted to help MDS or are you a chaperone for Alton?"

"It's possible to be both," Nancy assured them.

Becca turned back around in her seat and pulled a book from her backpack. It had been a gift from Joseph and Rebecca Byler. "You'll be gone three weeks, and your library books would be past due by the time you got back. This way you'll have something to read on the bus."

The front of the novel showed a mountain pass covered in snow, and across the spine were the words *Christian Fiction*. Becca wanted to lose herself in the story and forget all of her doubts and fears about the trip. But she also wanted the book to last, and this was only the first hour of their journey, so she placed the book in her lap, resting her hands on it but not yet opening it.

They had been traveling less than thirty minutes when Sarah made a desperate dash to the bathroom facilities at the back of the bus.

"Would you like me to check on her?" Nancy asked.

"*Nein*. I can do it." Becca hurried down the aisle.

Sarah opened the door after Becca knocked and asked how she was doing. They both crammed into the tiny bathroom where they could have a bit of privacy. Sarah insisted she was okay, though she was pale and a bit shaky.

"I have some crackers in my lunch sack." Becca wet a paper towel, wrung out the water, and handed it to her. "Maybe that will settle your stomach."

"*Ya*, okay. *Danki*."

"I'm going to use the restroom while I'm back here, but you go ahead and find what you need in my bag."

"*Mamm* sent a can of soda instead of tea. She knows I have trouble in *Englisch* cars sometimes."

"And a bus is probably worse than a car." Becca was suddenly glad that Sarah had come with them. She missed being with other girls. The farm could be a rather lonely place.

But when she walked back toward her group, she found that Alton had taken her seat, leaving his seat beside Joshua vacant.

Less than an hour into the trip with probably another ten to go, and already she was forced into close proximity with the man she'd begun having feelings for several months ago. The same man who cared nothing for her—at least nothing out of the ordinary. It was going to be a long trip.

CHAPTER 24

*J*oshua had barely slept the night before. He'd tossed and turned, worrying about Alton, about the trip in general, about the farm while he was gone, and about being in close proximity with Becca.

He fell asleep after they crossed the Texas border, and when he woke to find Becca still sitting next to him, he was disoriented and embarrassed.

"Don't worry," she said. "You didn't drool."

"I was out, though."

"You were."

"How long did I sleep?"

"Well, it's almost lunchtime. Look. We're in the Dallas area."

Joshua leaned forward to see past her and out the window.

"It's the big city, *bruder*. Not many tractors here." The words were barely out of Alton's mouth when a large cattle truck passed them, full of Hereford cows.

"Dallas may be a large city, but there are plenty of farmers and ranchers in the surrounding area." Nancy had stuffed her knitting back into her bag and was eating from her lunch sack. "We'll be stopping in the downtown area and changing buses. There will be a few street vendors as well as snack machines in the bus terminal, but we'll only be there for twenty minutes, so don't dawdle."

Nancy had obviously received more detailed information than

they had. All Joshua knew was that it was an eleven-hour drive, combined with eighty minutes of bus changes and fuel stops. He figured they would be pulling into Port Aransas just before sunset.

The bus chugged to a stop, and everyone spilled out, grateful for the chance to stretch their legs.

"Remember to take your things," Nancy called after them. "I'll confirm which bus we're continuing on and stand outside it."

Joshua wanted to put a little distance between himself and Becca—at least until he figured out what to say to her. But as he walked out from beneath the covered awning outside the bus station, he felt distinctly claustrophobic. Tall buildings consisting mostly of reflective glass towered above him on all sides. He craned his neck to see the sky, which was a robin's egg blue. The road that passed in front of the bus station was a world unto itself—teeming with people hurrying down the sidewalk. The street was crowded with cars, trucks, bicycles, and cabs—a startling abundance of different types of vehicles.

"I'm trying one of those hot dogs." Alton pushed past him and made a beeline for a street vendor as if he had done that a dozen times before. And maybe he had. What did Joshua actually know about his brother's life? He seldom asked questions because he didn't want to hear the answers.

Alton went up to the window and ordered "a dog, fully loaded." Whatever that meant, the smells were wonderful. Joshua had already eaten a good portion of the lunch their *mamm* had packed long ago.

He was surprised to find that Sarah and Becca had followed them out of the terminal.

"Want a hot dog?" he asked.

Sarah shook her head. "I still have plenty of my lunch."

Becca hesitated, and then she said, "*Ya*. I do. But no onions!"

Joshua smiled and hurried off to collect their order.

The girls turned and started back toward the terminal. Becca called over her shoulder, "We'll meet you on the bus!"

"Where are they headed?" Alton asked.

"No telling." Joshua ordered a hot dog same as Alton's, and then he ordered Becca's. Thinking she might be hungrier than she was admitting, he also ordered two bags of chips and two Cokes. Before paying, he grabbed a couple of candy bars.

"Hungry?" Alton asked skeptically.

"It's not all for me."

Alton grinned but didn't offer any other comment, apparently realizing that Joshua wasn't in the mood to be teased.

When they had all reboarded the bus, Alton again sat next to Sarah. "Since you have Becca's lunch, this only seems logical," he said to Joshua.

It was obvious that Alton was angling to sit next to Sarah—either because he was interested in her or possibly because he hoped to avoid his brother. Sarah rolled her eyes as Alton settled into the seat, but Nancy had no objection, and Becca didn't seem to mind one way or the other.

She was somewhat alarmed at the amount of food Joshua was carrying.

"Are you starving?"

"Well, *nein*, but I wasn't sure if you'd want chips, and it seemed a drink was necessary in order to wash down the hot dog—"

"And the candy bars?"

"Ah. Those are for later. I hear Texas is a big state, and we might not have a chance to buy more food."

Becca grinned even as she muttered, "I guess we'll work off the calorics tomorrow."

Then they were rolling again. Soon they had left Dallas behind. The bus continued down the interstate and stopped briefly at Waco, Temple, and Austin. They pulled into the bus terminal briefly in San Antonio, again in the downtown area. All four of them crowded close to the window in order to catch glimpses of the River Walk. Then the land flattened out and they entered cattle country.

"Big ranches out here," he said.

"*Ya*? My *grossdaddi* told me there's a small community of Amish in Beeville."

"We'll pass fairly close to it. To the west, I believe. In fact, I wouldn't be surprised if some from the Beeville community are helping at our work site."

"How do you know so much about Texas?" Becca asked. She had taken the window seat when Joshua left to use the restroom. Now she cornered herself against the window and the wall of the bus and studied him. It made him a little nervous to be the focus of her attention, but he also found he liked it.

"Not so much. Just what I read in the *Budget*."

"Read the paper, do you?"

"Usually several times because there isn't much else to read." He nodded toward the novel she was holding in her lap. "I see you like to visit the library."

"Guilty. Sometimes I have trouble falling asleep at night."

"Books help you sleep?"

"Well, not exactly. They keep me awake because I want to see what happens to the characters, but at least they take my mind off the fact that I can't sleep."

Joshua didn't know what to say to that, so he nodded and glanced past her out the window.

"Do you ever have trouble sleeping?"

"Me? Not usually." He started to tell her about the night before but decided she probably didn't want to hear his problems. "I think working in the fields helps. Most of the time, even if my mind wants to wrestle with things, my body insists on sleep."

He didn't add that often while he was on the tractor his mind dwelled on subjects best left alone.

And then they were talking naturally, and Joshua forgot to be nervous. They discussed the recent slew of marriages in their community, what they were looking forward to about summer, and how members of their families were doing. Finally, they started talking about the mission and what they expected to find when they arrived at the Texas coast.

Joshua was surprised when the bus began to slow down, and then they were entering the area of Aransas Pass. Up to that point, they hadn't seen much to indicate that Hurricane Orion had marked a path across the area. There had been a few of the large highway signs blown down, and one house in the distance had been destroyed by a small tornado spawned by the storm.

"Eleven tornadoes raked through Texas as Orion moved inland." Nancy's voice had taken on a solemn tone, and Joshua tried to remember if she'd always lived in Cody's Creek. Then it occurred to him that her farm was one of the places hit when the twisters came through in the fall the year before. He didn't think she'd sustained a lot of damage.

He'd volunteered at many of the job sites in their area. Samuel Schwartz had been the one most affected. Not only had he lost all of his crop, but his niece had been hurt—paralyzed, in fact.

As they were unloading their things from the bus, he noticed more signs of the hurricane. Several buildings next to the bus stop were in the process of being rebuilt, but gaps remained between most of the structures, places with a foundation but no building at all. Had that been the result of Orion?

A white van pulled up behind the bus. On the side of it were the letters *MDS*, and below that the words *Mennonite Disaster Service*. Next to the letters was a blue circle. Within the circle were two hands clasped in a handshake. The background consisted of a white cross. Their team leader introduced himself as Jim Snyder. He thanked them for coming and said they would have an introductory meeting in the morning to answer any of their questions.

He looked a few years older than Joshua—thirty or thirty-five, tops. He wore no beard, but then that didn't mean much. He could be married or not. The Mennonite rules regarding beards, dress, and technology were much more flexible than Amish rules.

As Jim explained that they would be traveling to Port Aransas via a ferry, Joshua looked around. The trip had gone much faster than he had expected, though he imagined that was because he had been sitting next to Becca instead of Alton.

Alton had slept through so much of the trip that he now looked bright eyed and bushy tailed.

Sarah was once again chewing on her thumbnail, something she seemed to do whenever she was nervous.

Nancy clucked—yes, actually clucked—and herded them all toward the waiting van.

But it was Becca that Joshua watched the most closely. When she stepped out of the bus and breathed deeply of the sea air, a smile spread across her face. He realized, not for the first time, what a beautiful woman she was. He heard Levi's words, "If you keep waiting for the right time, you may never begin."

Was that what he had been doing? Waiting? Stalling? Allowing his fear to restrict his hopes and dreams?

Because at that moment he couldn't think of a single reason not to court Becca Troyer.

CHAPTER 25

*B*ecca wasn't sure what she had expected the Gulf of Mexico to look like. Certainly she'd read about the ocean, the beach, and the rolling waves, but the reality was completely different from the descriptions.

After the MDS van drove onto the ferry, Jim told them they could get out and walk around the boat. Becca was more tired than she would have thought possible. After all, she hadn't done anything but sit all day. Perhaps that explained her disorientation. It was almost as if a fog had settled over her brain.

She stumbled when she stepped down out of the van, but Joshua caught her. "Careful, Becca. You don't have your sea legs yet."

"Sea legs? Didn't know I needed to bring those."

He waited until he was sure she was steady on her feet, and then he followed her to the side of the ferry. She had trouble processing so many different sights and sounds at once. The cry of seagulls filled the sky, and a few children standing at the end of the boat reached into a bag and pulled out pieces of bread. The birds dipped and dived, plucking the bread from the outstretched hands before flying back out over the water.

The sun had nearly finished its journey toward the horizon. A vast array of colors splashed across the evening sky and then bounced off the water. Becca realized her mother would love to draw what she was staring at, and that thought made her suddenly homesick, though she'd been away for less than a day. She'd brought her journal. It occurred to her that she could write down descriptions of what she was seeing. Perhaps if she were detailed enough, her mother would be able to paint a set of coastal cards.

"Not a bad place to serve on a mission team," Joshua said.

Becca swiped at hair that was pulling loose from her *kapp*. "It looks so peaceful. It's hard to imagine a storm that could cause so much destruction."

"Most of it was over in Corpus and on the island." Nancy had walked up beside them. "There was also quite a bit of destruction in Kingsville which is to the southwest. By the time the storm turned inland, much of its fury was spent."

"Other than the eleven tornadoes." Joshua opted to hold his hat rather than risk losing it.

"Yes, the tornadoes caused some damage but no loss of life. Unlike the actual landfall of Orion—which took twenty-four souls."

Alton and Sarah had moved closer and were listening solemnly. Becca was sure that each was remembering the tornadoes that had struck their small community. Compared to the destruction Nancy was describing, theirs seemed minor. But then tragedy was never minor when it happened to someone you loved.

"What are we going to be working on?" Alton asked.

It was the first indication Becca had seen that Joshua's brother had any interest in their mission. At one point during their bus trip, while Alton was asleep, Joshua had shared with her the fact that this was her grandfather's idea. When Joshua had asked Alton about going the day Levi had visited their farm, Alton had merely shrugged and asked, "Do I have any choice?"

Joshua hadn't considered that a rousing sign of enthusiasm, but Becca wasn't sure what he could have expected. No one liked being given an ultimatum, and that was basically what they had done to Alton—though for good reasons, she was sure.

Now Alton stood, bracing his hands against the side of the boat and closely watching the approaching shoreline. It occurred to Becca then that perhaps Joshua's brother was merely bored back home. Certainly that could happen. She felt that way at times—an itch of restlessness, the occasional daydream about what life might be like elsewhere. It wasn't a sin to wonder about other people and places.

Could it be that the life of a farmer was not the life Alton was meant to live? And if so, perhaps he could find his calling here, in Port Aransas, while they worked to alleviate the pain and suffering of others.

Then he turned and winked at Sarah, and Becca's lofty ideas popped like a balloon at a birthday party. It could be that they would be lucky merely to keep Alton out of trouble, and she planned to watch him closely with Sarah. That girl had been through enough without having her heart broken because she was the only available Amish girl around.

Which wasn't quite true.

Becca was available, but the thought of herself in a relationship with Alton caused laughter to bubble from her lips.

Joshua glanced at her, an eyebrow raised in question, but she only shook her head. They were nearing Port Aransas, and it was time to climb back into the van.

The tiredness she'd felt before had fallen away, and her mind began to clear as a ripple of excitement pumped through her veins. Three weeks living on a beach sounded like a real vacation to her. No gardening. Only her own laundry to do. And mostly they would eat light—cereal and sandwiches and such, so the cooking would be minimal. She hadn't realized how much she needed a change until she hurried back into the van and buckled her seat belt, feeling like one of the characters in the books she loved to read.

It was just the six of them in the van. Nancy was up front, sitting next to Jim. They were talking about the weather and the work that lay ahead. Sarah and Alton were discussing what they hoped to do while on the island—beachcombing for Sarah and surfing for Alton. Joshua sat beside Becca. He'd leaned forward to ask Alton what, if anything, he knew about staying upright on a surfboard.

And then the ferry docked and the attendants began motioning for the vehicles to drive out onto the street. As they trundled past the dock area, suddenly everyone in the van fell silent.

In vacant lots along the road, piles of debris were stacked up six, eight, even ten feet high. Certainly taller than Becca. To her it looked like a towering mountain of trash. In the fading light, she could just make out boards, parts of a ship, a couch, even a ragged teddy bear thrown onto the heap.

"Why hasn't the debris been carted away?" Joshua asked.

"Oh, it has been," Jim replied. "They've been taking off more than a hundred trucks a day since Orion hit. But every day people bring more. These are the designated lots for dumping, or people can wait until the disposal company reaches their property."

"But Orion hit seven months ago," Sarah said.

"True. It's hard to conceive the amount of debris when you have a hurricane like Orion. The wreckage you're looking at is a result of wind damage as well as flooding. We saw this in Galveston as well. After Ike hit in 2008, the Gulf Bank debris collection site received an average of four hundred and fifty trucks a day. A year later, they were still receiving truckloads from the damaged areas."

About half of the buildings on the road they traveled down were surrounded by yellow *Caution* tape. In other places, the site had been cleared of debris, and only a concrete foundation indicated that something had once existed there. They passed three, then four, and five buildings that had survived the storm—seemingly unscathed. Five buildings in the ten-minute drive it took them to reach their destination.

Temporary structures had been built in some places. Apparently, groceries were being sold out of trailers, but they looked nothing like mobile buildings Becca had seen before. She'd looked up FEMA trailers at their local library. Those had looked like small mobile homes. These structures were quite different. When they slowed at a light, Becca saw the letters *FEMA* written on the side of one. Then she noticed that similar structures were everywhere. They were serving as stores, medical offices, and even homes. Many were stacked two and three stories high, and to Becca they looked almost like freight train cars—only nicer and with doors and windows.

Jim turned down a street, continued for another block, and then pulled up to the curb and parked.

More temporary structures were stacked two high on the south side of the street, and cleared home foundations sat on the right. Two homes had been rebuilt. They looked cozy and efficient, and they provided a beam of hope in an otherwise desolate picture. Next to those two homes was an empty lot, followed by three other homes that were in various stages of completion—one looked nearly finished, though there was still scaffolding along one wall. Another had the frame up but little else. And then there was a third where nothing had been built, but boxes of supplies sat waiting, covered with a tarp.

Which one would they be working on? And who were the people who would eventually live there?

Becca's mind filled with questions as they made their way out of the van. She wondered where they were supposed to sleep and eat and bathe.

As they stood on the street, an elderly gentleman with a black dog pulled up behind them. He was driving a pickup. The dog waited for permission, though it was clear it wanted to run and welcome them. At least Becca hoped it had a welcome in mind. The beast was rather large, but it didn't look like an attack dog.

The night was quiet, with little traffic noise, so she could hear the man as he opened his door and said, "Come on, Quitz. Let's meet the new folks."

CHAPTER 26

*C*harlie tried to not be critical of the folks standing in front of him. He'd helped coordinate work sites with MDS for months now—the good folks of Mennonite Disaster Services had arrived within days of Orion, and they had done amazing work. This time was different though. These people would be working to finish Alice's house.

Did they have any experience at all? Could they be counted on to show up rather than skipping a shift to play in the sand and surf?

Would they be able to finish Alice's house in time for her to move into it in two weeks as she'd planned?

He pushed his worries to the back of his mind and hurried over to say hello.

"I'd like you all to meet Charlie Everman and Quitz," Jim said. "He acts as a liaison between the people we're helping and MDS."

"I'm a retired English teacher and a longtime resident of Port A." Charlie stopped to clear his throat, as he fought to hold his emotions at bay—emotions that too often intruded upon his day and stole his sleep at night. "In other words, I'm an old codger who hangs around the job site."

Laughter sprinkled throughout the small group.

Jim slapped Charlie on the back and then made introductions. "Nancy has experience working with MDS before."

The older woman nodded slightly.

"Joshua and Alton are brothers, and this is their first mission trip."

Joshua was the older of the two and also looked to be more serious. Alton kept whispering to the smaller of the two girls.

"Sarah and Becca are from the same community as Joshua and Alton. In fact, they're all from Cody's Creek, Oklahoma."

"I've never heard of it," Charlie admitted.

The group smiled knowingly at one another, as if they'd heard that response before. They must have come from a fairly small town.

Joshua said, "We're to the east of Tulsa."

"Tulsa I've visited," Charlie said. "Thank you for coming. Actually, one of the homes you'll be working on, the one that is seventy percent done, belongs to a very dear friend of mine. You'll meet Alice and the kids this weekend. Until then, they send you their deepest thanks."

He swiped at his eyes and pulled in a deep breath.

The group seemed to sense that this was an emotional moment for him. Then one of the boys spoke up—Alton, if Charlie remembered correctly. He looked to be about seventeen or eighteen with a thin build, blue eyes, and blond hair. "What's the dog's story, Charlie?"

The Labrador pressed against Charlie's leg when he reached down to touch the top of her head. "She was to be our last dog, which is why we named her Quitz."

Again polite laughter filled the night.

"She saved me. I suppose you could say she's an angel sent by God—an angel who has been with me for years now." His eyes flicked toward the ocean. "She literally plucked me from Orion's waters, but that's a story for another day."

There were groans and accusations of Charlie being a tease, but the group seemed to relax. The ice had been broken, and they were a team now. At least Charlie hoped that was the case.

"I'll take the guys to see their luxury accommodations," Jim said.

"And I'll escort you ladies."

They crossed the street to the FEMA trailers, and Jim and his charges climbed up to the second level. Jim spoke with the two Amish boys—though Charlie supposed they were not boys but men. He needed to quit thinking of anyone under thirty-five as a boy. Joshua and Alton followed Jim into their trailer.

Charlie pulled a key out of his pocket, unlocked the door, and then he handed the key to the older woman.

"*Danki.*"

He'd learned from previous work crews that *danki* meant *thank you*, but he only knew how to respond in Texan. "You're quite welcome, ma'am. If you don't mind my coming in, I'll point out a few of the features."

Charlie pushed the door open, allowing the women to enter in front of him. He followed them into the sitting area. They could hear Joshua and Alton and Jim upstairs, but the sound was muffled. The emergency shelters were surprisingly well insulated.

"These are nothing like the trailers I've stayed in before," Nancy said.

"You've worked with FEMA in other areas?"

"*Ya.* Many times."

"Our mayor was very insistent that he did not want the old-style trailers brought here." Charlie glanced around. The structure looked exactly like his, only a little larger. He was in a one bedroom. This particular model had two bedrooms, one bathroom, a small kitchen and dining area, and a living room. "With the old trailers, there were many reports of formaldehyde problems, and although those court cases have yet to be settled, our mayor didn't want to risk it."

"There were health hazards?" Becca asked.

"They say. Mayor Sapp had done some research in case such a thing as Orion happened. He felt very strongly that the old FEMA trailers should not be brought here while there was even a possibility that they posed a health risk, and Governor Benton put her weight behind the request. These models are actually Urban Disaster Trailers. They were designed for use in densely populated areas and tested in New York City."

"And yet you have them here, on an island."

"True. Life is full of irony."

"There are bedrooms?" Becca asked.

"Down the hall. Two of them as well as a shared bathroom. From here you can see the kitchen and dining room."

"We can go out on the patio?"

"Yes. Let me show you how to unfasten the lock." He did so, and then he pushed the sliding glass door open.

Both girls stepped out into the night. The boys must have done the same, for Charlie heard a call from above and then the girls were shouting back.

"They're young, but they will be *gut* workers," Nancy said.

"I'm sure they will. You can't know how much this means to the folks of Port A. Everyone who lost their home put their name on a list. The folks on the list are then ranked by the most severe need to least. The Red Cross sends teams as well as many charity organizations like yours."

Nancy nodded sympathetically, or it seemed so to Charlie. She said, "The destruction was quite widespread."

"It was. And to be fair, Corpus Christi is the more important site due to shipping and health care facilities."

"So you've had to wait."

Charlie shrugged. "In God's time," he murmured.

When the girls stepped back into the room a few moments later, Charlie gestured in the direction of the kitchen. "There are some supplies in the refrigerator and pantry. Nothing fancy, but enough to get you through dinner tonight and breakfast tomorrow. In the morning one of us will take you to the grocery store for shopping."

"Is the store another trailer?" Becca asked.

"Yes. Several trailers were combined to make a retail space."

Though Nancy was doing her best to be polite, her face appeared quite drawn and she blinked rapidly. In other words, she looked ready to drop in her tracks. No doubt they had been up since sunrise and traveling could be exhausting. A twinge in Charlie's shoulder reminded him that it was late and he should be heading home himself. The doctor had warned him that old bones mend, but they don't often heal quite like they were before the injury. Charlie considered his shoulder to be a daily reminder that God wasn't done with him yet.

Quitz had sat quietly by the door through their entire exchange, but now she whined softly.

"I'd best be taking her home. I wish you all a good evening, and thank you again for coming."

He stepped out into the night and walked over to his truck. It wasn't his pre-Orion pickup, but it was similar. It was approximately the same age, and he'd been lucky that his friend, Bill Rogers, had been able to locate it for him. Vehicles, along with practically everything else, were difficult to acquire in the weeks and months following Orion.

Bill and Ann had provided a home for Alice and the kids until they could find an apartment in Rockport. Charlie had remained in the Corpus area, not wanting to leave Moose while he was in the hospital. When his friend took a turn for the worse and died, Charlie had stayed even longer to take care of the funeral arrangements. It was a dark, difficult time, and knowing that Alice and her grandchildren were taken care of was probably the only thing that made it bearable. Bill and Ann were what Charlie thought of as good people—ready to lend a hand whenever one was needed.

Quitz waited when he opened the passenger door of the truck, and Charlie stooped to help her up. Coming out of the vehicle was no problem for the dog, but jumping in was difficult, especially in the evenings. It seemed that Orion had taken its toll on Quitz. Charlie knew it had taken a toll on him as well, but he hoped that with time and God's mercy they both would heal. And he prayed that the new home he sat in front of would ease the burdens Alice carried.

It was with Alice and the kids on his mind that he turned and made his way back across town to his own urban disaster trailer.

CHAPTER 27

*J*oshua woke well before daybreak, and why wouldn't he? All of his life he had risen before the sun was properly over the horizon. He was a farmer at heart, and his sleeping patterns reminded him of that. He left his room and made his way into the kitchen, thinking of the work ahead of them.

Over the years he had helped with several barn raisings and even lent a hand in the building of houses. Those houses had been farmhouses, though. They had been rambling structures that were added on to as needed or else large, two-story boxes in the typical Amish style. From what he'd seen last night, they would be building small houses, probably two-stories high, on small lots. He couldn't imagine living that close to another family. Neighbors could practically reach out the window and shake hands with one another.

But he also couldn't imagine the destruction and violence of Orion. They had seen a little of the devastation as they had driven from the ferry to the job site yesterday, but he suspected that was only the tip of the iceberg. He made coffee and foraged in the pantry, coming away with a box of Pop-Tarts. While he waited for the coffee to drip through the machine, he prayed that God would bring success to their work, that no one would get hurt in the process, and that his brother would grow up.

That last item seemed a large request for a single day, so instead he prayed that God would care for and direct his brother's path. Then he remembered something their minister had said about thanking God, not just asking for things as if their Creator were a modern-day genie in a bottle.

So Joshua took his coffee to the small patio, watched the sun come up, and thanked God for the things in his life at that moment. The slabs awaiting work across the street. The sound of the ocean waves in the distance. The tangy smell of saltwater.

He slowly became aware of Becca and Sarah and Nancy moving about downstairs, probably rummaging for food as he had. He could hear doors softly opening and closing, and the melody of their voices quietly calling out to one another.

He thanked God for this opportunity. He had never wanted to leave the farm in Oklahoma. He was content working in the fields and barn. But he had to admit that this was an interesting experience. Perhaps one day he would tell his grandchildren about his mission work at the Texas coast.

That thought brought a smile to his face. He would need children before grandchildren, and a wife before children. His thoughts turned to Becca, and then she was calling up to him. "Joshua, we have no sugar. Do you have enough to share?"

"I'll be right down."

He stopped in his brother's room, turned on the light—which still seemed a curious thing to do—and clanged his spoon against his coffee cup. Alton raised up long enough to throw a pillow at him before he huddled back beneath the covers. The bedrooms had no windows, and the darkness would be reason enough for Alton to sleep all day.

"We're to be at the job site by seven thirty."

"It's across the street," Alton muttered.

"Indeed. I suppose I'll have to go downstairs alone to enjoy the girl's company as I eat my *wunderbaar Englisch* breakfast."

The word *breakfast* seemed to capture Alton's attention. He popped up and made more of an effort to open his eyes. "I'm starving. What did you find to eat?"

"Looks like bread and sugar." Joshua held up the box of Pop-Tarts. "It's better than nothing."

"Coffee?"

"Already made."

"Shower?"

"If you want one, but you're just going to get sweaty. There is work to do, you know."

For his answer, Alton sank back onto the mattress and pulled the covers over his head. It occurred to Joshua that his brother could probably sleep through anything. He started to correct him, to remind him of the forty hours a week he had promised to spend on the job site. But Alton wasn't listening and his words would be wasted, so he saved his energy. Walking to the kitchen, he picked up the container of sugar and made his way out of their trailer and down the stairs.

He knocked lightly on the women's door, which was quickly opened by Sarah. She looked perky and ready for the day. He'd wondered during the bus ride if she might be sick, the way she had dashed for the bathroom, her face pale with a sheen of sweat across her brow. But today she looked as if she felt fine.

"Come in. Becca is cooking oatmeal."

"Oatmeal?" Joshua's stomach grumbled on cue. "All I found was a box of Pop-Tarts."

"We have plenty, Joshua. Come and join us." Becca had changed into a different set of clothes. The dress she wore was a pale blue and covered with a white apron. He assumed it was her work clothes because the fabric was a bit faded, but it had been freshly laundered and to Joshua she looked as beautiful as she had the day before. That thought embarrassed him, and he busied himself refilling his coffee cup with the brew Sarah pointed to.

"Breakfast sounds *gut*, and I can always drink more coffee."

"Oatmeal will stick with you better than those little sugary pastries," Becca said.

"I can eat both."

"I'm sure you can, Joshua." Nancy walked into the room and surveyed the group. "I see we're all here except Alton."

At that moment, they could hear the sound of water rushing through the pipes.

"He decided to shower first."

"Before working?" Sarah asked.

"I believe he was looking forward to only sharing a bathroom with one person. Lots of hot water."

That led to a conversation of how many siblings were at home and the things they had tried in order to ensure there was enough hot water when they took their baths or showers. All of the Amish in Cody's Creek had indoor plumbing, but water without an electric pump ran gently from the tap. Hot water, heated by either a gas heater or an outdoor firebox, was always in short supply.

They had finished their meal, and Joshua was helping to clean up when Alton popped into the room.

"Breakfast?" he asked hopefully.

"I left you a bowl in the microwave," Becca said.

Sarah joined him at the contraption to show him which buttons to push.

"Rather like glue." Alton frowned at the bowl and then took another bite.

"You'll find that freshly cooked food is often better than something heated in the microwave," Nancy said. "Though I'll admit it is nice to be able to warm up a cup of coffee."

Alton stood up, pretending to wash out his bowl—a task he never did at home—and used the opportunity to whisper something to Sarah. Whatever it was, he caused her eyes to widen as she shot him a look akin to what his mother might have done.

Joshua wondered whether he needed to worry about Alton flirting with Sarah. Was he already acting inappropriately?

At that point, Joshua realized he could easily spend the entire trip worrying over his brother. He supposed that was why he'd come, but now that they were in Port Aransas he realized he did not relish the task at all. At home his parents and sisters could also keep an eye out for Alton's antics. Here, Joshua alone would be responsible for dealing with any trouble Alton managed to find.

Fortunately, he didn't have much time to dwell on that worrisome thought. Nancy was herding them out the door, and Joshua looked out to see that a small group had gathered across the street at the job site.

There were close to a dozen people by the time they joined the other volunteers—Jim, Charlie, their Amish group of five, and another four workers who didn't look Amish. It was MDS leading the work, so Joshua assumed that the others would be from a Plain community. The three additional men and one woman looked to be Mennonite. Their dress was conservative, but the woman wore only a sheer head covering with no strings—almost like a kerchief. The men didn't have beards, though two of them sported wedding rings. They were plain gold bands. Joshua had read that some Mennonite couples wore them while others didn't. Like the Amish communities, the Mennonites changed their traditions, albeit slowly.

All of those thoughts swept through Joshua's mind as they formed a circle and Jim led them in a short devotional. Appropriately, he'd picked Colossians three, the twenty-third and twenty-fourth verses. "'Whatever you do, work at it with all your heart, as working for the Lord…'" Joshua cast a look at his brother, who was staring off in the direction of the ocean. "'Not for human masters, since you know that you will receive an inheritance from the Lord as a reward.'"

Becca glanced up and met Joshua's gaze.

"'It is the Lord Christ you are serving.'"

There were several murmurs of agreement and then they were singing, which surprised Joshua. This was looking more and more like a barn raising back home. After the devotional time was finished, those thoughts quickly faded as Frank, a Mennonite man of around forty, asked him if he'd ever used an electrical power saw.

And then Joshua was focused on the job site, looking forward to learning how to use new tools. Though there was a slight breeze, already he was sweating in the coastal sun. He had no time to worry about Alton or to doubt whether this trip would work to settle his brother's wandering ways. Instead, Joshua's mind and heart and all of his energy was focused on rebuilding homes.

CHAPTER 28

*B*ecca enjoyed the morning devotional. The Scriptures helped her to focus, and the singing calmed the nerves of excitement in her stomach. Once the devotional time was over, Jim launched straight into discussion of their work.

"Obviously, these are complete rebuilds we will be working on." He made introductions, though Becca wasn't sure she could keep the men's names straight. Frank Bear was the older, larger man. That she could remember. But Brady Denning and Simon Cottrell— or was it Brady Cottrell and Simon Denning? She was already forgetting.

The Mennonite woman was the only female in the group she didn't know, so she should be able to recall her name easily enough. It was Eva Holsteiner, and she looked to be the age of Becca's mother.

"I'll go into more detail about the job site in a few minutes," Jim continued. "But just to remind you, we currently have three different teams working in the area—two here on the island and one across the bay."

"Will the other island team be here on our street?" Joshua asked.

"They won't. They're working downtown, but we typically get together for Friday night dinners. You should be able to meet everyone this evening. We're having a simple get-together on the beach, which will include a cookout." He nodded toward Becca's group. "Something for you to look forward to after your first day of house building. Also, I want to remind everyone that MDS provides your housing, meals, and work materials. Any exploration you do on the weekends will be on your own dime."

Alton nudged Sarah.

Becca wondered if that was what they had been talking about earlier. Had Alton asked her to go on some sort of sightseeing trip?

And then Jim was handing out assignments to Frank, Brady, Simon, and Eva. Finally, he turned back to Becca's group. "This is our normal schedule. You'll eat breakfast on your own, and we'll meet here by seven thirty for a short devotional. Then I hand out assignments. This morning I want to spend a few minutes walking you through each house and answering any questions you have about MDS."

He led them into the first house, which from the outside looked to Becca to be nearly finished.

"This house belongs to Alice Givens. She's the legal guardian for her two grandchildren, so she chose a floor plan with three bedrooms. That makes the upstairs rooms smaller, but it's an efficient design and Alice is very pleased with it."

"The home owners choose the floor plan?" Joshua asked.

"They do. We have a few basic plans, but we will adjust them according to the owner's wishes as long as it's practical and can be done at no extra cost. As I'm sure you noticed, these lots are small, so many residents are going with the two-story plan. However, we have an older couple next door and a handicapped woman in the third house. Both have opted for the single-story plan."

"Most Amish houses are built with the same floor plan," Alton said. "How do you adjust the layout design? What sorts of things can you change?"

Jim tapped a finger against the clipboard he was holding. "Well, for instance, our standard two-story, fifteen-hundred-square-foot house has a parka closet…"

Becca started to raise her hand, but Jim anticipated her questions.

"Coat closet. It's something that's appreciated in northern homes, but here in Texas most residents don't want it. By taking that out, we're able to give them a slightly larger living room."

As they walked from the living room to the kitchen, Becca realized the house wasn't nearly as complete as she had thought. The outside was practically finished, but the inside still needed paint, flooring, fixtures—it needed basically everything. Would they be able to finish it in two weeks and still be able to work on the other houses?

"Alice met with me last week and picked out her countertops and kitchen fixtures. Either myself or Charlie…" he nodded toward the front door, where Charlie and Quitz were just coming into the house. "One of us will go to the mainland to pick up the supplies."

"It's surprising that you allow residents to choose such things," Joshua said.

"We realize that's a bit unusual, but we want the owners to feel that this is their home, and that they have a say in the design and building. As long as we stay within our budget, it's not a problem."

"Do the owners work on the homes?" Alton asked.

"Usually they do not, for a variety of reasons. Medical conditions, family obligations, depression." He ticked the causes off on his fingers, and Becca began to fully realize the needs of the people they were ministering to. "Grief is a major obstacle for many of our families. Some have no construction knowledge at all but want to participate. They will come by in the evenings and clean up the job site, put away tools, sweep, and even bring food they've made."

There were no additional questions, so Jim suggested they move to the house next door.

When Becca walked inside, she realized that by comparison Alice's house was nearly done. This house didn't even have walls. There was no roof yet, so it felt as if she were still outside. She could look up and see the bright blue sky.

Jim walked them through the framed rooms, pointing out how it differed from Alice's house.

"We have several community partners, including the Red Cross, Salvation Army, and local churches."

"What type of churches?" Nancy asked.

She'd been fairly quiet since the tour began. Becca remembered that she had worked on several MDS projects, so she'd probably seen similar job sites and was familiar with how MDS worked. Did the community partners differ depending on the location?

"Here in Texas, there are quite a few religious affiliations that have chosen to partner with us—Catholics, Episcopals, Baptists, Methodists—pretty much everyone who had a presence in the community. They provide funds that make our projects possible. We also work with FEMA to help residents receive government aid, which can be a daunting process."

They exited out the back door and walked to the final site, which consisted of a concrete slab. "As I mentioned, this home will require additional modifications because the owner is in a wheelchair. We'll need wider doors, a ramp in the front and back, and we'll have to meet ADA building code."

Alton glanced at Joshua, who shrugged.

"ADA is the American Disabilities Act. Their standards establish design requirements for handicapped persons."

"Sounds like a lot of paperwork," Joshua said.

"It is, and that's one of my jobs." Jim smiled. "I'd rather be swinging a hammer, but someone has to tackle the truly terrible tasks."

They were all now standing back out on the sidewalk.

"Once I hand out your assignments, I usually leave the site to check on the other groups, stop by the office to handle paperwork, head over to the mainland for supplies, that sort of thing. If you have any questions, ask Frank or Brady. They've both worked with me on several sites."

The two walked by, carrying lumber from a delivery van that had appeared while they were touring through the houses.

"*Ya*, we're old hands at this," Frank said.

Brady squinted at his friend in offense. "Careful who you're calling old."

"They also have a phone and my number in case you need to reach me for any reason." Jim glanced down at his clipboard. "All right. Let's go over your assignments for the day."

CHAPTER 29

*B*ecca had thought she'd be shopping for groceries with Nancy or perhaps fixing meals, but it seemed that Eva was in charge of that. She and Nancy hurried off to her car, heads together as they worked on a shopping list.

Sarah, Becca, and Simon were assigned to the first house, the one that looked nearly finished.

Within moments Joshua was deep in conversation with the other two men—Frank and Brady, and they were walking toward the second house, which had only a frame.

Jim and Alton were headed toward the last house. She couldn't imagine what they would do to it, since there was only a concrete slab. She didn't have much time to worry over Alton's assignment, though, as Charlie was already talking about what they hoped to accomplish in the next few hours.

"All the drywall is hung," he said. "Our goal is to do nearly all the painting today and then we can start laying the floor next week."

He led them into the house, Quitz walking patiently at his side.

"Did Alice pick out the color of paint?" Sarah asked.

"She did, though MDS buys three main colors in bulk quantity—white-white, off-white, and eggshell white."

Everyone laughed.

"The choices may be limited, but when a person has a say in what

169

color goes up on his or her walls, it helps to restore their dignity—even if it is only the choice between three types of white."

"Alice and Charlie aren't related, but you'd think they were the way the children look up to him." This from Simon, who had already been on the job a week.

"I care about them," Charlie admitted. "And I hope we can have them in their home soon. Commuting from the mainland every day takes its toll. It adds more time to Alice's workday and gives the children less time to do homework, play, and rest."

As an afterthought he added, "They currently live in a tiny apartment on the mainland. They were lucky to get it, but the children are anxious to move back into their own house."

"We'll work hard, Charlie." Becca found herself looking forward to the task as she accepted a brush, stirrer stick, and can of paint.

The morning sped by. Becca's job was to paint the boy's room. All of the rooms were the same color—Alice had chosen the eggshell white. As Becca painted, she imagined C.J.'s room with baseball posters on the walls and dirty socks on the floor. Charlie had told her that C.J. was the worrier of the family, and that he wanted to make sure everything was okay for his grandmother and sister. It was with that image in her mind that she painted his walls.

She was surprised when Eva called them to lunch. "Next week you'll each pack your own lunch except for Wednesday, when lunch is provided by one of our residents. As for today, you couldn't very well put together a lunch without groceries. Nancy and I have stocked your kitchens and made sandwiches for everyone."

A rousing chorus rang through the group—"Thank you" and "We appreciate it" and "Looks *wunderbaar* good."

Becca immediately began devouring her sandwich. She couldn't remember the last time she was so hungry. Focusing on the food and how good it felt to rest, she didn't notice Simon making his way toward her until he was standing in front of her.

"Mind if I sit here?"

"Of course not. You're as welcome to the curb as I am."

Simon's eyes crinkled in a smile as he plopped down to the right of her. She'd noticed he did that a lot—smiled, that is. He seemed like an affable fellow.

"How did your painting go, Becca?" Joshua sat on her left, took a huge bite of his sandwich, and waited for her answer.

"Maybe I wasn't painting. Maybe I was sawing boards."

She reached over and brushed sawdust off his shoulder.

"Maybe so." He drank half of his bottle of water. "But you're wearing paint on your nose, so I suspect you were working with a paint brush, not a saw."

Simon laughed, and Becca rubbed at her nose with her napkin.

"It's on your face too," Joshua said, shrugging. "No use worrying about it."

She rolled her eyes and returned her attention to her sandwich. Joshua and Simon talked about what they did back home. Joshua described the farm. He described the terrain, how many acres they had, and how the land differed from what he'd seen of Texas.

Becca had never noticed how his expression relaxed and his eyes lit up when he talked about home. She hadn't been around him that much before, only seeing him in large groups—church services and community gatherings where she mostly stayed with the women. When he described their crops and horses, a richness came into his voice, and it seemed as if he were describing a person rather than a place.

Simon explained that he and his brother owned a business in their hometown of Seminole. "We build houses. I do most of the interior work, and my brother hires a crew to help with the actual framing, though I can do that in a pinch."

"So you're an expert painter?" Becca teased.

"I suppose I am. I can certainly clean a paint brush better than most." He grinned at Becca. When she'd left her paint brush on top of the opened can of paint, he'd explained to her the importance of closing the can and properly cleaning her brush—even for a lunch break. Simon stood and stuffed his hands into the pockets of his jeans. "I'm off to check out the cookie selection. Can I bring you anything?"

Becca shook her head, though she thought that probably it would have been all right to eat a few. Surely she'd burned a lot of calories with all that painting. Joshua said he'd grab some in a minute.

When Simon had walked away, Joshua leaned closer and said, "Careful, Becca. I believe Simon has his eye on you."

"What?" Her voice squeaked as she looked left and then right.

"Just saying. A pretty girl like you would naturally interest a man like Simon."

Did Joshua just call her pretty? She shook her head to clear it, and then she forced her voice down to a normal volume. "And what kind of girl would interest a man like you?"

The question popped out of Becca's mouth like grease from a pan, and she nearly groaned in embarrassment. Why had she asked such a thing? She couldn't tell if he noticed her embarrassment. He was staring over at the trailers they had slept in and scratching his jaw.

"Me? Can't say I've thought about it a lot. I suppose I want a girl who can make a good sandwich, keep a clean house, care for my children, and maybe sew my clothes."

"Is that all?"

"There might be more things. I could draw up a list if you like."

"A list?"

"In case you were thinking of applying for the job."

This kind of talk wasn't like Joshua at all. What happened to the quiet young man from their community? What happened to the shy guy on the bus? Maybe it was the ocean air, but he was certainly acting peculiar.

Before she had time to ask him about the abrupt change in his personality, he stood, winked at her, and held out his hand. "Care to accompany me to the cookie table?"

Becca decided that was a pretty good idea, so she allowed him to pull her up from the curb and together they walked over to where the food had been laid out on a makeshift table.

But later that afternoon, as she was painting Shelley's room, what kept going through her mind was the way Joshua had winked, smiled at her, and held out his hand.

CHAPTER 30

*B*ecca helped Sarah to braid her hair after she had taken a shower. Of course both girls could take care of her own hair, but it was so much nicer to help each other. It reminded Becca of home when her mother would sit on the bed next to her, braid her hair, and speak of the day's events. As Becca ran the brush through Sarah's hair and separated it into plaits for braiding, she felt closer to her—as if they knew each other much better than they actually did.

"Did you enjoy your work today?" she asked.

"*Ya*. I never imagined that I'd be hanging drywall."

"You should have seen the look on your face when Frank appeared and asked for your help next door."

"I've watched many house raisings. Both painting and hanging drywall always seemed like a man's job." Sarah glanced over her shoulder. "I liked it, though. I liked the way it felt to hammer the nails into the panels, and using the screw gun was fun. It was good to be doing something that required all of my attention and energy, you know?"

"I do, but my arms are sore already. You wouldn't think painting could use so many muscles."

"This is nice," Sarah said. "At home, there's always work, but it's the same work every day. Some tasks change with the seasons, but they are still the same chores we did the year before."

"I've certainly never painted two rooms in one day. I don't think I've ever painted anything, actually."

Sarah sighed. "It was *wunderbaar* to do something different."

Becca murmured in agreement, and then she held the mirror up so that Sarah could see her hair.

"Looks *gut. Danki*. Now hand me the brush, and I'll do yours."

Neither had washed their hair. They would do that the next day when there would be time to let it hang loose to dry. Becca thought it had felt wonderful to stand in the shower and wash the dirt and paint and sweat of the day from her body.

"I worried I might be too tired to go tonight, but now I'm looking forward to it."

"So am I." Sarah ran the brush gently from the top to the bottom of Becca's waist-long hair. "I like how wavy your hair is."

Becca laughed. "You wouldn't if you had to corral it every day. Sometimes it just pops out of my *kapp*."

Nancy tapped on the door and reminded them that Jim's van would be leaving in ten minutes.

"Do you like Simon?" Sarah asked.

"Like him? I suppose. As much as anyone else."

"Oh, Becca. Surely you can tell that he likes you more than simply as a new friend."

"I don't know." Becca thought of what Joshua had said at lunch. "To be honest, boys still confuse me, even though I'm practically a spinster at the age of twenty."

Sarah handed her the brush and began to plait her hair. "*Mamm* reminds me of my age often, as if it will spur me to choose a man and settle down."

"I'm not sure I'm ready for that."

"I'm certain I am not."

"So nothing serious is going on between you and Alton?"

Sarah coiled the braid around the top of Becca's head, pinned it, and fetched her *kapp* from the dresser.

"Alton is…different. He says funny, unexpected things. Like this morning. He said that my eyes were prettier than the Texas sky."

"He's a flirt."

"Yes. But it's nice to be flirted with sometimes. Back home, every-one treats me as if I'm breakable. I suppose because of..." She hesi-tated, her eyes meeting Becca's in the small hand mirror. "Because of my eating problems."

Having fastened on her *kapp*, Becca replaced the mirror and brush on the single dresser they shared. The room was barely big enough for it. A nightstand sat between their twin beds, and there was a straight-back chair next to the dresser. The furniture was so sparse that it felt like home, only there weren't quilts on the beds—instead, they had freshly laundered sheets, a thin blanket, and a light comforter. Becca supposed their covers were much more appropriate for Texas weather, but she missed the nine patch quilt that had adorned her bed since she was a small girl.

There was no window in the room, so they used the electrical lights whenever they weren't sleeping. It seemed odd to Becca, but she did like the small lamp on the table between their beds. She wouldn't have to read by flashlight, though the night before she'd fallen asleep without even opening her book.

She turned to Sarah, sat beside her on the bed, and pulled her hands into her lap. "How are you feeling? I don't ask often because I don't want to pry, and I assume you are tired of folks asking."

"No one asks, Becca. It's as if my eating disorder is a subject that must not be broached. Sometimes I want to wear a blouse that pro-claims *I'm Skinny but Alive*."

"So it's still difficult?"

"It's a struggle to eat normally if that's what you mean. Some days are better than others. Today was a *gut* day."

Becca wrapped her arms around Sarah. "I'm glad you're here. Glad you came with us."

"I'm glad I learned to hang drywall."

They both laughed and then hurried out to join Nancy. The six of them settled into the van—the same one that had fetched them from the bus station. Nancy again sat up front next to Jim, Becca and Sarah took the middle seat, and Joshua and Alton were in the back. They talked about their work and the progress they had made on their respective houses. Alton asked the girls if they had brought their swimming suits. They hadn't. Becca didn't own a suit, and she doubted that Sarah did either. Apparently, Alton had walked to a nearby store at lunch and purchased swim trunks.

When the van pulled off the main road and headed toward the ocean, they all stopped talking, intent on the scene unfolding in front of them.

At first there were rows of lots with empty slabs of concrete.

Then there were properties where the debris had not yet been cleared. Many of these still had portions of houses that had tumbled under Orion's fury.

Finally, there was only sand. Jim pulled into a parking lot and parked the van. "I hope you enjoy our picnic on the beach. Watch out for jellyfish, and remember the bus leaves at nine o'clock sharp. If you're not back here by nine, you'll either have to walk or find a different ride."

They helped carry supplies to the beach—a cooler, several lawn chairs, and towels in case anyone decided to swim. The day had been warm but was cooling quickly. Becca wasn't sure she would want to get wet even if she did have a swimsuit.

They walked past sand dunes that were covered in yellow flowers and then the Gulf of Mexico was in front of them. The waves rolled and crashed. The darker blue of the water extended as far as she could see until it met the lighter blue of the sky. The wind was stronger on this side of the dunes, and the briny scent of saltwater filled the air.

Becca followed the group, her walking slowed as her feet sunk into the sand. She had worn sandals, but she longed to yank them off and walk barefoot. Then she remembered Jim's admonition about jellyfish. What did they look like? What would happen if she inadvertently stepped on one?

Those questions would have to wait, as she was soon surrounded by a large group of people—the two other groups that Jim had mentioned. There were Amish, Mennonite, and *Englisch*. They all seemed to know one another, and though they introduced themselves, Becca didn't even try to remember their names. They floated in and out of her mind like sand sifting through her fingers. Nancy had told them that the other two groups would be rotating off at the end of the week. There didn't seem to be much reason to work on remembering their names because they would soon be gone.

Everyone was nice enough. All were in high spirits because it was Friday and they would be able to rest the next day. Within such a large group, the people of Becca's group suddenly felt like family—even Frank, Brady, Simon, and Eva.

Someone had started grilling hamburgers over a charcoal grill, and Becca's stomach grumbled. Part of her mind realized she wasn't worrying about food anymore and whether or not she should restrict her calories. She reached to fill her plate with chips, guacamole dip (something she'd never tried before), and fresh vegetables. It felt good to eat after such a long day's work.

Soon the hamburgers were done and everyone was pulling them from the grill, adding mustard, ketchup, onion, pickles, and even chili. Before she'd taken her first bite, one of the ladies from the downtown group said, "We brought ice cream for dessert."

Everyone groaned except Alton, who said, "Before my second hamburger or after?"

"You can eat it whenever you want. It's in the large red cooler—and it's Bluebell, a Texas specialty."

"We worked on a MDS project in Bastrop once." Brady pushed up his large glasses and offered a rare smile. "It was only an hour from the little creamery in Brenham. Now that was a great Saturday field trip."

"We brought six different flavors, including Butter Crunch, which is a flavor they rotate into the summer production." The woman was not Amish or Mennonite, but she seemed quite familiar with MDS and Texas ice cream. "Save some room. You're going to want to try it."

As they ate in a circle around the campfire, everyone began to tell stories about funny events on the job site and families they remembered helping. Someone pulled out a guitar and started to sing, and the fire grew brighter as the sun faded from the sky. Becca looked down and saw that her plate was empty. She glanced back out at the ocean. She wanted to go walk there, but Sarah was already gone, having left a few minutes earlier with Alton, who had indeed switched into bright green trunks. She didn't know if she wanted to walk to the water alone. What if she became lost? What if she stepped on a jellyfish?

Shaking her head, she practically laughed at herself. She sounded like a small child—afraid of her own shadow. In fact, she could look up and see young children with their parents, laughing as their feet touched the surf.

So she stood, kicked off her shoes, and walked toward the waves. The first time the water splashed over her feet she jumped backward and nearly fell into Joshua. Beside him was Simon, and they were both laughing at her, which she didn't mind so much. It was nice to be with friends, nice to have these quiet moments walking along a Texas beach.

She decided to ignore the butterflies batting against her stomach and enjoy the evening. As her mother had said, these would be memories she'd have for a lifetime, and she wanted them to be good ones.

CHAPTER 31

*C*harlie had fallen into a routine. He would rise at his usual time Saturday morning—actually, every morning was the same time with Quitz. After feeding the dog, he'd pour himself a cup of coffee and stand on the patio of his urban disaster trailer. The name still made him shake his head. They had certainly suffered a disaster, but they were far from urban. Still, the one-bedroom trailer was sufficient for him and Quitz. He was grateful not to be commuting from the mainland.

As he drank his coffee, he tried not to dwell on the pile of debris next door. His entire home had collapsed. Much of it had disappeared and been replaced with debris from other parts of the island. The first few weeks after he'd returned, he had tried to dig out what could be salvaged. What he'd found had been waterlogged—ruined. The task finally became too depressing. It was all trash and would need to be hauled to one of the debris disposal sites. What was the hurry? It wasn't going anywhere.

The important thing was that he was alive. He had that to be thankful for each morning, and he was. He could rebuild if he decided he wanted to do so. His life was full of too many questions at this point, and there was no real hurry.

After his coffee, he'd rustle up something for breakfast—usually a bagel or bowl of hot cereal. Then he'd clip Quitz's leash to her collar, take her for a short walk along the beach, and return home to pack a lunch. Three times a week he stopped off at the diner for coffee and to check on Alice. Then he would drive over to the job site.

Charlie especially liked Saturday mornings. He was able to survey the progress without being in anyone's way. He understood that no one needed an old man underfoot, slowing them down. A year ago he might have tried to help with the construction, but his shoulder hadn't yet healed enough for that.

Sure, he did errands for Jim. And he helped the new group in any way he could. But it irked him that he couldn't climb up on the roof, carry in the drywall, or lay flooring.

Regardless, he went to the job site every Saturday morning, walked through the houses noting progress, and made a list of questions to ask Jim if there was anything that seemed out of place. He thought of himself as an overseer, but that wasn't quite right. It was more that he was an advocate for the people of Port Aransas. He'd suffered through the storm with them, and he had to believe that God had a reason for the fact he had survived when some hadn't. That reason might be to help see families resettled into new homes. He certainly had the experience to understand what they were going through.

But the restrictions in his activities rankled him. Who would guess that a shoulder could cause so much trouble? The bone had been cracked as well as dislocated. Old bones healed slowly. Perhaps God was using his injury to teach him patience.

"God has forced our hand, Quitz. We're slowing down whether we want to or not."

They pulled up in front of 423 Sea Side—the site of Alice's house. It was the same lot she'd owned before Orion, but now everything looked completely different. If he were honest, Charlie would admit that in some ways it looked better. The neighborhood had been on the downslide before the hurricane hit. The storm had cleared away both the good and the bad.

Tidy houses in a row winked at him from the sidewalk—some complete, some not begun, and some—like Alice's—nearly ready for the owners to move in. The lot beside hers was empty. Charlie knew it was for sale. The folks who owned it had decided not to return to the island. He had contacted them and found out the price, something he could easily afford. But should he move? Would Alice want him to? And what about his place on the beach? What would Madelyn want him to do?

"The world doesn't stand still, Charlie." Her words were a constant reminder in his heart.

He stepped into the house and was surprised to see Joshua there. After greeting Quitz, Joshua looked down at the two bags of donuts he held and pushed one into Charlie's hands. "I have no idea why I bought so many. We don't have these often in our community. It's too far to town. I woke early and took a walk—"

"You can smell Mr. Kim's donuts from a mile away."

Joshua smiled and popped a donut hole in his mouth.

"You're off today, Joshua. I thought you'd be sleeping in."

"My *bruder* is. He can sleep through several meals if we let him."

"Youth."

"*Ya.* I suppose."

"But you aren't one to do that."

Joshua shrugged. "I'm a farmer. It's in my blood to rise early, work hard, and collapse on the couch when the day is done."

"Hmm. Amish life doesn't sound too different from that of a Texas farmer."

"It's probably not."

Charlie wondered why Joshua was here. Why had he come to help a small town in southern Texas? Most of the MDS volunteers were either young—teenagers or twentysomethings—or they were older, retired folks like himself. They also had some regulars, such as Simon, Frank, Brady, and Eva. They lived in distant Texas towns and felt a kinship to the people in Port A. They wanted to help and would probably keep returning until there was nothing left to do.

"Tell me about Alice and the kids," Joshua said.

"Good family. She works at the Shack."

When Joshua's eyebrows rose, Charlie chuckled. "It's a diner. We'll eat there soon. Maybe next week. Excellent home-style cooking."

"Sounds like my kind of place." Joshua paused and then asked, "How do you know Alice? It's plain she means a lot to you."

"She does, and so do the kids—C.J. and Shelley." As he munched on a donut, Charlie described the children, their ages, and their activities in school. The men walked through the rooms, and Charlie noted that the painting was finished. He nodded in approval. The flooring could be laid on Monday. They were making good progress.

They had stepped into C.J.'s upstairs bedroom and were looking out the front window. From there they had a good view of the street and the neighborhood beyond. They were too far from the ocean to catch sight of it, but Charlie knew it was there. Like a heartbeat it seemed to provide a background for most of his life. Perhaps it was that thought that caused him to share more than pleasantries with Joshua.

"My wife, Madelyn, and I moved here when I was twenty-two years old. We were newlyweds. It was my first teaching job."

"She's passed?" Joshua was now facing him, though Charlie continued gazing out the window.

"Yes. Three years ago—nearly four now." It surprised him that the words came out so evenly, as if he weren't describing the day his life had change irrevocably. "Love is the most important thing, son. Don't ever pretend that something takes precedence over it. Even the Good Book says as much. Faith, hope, and love…"

"But the greatest of these is love."

Charlie was a little surprised that Joshua knew the Scripture. It seemed a thing from a lost generation—memorizing the words from God's Book.

"After Madelyn passed, I suppose I was a bit lost. I was retired then and unsure what to do with my time."

"Alice helped you."

"She did. I would go to the diner several times a week. She always had a pleasant attitude and ready smile. Eventually she began to tell me about the kids—her grandkids."

"So she's like a daughter to you."

Charlie smiled. He'd often thought the same thing himself.

"And Shelley and C.J. are like *grandkinner*."

Grandkids? Probably, but before Charlie could ask, a Dodge Neon drove up and C.J. and Shelley tumbled out of the car. Quitz had been waiting patiently, but at the sound of the car door she looked to Charlie, who nodded once. She hopped up and bounded down the stairs and out the door.

Charlie rolled up the top of the donut bag and handed it back to Joshua. "Let's show the kids how much progress you've made."

CHAPTER 32

*J*oshua hadn't known a lot of *Englischers* in his lifetime. Certainly Amish and *Englisch* lived side by side in Cody's Creek, but other than interacting at work, most kept to themselves. Maybe occasionally they traded produce with one another. An Amish man or young woman might take a temporary job at the Cheese House. Men sometimes worked on a building for an *Englisch* farmer. Women would occasionally commission a sewing or quilting project. An *Englischer* looking for temporary work might even show up and help with the harvest. But by and large their lives remained separate.

One *Englischer* in their community, Brian Walker, had become Amish. That had surprised everyone. Most thought he wouldn't last, but he had. Not only that, but he'd been asked to teach at their local school, and he'd eventually married a girl from their community. But Brian seemed Amish to Joshua—wearing their clothes, slowly learning their language, living their plain and simple life.

Charlie Everman was most certainly *Englisch* through and through. Joshua watched the old guy hobble carefully down the stairs. Twice he paused to rub one of his shoulders, which hinted of a past injury. But there was little doubt that his mind was as quick as it had ever been. He wasn't focused on his own problems, either. As soon as the car had driven up, Charlie's attention had turned toward the people outside. When they reached the door, the children barreled into him, much as Joshua had seen Amish children run up to their *daddi* after a church meeting.

Would his life be like that?

Would he have children who would spend lazy Sunday afternoons with his parents?

His mind brushed back over the Scripture Charlie had mentioned, "Faith, hope, and love." He hadn't given it much thought. Occasionally he would wonder if he'd ever marry, but in the day-to-day business of working a farm the thought usually got pushed to the back of his mind. Since he'd left Cody's Creek, he'd certainly spent some time thinking about it. Maybe it was the hours spent in idleness on the bus. Or maybe, possibly, it was being in such close proximity to Becca Troyer.

The children's voices brought his mind back to the present.

Although he could relate to them, his first glance at Alice revealed that she was nothing like he expected. Her brown hair, tinged with gray, was cut in a straight, short fashion. Her hairstyle and clothes (she wore jeans and a faded T-shirt), made her seem much younger than the grandmothers he knew. Had being a mother to the children kept her young? And what of the children's parents?

Before he could spend any more time puzzling over the situation, Charlie was introducing C.J., who studied him seriously and then stuck out a hand for shaking.

"You're Amish. Like Mennonites but different."

"*Ya*. That is true." Joshua shook the young boy's hand.

"You don't have a beard unless you're married, so you're not married."

"Mind your manners, C.J." This from Alice, who was standing close by, squinting into the glare of the sun.

"Your grandson is correct." Joshua stuck his hands in his pockets as he nodded hello at Alice. "I'm Amish and I'm not married."

"The first week that MDS was here, C.J. had the Mennonite community pulled up on his computer and was learning all about them."

"But I didn't find as much online about the Amish."

"I'm happy to answer any questions you have if I know the answer." Joshua squatted down beside the little girl, who was petting Charlie's dog. "You must be Shelley."

She nodded but didn't say anything.

"My friend painted both of your bedrooms yesterday."

Shelley's head jerked up, causing the ribbons around her ponytails, worn high today, to sway back and forth. "Can I see?"

"Ask your *mammi*."

"That's not my *mammi*." Shelley giggled. "That's my nana."

The grown-ups laughed and C.J. rolled his eyes.

"Can I take her up, Nana?"

Alice looked to Charlie, who nodded.

"Sure," she said. "But careful on the stairs."

"The banister was added to the stairs on Wednesday," Charlie assured them. "All of the tools have been picked up. Watch out for any stray nails, though. I'm not sure those tennis shoes would stop them."

"A nail would have to be standing straight up to go through our shoe." C.J. scuffed his foot against the ground, and then he added, "But we'll be careful."

The two children raced inside, Quitz close on their heels.

Alice turned to Joshua. "Thank you for working on our home."

"It's a pleasure to be here. Port Aransas is quite different from Oklahoma. We're enjoying the change of scenery."

"I hope you'll have some time to take it all in."

"We had a picnic on the beach last night." Joshua's thoughts again drifted to Becca. They had walked for more than an hour—looking for seashells and avoiding jellyfish. The waves had washed over their bare feet, and the night had grown cool. They had eventually returned to the fire and listened to a young man who had brought a guitar. He'd sung about Texas nights and lost love and cowboys.

"Let's go inside." Charlie took a package from Alice's arms. "I'll carry that. What did you bake?"

Joshua learned that Alice brought baked goods for the work crew every Saturday morning. The sack was filled with loaves of cranberry-orange bread, chocolate chip cookies, and brownie bars. Perhaps she wasn't so different from the grandmothers back home after all.

Soon Sarah and Becca had joined them, with Nancy not far behind. Alton was the last of the group to stumble out, looking as if he'd barely managed to pull his suspenders over his shoulders. There was another round of introductions. C.J. seemed particularly taken with Alton, who had found a football somewhere and was passing it back and forth to the boy. When had Alton learned to throw a football?

Before Joshua could ask, they were moving to the girls' trailer for coffee and to eat the goodies from Alice's bag. They barely fit into the tiny space. Some sat in the kitchen. Others moved out onto the patio. The children lay on the floor in the living room in front a television set, which had been tuned to cartoons.

"I'm surprised to see you up before noon," Joshua said to Alton. He'd meant it as a joke but quickly realized that his voice had a nagging ring to it. Trying to lighten the mood, he added, "Maybe you smelled the sweets Alice brought us."

"I actually have things to do today, *bruder*."

Alton and Sarah exchanged glances, but neither elaborated on what the "things" were that Alton had to do. Joshua was curious, but then decided he'd rather not know. They had been on the island less than forty-eight hours. Even his brother couldn't find trouble that fast.

Becca moved to sit next to him, and thoughts of his brother fled. They would have three weekends to enjoy Port Aransas because volunteers didn't work on Saturday or Sunday. No use wasting time worrying over Alton's antics. Sarah brought over a tourist map she'd found in the trailer. Together they opened it up and planned their adventures for the day.

Once they had settled on a course, Joshua asked Alton if he would like to join them. He shook his head and reached for another piece of cranberry bread. "Can't. I'd love to, but I can't."

And with no more explanation than that, he turned and walked from the room.

CHAPTER 33

What is Alton planning on doing today?" Becca asked Sarah.

They were sitting outside a tourist store with a giant fiberglass shark out front. The store was one of the few structures that had been rebuilt along the main road, and a poster on the window explained that the plastic shark had been specially ordered to replace the one lost in the hurricane. The aisles were packed with shirts, swimsuits, and ball caps. They hadn't purchased anything, but they'd had a good time looking around and laughing at the slogans on the T-shirts: "Life is better on the beach," "Beach out," "I love Port Aransas," "Orion came. Orion went. We're still here."

Becca liked the last one. It showed a stubborn spirit, a refusal to be run off your land. Whether it was smart or merely arrogant she wasn't sure, but she could definitely relate.

Though no one in their group owned a camera, or even a phone with a camera, they had enjoyed jumping in and out of the huge shark's mouth and laughing at one another. Even Joshua had seemed to finally relax. Now they sat with ice cream cones and enjoyed the feel of the sun on their faces.

Sarah took another lick of her raspberry truffle. The sight of her eating warmed Becca's heart. It seemed that her friend was able to put aside her own worries, or at least she had for a time. Maybe island living did that for a person.

Sarah hadn't immediately answered Becca's question about Alton, but finally she shrugged and said, "He had a job."

"A job?" Joshua practically choked on his mint chocolate chip.

Becca continued eating her peanut butter swirl. This should be interesting. It hadn't taken long to notice how much Joshua worried over Alton, but honestly, what could he do? In her opinion, he should relax and enjoy his day. She didn't share her thoughts, though. Instead, she watched, listened, and enjoyed her ice cream.

When Sarah didn't offer any additional details, Joshua finished his cone, walked over to the trash can, and dumped in his napkins. Maybe he needed the time to calm down, as his complexion had turned a bright red. Walking back to the girls, he stood with his hands at his side and a scowl on his face.

"What kind of job? Where? How? And why would he even want one?"

Sarah cocked her head to the side and then said, "Landscape work at some condos, I don't know, and to rent surfing equipment."

"Landscape work?"

Sarah nodded.

"He told you this?"

"He did. He asked me to watch him surf later."

"Are you going?" Becca asked.

"Maybe. It might be fun, though I suspect he'll spend more time falling off the board than actually surfing."

"It certainly looks like a complicated thing to learn." Becca couldn't help wondering what that would feel like—to stand up as the waves carried you toward the land. Probably it would be exhilarating until you ended up taking a spill and swallowing gallons of saltwater. Falling would be no fun at all.

"I'm not even that *gut* on a bicycle," Becca confessed. "I doubt surfing is in my future."

Joshua was staring at them as if they had lost their minds. "You two act as if this is completely normal. As if every person who comes on a mission trip finds a side job."

"Maybe it will keep him out of trouble." Sarah stood and brushed her hands against her dress. "Where are we supposed to catch the bus?"

They had seen on their map that Port Aransas had begun offering a local bus service. Their plan had been to take the bus downtown and then spend the morning walking the streets. It had taken less time than they had expected. Most of the structures were still in some process of being rebuilt. They walked past the job sites for several churches, the post office, and the local museum. Schools had been set up in portable buildings. A large sign announced that construction on a new facility would begin on June first. At many of the locations they passed, crews were working even though it was Saturday.

MDS seemed to be the only organization that didn't work on weekends. Becca wondered if the crews they passed would work on Sundays as well. In Cody's Creek, two of the restaurants and the grocery store remained opened on the Sabbath, but all of the other establishments closed. It was something she especially enjoyed about Sundays—the peace and quiet and lack of bustle, not that she ever saw much bustle from her parents' farm.

They moseyed down the street and passed a place that looked as if part of it had withstood the storm.

"Let's check it out," Sarah said.

The Tarpon Inn had rooms for rent as well as a restaurant and office/lobby area. A historic marker in front of the building explained that it was originally built in 1886, and President Franklin Roosevelt had once stayed there while he was in the area fishing for tarpon.

"What's a tarpon?" Becca asked.

"I have no idea." Joshua held the door open for her and Sarah.

The person behind the desk was friendly. She pointed out the two walls inside the reception area that were covered with tarpon scales. Penned on each scale was the signature and hometown of the angler who had caught it. President Roosevelt's scale was covered with a plastic shield to protect it.

"So the inn survived the storm?" Joshua asked the girl.

She was probably Becca's age, with piercings in her right eyebrow and hair streaked pink. Somehow it seemed normal in a beach town, and Becca found herself liking the girl and her open demeanor.

"Sort of." Jocelyn—her name tag was pinned to a psychedelic T-shirt—leaned on the counter and pointed to some of the photos caught beneath its glass. "We lost some of the back building, and had damage in others, but we're still here—which is more than most of the island can say."

"Why do you think that is?" Becca asked.

"I'm not really sure." She popped her gum, reminding Becca of her grandfather. "The inn was rebuilt in 1923. At that time, the pilings were placed in concrete." She shrugged. "Maybe we're on higher ground, maybe we got lucky, or maybe…maybe God knew this place would be needed."

It seemed funny to hear someone with piercings and pink hair talk about God, but then Becca realized she was wrong to stereotype someone because of how they looked. After all, Jocelyn hadn't said a thing about Becca's dress or *kapp*.

"This place has served as the headquarters for the Red Cross, Salvation Army, and even National Guard. After Orion, it was the only place people had to stay."

Joshua thanked her for her time. Sarah finished browsing the jewelry section, and Becca followed them both out of the inn.

They continued walking, passing a sign that pointed to the Marine Science Institute. "Simon mentioned that part of the university is still standing." Joshua smiled at both girls. "Care to walk there? It's only a half mile farther."

Becca groaned and Sarah shook her head vigorously.

"My feet are ready to let the bus take us somewhere." Becca looped arms with Sarah as they set off down the street.

They were at the bus stop in less than five minutes. The bright yellow vehicle arrived, and they each showed their pass as they climbed aboard. The day pass had cost only five dollars, which seemed like a good deal because they couldn't possibly walk everywhere they wanted to see. The bus itself was actually only a little larger than a van. On its side was an advertisement which said "Port A—Bigger and Better." Painted in the background was an outline of some buildings, and next to that a pristine beach.

The driver was friendly enough. He looked to be close to Charlie's age—whatever that was. He explained that there were only three buses in commission at the moment. "But there will be many more once summer vacation begins. I suppose you all won't be here then."

"We leave on the twenty-seventh," Joshua said, sitting down next to Becca.

Sarah sat behind them and peered out the window.

"I'm sorry you're upset about Alton." Becca glanced at him, trying to figure out his mood.

Joshua rubbed the back of his neck. "I'm responsible for him."

"But he's grown."

"Supposedly."

"Are you worried about his surfing?"

"I worry about everything. Mostly that I can't keep my eye on him at all times. He…he has a history of getting into trouble when he's alone."

"But he's working," Becca reasoned.

"With whom? How did he even hear about this job?"

"From one of the boys we met on the beach last night." Sarah leaned forward. "He seemed nice enough, though he had a lot of tattoos."

Joshua groaned. "If Alton comes home with tattoos, my *mamm* will faint."

"I imagine your mother is made of stronger stuff than that." Becca turned and smiled at Sarah. "Besides, he'd have to tattoo his neck or hands for anyone to see it back home. Our clothes cover most areas."

"You girls sound like you're on his side. You don't know how much trouble he's been in, or how I'll have to answer for any trouble he gets into here."

"Surely your parents can't blame you for what Alton does or doesn't do." Sarah sat back, as if she'd said all that needed to be said on the subject.

And maybe she had a point. Becca couldn't stop Joshua from worrying any more than she could stop Alton from finding trouble—if that was what he was looking for. It seemed to her that Alton was more interested in trying new experiences, and she didn't blame him for that. Plus, he could have stolen a surfboard—now that would have been bad. Working so that he could rent one? That seemed harmless enough to her.

So instead of attempting to talk Joshua out of his worries, she hopped off the bus, walked along the seawall, and allowed herself to be amazed by the size and number of barges passing by the jetty. A pelican turned to stare at them but made no attempt to fly away. The three of them walked out onto the rocks where some people were fishing, and Joshua started a conversation with an older gentleman about what type of bait he was using and what kind of fish might be caught.

Becca was standing near them but not paying attention until the man began to speak of Orion. "Two days before the hurricane hit, the old-timers knew what was about to happen. The fish, they were so thick you could look down and see them here—like so many pebbles stacked up in the surf."

The old man cackled, showing that several of his bottom teeth were missing. "We came out in a hurry and used buckets to scoop them up. Quite the beach party we had that night—grilling fish and laughing in the face of danger."

"Did you stay here on the island through the hurricane?"

"I might be old, but I'm not a fool. We were off well before he struck land, though some weren't." Now his tone softened and his eyes sought the horizon. "Some didn't make it, and that is a tragedy for sure."

Joshua murmured something that Becca couldn't hear.

The man's toothy grin returned. "The fishing isn't as good today as it was that day. I don't suppose it ever will be. But our weather this week? It's about the best we could hope for."

Joshua wished the man a good afternoon, and when he stepped closer to Becca, he reached for her hand, twining his fingers around hers. She was surprised but didn't pull away. She rather liked the feel of her hand in Joshua's. She liked that the look of concern over his brother had fled and in its place was a thoughtful, peaceful expression.

They walked along the jetty, the water splashing up and over their feet, and enjoyed the rest of the afternoon before they boarded the bus again.

The day had been very nearly perfect, but then they stepped off the bus and rounded the corner, heading down the street toward their trailers. That was when they saw the police car parked in front of where they were staying.

And suddenly the perfect glow of the afternoon fell away.

CHAPTER 34

*J*oshua didn't run, but he did hurry toward the trailers. Becca and Sarah jogged to keep up with him.

What had Alton done now?

Joshua felt a stab of resentment that he couldn't enjoy one afternoon without dealing with his brother's antics.

And beneath those thoughts were more serious ones. What if Alton had been hurt? Should he have let him go off alone? How would he explain this to his parents?

By the time they reached the front of the house, the officers were standing outside talking to Jim. They wore dark blue jackets with the words POLICE and ICE in large white letters across the back. Alton was nowhere in sight.

"What's wrong? What's happened?" Joshua was practically breathless after hurrying down the street. A part of his mind was aware that Becca and Sarah had come to a panting stop behind him, but his attention was focused on Jim and the officers.

"Joshua, this is Officer Nesbic and this is Officer Bailey." Both men nodded their hellos. They were the same height, but Nesbie was heavier and older. "They are both Immigration and Customs Enforcement officers."

Joshua didn't know what to say. ICE? What could they have to do with his brother? He never for a moment questioned that they were standing outside their trailer because of Alton. The past did often repeat itself, and it seemed that the situations they'd endured in Oklahoma were popping up in Texas. But ICE?

"Joshua is Alton's brother," Jim explained.

"Is he in trouble? Is everything all right?"

"Your brother's fine." This from Nesbie. "There was a situation at the place he was at this morning."

"We were investigating another matter, and in the process checked that everyone working was eligible to do so."

Joshua didn't say anything. He didn't know what to say to that.

"Your brother had no identification papers." Bailey pulled out a small notepad and read from it. "He said that Mr. Snyder could vouch for him and that he'd filled out forms in order to work on this site. We were checking out his story."

"Most Amish don't own a driver's license," Joshua said.

"Yes, so Mr. Snyder explained."

When the officers didn't offer anything else, Becca stepped forward. "So we're *gut*? No one's in trouble?"

"No one's in trouble," Nesbie agreed. "However..."

He glanced at Bailey, who nodded.

"The people your brother has chosen to hang around with have been in trouble before. There's a reason we were out there this afternoon."

"What—"

"I'm sorry, but we can't provide details even to family," Bailey said.

"We understand you're visitors here, and we appreciate the work you're doing." Nesbie's gaze drifted to the partially completed homes across the street and then back to Joshua. "You might want to have a talk with your brother. We'd hate for him to get caught up in something illegal."

Joshua scrubbed a hand across his face and then thanked the two officers. When they had returned to their vehicle and driven away, Jim said, "Joshua, would you like me to have a talk with your brother?"

"*Nein*. He's my responsibility."

"Well, don't be too hard on him. He couldn't have known."

"He should have known!"

Jim studied Joshua for a moment. Then he said, "Remember, he did nothing wrong. Working for the day to earn money shows that he's motivated and that he's not lazy. He's done good work here, and I wouldn't want him to have a bad experience with MDS simply because of a small misunderstanding."

"I'll try to remember that."

"Great. We'll leave for dinner at six. Local business owners like to treat each team to dinner on Saturday nights. I think you'll enjoy the Fish Place."

Jim walked away, and Joshua stood there in the late afternoon sun wondering what he was going to do about his brother. Becca and Sarah stood on either side of him, but he knew he needed to talk with Alton alone.

Sarah murmured something about cleaning up and moved toward her trailer. Becca held back, as if she wanted to say something. But when Joshua looked at her, she simply reached out, squeezed his arm, and walked away.

He climbed the stairs and then hesitated before opening the door, pausing just long enough to send up a brief prayer for wisdom and patience. He stepped inside and found his brother lounging across the sofa, the television turned on to a baseball game. Joshua picked up the remote, muted the sound, and sat down across from Alton in the room's only other chair.

"You look like *dat* with that expression on your face."

"Tell me what happened."

"Nothing."

"Something happened."

"It didn't."

"Then why were the police here? Why were immigration officials standing outside and talking to Jim?"

"I explained it to them, and they explained it to you. I know how the conversation went."

"And you didn't feel the need to come outside and defend yourself?"

"Not for a third time. *Nein*, I didn't." Alton sat up, grabbed a tennis ball off the table, and began to bounce it against the opposite wall, which seemed to calm him. That was Alton—he simply couldn't abide sitting still. Even when he'd been watching the baseball game, when Joshua had first walked into the trailer, he'd been jiggling his leg.

"Explain it to me. Like you did to them."

"Joshua, there's nothing to say. I had a job planting flowers at one of the big condos farther out of town."

"Where did you get this job?"

"Why does it matter?" He threw the ball against the wall and caught it. "On the beach, last night."

"And they just offered you a job? Someone they didn't even know?"

"It's not a skilled position." Alton threw and caught the ball again before dropping it on to the coffee table. "These guys were surfing. I wish you could see them. It's pretty amazing what they're able to do. So I watched, and then I asked how I could learn."

"You're going to break your neck."

"Maybe, but first I need a board. Turns out you can rent them by the week, but as you might guess I don't have a lot of extra money stashed with my change of clothing."

"It's a complete waste of good money if you ask me."

"When I mentioned that I couldn't afford to rent a board, they said that maybe they could throw some work my way. The job pays ten bucks an hour, and I can do it on Saturdays or a couple hours after we knock off here during the week."

Joshua closed his eyes, rested his head against the back of the chair, and tried to think of a way to argue with his brother. In the face of Alton's enthusiasm, he always felt so old—and tired. Finally he said, "Why were the ICE officers there to begin with?"

"Didn't say. One of the teams had a dog, so I assume they were looking for drugs."

Joshua groaned.

"But they didn't find any. Spider Nix—"

"Spider?"

"I'm not sure that's his real name. Well, I suppose his last name is Nix."

Joshua immediately envisioned a man with a giant spider tattooed on his arm. He decided he didn't want to know.

"Spider says they're harassed like that sometimes because they do the hard work around here, the work that people want done but don't want to dirty their own hands on. It's very hypocritical if you ask me. It's as if they don't want their town tainted with lower-class working folks."

"And you believe that?"

"If this afternoon is any indication, it may be true. But none of that involves me. I just put in my hours—" He spread his hands out in front of him, studying the dirt under his nails, or was it sand?

"I work and collect my hourly wage." He pulled out a small wad of money and tossed it on the table. Ten dollars an hour. He may have made eighty bucks. "Now I have enough to rent a board. If I work a few more hours, I could afford a few lessons. Who knows? Maybe I'll have a little fun while I'm here."

Joshua wanted to argue with that, but was he being too stern? Was it any of his business what Alton did in his off time? Jim didn't seem to mind.

While he was puzzling it over, Alton left the room. Soon Joshua heard the sound of the shower running. At home, they took a complete bath once or maybe twice a week. There simply was not that much hot water.

Still, those things were not his business. If Alton wanted to pretend he was *Englisch*, take showers twice a day and rent a surfboard, what could Joshua do about it? Nothing. What should he do about it? Again, probably nothing.

He remembered Becca's expression and the way she had walked away without another word. What was it she had said on the bus? "Surely your parents can't blame you for what Alton does or doesn't do."

He didn't know about that. Somehow he had always felt responsible for Alton. Some days his life resembled that of a twenty-seven-year-old man with a seventeen-year-old kid. He'd been his brother's age himself only a few years ago. Alton was determined to take a different path than he had, but Joshua had no idea if it was his place to intervene.

He did know that he was starving, and dinner at the Fish Place sounded pretty good. Maybe he'd even indulge in another shower. After all, tomorrow was Sunday. And tonight? Well, tonight he'd be sitting beside pretty little Becca Troyer if he had anything to say about it. It wouldn't hurt to smell clean.

CHAPTER 35

The Fish Place was everything Becca had imagined and more.

It was a restaurant perched over the water and situated next to an area where boats were docked. As they had walked in, Becca had lagged behind the others to stop and stare out at the many types of fishing and recreational vessels. They sported names like *Serenity*, *Gale Force*, and even *Orion*.

"Next weekend we'll take you on an outing to see the lighthouse." Jim paused beside her. "They're a sight to behold, don't you think?"

"They are, and I'd love to go for a ride, though I'm only a passable swimmer."

"We haven't had a boat capsize yet." Her expression must have revealed her alarm, because Jim laughed and said, "No worries. All vessels are required to provide life jackets for anyone who would like to wear one. If the gulf waters make you nervous, it may be a good idea."

The night only got better from there. The people consisted only of what Becca thought of as *their group*. Frank, Brady, Simon, and Eva sat on one side with Jim on the end. She sat between Sarah and Joshua, and on the other side of Sarah was Alton. Nancy sat at the end of the table across from Jim.

Alton seemed in fine form, in spite of the issue with the police. The incident had sounded harmless enough from what the officers had said, but Becca had known from the tightening of Joshua's expression that the two brothers were about to have a big row over it.

And apparently they did. Through the open windows, the raised voices were clearly heard.

"It's so uncomfortable to know something you're not supposed to." Sarah fidgeted with her *kapp* strings. "Then when someone finally confides in you, what do you do? Act surprised? Admit you know? Ack. I'd rather sit on the patio."

"I don't think we need to hear anyway," Becca said as she followed Sarah out to the chairs that were sitting in the shade of the boys' balcony. "We can guess what they're saying. Joshua will tell Alton he needs to grow up."

"And Alton will tell Joshua to lighten up and have some fun."

"Then Joshua will remind him that they promised their parents they would stay out of trouble."

"Those two remind me of my little *bruders* at home—always fussing." Sarah laughed, but then a preoccupied look came over her face.

"Homesick?"

"Well, when I'm home, my thoughts often drift to other places. Now that I'm here, I keep thinking of home."

They sat in the warm afternoon sun, enjoying the coastal breeze and the sounds from the ocean. Eventually Sarah crossed her arms on the table and rested her head on her arms.

"Are you okay?"

"I guess."

"You don't look okay."

"I'm only tired. Maybe I need to lie down."

"You're not sick?"

"No. I don't think so."

Sarah went inside, and Becca followed soon after. She was surprised to see a letter to Sarah sitting on the table. She must have read it while Becca was standing outside with Joshua. Had it upset her? The return address said it was from her mother. She thought back over what Sarah had just said, about knowing things that you weren't supposed to, and decided not to snoop.

Snooping was wrong anyway, even if you had a good reason—such as concern for your friend.

Becca would have liked to have known what was in the letter. Was it important? Sarah's mother must have sent it the same day they left in order for it to arrive so quickly.

She only hoped that whatever was in it wasn't the cause of Sarah's change in mood. It seemed to Becca that her friend needed a rest, and perhaps not hearing from home would be better.

Becca was reminded of that letter as she watched her friend enjoy their meal at the Fish Place.

Sarah had seemed better when they climbed into the van for dinner, and she was eating her food. The meal was served family style. Joshua passed her platters of grilled tuna, sautéed shrimp, and even fried frog legs. Side dishes included fried potatoes, hushpuppies, and a giant bowl of salad.

"How did this place survive the storm?" Nancy asked.

"It didn't." The owner had stopped to see how they were enjoying the meal. He was an older man with weathered skin and deep blue eyes. Jim had introduced him as Stu Harrison.

"Everything you see here? New. All of it's new."

"How did you rebuild so quickly?" Alton asked.

"A good question." Stu crossed his arms and looked out across the room. The place was full of customers, and there was a line of folks waiting out the front door. "The truth is that I'm incredibly lucky—or blessed, depending on how you look at it. My nephews own a construction firm in Houston. They were one of the first work crews on the island. The Fish Place was rebuilt before most people had finished digging out from under the rubble."

"Are your nephews still here, working on the island?" Joshua placed his elbows on the table and leaned forward.

It was easy for Becca to see that he was taken with the place. The food, the sound of the waves outside, and the general ambience had helped him to relax. He hadn't sent a worried look Alton's way in more than an hour.

"No," Stu said. "They're back in Houston. They had jobs contracted out for the next three years. Their coming here was a real sacrifice and caused them to work many nights and weekends to catch their other projects back up to where they were supposed to be."

"Family first," Nancy murmured.

"Yes, I suppose that's true. However, even I was surprised at how quickly and how well it was done."

Stu thanked them again for coming and then hurried off to check on something in the kitchen.

"This restaurant was one of the first establishments to reopen on the island." Jim glanced around at the room filled with people. "Stu could have taken advantage of that. If he'd raised his prices, he still would have had plenty of customers."

"But he didn't," Joshua guessed.

"No. In fact, he offered a discount for residents who lived on the island or anyone who was working on a rebuild, which was basically everyone. One of our first rebuilds was for a neighbor of his. When he learned about MDS, he searched for ways to help, and he's followed through on all of those commitments. An organization like ours depends on contributions from others."

"Do you bring all the work crews here?" Becca asked.

"We do. Stu insists on providing a free meal for each MDS work crew. The other crews you met at the beach came a few weeks ago."

"They mentioned last night how much we would love this place." Simon was talking to Jim, but he glanced back and forth between Becca and Joshua. Had he guessed that she had feelings for Joshua? Becca blushed at the thought and then immediately stared down at the table so that he wouldn't see her cheeks redden.

"Stu wants to meet and thank every person involved, and he says that feeding you is the best way he knows to do that. From the amount of food you ate, I guess he's right."

"I feel like a beached whale." Alton relaxed back into his chair and patted his stomach, which looked quite flat to Becca. "Tell Stu he outdid himself."

Joshua leaned forward and glanced at his brother. "*Ya*. Wait until we tell *Mamm* about the frog legs."

"Tastes just like chicken," Alton said in a deep voice.

They both laughed over some shared family joke. Becca was relieved to see them getting along so well. Perhaps the argument they'd had before dinner hadn't been as bad as she'd imagined. Some folks raised their voice to let off steam. But had that been Joshua or Alton?

Brady was telling a story about frog gigging while they were working on a MDS site in Jasper.

"Where's Jasper?" Becca asked.

"Southeast Texas." Frank pushed up his glasses. "Nearly to Louisiana. It's an interesting place."

"That was my first mission trip." Eva carefully folded her napkin, and then she added, "What I remember most is the snakes. We have some in west Texas, but nothing like what they have in Jasper."

Becca hadn't thought much about snakes. She didn't want to either. It was enough to worry about jellyfish, though she'd learned to watch for them and walk around them. Suddenly there were so many things she wanted to share with her mother that she felt a wave of homesickness.

Before she could wallow in it, their server brought over a tray of desserts. Becca opted to share a piece of key lime pie with Joshua. She turned to see what Sarah wanted, but the chair next to her was empty.

"Where's Sarah?" she asked Alton.

He shrugged his shoulders. "Bathroom?"

By the time her coffee and pie had arrived, Sarah still wasn't back. Becca excused herself and hurried to the ladies' room. She opened the door and heard the unmistakable sound of someone retching.

But when Sarah came out, she insisted that she was all right, that the tuna maybe hadn't agreed with her stomach. Doubts whispered in Becca's mind. Was this what Sarah's eating disorder looked like up close? She'd read about girls who ate normally but then forced themselves to throw up. Was that what had happened to her friend?

Sarah had already left the restroom. Becca used the facilities and then washed her hands. As she made her way back to the table and sat, it seemed that Sarah purposely avoided her, turning all of her attention to Alton. Joshua proclaimed the key lime pie excellent and teased Becca that he'd almost eaten her half.

He was right. The taste was exquisite—sweet and creamy with just a touch of tartness. She almost enjoyed it, but her thoughts kept turning to her friend and the possibility that she might not be as well as she pretended to be.

CHAPTER 36

*T*he next day, Sunday, their little group attended a nondenominational church service at the state park. Although it was different from what Joshua was accustomed to, the Scriptures and the hymns had been familiar.

Then the first part of the week passed in a blur. During the day Joshua immersed himself in the work, which he found quite different from farming but still quite satisfying. He supposed as long as he was outdoors, he'd be content.

His brother continued to disappear at the end of the workday—ostensibly going to plant flowers at the large condos. Joshua had seen a glimpse of them when they had gone to the beach on Friday. They looked like giant hotels to him. Did people actually live there? He couldn't imagine. Surprisingly, a few of them had withstood Orion's wrath, though much repair work had to be done before they would be habitable again.

He enjoyed the work and the time with Frank and Brady and Simon, but what he looked forward to the most was the evenings.

On Monday they had taken the bus to the beach. Sarah and Becca had hunted for seashells while he'd enjoyed the beach, the surf, and watching folks fish. He had to admit, the fishing looked like something he would enjoy. Then on Tuesday evening, Simon had surprised him by showing up with a fishing rod. "Want to give it a try?"

"*Ya*. Sure I do."

Sarah and Becca had begged off going, claiming they wanted an evening to wash their clothes and rest. He later heard Becca talking to Eva about going over to the mainland for a little shopping. The thought made him smile. What woman did he know who didn't like shopping?

Within a half hour, he and Simon had found a relatively empty stretch of beach.

"We'll do a little surf fishing first. Then we'll try it from the jetties."

"Anything I need to know?"

"If you've fished before, you'll get the hang of it pretty quickly." Simon handed him a baggie and instructed Joshua to loop it through the fastener that held his suspenders. "Fish guts. It's good for catching trout and maybe even redfish."

With his pants rolled up and wearing his Amish hat, Joshua felt like a true tourist, but that didn't matter. What mattered was the wind, the sea, and the fish waiting to be caught.

As he began walking into the surf, Simon cautioned, "Be alert as to what's around you. They don't have sharks in this close, but a friend of mine was once wrapped up by a man-of-war. He came out of the water trying to beat it off with his fishing pole."

"Did he live?"

"Sure. A little meat tenderizer on the wounds and he was fine, but he wasn't allergic to them."

"What if I'm allergic?"

"We don't want to find out. Just stay aware of what's going on around you."

The story of the man-of-war should have changed Joshua's mind. Surely the responsible thing would have been to sit on the beach and watch Simon fish. But there wasn't a chance he was going to do that. Adrenaline pumped through his veins, filling him with confidence. He could just imagine taking a big catch of fish home and frying it up for the girls.

He ended up catching two nice-sized trout and three that were too small to keep. Simon had brought a cooler, and they placed the trout under the ice, adding what he'd caught to it. "Makes for a good breakfast or dinner," he said. "Want to try the jetties?"

"Of course."

"You're going to want to keep your eyes out for snakes. Especially with the warmer weather, they will often come up on the rocks."

Joshua's life had become an adventure story like the books Becca liked to read. He could hardly wait to get back to the trailer and tell her about this. But once he was on the jetty, all other thoughts fell away. He stopped worrying about Alton. The work still to be done on the houses seemed like a distant concern. Becca was a pleasant memory that tickled his mind.

His attention was filled with the experience as they walked to the end of the jetty and baited their hooks with live fish.

"Before the storm, you needed a license to fish here," Simon said. "But there's a temporary waiver on that, mainly because it's difficult to get a license with all the buildings blown over. Even the state park offices was demolished by Orion."

"So you've done this before?"

"Sure. I enjoy working for MDS. It's a good use of my free time when things aren't busy back home. But I also come here because I love the fishing."

Simon caught four more trout and a catfish, which he threw back because it was on the smallish side. By the time they packed up to leave the jetty, they had a total catch of ten. "That's good. Our limit is ten each, so there's no problem if we're stopped."

"Why would we be stopped?"

Simon shrugged. "Some people try to fish commercially, and you need a special permit for that. Who needs more than ten fish?"

"*Gut* point."

Simon stopped at the fish cleaning station and showed him the quickest way to clean the trout.

"How do you cook it?" Joshua asked.

"Salt, pepper, and lemon in a pan with a little oil. You're going to love it."

They made their way back to the car that Simon shared with the rest of his group. When they reached the trailers, Joshua thanked him. "I'll have some great stories to tell when I get back home."

"You will, and when you get a hankering for more trout, maybe you'll come back to the job site."

Together they carried the cooler inside and then bagged and stored the fish in the refrigerator. Joshua walked Simon back out and thanked him again for the evening. He intended to head up to his room and to bed. It appeared Alton wasn't home yet, but it didn't bother him as much as it would have earlier. That was what four hours of fishing could do for a man—help him forget his troubles.

He noticed a light on the girls' patio and walked that way. Becca was sitting outside alone, reading her novel.

"Can't do that inside?"

She looked up in surprise. "I didn't hear you walk up."

"Quiet as a cat, that's what I am."

Becca closed her book and waved him over. "Come tell me about your fishing."

So he did. As he described himself standing in the surf, glancing around for man-of-wars and reeling in the trout, she pulled out her notebook.

"You're going to write about it?"

"I'm keeping a sort of journal for my *mamm*. Maybe she can draw or paint something I've seen."

"That's thoughtful of you."

Becca shrugged. "I wish she could have come. I found out my parents met on a mission trip. I think I understand her better now that I've been here."

"I was thinking along the same lines tonight. Maybe I understand my *bruder* a little better. Coastal fishing was a whole new experience for me. It was exciting, and that made me wonder if Alton feels the same way when he's surfing."

"Probably."

"I only wish—" Joshua shook his head. This was no time to bring up his regrets about Alton's behavior.

They spent the next hour talking about their families, their homes back in Cody's Creek, and the work they were doing in Port Aransas. He finally glanced at his watch and was surprised to see it was nearly eleven. "I'd never stay up this late at home," he admitted.

"At home you're up well before dawn."

"True. Here we sleep in until at least six thirty."

Joshua suddenly realized he wanted to kiss Becca. They had both stood, and she'd opened the door so that he could walk through the house rather than vaulting over the patio railing.

When he paused next to her, she looked at him, her eyes widening, and then she looked away.

Did she want him to kiss her? Did she care about him the way he was beginning to care about her?

He stepped closer, put his hand under her chin, and lifted her face to his. And just as he was about to press his lips to hers, a truck pulled up out front, bass pumping, music blaring, Alton laughing.

The moment between them dissolved. Becca sighed, and Joshua followed her into the house and out the front door.

Suddenly there was something he wanted much more than the trout in the zippered baggies in his refrigerator. He wanted more time alone with Becca. He walked upstairs, following his brother, who was laughing and describing his latest surfing attempts. As he half listened, Joshua vowed to himself that the next time he had an opportunity to kiss Becca, he would ignore anything else and follow his heart.

CHAPTER 37

*C*harlie had looked forward to the Wednesday luncheon all week. On Wednesdays one client shared their story with the volunteers. Although Charlie wasn't technically a client—his home still hadn't been rebuilt—he looked forward to the chance to tell what had happened to him on that fateful day. He felt like the main character in *The Rime of the Ancient Mariner*—a lyrical ballad he had taught to many high school classes. It was the longest poem Samuel Taylor Coleridge had written. Though it had been penned in 1797, Charlie took solace in the fact that much of man's troubles and triumphs remained the same—which in turn reminded him of the book of Ecclesiastes.

"'There is a time for everything, and a season for every activity under the heavens,'" he quoted. There was no need to look up the passage from the third chapter of Ecclesiastes. He'd memorized it long ago. "'A time to be born and a time to die, a time to plant and a time to uproot, a time to kill and a time to heal, a time to tear down and a time to build.'"

Though physically he continued to struggle with the pain in his shoulder and arthritis throughout his body, Charlie's voice remained strong. As in those days when he was a teacher, his tone and emphasis captured his listeners' attention.

"No doubt you've heard those words before, but they sound different sitting among piles of lumber and roof shingles."

"Too many roof shingles," Alton muttered, though a smile belied his tone.

Alton had been carting stacks of shingles up and down ladders for more than two days. He actually seemed content, and his occasional petulant look had vanished. In short, he was a good volunteer and had been invaluable around the work site. Though he continued to fight with his brother about his evening activities—Charlie had heard some of the arguments himself—he was quite dedicated to the work they were doing, at least between the hours of eight and five.

"And too much gumbo," Jim added.

Their lunch had been provided by the family who would own the house next to Alice's. The giant pot of seafood gumbo and pans of corn bread were their way of thanking the workers.

"It's good that you're tired and full," Charlie said. "That means I have a captive audience."

Laughter spread through the group like the breeze that cooled the day. Charlie thought they were a fine team, numbering eleven, when you included Jim and himself. Quitz turned once, twice, and then three times before she plopped to the ground at Charlie's feet.

"Quitz has heard this before," Charlie joked, but then his tone became serious. "And she's an important part of this story. If you don't believe that God can use animals...you may reconsider the idea after I share my experience."

He had their attention now. He described the week before Orion landed, how few believed tragedy could strike them, how some had even placed bets on when or if the storm would arrive. "That seems incredibly naive now, but you have to remember that prior to Orion, only two major storms had hit the island in the last forty-five years.

"I wasn't here for Allen in 1980. I evacuated like everyone else. Three people died, and there was more than six hundred and fifty million dollars in damages." He paused long enough to let the numbers sink in. "I was here for Celia. The island took a direct hit from her in 1970. Those days completely changed the path of my life. Or I should say, God changed the path of my life on that day."

Becca scooted closer to Joshua, who squeezed her hand. It reminded Charlie of those early days with Madelyn. His heart still ached at the loss of her, but he enjoyed seeing young love—even when those involved didn't realize what had happened to them yet.

"My wife, Madelyn, and I were new to the island when Celia wrought her destruction—winds steady at 160 miles per hour, gusts up to 180. Tragically, 13 souls were lost and the damage exceeded 500 million." His mind stretched back to August 1970, and it was as if he could see the way the island had been then.

"We hardly knew anyone, and we certainly didn't understand the ferociousness with which nature can attack an area." He glanced over their heads, at the street and the area beyond. "There were fewer people living on the island then, but after the storm...after it had nearly destroyed our lives, we understood what it meant to be a neighbor to one another. There was no choice but to depend on the man or woman standing next to you. We cleaned up debris for one another, cooked for one another, even lived with one another. FEMA had no urban disaster trailers back then."

More laughter, but now they were watching him intently.

"Those times were difficult, but we pulled together as a community. From that storm were born friendships I couldn't have begun to imagine. I was a young man—only twenty-two years old, and I was pretty sure I could handle things on my own. Celia taught me to accept the grace and help of others. God...well, He taught me that I'm safe in His hands, even when my life is turned upside down."

There were murmurs of agreement.

"I think I knew that Orion posed a threat. I remember walking with Quitz on the beach just days before the storm hit. I recall thinking back over something my wife used to say—that life moves on. Maybe I was thinking that it had already moved on for me. But there was Alice, and the kids..." He waved toward their house, which would be ready to live in before this work crew returned to their homes.

"I made sure that Alice and Shelley and C.J. were safe, that they had a place to go farther inland. And I planned to leave too, but there were a few other folks, some stubborn old-timers, who I needed to check on." He told them of finding Moose Davis and of the man's diminished mental abilities. He described how they had been forced to swim over to the community center when Moose's house broke apart.

"The water was cold, but the rain had suddenly stopped. We were in the eye of the storm. I looked up…looked up and saw starlight." His voice faded as his eyes sought the sky. Finally, he cleared his throat and continued. "We knew it was risky to try to swim to the community center, but in truth we shouldn't even have still been here on the island. At that point, I think we understood our chances of survival were slim. Moose told me that we would *live together or die together*, and that sounded all right with me. There are worse things than dying with a friend in a place you love. When I faced death though, it awoke something in me. Suddenly, I wanted to live. I wanted to watch Quitz grow old and to see Alice's grandchildren into adulthood."

Tears stung his eyes. He brushed them away unashamedly. It didn't matter if these people saw how he felt. What mattered was that he shared with them the truth that God had impressed upon his heart.

"We'd found some old boogie boards up in the attic, and when the roof tore off and the walls began to come apart, we jumped. The water was moving faster than I imagined. At one point the board slipped from my hands, but Quitz snagged my shirt sleeve and pulled me back up." He held up his hands as if to ward off any argument. "I know. That sounds impossible, but she did. She was riding that board like a world-class surfer, and she snatched at my sleeve and tugged with all her might. It was enough to pull me back toward the board, and then I was able to grab hold."

He described how he'd hit the building, how that had dislocated his shoulder. He told them about the other people they met in the community center. "Besides me and Moose, there was Lamar Johnson—you may have met him when he stopped by yesterday. Also a young family—Dale and Angela Northcutt and their little three-year-old daughter, Sophia Claire. And Kurt Jameson—a good man who still works here in Port A."

"Did they all make it?" Sarah asked. Her eyes were wide, and she'd leaned forward during the telling of his story. "The little girl...did she make it?"

"She did. Sophia Claire and her family decided to move permanently to Corpus."

"And we know Lamar is still here," Alton said.

"He is."

"What of Moose?" Joshua asked.

"My friend Moose, he made it through the storm...though, as you may know, twenty-four did not. We heard some of those people that night as we sheltered in the community center. We tried...we tried to save the ones we saw floating by, but...it wasn't possible." This was always the hard part for Charlie, but he also knew that it was the important part. He needed them to understand that God had indeed had a plan, even when parts of it still made no sense to him.

"Moose developed pneumonia, and his system was already compromised from the dementia that he'd tried to hide from everyone. I don't blame him for that. Moose was a good man, but as I mentioned, he was stubborn. He was hospitalized in Corpus and died eight days later. He isn't one of those included in the death toll of Orion, but he may as well have been."

"You miss him," Becca murmured.

"I do. And I've spent many a night wondering why he died—why other good people died—and why I lived." He cleared his throat, reached down, and patted the top of Quitz's head. "There were seven of us huddled there that night. We needed each other. It took all of us to find supplies, to protect the child, to set up a barrier around us for when the windows blew in. It took each of us praying and caring for the one to his left and the one to his right."

He thought of Sophia Claire and the picture he'd received of her recently. She was a beautiful girl and would now grow into a lovely young woman. Alice and her grandchildren would be able to return to their home.

"My story, like the others you will hear, is one of survival. As my wife said, life moves on, but we know and believe that God is by our side regardless. I don't know why God Almighty chose me that night, but I believe He did. Same as I believe He chose you to come here and help. We're all an integral part of His mighty plan, even Quitz."

He stepped aside and sat in the chair next to his dog. There was a smattering of applause, and one by one each person came by and thanked him for sharing his story. When Becca stopped in front of him, tears shining in her eyes, she leaned forward and hugged him. Softly, she said, "Thank you, Charlie. I needed to hear that."

Which was pretty much all Charlie could ask of his life and his story, that it would serve to guide someone else. That it would restore and bolster their faith, even when they were facing terrible storms.

CHAPTER 38

*L*ater that day Becca and Joshua took a walk out to the beach. They had discovered it was easy to catch a ride with one of the workers as they left the job site. All they needed to take with them was a blanket to place on top of the sand, sunscreen, a bag for Becca's growing seashell collection, and dinner. For their ride home, they could catch the city bus that stopped at the fishing pier on the hour.

Becca had found that her skin blistered instead of tanning. She definitely didn't like the bright-red-lobster look, and she'd listened to Nancy's warnings about skin cancer. Though her dress covered most of her legs, Becca worked the sunscreen into her arms as soon as they arrived and every hour afterward.

"Your freckles like the Texas sun," Joshua teased.

Becca felt along her cheekbones and the bridge of her nose, as if her fingertips could press the freckles back into place.

"*Nein*. I like them." Joshua grabbed her hand, uncurled her fingers, and placed on her palm a large portion of a sand dollar.

"Oh! It's the biggest piece yet. When did you find it?"

"Earlier, while you were playing in the surf."

"I was looking for shells." She gave him her most serious look but then burst out laughing. "All right. I was enjoying the water splashing over my feet."

"Like a child." He lay back on the blanket, tilting his hat over his eyes to block out the late afternoon sun.

"Is that such a bad thing?"

"Being childlike? *Nein*. It's a *gut* thing. Remember your *daddi* preaching on it last month?"

"'Blessed are the peacemakers, for they will be called the children of God.'"

"*Ya*. You're like that."

"I'm a peacemaker?"

She thought he wouldn't answer, but then he said, "Maybe."

"Maybe I need to be, considering the way you and Alton argue."

"Let's not ruin the evening talking about it."

Becca studied the sand dollar, running her fingers around the edge and then across the middle. "Shelley colored a picture for me. Alice brought it by today when she stopped to talk to Jim. The picture is of a sand dollar, and beside it was printed the legend of the sand dollar."

"Legend?" Joshua yawned, and Becca poked him in the ribs.

"Pay attention and I'll tell you about it."

"Oh, *ya*. I'm awake." He raised up on one elbow and blinked his eyes several times.

Becca laughed and turned her attention back to the sand dollar in her hand.

"There are four holes."

"I only see three."

"But you can see where the fourth would be. Three of the holes represent the nails that held Christ on the cross."

"Hmm."

"And this larger hole near the top represents the Roman spear that pierced His side."

"Shelley did this in school?"

"Apparently they had several coloring sheets that portrayed different legends pertaining to the sea. She picked the sand dollar because her nana likes them."

Joshua traced his forefinger down the inside of her hand, from her wrist to the center of her palm where he drew a circle. Funny how such a thing could cause her heart to beat faster.

"There's more."

"I'm not surprised."

Becca pointed to the center of the shell. "On this side we have the Easter lily, and at its center is a star."

"Like in the Nativity story."

"Yes. And on the other side—" She turned over the sand dollar. "This is the Christmas poinsettia."

"It's a *gut* story," Joshua said.

"The legend says that if you find a whole one and break it open, you will release five white doves that spread God's *gut* will and peace."

"I'd like to break open a loaf of bread. What did you bring for our dinner?"

"I tell you a beautiful story, and you're thinking of dinner."

"I tried to pay attention, but my stomach is grumbling."

"Now you sound like a child." But she pulled her backpack closer and unzipped it. "Let's see, I don't have a loaf of bread, but I do have two bananas."

"Monkey food."

"One jar of peanut butter."

Joshua grunted.

"And four pieces of bread." She pulled out the items and set them on the blanket between them. "What did you bring?"

"I found you a divine seashell. What more do you want from me?" He laughed when she pushed him over. "All right. Don't get violent."

He had brought four oatmeal raisin cookies from one of the clients, two Thermoses of cold milk, and a bag of chips.

"Ack. Junk food."

"Chips replace necessary salt I lost while hammering shingles."

"Uh-huh. Well, we can make peanut-butter-and-banana sandwiches, have some of your chips, milk—"

"And cookies. Sounds like a feast."

It felt like a feast to Becca. As she watched children run in the surf and the sun set over the gulf waters, she was almost able to stop worrying about Alton and Sarah.

For the last two nights, Alton had come home very late. One day he fell asleep during lunch. He and Joshua got into a big row about that as well as the fact that he was once again smoking. Most days Alton missed breakfast and stumbled out of the trailer as they were finishing their devotional time. But once he was awake, he was a good worker. She wasn't sure Joshua could see that.

Sarah was another matter entirely. Something was bothering her, and Becca wished she knew what it was. She'd tried asking Nancy, but her *aenti* had been no help at all. If she knew, she wasn't sharing.

Once Joshua had finished his dinner, he proceeded to bury her feet in the sand. It was a warm, cozy feeling. Becca could almost close her eyes and forget the troubles that worried her mind and stole her sleep.

When they were finished playing in the sand, Joshua helped her store their trash and then pulled her to her feet. They made their way down the beach toward the fishing pier. Once there, Joshua walked out to ask if they were catching anything and what bait they were using.

Becca hadn't realized Joshua was such a fisherman, or at least he seemed interested in it. If his excitement the night he'd caught the trout was any indication, she suspected he was itching to give it another try. Nancy had promised to cook the fish for dinner the next evening.

If they were to marry, would he catch fish from the pond and bring it home for her to fry? The thought popped into her head and she giggled. A few evening walks on the beach had her mind turning to marriage. Perhaps the afternoon sun had made her a bit loopy.

Joshua walked back to where she was waiting, and they turned toward the bus stop.

Becca sensed the moment his posture changed—as if an instant tenseness had swept through his body. Looking up, she saw his jaw clench, and then she glanced in the direction he was staring. At first she saw four *Englischers* pulling surfboards from the back of a truck, but then she looked again and realized that one of them was Alton.

CHAPTER 39

*J*oshua would recognize his brother anywhere under any circumstances, yet he could hardly believe that the person standing before him was Alton.

The clothing was part of it—the long swim trunks he'd worn the night of their beach cookout, a white sleeveless T-shirt, and flip-flops. Where had he purchased them? And why? He'd never get away with wearing such clothes in Oklahoma, even if he was still indulging his *rumspringa*. Then there was the seven-foot surfboard he was holding. It gleamed in the lights of the parking area—a sleek, off-white board sporting a yellow-and-blue design.

He'd known his brother was surfing, but seeing him that way—seeing him standing there like an *Englischer* about to trot off into the ocean—caused Joshua to gape in amazement.

He wasn't surprised when the situation grew worse. It was bad enough seeing his brother with this gang of thugs. Did he have to talk to them too?

But Alton didn't pick up on his brother's attitude. He offered a small wave, and then he and his three friends walked toward them.

"Hey, bro. Surprised to see you here."

Bro? Had Alton just called him *bro*?

Joshua gave a short nod, trying to figure out what to say. What he was seeing made no sense to him. What Alton was doing made no sense at all.

Not a big deal was what Jim had said.

Give him space was Charlie's advice.

I'm a peacemaker? Maybe I need to be. Becca's earlier words pulled Joshua to his senses.

"We were out for a walk." He nodded toward the surfboard. "That's what you're spending your money on? A fancy board?"

"This is it. Isn't she beautiful? I've been keeping it in the bed of Spider's truck. Seemed easier."

Spider was everything Joshua had imagined, only worse. He was probably six feet two, with muscular arms and legs and skin bronzed from the coastal sun. His hair was fashioned in dreadlocks, or so Joshua had heard them called. The long, matted coils of hair snaked down his back. He wore no shirt, which revealed that his chest was completely tattooed—and yes, there was a spider in the center and intricate webs radiating out from it. Several earrings adorned one ear, and a scruffy beard completed the picture. So this was his brother's new best friend.

"Nice to meet you, Joshua. Alton's told me a lot about you."

The man held out his hand and Joshua shook, though he had to resist the urge to wipe his palm on his pants afterward.

"Are you Sarah or Becca?"

"Becca. Nice to meet you." She seemed to have recovered more quickly than Joshua. She actually smiled at the three men standing in front of them, and she didn't look a bit embarrassed that they were practically naked.

"Cool dress." This from the boy standing on Alton's other side. He couldn't have been seventeen and was trying to grow a goatee, but the result was only a few sprigs of hair. His head was shaved, and his eyes had a glassy look to them.

"Don't be rude, Dax." Spider's voice was a soft, gentle reprimand. "Joshua and Becca, this is my friend Dax, and behind him we have Zach."

The third man looked the most reputable—maybe twenty-five with clean-cut hair and no visible tattoos. He was focused on wiping down his board, though, and barely nodded a hello.

Joshua felt as if he'd stepped into his worst nightmare.

Becca tugged on Joshua's hand. "The bus is coming."

"We have to go."

"Sure. That's cool. Peace, bro." This from Dax.

"Y'all have a nice evening." Spider hefted his board and started toward the beach, Dax and Zach in his wake, leaving Alton standing between his new friends and his family.

"We're off to catch some waves. I guess I'll see you back at the trailer."

Joshua's anger returned in a flash. For a moment his emotions actually blurred his vision. He stepped toward his brother and hissed, "These are the people you're going out with every night? A druggie, a loser, and his sidekick?"

"You don't even know them—"

"I know enough."

"Because of what, Joshua? Because of their tattoos or their hairstyles? Have you ever stopped to think that people can look different and still be *gut* people?" Alton stepped back. "You embarrass me. You know that?"

Before Joshua could respond, Alton turned and walked off after his friends.

Becca tugged on his hand again, and he turned to see a line of people climbing onto the bus. He and Becca ran and trundled up the steps just as it was about to pull out. Nearly every seat was filled—teens, families, and even a few older people. Though they were all talking to one another, Becca seemed content to stare out the window.

Joshua was grateful she didn't try to talk to him about what had just happened. He realized that now was probably an important time to keep his mouth shut. He needed to calm his temper before he spoke. He cared about Becca, and it infuriated him that she'd been subjected to the stare of a stoned-out surfer.

How to tell her that? Or did she even want to hear?

Now that she'd finally seen Alton in his glory, seen him as he spit on their Plain life, maybe now she would understand Joshua's anger without him having to explain.

The bus stopped at the end of their street. They got off, Joshua carrying the blanket and his backpack. Soft voices spilled through the night, and he could just make out Sarah sitting on the patio with Nancy. As they drew closer, he could see that they were playing a hand of Dutch Blitz.

Becca still hadn't said a word. Joshua tugged on her hand and pulled her across the street to some lawn chairs that had been placed on Alice's front porch for workers to rest in.

"I'm sorry, Becca."

"For?"

"For the fact that you had to see Alton like that. Also that those *Englischers*...that they embarrassed you."

"But they didn't."

"What do you mean?"

"I mean they didn't embarrass me. I'm Amish, Joshua. It's not the first time someone has commented on my dress."

He could only stare at her, unsure of what she was getting at.

"If you want to apologize to someone, I think you should save it and apologize to Alton."

"What?" His voice rose in disbelief. This could not be happening. Becca could not be taking Alton's side. Had the whole world gone mad?

"Oh, Joshua." Becca sank into one of the lawn chairs and then popped back up. "Weren't you even listening to Charlie's story earlier today?"

"What does that have to do with this?"

"It has *everything* to do with this." She crossed her arms and stared across the street. When she finally turned to look at him, her voice had gone soft but the furrows between her eyes had deepened. "Life moves on, remember? But *Gotte* still has a plan for each of us. Alton is no longer a child that you need to follow behind and correct. He's a man, and he needs only your steady influence in his life and the certainty of your love as part of his family. He doesn't need your approval or disapproval."

"But I don't approve." The words fairly exploded out of him. "How can I? *Mamm* and *Dat* would be horrified to see him as we did tonight."

"Because he was holding a surfboard?" Becca shook her head and started to walk away. She'd made it a few feet when she spun back toward him. "Did you even notice that his shorts were longer than the others? He must have picked the most conservative pair he could find, and it's not as if one can surf in Amish clothing."

"He shouldn't be surfing at all."

"He had no tattoos, no earrings, and he spoke to us kindly. You were the one whose tone was bitter and accusatory. Alton's only fault is that he has friends you don't approve of—people you have judged even though you know nothing about them."

"You don't understand."

"Perhaps. Or perhaps you are stuck in the past. Like a child, you shut your eyes and refuse to see that your *bruder* has grown up. Maybe he is making different choices than you or I would, but they are his choices to make. You think by pouting you can change the way things are."

"There is no need for you to talk to me this way."

"But there is."

When she stepped closer, he saw the compassion in her eyes. It made one part of him want to reach out and pull her into his arms. It made another part of him want to storm away.

"I'm your friend," she said. "And that is why I dare to speak to you this way."

Joshua watched her turn and walk across the street and into her trailer. He sat in the lawn chair, confused, dazed, and unsure of what had just happened.

As the lights across the street winked out, he wondered if he'd just broken off the relationship with the woman he was beginning to love. But how could he love her if she couldn't even stand by his side during serious family matters?

He shook his head. It was fine to listen to an old man, but Charlie wasn't in the middle of a family crisis. As for Becca, in many ways she approached life simply—like a child. It was certainly entertaining to quote legends that spoke of breaking a shell and releasing God's peace.

A child's fairy tale.

In Joshua's experience, things had never been quite that easy.

CHAPTER 40

The next few days passed in a haze of confusion for Joshua. He focused on the mission work—on hammering shingles and laying floor. At one point he was working in Alice's kitchen with Alton on his left and Becca on his right. Sarah was in the next room, gently humming as she screwed on the plastic plates that covered the electrical outlets.

In the kitchen, they struggled not to speak to one another.

Alton had continued to work diligently each day and leave as soon as the hands of the clock struck five in the afternoon. His brown hair was beginning to take on a bleached look, and his skin looked more like that of a native Texan than that of an Amish farmer from Oklahoma. Alton had not mentioned the scene on the beach, and he'd stopped arguing with Joshua. Whenever Joshua brought up his activities or his new friends, he simply walked away.

Becca had been polite but distant.

Joshua's anger fueled his attitude for the first twenty-four hours, and then he began to doubt himself. Give up Becca over an argument about his brother? That would be foolish. But he was clueless as to how to set things right. He had no idea how to fix either of the relationships that now seemed broken.

On Friday afternoon, before they were to knock off for the day, Charlie arrived with Quitz trailing faithfully at his side. The old guy was a regular at the job site, and Joshua found himself looking forward to seeing him and talking with him.

"Did you get the sod laid out back of Alice's house?"

"We did. Let me show you."

They walked around the little house. In Joshua's opinion, the yard was pitifully small. He thought of their farm in Oklahoma, of the swings his father had hung from the limbs of the oak tree near the barn and the trampoline that he and his brother and his four sisters had jumped on, sure that they could somehow reach the sky.

"Looks good. You all have done excellent work. I have to say, I don't think I've seen a more dedicated crew."

"Even Alton?" The words slipped out, unbidden.

"Yes. Certainly." If Charlie was surprised, he didn't show it.

"I suppose he's been somewhat useful."

"Son, is there something you'd like to talk about?"

"Family problems. You wouldn't—"

"Wouldn't understand? Do you say that because I had no children or because I'm *Englisch*?"

"That was insensitive of me, Charlie. I'm sorry."

"Apology accepted."

"I only meant that I don't think you can understand what it means to be Amish and why my *bruder*'s actions are hurtful and wrong."

Charlie sighed and then walked Quitz around the perimeter of the yard. The dog sniffed in every corner, left her mark along the back property line, and barked once at a bird that landed in a nearby bush. The bird spent a moment squawking and scolding the dog before flying away, causing Joshua and Charlie to laugh.

"She never catches them?"

"No, and if she did my guess is she'd have no idea what to do with it."

They walked into the house, Charlie complimenting the work on the kitchen floor, and then they made their way upstairs to the bedrooms.

"Alice is going to be so pleased. Their plan is to move in next weekend."

"Should be doable, but you'll want to check with Jim."

They walked through each room before making their way back downstairs and outside. As they exited the house, Alton emerged from their trailer—cleaned up and ready for his night of surfing. He crossed the street and called to Quitz. The dog looked up at Charlie, who nodded once. When Quitz reached Alton's side, he pulled a dog biscuit from the pocket of his swim trunks and handed it to her.

Quitz trotted back to Charlie, waiting to eat the biscuit until she was again standing by her owner's side. Alton waved once and then continued down the street.

"Your *bruder* is kind to remember such a thing—a biscuit for a dog. It sounds so small, but to this old girl…" he laid a hand on the top of her head. "It makes her day a bit brighter."

Joshua didn't know how to answer that, so he remained silent.

"You know I worked with teenagers for many years. Sometimes the ones who did what I hoped—went off to college or took a promising job—ended up sliding into a lifestyle that would take them years to crawl out of."

"I hope this story isn't going to end by telling me surfing is a *gut* thing."

Charlie shrugged. "Other students, they went the alternative route. They followed their dreams, indulged an unconventional skill…" He broke off, and then he stuck his hand into his pants pocket, jingling his change. "One boy was a skateboarder. Alex had excellent scores on his SAT and could have picked his college, but that wasn't his dream. He just wanted to skate. Last year, he received a sponsorship to the X Games."

"So you're saying I should let Alton follow his dreams even when they're ridiculous and can only bring misery to his family."

"I'm telling you that sometimes we think we know what's best for someone else, but we don't." Charlie turned and looked at him directly. "As the oldest brother, I'm sure you often do know what's best for Alton and even the sisters you've told me about. Sometimes. No one always knows what's best though. Let me ask you a question, and I want an honest answer. Have you prayed about this?"

"I ask *Gotte* every night to bring my *bruder* back into the fold—"

"That's not what I'm talking about, Joshua. Have you prayed for yourself? That God will give you a clear perspective and heal your relationship with your brother?"

When Joshua didn't answer, Charlie slapped him lightly on the back. "Perhaps you should start there."

CHAPTER 41

*B*ecca walked into her trailer dusty and tired after a long week of work, but she also felt curiously satisfied. Her assigned jobs had certainly turned out different than she'd expected, and in spite of the current strain between her and Joshua, she was glad she had come.

Nancy sat at the table, working on some needlework. "Pillowcases for Alice."

"She'll appreciate that. She seems like a very nice woman."

"That she does."

Becca sat down and slipped off her shoes, nearly groaning as she did so. "I thought farmwork was hard, but that's nothing compared to nailing hurricane joists."

"I saw you working on house number three."

They had taken to calling Alice's house number one, her next-door neighbor's number two, and the one at the end—the one with the least amount of work done—as house number three. The lot on the opposite side of Alice's was still empty. Becca wondered if it was because no one owned it or if the people weren't sure they wanted to rebuild on the island. Although she loved it here, she couldn't imagine living somewhere that could place you in the path of a hurricane.

"Tornadoes in some places, hurricanes or earthquakes in others," her mother had said in a recent letter. "We place our lives in *Gotte's* hands wherever we choose to live."

Nancy tapped a letter on the table, bringing Becca back to the present. "Another one from Sarah's *mamm*. Take it in to her when you go?"

"Sure." But Becca didn't reach for the letter. "Do you think it's a little odd? That her *mamm* writes her every day?"

"Perhaps."

"She's taken to not opening them. They're stacked in a pile on top of our dresser."

"Could be she needs a break from her situation in Cody's Creek."

Becca thought about that for a few minutes. What was going on in Sarah's life? Was this mission trip an escape for her? And how could she help?

She decided to start with a cup of hot tea.

Nancy said she wasn't thirsty, so Becca made two cups of lemon-flavored tea, put them on a tray, and added a small jar of honey, a spoon, the letter, and a plate of sugar cookies. Balancing it carefully, she walked down the hall to the other end of the trailer.

She didn't knock—after all, it was her room too. But she did make certain that she made a bit of noise outside the door before she entered.

When she walked into the room, Sarah was sitting on her bed, pretending to read a book, though her gaze had been locked on a spot on the wall instead of a page. The paperback was something she'd found on the shelf in the living room.

"*Gut* book?"

"If you believe an Amish girl might run off to Hollywood and become an actress in a James Bond movie." Sarah wiggled her eyebrows.

"It's *gut* to see you smile. I brought you some tea."

"*Danki.*"

"And another letter."

Sarah nodded but didn't reach for it. She did add a teaspoon of honey to her cup of tea.

"At home my folks drink coffee," Sarah said. "I've never been much of a tea drinker."

"I like it."

"So do I, and Alice says that local honey will help with allergies."

"You don't have allergies."

"True, but if I did it would help."

Becca sat on her bed, resting her back against the wall and facing Sarah. She realized in that moment that she truly liked the girl across from her.

"I've never had a *schweschder*," Becca said.

"Or *bruder*. You're that rare thing in an Amish community."

"Indeed I am."

They both giggled.

"The last week has felt like having a *schweschder*, though, sharing this room with you. I kind of like it."

"That's because urban disaster trailers have plenty of hot water. Otherwise, you'd be glad you're an only child."

It was their constant refrain and one of the only negative aspects they brought up about Amish life—though Becca wouldn't change her simple life for any amount of hot water. Still, it was nice to be able to enjoy a steaming shower or bath anytime she wanted. One of the perks of doing mission work, she supposed.

"You have three little *bruders*?"

"Four." Sarah's voice took on a somber tone.

"How old?"

"Six to Eighteen. *Mamm* spread us out."

"I don't mean to pry, and we don't have to talk about it, but…what's with all the letters from home?"

Sarah sipped her tea. She hadn't yet reached for the most recent letter. Finally, she set her cup back on the tray that Becca had placed on the night table between their beds. Sitting back down, she turned so that her back was against the wall and she was facing Becca. The room was so small that with them both sitting on their bed sideways, their feet nearly touched.

"You've met my *mamm*."

"Yes."

"She's not quite as…put together…as she seems during church."

"I'm not sure what you mean."

Instead of answering, Sarah asked, "Do you know about my *dat*?"

"Know what about him?"

"Then you don't." Sarah picked up the book and flipped it over and then over again. "He's been sick for as long as I can remember."

Becca couldn't recall Sarah's father being sick. In fact, he'd helped at the last barn raising. She didn't know what to say, so she murmured, "I'm sorry."

"It's not something we talk about. When he takes his medicine, he's okay, though a bit sleepy and somewhat distant."

"And when he doesn't?"

Sarah reached up and pushed back her blond hair. She'd taken off her *kapp* because she was in their room. Becca couldn't help noticing that her hair was always precisely braided. If it became mussed at all, she would quickly take it down and rebraid it. Sometimes she worked the braids so tightly that they pulled the skin taut around her hairline.

"When he doesn't, then…then there is no telling what will happen. Sometimes he screams and hollers, sometimes he accuses us of poisoning his food and trying to kill him, and other times he weeps."

"I had no idea."

"It's something we don't talk about except to his doctor and the bishop."

"*Daddi* has never mentioned it to me. Isn't there something he can do?"

"A few times he has intervened. Once he took us somewhere else to spend a few days. And of course he strongly encourages my father to stay on his medication, but no one can force him. After all, he hasn't done anything illegal yet."

"We can't wait for that! Surely something can be done now, before…before things become any worse."

Sarah met her gaze, her lips trembling and tears shining in her eyes. "I figured you knew. I guess I thought everyone knew, but apparently the Amish grapevine hasn't spread the word."

"If it did, I must not be plugged in." On an urge, Becca stood up and moved over to her friend's bed and sat beside her so that there was only the book sitting between them. "Is that what the letters are about?"

"My *mamm* does her best. I suppose the situation has worn her down over the years. Bishop Levi says hard times can make you stronger, but they can also sap your strength and cloud your outlook. For my *mamm*, I'm afraid it's the latter."

"Why does she write you every day?"

Sarah laughed, but there was no merriment in the sound. "Some days she is begging me to come home, asking me how I could dare abandon her. Other days, she is assuring me that I should stay."

Becca thought of her own parents. Both were a calm, reassuring presence in her life. What would it be like to live with two adults who couldn't be depended on? Did that make Sarah the mother figure in the family? Did she carry the full responsibility for her four siblings?

"We never know what will set him off." Her voice had taken on a soft, faraway tone, reminding Becca of the lonesome train whistles she sometimes heard late at night. "It could be that our hair isn't braided correctly or his food has grown cold. One moment he might be smiling and telling you how proud of you he is—and then in nearly the same breath he becomes this bitter, angry, unreasonable man that I am sure I cannot be related to."

Becca reached across the book and twined her fingers with Sarah's.

"The first day I made myself throw up was after he accused me of being pregnant." Sarah chewed her bottom lip. "I wasn't interested in boys at all. This was the summer between seventh and eighth grade. Something in my mind clicked. If he thought I looked pregnant, then I'd assure him I wasn't. I'd become so thin he would never accuse me again."

"I remember your being sick, and…going away for a while."

"The bishop convinced my parents I needed intervention. He arranged transportation to one of the hospitals in Tulsa where they specialize in teens who need better coping techniques."

"Did it help?"

"I suppose." Becca stared down at their hands. "I've learned when my mother's emotional traps become too much for me to endure that it's okay to step back. That's why I don't open all of her letters. Once I see that she is lashing out at me instead of dealing directly with my father, I try to create distance. It works better here than at home."

"I'm so sorry."

Sarah smiled, gently removed her hand from Becca's grasp, and tapped the top of the book. "Don't worry about me. I may one day live in Hollywood and star in a movie about spies."

Becca laughed with her, though her heart was aching at the revelation Sarah had just shared. She stayed in the room a few more minutes, and then she excused herself and walked down the hall to take a shower.

She'd thought she understood Sarah, that she knew her problems and presumed to think—in her heart of hearts—that Sarah should just "get over it." How hard was it to eat? Why make such a big, dramatic thing of the process?

Becca had never said those thoughts out loud, but they had occasionally crossed her mind. Now she understood that very few things were as simple as they seemed. Obviously, Sarah was still struggling with her eating disorder, and it was directly related to the situation at home. Where was the escape from that? Did she have any say in what her future would be like?

Would she continue to be buffeted between the two people who were supposed to protect her from the world? Was not eating or throwing up her food Sarah's way of saying *I can control this when I can't control anything else*?

As steam filled the bathroom, Becca prayed for her friend. For healing and peace for Sarah, and for clarity in her own mind and heart.

CHAPTER 42

Charlie stood next to the sixty-five-foot fishing/tour boat and helped the Amish gals board. Sarah's eyes were serious and taking in everything they could see, but at least a hint of a smile brightened her face. Becca kept close to Sarah and laughed when Quitz nudged her hand.

"I don't have anything for you to eat, Quitz. Ask Alton."

For an answer, Alton reached into his pocket and produced the requisite treat. Quitz sat and cocked her head, waiting until Alton offered the dog biscuit.

"Smart girl," Joshua said.

"She likes to think so." Charlie winked and turned to help Alice aboard.

"Are you sure there's room for us?" she asked.

"Yes, I'm sure. Even with all the workers here—"

Frank, Brady, Eva, and Simon were already seated next to where everyone was boarding.

"You're not taking this excursion without us," Simon joked.

"Indeed, Simon has been talking about it for days." Eva poked him in the side with her elbow, and Simon jumped to the side to avoid the jab.

There was a time when Charlie had thought Simon was interested in Becca. Perhaps he'd imagined that as he'd noticed no unusual interaction between them lately.

"Are we ready?" Jim asked. He'd brought up the end of the line, and stood counting heads before he boarded the boat.

"We are. Just assuring Alice and the kids that there's plenty of room."

"Of course there is, and we want you to join us. I've been asking for weeks. Remember?"

"Come on, Nana." Shelley pulled on her grandmother's hand as C.J. hurried aboard ahead of them.

Charlie noticed that the boy headed straight to Alton's side. There was something about Alton that C.J. liked, that he related to. It was interesting to watch the two of them. It seemed to Charlie that Alton could do with a little hero worship. Perhaps having someone look up to him would help Alton to find his path in life.

The captain of the vessel, whose stage name was Captain Hook, welcomed them aboard. Charlie found a place to sit between Alice and Jim. Shelley whispered something to her grandmother, and then she ran to squeeze between Sarah and Becca.

"Thank you for boarding our vessel. The first thing I want to point out is that a life jacket is located beneath each of your seats. We have calm waters for our trip, but if you're more comfortable wearing a flotation device, then you're certainly welcome to get it out now."

Charlie glanced at Becca, but she hadn't reached for hers yet. She did glance down at the bin beneath her seat to make sure it was there.

"Our tour this evening will take us out past the St. Jo Island and the Port Aransas jetties. We'll also see the Lydia Ann Lighthouse, which is still standing even after Orion's attempts to send her to the bottom of the sea."

There were a few cheers of "Let's hear it for Lydia!" and "Lighthouses rule!" It pleased Charlie to see everyone in such good spirits. The weather was fine, and the evening was warm enough that no one needed more than a light jacket. He hoped they would enjoy seeing some of the coast he loved so much.

"Have your cameras ready," the captain said. "We will likely see bottlenose dolphins, and we should make the lighthouse just as the sun sets."

"Why is your name Captain Hook?" Alton asked. "Seems to me that you still have both hands."

C.J. giggled and Shelley slapped her hands over her mouth. Charlie had caught her watching *Peter Pan* on her grandmother's tablet just a few weeks ago. No doubt she was thinking of a different Captain Hook.

"I'm so glad you asked." The captain's voice grew mysterious. "We'll be putting the trawl net down so we can pull up a good sampling of the ocean life for you to see. Always be careful, though. I might have both of my hands, but One-Armed Pete wasn't so lucky."

Pete waved at them from the end of the boat. He was dressed up as a pirate, with a patch pulled up above his eye, blousy pants, and a white cotton shirt. When he waved his right arm, which ended in a stump, several gasps were heard throughout the crowd.

"Pete will tell you his story when he pulls up the trawl. As for mine?" The captain fingered his right earlobe, from which hung a long, sparkling jewel. "I was caught in the ear with a fish hook, so now I wear this earring as a reminder to be on the lookout for flying objects."

The captain wished them a good journey and then excused himself to pilot the boat.

They set off at a slow pace, but it was only moments before their guests were oohing and aahing over the dolphins as they leaped out of the water. They seemed to keep pace with the boat. One jumped high and then flipped over before splashing down. Charlie was reminded of the time he and Madelyn had gone to SeaWorld together. He glanced across the boat and noticed Becca step away from the others and write something in a small journal she carried.

"It's for her mother," Alice explained. "She's an artist. She paints and draws cards and small landscapes."

"Sounds unusual for an Amish woman."

"Perhaps. Becca is determined to write down every possible detail of what she's seeing so her mother can use the information for a new line of cards that has to do with MDS."

Charlie shook his head. "I'll admit I didn't know much about the Amish before this group arrived. Mennonite, sure. They have been helping us practically since the day Orion landed."

"They've all been a real blessing."

"Indeed they have, but this group has opened up my eyes to some things."

"Such as?" Alice smiled at him, swiping at the strands of gray hair that had escaped the baseball cap she wore.

"Oh, I don't know. Young love." He threw a pointed glance toward Joshua, who was watching Becca write in her journal.

"I'd noticed that."

"Also how a community can have a hand in raising a child." He nodded toward Shelley.

"She adores Sarah and Becca."

"And that God brings people into our lives for a reason."

C.J. was laughing, using his grandmother's phone to take a photo of Alton, who was hamming it up and pointing toward a dolphin. Although Nancy, Joshua, Becca, and Sarah usually avoided the camera, Alton seemed to have no qualms about having his picture taken. Becca had explained to Charlie that the rules were a bit more lax when they were enjoying a vacation or trip away.

"Though pride is always to be discouraged," she had hastened to add. "We wouldn't carry photos of ourselves around in our wallet."

He was learning that the Amish understanding of living a simple life extended to nearly everything they did.

"I'll agree God brought every person on this boat into our lives for a reason," Alice said. "I'm so glad you recommended my name for the MDS program."

"Now, don't give Charlie all the credit." Jim finished taking pictures for the Mennonite group. He handed the camera back to Eva and plopped down on the other side of Alice. "Surely my wonderful analytical skills would have pulled your name from the pile even without Charlie's input."

"You're an analyst?" Charlie scratched his head. "I always thought you were just some construction guy who had stumbled onto the island and needed a job."

Jim tilted his head back and laughed.

It felt good and right and like a rich blessing to tease a friend. To see a smile of satisfaction on Alice's face. To feel the wind against his skin, smell the ocean, and enjoy the waves gently rocking the boat.

Quitz lay at his feet, her head on her paws.

The sun was indeed setting as they made their way past St. Jo Island and toward the Lydia Ann Lighthouse. He'd seen it twice with Madelyn. The first time had been on a boat like this one. The second time they had signed up for a tour that required them to take a boat out, dock, and walk up to the structure. He realized that his memories of Madelyn now brought him joy instead of pain. When had that changed? When had he learned to appreciate the memory of her instead of agonizing over the loss?

The captain again came over the loudspeaker and told them the details about the lighthouse. "She was built in 1857. Texas has a 400-mile coastline, and most of that is protected by barrier islands. Aransas Pass is one of the few gaps that allow access to the mainland. Congress authorized the building of the lighthouse in 1831 for a cost of $12,500. Most cars cost more than that now."

There was laughter from the passengers. Charlie could tell they were listening intently, though several continued to take photographs of the lighthouse as the setting sun splashed rays of color around it.

"At one time it was called the Lydia Ann Channel Light, and it was very important during the Civil War. In fact, the lighthouse passed hands many times from Confederate to Union and back again. At one point soldiers from the South removed the lens from the light and hid it in the marshes on the island. Then on Christmas 1862, Confederate General Magruder ordered the destruction of the lighthouse in order to keep it out of Union hands. Rebuilding began in 1867. If you have time, I highly recommend you take the tour of the lighthouse and learn more about it."

Charlie had been standing to get a better view. When he sat down, Shelley ran to his lap and crawled up in it, snuggling against him.

"I'm a little cold, Charlie."

"We can't have that." He shrugged out of his jacket and placed it around her shoulders.

Alice started to protest, but he stopped her. He counted it a joy to be able to help the child, even if it was just to ward off the evening chill.

"Anyone want to help drop the trawl into the water?" Pete asked.

C.J. looked back at Alice, who nodded but hollered, "Be careful!"

And then Alton was picking him up, holding him near the button that allowed the line to release. C.J. laughed as the net fell into the water. It followed in the wake of the boat, causing a bit of a ripple as it collected treasures from the sea.

And when Alton put the boy down, he stepped closer, nearly plastering himself to Alton's side. C.J. had indeed changed in the last few weeks. It seemed to Charlie that he'd allowed himself to be a child and let the adults handle the big stuff. That, for C.J., was a real mark of progress and healing. The boy had been through so much—being raised without a father, abandoned by his mother, and then finally having his home ripped away by a hurricane.

Yet he'd learned to trust an Amish man from nearly seven hundred miles north. Yes, it would seem that God had a hand in such things. And once the boy was moved into his new home, Charlie would finally rest easy.

CHAPTER 43

Joshua stood in front of Becca, casting a shadow onto the page where she was scribbling descriptions of all she saw.

"Better put that up and come watch One-Armed Pete."

Becca added two more words, clicked her pen, wrapped the elastic band around the small book, and stored the pen beneath the band. "You think I should? It may be dangerous."

"It may," he agreed. "But I imagine it's worth the risk."

Joshua was worried she would say no, that the distance he had created between them would continue. But Becca smiled, tucked her small notebook into her backpack, and said, "I'm ready!"

Pete was pulling up the trawl net by the time they reached the back of the boat.

"It's best not to let the net go too deep or stay in for too long," he explained. "That's how I lost my hand. Pulled up a shark."

C.J.'s eyes had widened to the size of quarters, and Shelley stepped closer to Sarah.

"But that's not the end of the story," Pete said. "I killed the shark, and later—after I was out of the hospital—I ate him! So I suppose you could say I had the last word."

He waved his stump in triumph, and the people gathered around clapped.

Joshua leaned toward Becca and whispered, "Think he's telling the truth?"

"Could be! He lost that hand somehow. I can't imagine going through something like that. I'm sure I'd find a different job."

Pete must have heard her, for he winked and said, "I've worked on fishing boats all my life. Didn't see any reason to stop doing something I loved because I had a single bad experience."

In fact, the man was wiry and muscular. The net he pulled up was brimming with different types of fish, shells, and even some plant specimens. He selected a dozen items, dumped them into two waiting buckets, and then he emptied the net back over the end of the boat.

"Follow me downstairs, and we'll look at what we caught."

Joshua reached for Becca's hand. She hesitated for a moment, and then she looked at him and smiled. It was enough to cause his pulse to race. She was going to give him a second chance. Relief washed through his mind and his heart. He hadn't realized how hard it would be to not speak with her each day, to not share the good and bad events at work. He'd quickly found out just how much he missed their walks on the beach.

"What are you laughing about?" she asked.

"It's only been three days since our argument, but it's felt like much longer. I'm glad you're not angry with me."

"I was never angry with you." She nudged her shoulder against his.

"Well, you certainly weren't happy with me." He held up a hand to stop her protest. "I don't blame you. I was being bullheaded."

"Yes, you were." Her laugh mingled with his. "We can talk about this later. I want to see what Pete put in those buckets."

"And describe them in your journal for your *mamm*?"

"Exactly."

By the time they had descended the stairs, Pete had dumped the buckets onto an odd type of table. The top of the table was recessed two to three feet and the area had been filled with saltwater. The fish from the buckets swam back and forth.

C.J. and Shelley weren't the only curious ones. Joshua noticed Alice reach forward and touch one of the fish as it swam by. Shelley glanced up at her grandmother, and a smile spread across the child's face. It occurred to Joshua that when you lived in a place, you worked and went to school and went about your daily life, but often you missed out on the little pleasures that visitors enjoyed. He was glad Alice and her grandkids had come. They seemed as much a part of their group as Charlie or Jim or the Mennonite folks.

"This here is a flounder. I suppose most of you have seen or eaten one of these." Pete dropped the fish and reached for a smaller specimen with his good hand. "Of course, this is a shrimp. I like mine battered and fried."

There were several murmurs of agreement. Joshua realized that Pete was actually quite good with the crowd. He was instructing them as well as a teacher in a classroom. No wonder he had returned to his job after his accident. His skin was weathered, his speech that of common people, and his love for the sea quite evident.

Pete reached into the tank and picked up a fish that was flat, about the size of a dinner plate.

"This is a stingray. It has a barbed stinger on its tail." Pete carried the fish to a tabletop behind him and snipped something off. He held the fish up, so that they could see its underbelly.

"I removed the stinger—"

"Did that hurt?" C.J. asked.

He returned it to the water. "I don't think so, and it will grow back. Some people say it's wrong to remove the stingers, but I think that it's good to teach people about fish. I wouldn't want you getting hurt, though. Now you can touch this one or even pick it up."

"How big do they get?" Shelley asked.

"Giant ones can be more than sixteen feet across and weigh more than a thousand pounds."

Becca glanced up at Joshua, a comical look on her face.

"Worried about putting your toes in the water now?" he teased.

"We don't see the monster size here in the gulf. At least I haven't." He again picked up the stingray as it swam by. "They hide under the sand. Their eyes are on top, but their mouth is on bottom."

He flipped the fish over, and they all leaned forward, staring at the little mouth.

"Because they're buried in the sand, they can't see their prey. Instead, they smell it."

"They smell us?" Shelley asked.

"Well, mostly they aren't interested in little girls. Stingrays eat small fish, snails, clams, and shrimp. It's okay for you to touch it and even pick it up. Just don't leave her out of the water too long."

Alton had picked up the stingray and was holding it for C.J. and Shelley to touch. He moved next to Becca. Joshua almost laughed when she hesitated, but then she reached forward and ran a finger gently over the top of the fish.

"I never thought I'd touch something like that," she whispered.

"The sea is amazing. It's full of a wide variety of God's creatures. Just be sure to respect all people and animals, and give them plenty of space if they have big, sharp teeth." He waved his stump again. "Best to learn from my mistake rather than endure the consequences of your own."

"Learn from my mistake..." Those words echoed in Joshua's mind as he watched Becca and Sarah *ooh* and *aah* over starfish, crabs, and even the stingray.

The last fish Pete held up was small and practically spherical in shape. "This is a puffer fish."

Shelley giggled and leaned forward, gripping the edge of the table.

"His best defense is that he can fill his stomach up with water. When he does, he becomes like a spiky ball, which is not too good if you're a bigger fish trying to eat him."

Pete again encouraged them to touch all of the fish, including the puffer. And then he reminded them once more that the ocean was a wonderful place and not to fill it with their trash. "Leave it like you find it," were his exact words. "Better yet, if you see some trash, pick it up and take it home with you."

The captain came over the ship's loudspeaker, telling them they would be docking in twenty minutes.

"I want one more look at the ocean," Becca said.

So the two of them went upstairs and stood at the side of the boat, watching the lights of Port Aransas come closer and the darkness of the sea recede. The sky was ablaze with starlight, the moon a mere crescent on the horizon. A light breeze had sprung up. Looking around to make sure no one else was close by, Joshua moved behind Becca and put his arms around her.

Instead of acting surprised, she snuggled into his embrace.

Could this be happening to him?

Was he falling in love with Becca Troyer?

And was it possible…a prospect that surely rivaled the wonders of the universe…was there a chance she loved him too?

CHAPTER 44

When Becca heard footsteps coming up to the main deck, she reluctantly stepped out of the circle of Joshua's arms. She didn't want to. She wanted to stay there, stare up at the stars, and enjoy the beating of his heart in rhythm with her own.

Joshua seemed to understand what she was thinking as he squeezed her hand once and then tugged her down on the seat next to him.

Soon they were surrounded by the others in their group, everyone talking about the fish below, the dolphins they had seen, and the lighthouse.

"Maybe we can go out to the lighthouse someday," Shelley said, sitting on the seat between Becca and Sarah, bouncing up and down.

"We travel home soon," Sarah reminded her.

"When?"

"In two weeks."

Shelley stuck out her bottom lip. "Why can't you just stay here?"

"Our family is in Oklahoma," Becca explained. "They miss us, and we miss them too."

"I'd miss Nana. I wouldn't want to be away from her."

"So you understand." Sarah reached forward and straightened one of Shelley's ponytails.

"I guess." Shelley had popped up, but she sat down again and snuggled next to Sarah. "But when you want to see a lighthouse or a stingray, you'll have to come back here!"

Becca and Joshua shared a smile.

They spoke of it when they had arrived back at their trailers and were sitting out on the patio. "It's almost as if those two are healing one another."

"*Ya?*" Joshua had foraged around in the kitchen and found a plate of cookies, a jar of peanut butter, some crackers, and a carton of milk. "I didn't know Sarah needed healing."

It wasn't her secret to tell, so Becca shrugged and changed the subject. "That's not exactly a balanced meal you have there."

"The milk balances it."

"Does not."

"Well…" Joshua popped a cracker topped with peanut butter into his mouth. "What do I need? Fruit? Vegetables? I think I saw a celery stick in there."

"We had dinner before the gulf tour. You had a giant platter of fried shrimp."

"Hours ago. A man needs constant nourishment."

"Does he now?"

"*Ya.* A *gut* Amish wife would know that."

Becca wasn't entirely comfortable with talk of wives, and she blushed at the thought that Joshua might be thinking along those lines. She did care for him, and she was glad they were no longer cross with one another, but—

"You have that worried look." Joshua's tone was no longer light and teasing. He pushed aside the snacks, crossed his arms on the patio table, and leaned forward to study her in the light that spilled from the dining room.

The heat on her face warmed until she felt that her ears were burning. She was grateful for the semidarkness, which didn't seem to keep Joshua from noticing her discomfort.

"Best to tell me than to chew on it."

"It's only that…what I mean to say is…well, I don't want to be presumptuous."

"I care about you, Becca. You know that, *ya?*"

"And I care about you."

"Then I'd like to know what's bothering you."

She pulled her hands into her lap and stared down at them. She couldn't see much, but it was better than looking into Joshua's eyes. "You know I'm an only child."

"I do."

"And perhaps that is the reason it bothers me so much."

"It?"

"Your arguments with Alton."

Joshua cocked his head.

"Could be it's normal for siblings." Now she rushed to explain, the words tumbling out of her mouth. "My *mamm* and *dat* and I, we don't argue in that way. One of us may be out of sorts, even a bit short tempered, but we quickly apologize and then…then harmony is restored."

Now Joshua sat back in his chair, but he continued watching her closely. She finally raised her gaze to his. What she was about to say was too important to diminish by staring away like a child.

"I wouldn't know how to…how to live in an environment of constant disagreement and dissension." The worries she had been afraid to admit even to herself spilled out. "Not that I'm saying we're ready to make such a commitment. Only I thought I should let you know…how…how it is that I feel."

Joshua took his time answering, but finally he stood, walked to her chair, and squatted down in front of it. He pulled her hands out of her lap and gently kissed her fingers. "I want to know how you feel, Becca. I want you to always be honest with me. Do you understand?"

She nodded, not trusting her voice.

He squeezed her hands one more time before he stood and walked over to the patio railing. After a few moments, he turned, crossed his arms, and studied her.

"So you care about me."

She could hear the smile in his voice. "I do."

"And I care about you."

Oh, how she wished she could see his expression.

"But you're worried that were we to court seriously, and even one day decide to marry, that you'd be agreeing to live in a contentious home."

"*Ya*." She joined him at the porch railing. Instead of looking at each other, they gazed up at the Milky Way.

"You're a wise woman, Becca. Probably more than you know."

"I'm not judging you."

"I can tell that."

The breeze tickled the hair escaping from her *kapp*. She batted her hair back into place. Soon they would be back in Oklahoma. How would their relationship change then?

"I hadn't stopped to think how my constant arguments with Alton might affect others. So often I focus on setting him straight, convinced he's going to land in some trouble that will hurt our family."

He turned and rested his back against the railing.

"You're not the first to talk to me about this. Jim tried. Charlie tried. And now you have tried." He cupped her face in his hands. "*Danki*, Becca. For caring enough to be honest with me, even about things I'd rather not hear."

"What will you do?"

"What I should have done long ago—pray about it." He lowered his head and brushed her lips with the gentlest of kisses.

Becca realized then that though the situation might not improve immediately, at least Joshua was willing to try. That was all she could ask.

CHAPTER 45

*O*n the second Sunday they attended Jim's church. It wasn't lost on Joshua that the minister spoke on forgiveness. Matthew, Ephesians, Colossians—he worked his way through the New Testament, showing time and again how God commanded the church to forgive. Then he reversed directions and took them through the Old Testament.

"We would do well to understand that the character of God is one of incomprehensible forgiveness and mercy and grace." The older man stood at the front of the room wearing jeans and a starched white shirt.

Jim had warned them that the service was a "contemporary one," meaning a full-fledged band led the song service and most of those in attendance wore blue jeans. Folks were friendly, coffee and donuts were served, and the little group from Cody's Creek were made to feel quite comfortable. It was another very different worship experience for them.

The message, though? It was something Joshua might have heard at home. The words wound through the walls of bitterness and anger he had erected around his feelings. The Scripture moved powerfully and found its way to the very center of Joshua's heart.

"The prophet Micah praises Jehovah when he cries, 'Who is a God like you, who pardons sin and forgives the transgression of the remnant of his inheritance? You do not stay angry forever but delight to show mercy.'"

Delight to show mercy.

Joshua realized as he bowed his head to pray that the key to his situation was in those final four words. It wasn't enough to forgive his brother or to be more patient. Micah was clear—God delighted in showing mercy to them, and as a Christian he was called to be as Christlike as possible.

Sweet peace flowed through his soul as he released years of pent-up bitterness. The time of prayer ended, and Joshua glanced around, wondering if the message had deeply affected those around him. But the service proceeded as if nothing had happened. As if God hadn't moved heaven and earth to soften his heart.

After the minister announced the blessing, folks began to gather their things together. Alton stretched as if he had been having trouble staying awake.

Joshua blinked, trying to reconcile everyday activities with the spiritual awakening he had just experienced. The words had been meant for him. He couldn't tell who else had been blessed by them, just as they couldn't tell that he had been cleansed from the inside.

Joshua glanced again at his brother, who was covering a yawn with his hand. More than likely he was exhausted. Though the rest of the group was home from the dolphin tour by nine that evening, Alton had said he'd catch up with them later and hitched a ride to the beach. It was in the wee hours of the morning when he'd collapsed on top of his covers, not even bothering to remove his clothes.

"I'm glad you came today," Joshua said.

Alton raised one eyebrow, waiting—no doubt—for the barb which usually punctuated every sentence. Joshua shook his head. He didn't want to be that person anymore. So instead of adding anything, he slapped Alton on the back and turned to speak with Becca.

The church was having a luncheon after the service, which they stayed to enjoy. Jim explained that while it wasn't Amish cooking, it was good, wholesome, Southern food.

"This fried chicken may be better than my *mamm's*," Becca admitted.

"Wait until you taste the macaroni casserole." Sarah smiled around a forkful, and something passed between her and Becca. Joshua didn't know what that was about. He probably didn't need to. What mattered was that it was a new day, and he'd finally learned to forgive and accept his brother.

Only…something wasn't quite right yet. There was something he still needed to do. With a sigh, he pushed his plate away, realizing that *the sooner begun, the sooner done*—wasn't that what his *mammi* used to say?

"Problem with the ham?" Nancy asked.

"*Nein*. It's only that I need to speak with Alton."

Alton, it turned out, was already outside playing basketball. When he saw Joshua, he passed the ball to a gangly teen and walked over.

"Need something?" he asked.

"Only to apologize."

Alton waited, and Joshua finally said, "I've treated you unfairly and unkindly, and I want your forgiveness."

"You do?"

"Yes."

Alton looked to Joshua's right and then his left, as if searching for a clue to this change of events.

"It's not a joke. I'm serious."

"I was just wondering if someone had stolen my brother and maybe replaced him with a look-alike."

"*Nein*. It's still me. Smart, good looking—"

"I'm more accustomed to old and cranky."

Instead of rising to the bait, Joshua only nodded in agreement.

"See? The Joshua I know and love would never have taken that."

"But you're right. I have been old and cranky."

Alton turned in a circle, as if he was still waiting for someone to jump out of the bushes and yell "Surprise!"

Then he stepped closer and pulled Joshua into a man-hug. "Forgiveness granted."

Tears clouded Joshua's eyes at the same time a giant smile spread across his face.

"Now let's see if you're any good with a basketball."

The afternoon passed quickly. They played two games, enjoyed a return trip to the food tables, and when the time of fellowship was over, they rode back to the trailers in the van. The day slowed as each person drifted off to their own restful activity, which for the Kline brothers meant an afternoon snooze—Joshua on the patio and Alton on the couch.

Then it was five o'clock, and Becca and Sarah were knocking on their door.

"We're going to look for shells. Want to come?"

"Of course." Joshua snatched up his hat, and then he thought to add some drinks to his backpack.

Alton yawned, excused himself to splash water on his face, and went with them, dressed in his swim trunks and a T-shirt. Joshua knew by the way he looked at his watch that he had other plans later.

For once it didn't bother him. His little brother might have made a few *Englisch* friends, and perhaps they were people that Joshua would have kept at a distance. But he wasn't Alton. He didn't need to judge what his brother did.

Delight to show mercy.

Joshua's heart was lighter and his energy was back because he wasn't spending hours arguing with Alton in his mind.

That was a blessing, a benefit he hadn't expected.

And he hoped, he prayed, that he could hold on to it should trouble find them again.

CHAPTER 46

$\mathcal{T}$rouble did find them again—and with amazing speed.

They had caught the bus, ridden to the beach, and walked down the shoreline. Becca and Sarah were obviously enjoying the afternoon. Alton kept checking his watch.

Joshua finally decided to end his brother's misery. "Need to be somewhere?"

"*Ya*. I told the guys...but I don't want to desert you with the girls."

"It's no hardship." Joshua laughed. "Go. Do what you had planned."

Alton seemed to hesitate, as if waiting for Joshua's usual refrain of caution and reprimand. Hearing none, he called out to the girls, waved goodbye, and jogged off in the opposite direction—toward the parking area.

Joshua walked with Sarah and Becca up and down the beach. There was a sand castle competition going on, and they were delighted to find elaborate edifices, full-sized mermaids, and even a dragon. The details created by the artists were incredible, and Becca quickly pulled out her notebook and began jotting down notes.

When they had seen enough and returned to walking down the beach, Sarah suggested they find Alton and watch him surf.

"I think he's getting pretty good. At least he told me he isn't pitched as often."

"Pitched?" Becca transferred her bag of shells from her left hand to her right. "What is pitched?"

257

"Thrown off, I imagine."

"All right. It might be *gut* to see what my *bruder* has learned in the last week."

And it was good to see.

They had no trouble locating Alton and his motley group of friends. They had left their shirts, towels, and various backpacks in a pile on the beach. Spreading their blanket next to the pile, Joshua, Becca, and Sarah sat and watched. They cheered when Alton rode the waves, and they covered their eyes and groaned when he crashed.

"It does look fun," Becca admitted.

"So you'd like to try it?" Joshua had once again been covering her toes with sand. He stopped, brushed off his hands, and acted as if he was about to stand. "I imagine we could rent you a board. Sarah probably has a few bucks on her and will help pay for it."

"I do and I will."

"And we'll see if the ocean pitches you."

Becca began giggling and shaking her head. The sun spread purple, orange, and red colors across the sky. Joshua realized that he was happy, truly happy for the first time in a long time.

And then the bark of a dog captured his attention.

The man with the dog was wearing khaki pants, a dark shirt, and a ball cap with letters on it. As he drew closer, Joshua could make out the letters ATF. The dog was a German shepherd and wore a vest with the same letters.

Sarah and Becca stared at the dog and the man, and then they glanced at each other and finally at Joshua.

He stood, brushed off his hands, and asked, "Can we help you?"

It was obvious that the dog was interested in something near them. He was on point, nose high and body visibly quivering. He barked once and then sat, waiting on the officer.

"I'm Officer Mendez. Are these your things, sir?"

"Some of it is." Joshua indicated the blanket they sat on, his backpack, and Becca's bag of shells.

"What about those things?"

Joshua glanced at the stack left by his brother's friends.

"*Nein*. Those aren't ours."

"Do you know who this stuff belongs to?"

He didn't. Alton's shirt was discarded in the middle of the pile, but Joshua didn't know which pack belonged to whom. Was he supposed to turn them in? Would his brother be in trouble? And what had the dog smelled?

Before he had any answers, Spider hurried up, carrying his board.

Water dripped from his dreadlocks, and if anything the setting sun only highlighted his maze of tattoos. "Is there a problem?"

"Are those your packs, sir?"

Spider shrugged.

"Are they your packs?" The officer stood with perfect posture, his feet six inches apart and planted firmly in the sand and his hands at his side.

The dog waited patiently next to him.

Spider stepped closer and pointed at a pack with a black widow stenciled on it. "That one is."

"And the rest?"

"Friends'."

"Are those friends here?"

Alton picked that moment to join them. He also hurried up to the group, shaking off water as he walked with his surfboard clutched under his arm.

"What's the problem?"

Becca and Sarah were now standing next to Joshua. Their group was beginning to draw curious stares from other folks on the beach.

"Do any of these items belong to you?" Mendez asked.

"Only the T-shirt."

"All right." The officer looked around to see if anyone else was approaching, but the onlookers kept a healthy distance, and Alton's other two surfing buddies had disappeared.

"My dog has alerted on something in this pile. According to Texas law, I have probable cause to search these bags."

"Search for what?" Alton asked.

"Drugs. He's looking for drugs, and the dog caught the scent of something, which gives him the legal right to search through the bags." Spider's tone was matter-of-fact. He gestured to the pile of bags and said, "Go ahead."

He made to pick up his bag, but the officer stopped him.

"Please take a step back, sir."

Spider's hands went up in a surrender gesture. "I've nothing illegal in my bag."

After another pointed look from the officer, he folded his arms across his chest and did as he was told. Alton stood between Spider and Joshua. He glanced at his brother and shook his head as if to say, "I've got nothing."

The dog immediately went to a black pack on the far side of the pile. Again he barked once and sat.

Officer Mendez angled slightly away from them and said something into the radio clipped to his shoulder. When he turned back to the group, he addressed them. "I've called for backup. I'd like you all to sit in a line there in front of me."

Joshua's head was swimming. Was it just this morning he'd had a revelation of forgiveness and grace and mercy? And now he was being told not to flee a scene because a drug dog had alerted on something in his brother's possession? That wasn't right, though. He knew Alton and was certain he didn't mess with drugs. Yes, he'd had the one instance with alcohol, but he'd promised that was in his past and Joshua believed him.

No, Alton's guilt in this scenario was in being naive enough to associate with disreputable guys, socialize with them, and think they were his friends. The absence of the other two surfers seemed glaringly obvious to him. The offending bag belonged to either Zach or Dax. After having met them, Joshua would bet it belonged to glass-eyed Dax, and for all he knew Spider was in on it as well.

It took twenty minutes for the backup officer to arrive. No one was surprised when Officer Mendez opened the black backpack and found a rather large baggie of marijuana.

"Is that…" Becca leaned forward, but Sarah pulled her back.

Joshua had an insane urge to laugh. Officer Mendez was explaining to Spider and Alton that they would have to go down to the station. He turned to Joshua and the girls and said, "You're free to go."

Had he simply believed them when they said the items weren't theirs?

Or was he quick to believe their innocence because of their Plain clothing?

And what of Alton, who was dressed like an *Englischer*? Even now he was placing his hands behind his back, being handcuffed, and then walking off to the police cruiser waiting at the end of the stretch of beach.

The real miracle of the situation was that Joshua wasn't angry with Alton. No, he'd left his anger back in the church pew, and he was done with it. But he did feel an overwhelming sadness. They had traveled a long way to immerse themselves in the rebuilding of Port Aransas homes and to do God's work, and now they were involved in the middle of a drug bust.

CHAPTER 47

"How did you get the surfboards back here?" Nancy asked.

She'd taken the details of the afternoon's events better than Becca would have thought. But then perhaps she'd seen a lot of strange happenings over the years. Certainly, Alton wasn't the first one to be involved in such a misunderstanding.

It was a misunderstanding.

"The officers allowed us to bring them home." Sarah fiddled with a cup of tea, not drinking it but rather turning the cup in her hands—perhaps drawing some comfort from its warmth.

"After the dog checked out Spider's truck," Becca added.

They were all once again sitting on the patio of their trailer. Nancy leaned forward to see past Becca. The large black truck was still parked at the curb.

"Joshua has a driver's license," Nancy said, as if explaining the truck's presence to herself.

"I do." Joshua stepped out onto the patio, pulling a chair from the dining room with him.

Becca and Sarah scooted their chairs closer to Nancy to make room for him. It was a tight fit, but Becca didn't mind. She wanted her friends close. She wanted and needed their strength and perspective. Back in Cody's Creek, she'd grown up accustomed to being alone except for her parents. Now she realized that she enjoyed being with her friends. She liked having them nearby to share her burdens, and Alton weighed heavily on her heart.

"That driver's license has come in handy more than once with my *bruder*."

Nancy surprised them all by chuckling. "I remember when the topic first came up about your obtaining your license. Levi wasn't sure that the rest of the church leadership would go along with it."

"It helps that we're in Oklahoma and not Pennsylvania," Joshua said.

"*Ya*, for sure and for certain. Some of the more conservative communities would never allow it, but we'd had a drought-plagued year. Most crops didn't produce and families were scrambling to make ends meet. The job you took helped to provide food for your family, and now that same license has allowed you to help your *bruder* twice." She picked up her cup of tea and sipped it. "I suppose God had a plan even in that."

"Hopefully, God also has a plan to keep Alton out of jail."

"Worry ends where faith begins," Nancy said.

"Maybe that's why I'm not worried." When they all looked at him curiously, Joshua went on to explain what had happened that morning at the church service. He ended with, "I don't mean to say I'm perfect now. I still slip into my old frame of mind, and more than once today I wanted to either give him a nice long lecture or shake him into his senses. But those moments are fewer and they pass rather quickly. I don't know how this will end, but I do believe God has a plan and it will work out."

"I was wondering why you didn't holler at him when we were at the beach." As soon as she said it, Becca wished she could snatch her words back. They sounded so uncharitable.

But Joshua didn't seem perturbed. He merely sat back in his chair, laced his fingers together behind his head, and said, "Yesterday I would have."

The quiet of the evening was broken by an approaching car, which turned out to be Jim's van. They all watched as Alton and Spider jumped out.

Joshua had left the keys in the truck as planned. Spider called out, "Thanks!" as he walked to his truck and drove away.

Alton turned back to the van and said something to Jim. They could hear the sound of Jim's solid, calm voice, but Becca couldn't make out what they were discussing. Then the van drove off, and Alton made his way toward their building. When he noticed them all sitting outside, he walked to the patio and hopped over the waist high railing.

"That was an interesting experience."

Joshua stood to fetch another chair, but Alton stopped him. "I've been sitting in the Port A jail for several hours. I'm happy to stand, though I could use a soda if you have one."

Becca hurried inside to pull a cold drink from the refrigerator. She'd shut the door to the appliance and was turning to head back outside when she bumped into Joshua, knocking her *kapp* askew.

"Careful now," he said.

"I didn't hear you walk inside."

"You didn't hear me ask if there were any cookies left?"

"*Nein.* I suppose I was distracted. My thoughts are scattered all over the place."

"Then we should unscatter them." He righted her *kapp* and then kissed her softly, briefly.

"I'm proud of you," she said when she could catch her breath.

"For?"

"Everything." She reached up and touched his face, and then she stood on her tiptoes and planted a kiss on his lips. Making no attempt to explain herself, she turned and walked back out to the patio.

Alton accepted the can of soda and took a long pull from it before setting it down on the table.

"What was the jail like?" Sarah asked.

"Same as an Oklahoma jail."

It occurred to Becca that he was the only person there who could make that comparison.

"Actually, it was a bit different because it was in a FEMA trailer, but the bars and bad furniture were the same."

"Did they charge you with anything?" Nancy asked.

"No. But we had to pass a few tests before they would let us go."

"Tests?" Sarah glanced from Becca back to Alton.

"Sure. First they checked our pupils. Then we had to tilt our head back, close our eyes, and count to thirty."

"Seriously?" Joshua shook his head in disbelief.

"Oh, yeah. If you're drunk or high, they say you can't do it. After that, there was the heel-to-toe-walking test and then the stand-on-one-leg test."

"Show us." Becca felt the urge to laugh. It all sounded so absurd. Alton might be a free spirit, he might be indulging his *rumspringa*, but take one look at him and you would know he didn't do drugs. Then again, she hadn't known anything was wrong with Sarah's father. She supposed people could become good at hiding stuff.

Alton stood, raised his right leg, and began to count. By the time he reached twenty they were all laughing.

"You look like one of the pelicans on the beach," Nancy said.

"I guess we were lucky. Because we passed all the tests, they didn't need to take urine or blood samples."

"Ack." Sarah crossed her arms. "I don't like needles."

"Once they'd confirmed that neither of us had anything to do with the drugs found in the backpack, we just had to fill out some paperwork and then we were free to go."

"Sounds like a lot of trouble for a bag of marijuana. I'm certainly against drugs, but..." Joshua shook his head.

"Turns out the bag also contained prescription and illegal drugs. They found some bottles of hydrocodone as well as some cocaine."

They were all silent for a few minutes. Becca thought she was just beginning to understand the implications of the police investigation.

If Alton had been found guilty, he may have had to stay in the Port A jail. It didn't bear thinking about.

"And Spider?" Joshua sat there, looking relaxed and studying his brother.

"The backpack wasn't his."

"So why did they take you both in?" Becca asked.

"Procedure. I guess we could have been lying, but when they opened the pack they found a scrap of paper with Zach's name on it. I think that was how he was paid. He'd leave the bag on the beach. The buyer would pick it up, and the money would be left in a post office box under Zach's name."

"Seems rather chancy," Sarah said. "Anyone could have picked up the bag."

"Maybe a tourist would. I think the locals know not to pick up bags that aren't yours."

"How did you learn all this?" Joshua asked.

"Spider. He's been aware of the growing drug problem in the area, but he had no idea Zach was involved."

"Wait." Becca rubbed her fingers across her chin. "Isn't Zach the clean-cut one?"

"He is." Alton seemed amused by their confusion. "Sometimes it's the clean-cut guys you have to worry about. Turns out the police have been watching him. They obtained a search warrant for his house and were headed out there as we left."

"To arrest him?" Joshua asked.

"Yes. For the sale and distribution of marijuana, prescription drugs, and cocaine."

"Wow." Sarah fiddled with the strings of her prayer *kapp*. "Just...wow."

"Unbelievable." Joshua leaned forward. "You're telling me the glassy-eyed kid who called me 'bro' and looked as if he hadn't been sober in weeks was not involved?"

"You're talking about Dax. Nah. He's clean."

"But he looked so..."

"Spaced? Yeah. He has terrible allergies and has been taking meds for it. We warned him about surfing that way, but he wouldn't listen. Turns out the combination of sun and saltwater made him pretty sick. A paramedic was called to help him."

"Tonight?" Becca asked. "On the same beach?"

"Yup. Busy place." Alton finished his soda.

"What are the odds?" Joshua asked. "What are the chances that Dax would get sick at the same moment that a drug-seeking dog sniffs out someone's stash?"

"I suppose they're low." Alton shrugged. "Odd things happen all the time, though."

"Maybe. Or maybe Dax was looking for an escape route, so he wouldn't be taken in and questioned."

"But there were no drugs in his bag." Alton stood and stretched. "I'm beat. Think I'll head on to bed."

Nancy and Sarah followed soon after, leaving Becca on the patio with Joshua, once again watching the stars adorn the Texas sky. She would miss these quiet moments with him when they returned home.

"Do you think Dax could be in on it?" she asked.

"I'm not sure. I don't know Dax all that well, and the fact that Spider came away clean—well, that surprises me."

"Because of how he looks?"

"Maybe. Probably." Joshua crossed his arms on the table and dropped his head.

Becca had to lean closer to hear the last thing he said.

"All I know is that Alton is too trusting, too naive."

Becca gave in to the urge to reach toward him and brush his hair back from his face. He looked up, smiled at her, and caused her heart to skip into a triple rhythm.

Joshua's expression turned somber. "I had a change of heart today, but that doesn't mean the world became a better, safer place. I'm afraid Alton is involved in something he doesn't understand at all."

CHAPTER 48

Charlie didn't want to be a bother at the job site, but it was difficult for him to stay away. There were plenty of other things for him to do during the week. The island was full of people who needed help clearing away debris. On Tuesdays and Thursdays he drove over to Rockport or Corpus Christi for supplies that folks needed. And he stopped by Alice's apartment on the mainland at least once a week to take dinner and check on the kids.

But the MDS site had an immense pull on him. He loved watching the young people work, and Jim was a good manager. He didn't stereotype as to what someone could or couldn't do. In the last two weeks, Charlie had seen little, graceful Sarah Yoder hanging drywall and big, muscular Joshua Kline planting flowers in the front beds of Alice's house. When you were finished with one task you were given another—whatever needed to be done. Gender or age weren't usually a factor.

That approach worked well with the MDS crews. It meant a lot of variety for the workers in addition to providing some good laughs for everyone watching. Alton's attempt to add shelf paper in Alice's kitchen was a case in point. He ended up with the stuff stuck to his arms from his wrists to his shoulders.

It was no wonder that Charlie enjoyed stopping by the site to visit, and Quitz trotted by his side, eager to see friends new and old.

But when Charlie showed up on Wednesday, expecting to hear the weekly testimony, the crew's mood was somewhat somber. He'd heard about the trouble at the beach with Alton and his friends. Although it hadn't resulted in any charges against the young man, it seemed to have put a damper on their spirits. There were fewer smiles and jokes, and everyone looked a bit tired.

The couple scheduled to give their testimony were Rodney and Jalynn Thomas. They brought large pots of seafood gumbo once a week, and their home was next door to Alice's. Charlie realized they had been Alice's neighbors for years, but he'd never taken the time to get to know them before the storm. Today Rodney and Jalynn stood up and told about the day they had evacuated from Port A.

The two were African-American and in their early fifties. Charlie knew they were both hard workers, as he'd seen their applications. They loved the island and would do their best to give back to the community.

"I drove a school bus until Orion hit," Rodney said, running a calloused hand across the back of his neck. "After that...well, we had some families come back to the island with their children, but not as many. Not nearly as many. The school district needed only half the bus drivers, so I was laid off."

"I found other work easily enough, but it wasn't what I was used to doing. I knew bus driving, knew my routes, and I was good with the kids. Suddenly, I'm hauling loads of debris across the island for half the hourly wage I'd made before. It's been a tough change. I miss the kids. I miss the job I once had, though there's always a chance that more families will eventually come back and I'll get rehired."

He cleared his throat and glanced over at his house, which would soon be finished. "This program has made it possible for us to stay on the island. We're grateful to MDS, more grateful than we can say. We appreciate what you all do every day. That's why my wife brings the gumbo and whatever else we can put together."

Alton groaned at the mention of gumbo, and Sarah said, "I told you not to go back for a third helping."

Soft laughter from the group helped to ease the intensity of Rodney's story.

Then Jalynn stood up. She was a larger woman, and usually wore polyester slacks with a T-shirt proclaiming some slogan. Today her shirt was psychedelic and said *Jesus Freak*. Her hair was cut nearly as short as Charlie's, and she wore dangly pink earrings. Charlie had met women like her before—mothers and grandmothers who took care of their children and grandchildren. It was obvious she was tough and didn't cave because of hard work. You could also tell that her faith had helped her hold her family together.

"First thing I want to say is praise Jesus, who has saved my soul, who protected my family, and who provided an island for us to come back to." Murmurs of "Amen" sounded from Charlie's left and right. "You all think you came here on your own, but I know differently. I know God brought you here."

A smile spread across her face, deepening her age lines but also softening her expression. It seemed to Charlie that she actually radiated the love of God. "And for young Alton, I saved you a piece of pecan pie for after you've digested those three bowls of gumbo. Lord, but that boy can eat."

Now there was open laughter and Charlie joined in. Alton put both hands on his stomach and said, "Give me another half hour."

"Oh, child, I'm not going anywhere." Her face grew more somber. "And that's what I want to talk to you about. I'm staying here. Rodney and I are staying here, and I pray to the good Lord each night that my children and grandchildren will return. Some folks may say we're crazy. Well, that won't exactly be the first time we heard such."

She slowly scanned the crowd, and when she met Charlie's gaze she nodded slightly. "Life is hard, amen? But the good Lord never gives us more than we can handle. What Rodney didn't mention was that times were hard even before Orion hit. I stayed home when my children were young. I was a homemaker and proud to be one. But once the children married and moved to their own place, I took a job cleaning some of the condos out on the beach."

White teeth and a large smile again. "I know you've been by them. Big, monstrous things. Houses that cost more than you or I will make in ten years. And I liked my job. I liked taking a place that was dirty, messy, and sometimes neglected and turning it into something sparkling and beautiful. Lord, but I would pray as I worked. Pray that Jesus would shine His love on all His children—the rich and the poor alike."

Rodney bowed his head and stared at the ground, as if he knew what was coming.

"Then I fell. It was my fault, and I won't be blaming anyone else. Got in a hurry and tripped over my own two feet walking out to my car. Broke my arm, this one I favor slightly. It was a bad break too—had to have surgery and pins put in. Now if I go through an airport screening machine, I'm going to set that thing off like fireworks on the Fourth of July."

Charlie noticed Becca lean over and say something to Joshua. Something about her mother and a broken foot.

"The worst part was that I couldn't work, and my job didn't provide paid sick leave. Some of the people I cleaned for gave me a few weeks' pay, which they didn't have to do. It was appreciated. Even though folks may be different, God can show us that we share a common decency. The medical bills…well, they were covered after we met our deductible. Our church helped us to do that, God bless them. But we had to let some things go. We had to tighten our belts."

Her voice dropped as she confessed, but everyone heard. They were transfixed on Jalynn and her story.

"We turned off the cable and started eating things we could catch, like that gumbo you just enjoyed. We stopped paying the flood insurance. Didn't know, couldn't even imagine the destruction of Orion. We fled in the path of that black storm—all of us went inland. What a sight we must have made—three cars stuffed with children and grandchildren and pets."

She tilted her head and glanced at Quitz. Charlie knew she was remembering that October day and that long trip, the road that seemed to stretch out forever. The evacuation routes that had turned both sides of the freeway into northbound lanes—escape lanes.

"We also took a few changes of clothes and some photographs. That's about all that would fit. When we returned—our home was gone. Our possessions had been scattered across the gulf. But our children were safe. Our grandbabies were healthy and alive. Praise God, amen?"

Now there was a rousing chorus of "Amens!" in response.

"We didn't know where we would live when we saw that our home was gone. How could we ever afford to rebuild? But we prayed. We prayed and we believed." Jalynn raised her hand to the sky, testifying to God's ways. "His grace is amazing. We'd never heard of MDS, but God, He brought us Jim. He brought us work crews with people from places we have never been. He brought us you—each one of you."

She reached down for Rodney's hand and clasped it with her own. "We will testify and tell of what you have done for us. We'll tell our children and our grandchildren and our neighbors. And when we do, we'll give the glory where it belongs—to our God."

The applause was thunderous.

Tears stung Charlie's eyes, but he didn't even attempt to wipe them away. Why would he? Gratitude and joy were not things to be ashamed of.

He stayed and helped for the rest of the afternoon, though there wasn't a lot he could do. His shoulder had ached worse than ever the last few days, probably because of a storm that was predicted to land before morning. Nothing dangerous. Just a south Texas squall.

It was when he was helping Joshua store the day's tools that he had the idea. "If you're not busy tonight, I'd like to take you out to see my place."

Joshua looked around confused. "No offense, but doesn't it just look just like ours? You're in a FEMA trailer, right?"

"I am, but that's not what I'm talking about. I'd like to take you out to see my home—my little piece of property."

Alton had walked up behind them. "Can I go too?"

"Of course."

"Not surfing tonight?" Joshua asked.

"The guys couldn't make it. I could go alone." He shrugged and added, "But alone isn't much fun."

Charlie thought it was more than that, but he didn't call Alton on it. The boy would share when he was ready to.

"Nancy made sandwiches for dinner. I'm sure there's extra."

"Sounds good."

An hour later the three of them were in the front seat of Charlie's old truck, Quitz sitting on the smaller bench seat in the back, her nose pushed out the partially opened window. Charlie drove out toward the state park, and then he turned on the road that led to his home. He tried to see it as Joshua and Alton might, but his memories of the past overlay the destruction of the present.

CHAPTER 49

*J*oshua couldn't have said what he'd expected to see, but it wasn't the heap of rubble Charlie parked in front of. It looked two, maybe three stories high. Parked a few yards away and to the south was a small FEMA Urban Disaster Trailer.

"Welcome to my place, or what was my place." As soon as Charlie opened the back door, Quitz leapt out and headed for the corner of the rubble where she marked the spot.

"Apparently Quitz still thinks of the place as home," Alton said.

"Yeah. There are more strays than before the storm, though Animal Control is doing their best to rescue them and reunite them with their families. Quitz catches their scent and has to reassert herself."

They all laughed as she ran to a different spot. The laughter helped, but it didn't mitigate what they were seeing. Charlie's place was a wreck.

A good part of the structure was simply gone. Joshua could tell where it had been because of the foundation, but what lay on top of it was rubble.

"You had a swimming pool?" Alton walked over and craned his neck back to stare up at what was clearly a water slide.

"No. All sorts of things landed here that aren't mine. Orion's sustained winds were 140 miles per hour, with gusts up to 155. Technically, it was a Cat 4, but it was at the top end of that category. It blew over nearly everything in its path, and the rising water finished destroying what the wind left."

"So this was all swept back from…" Joshua turned in a circle until he spotted condos farther down the beach. "From those?"

"Possibly. The debris was pushed inland and mixed with structures that had collapsed there. When the tide receded, things came out in different locations. I've found a street sign from Corpus Christi, someone's driver's license from Rockport, and even part of a business marquee from over in Copano Bay."

"How far away is that?" Joshua asked.

"Sixty miles by road, though I'm sure the storm took a shorter path."

"Why is all this still here, Charlie?" Alton waved toward the pile of debris. "You help at the job site nearly every day. Why aren't you taking care of your own place?"

"That's a good question, and I'm not sure I have any sort of answer." He paused, but then he changed topics. "Let me show you around."

He led them across the lot, pointing out where the house had been. He explained that all of the living area had been on the second floor, and he showed them how the windows had overlooked the gulf. He finally stopped at a small area that had been a vegetable garden.

"Madelyn loved fresh tomatoes, cucumbers, and even green beans. She planted all sorts of things. One year she planted small gourds, dried them, and turned them into bird feeders. The garden was something I kept going after she passed, though I can't cook nearly as well as she did."

He pointed to what Joshua recognized as a strawberry plant. Its green leaves and white flowers were a testament to the strangeness of tragedy, destruction, and its aftermath.

Charlie whistled for Quitz, and they all walked down to the beach.

"The property isn't very wide, but it is deep."

"Nice beachfront," Alton noted. "You could probably get a good price for it."

"I had several offers before the storm, and I've had one or two since, though they're offering a lot less. I expect that once the reconstruction is done the value will go back to what it was." He waved away the idea. "It's not the price that holds me here though. It's the memories."

The sun was beginning to set, a giant orange ball that dropped steadily toward the water. An enormous wall of clouds rose in the sky to the south. To Joshua, they were as impressive as any he'd seen in Oklahoma, and they were only what the locals called a squall. They promised to bring a good rain. He couldn't even imagine what Orion must have looked like.

"Great surfing spot, Charlie. You're making me wish I'd brought my board." Alton grinned sheepishly. "Though I have no experience surfing in these types of waves."

The white caps rose and crashed, leaving a foamy residue. Indeed, they were higher than normal, higher and more dangerous. Was that the reason Alton hadn't surfed tonight? Had he actually used common sense? Joshua regretted the thought as soon as he acknowledged it. His brother had worked hard all week, and there had been no further contact from the police. Perhaps they were out of trouble as far as the drug charges were concerned.

Charlie walked over to a large tree trunk. No doubt it had been dumped there by Orion. He sat, picked up a small stick and threw it for Quitz. The dog loped down the beach, but when she brought it back, she dropped it several feet from Charlie and sat, her head resting on top of her paws, her eyes on her owner.

"That means she's tired," Charlie said.

"This must be hard on you two." Joshua sat beside him. "Living in a FEMA trailer when your home is wrecked."

"Yes and no. Yes, we miss the place, but no in matters of convenience. It's probably better for both of us not to have to go up and down the stairs multiple times each day. Quitz has hip dysplasia. I give her a pill for it each night, but there's not much they can do other than a total hip replacement."

"Sounds expensive."

"Yeah, it is, but money isn't the only consideration. At her age surgery has it risks. Sometimes…well, sometimes it seems wiser to choose the problems you know how to deal with."

"And you?" Joshua joked.

"I'm just getting old. I can still make my way around a job site, though." Charlie laughed and dug his foot into the sand.

Alton had been standing, studying the surf, but he finally turned his attention back to Charlie. "Is that why you haven't rebuilt? Because of health reasons? You had flood insurance, right?"

"Sure. I received my compensation already. I could start any day, I guess. But there are a lot of things I haven't figured out yet."

Alton sat on the sand. When he did, Quitz stood and padded over to his side. She turned once, twice, and then a third time before curling up beside him, her tail thumping, her eyes nearly closed.

"What kind of things?"

"Do I need a place as big as what I had? Is that the best use of the insurance money? Is selling out to one of the big condo owners the right thing to do? While I wouldn't want to live in one, they provide a lot of jobs for locals, and they allow people from all over Texas to enjoy the beach. Maybe a condo here wouldn't be such a bad thing."

"Are you thinking of leaving the island?" Joshua asked.

"No. But there are plenty of other properties. We could move closer to town, closer to Alice and the kids. I've even thought of purchasing the empty lot next door to hers."

"In the meantime, why don't you let us help you clear this wreckage away?" Joshua glanced from the giant pile of debris to Charlie. "There's no telling what we might find that could hold memories—"

"My memories are here." Charlie tapped his heart. Then he glanced out at the ocean. "I stopped by the house to pick up the bag I'd already packed as well as some things for Quitz. At the last minute, I glanced around the room and saw a picture, one that was particularly special. I grabbed it and put it with the other things I wanted to take with me."

"What was the picture of?" Joshua asked.

"Madelyn and me and Quitz. We were walking down the beach, and Madelyn stopped to ask someone to take our picture with her cell phone. She was like that. She would talk to just about anyone. After the person had taken it, Madelyn turned to me and made me promise that I would always remember to treasure the blessings in this life."

Joshua could tell it was an emotional memory for Charlie. He swallowed, as if his grief threatened to rise and choke him. Slowly the customary smile returned to his face. "That picture meant a lot to me because we'd found a place in our life where we were happy, where we were satisfied. We took it probably three months before she learned about the cancer."

"I'm so sorry, Charlie." Joshua realized that so many of the things that he worried about were minor details. He actually had very little to fret over.

"The picture was in my bag, and the bag was swept away along with my old truck. They found the truck across the bay. It had come to rest in a playground, right on top of a merry-go-round."

"And the bag?"

"Gone. It floated away in the surge, I suppose. The truck's windows were shattered, and a tree lay inside the cab." He waved at the debris in front of them. "I thought I needed the things in my home, but I don't. And I thought I needed that bag, and the picture of my life, of Madelyn."

"Wouldn't you like to have them?" Alton was studying him closely.

"I would. But whatever is under that pile of rotten wood is ruined. The memories I hold in my mind and my heart, they are like new."

Alton nodded as if he understood, but Joshua wasn't sure he did. How did Charlie resist cleaning up this mess? He was a hard worker, and even Joshua had been able to see in the two weeks he'd been there that Charlie had a lot of friends. He could get the help if he wanted it.

"That's not why I brought you out here though, to show you what I've lost. I brought you here to show you what a difference you are making in peoples' lives. The families whose houses you're working on—they lost every bit as much as I did. The difference being, they didn't receive an insurance check."

He leaned forward, elbows on knees, and looked from Joshua to

Alton. "We can argue about how they should have kept their insurance premiums current, but it's a moot point. The fact is, they need help and you're providing it. That's something you both should be proud of. I'm certainly grateful for you and the girls and all the workers with MDS. They're not the only ones, either. We've had Red Cross, Baptist Men, and Methodist response teams. That terrible storm from the gulf sought to destroy us, but instead it brought together a special group of people and allowed them to minister to others in need."

Charlie smiled, slapped his leg, and stood.

"That's it?" Alton stood too. "You brought us out here to give us a pep talk?"

"Yeah. You both looked like you could use one today."

They walked back toward the truck, side by side, the light fading and raindrops beginning to splatter the pavement.

Joshua wasn't sure he felt pepped up. Sunday's highs and lows had exhausted him, and the work had been somewhat grueling the last few days. In addition, he was beginning to miss home—wondering about his crops and even counting the days until they left.

But as they drove away from the beach, he realized he was glad he'd come. He had a new appreciation for the old guy driving them back to their trailer and for the people in Port Aransas, Texas, who had endured the worst that nature could throw at them and refused to be defeated.

CHAPTER 50

*B*ecca lay in bed, awake but not yet willing to open her eyes. Thoughts of going home filled her with a wide array of emotions, and she wanted to think about them before the day's activities began. What exactly was she feeling?

Excitement to see her parents again.

Worry for Sarah and the situation she was returning to.

Uncertainty about her and Joshua. Were they courting? Would he continue to care about her in Cody's Creek, or was it just that they had been thrown together for a few weeks?

How would Alton act once they returned? Had the trip matured him or only taught him new ways to find trouble, to indulge his *rumpsringa*?

Even with these questions, she was sure of two things. The trip had given her a new compassion for people who were far from her home, and she cared deeply for Joshua Kline.

Joshua and Alton had visited the site of Charlie's home on Wednesday. Joshua had come back to the trailer and told her and Sarah and Nancy all about it. Alton hadn't joined their evening discussion as he usually did. Begging exhaustion, he'd gone to bed.

On Thursday they had all worked with increased vigor, though their activities had been limited to indoor work while rain pummeled the ground.

Becca realized with a start that it was Friday. Feelings of excitement surged through her veins. She sat up in bed, trying to remember why this day was special. Sarah stood next to their dresser, already dressed and braiding her hair.

"Looks like a *gut* day for Alice to move in," she said. "The rain has stopped, and the weather forecast calls for abundant sunshine."

That was it. That was what she was so excited about. Alice and Shelley and C.J. were to begin the move into their new home today.

Alice had taken the day off from the diner.

Half of the MDS team was going to the mainland to help move her boxes and furniture. Sarah, Becca, Alton, Nancy, Jim, and Simon were to travel over in the van.

Becca jumped out of bed and pawed through her bag of clothing, searching for clean things to wear and wondering if she had time for breakfast.

"You can slow down. Jim said he'd meet us out front at seven thirty." She nodded toward the clock between their beds. "You still have forty-five minutes."

Becca impulsively threw her arms around Sarah. "It's a *gut* thing you were here moving about or I might have slept until noon."

"I doubt that."

"I've never been so tired before. Building houses is hard work."

Becca gathered up her things and hurried down the hall to their shared bathroom. Ten minutes later she was at the table, drinking her first cup of coffee and trying to choose between the donuts left over from the day before or a piece of fruit.

"You'll probably need both," Nancy clucked. "Actually, I have time to fix you some eggs."

"There's no need—"

But Nancy was already pulling out a skillet. Within moments the sizzling smell of fried eggs awakened Becca's stomach. She jumped up to fix a piece of toast to go with them. Sarah had fled the room as soon as the eggs hit the pan. Becca was learning that certain days were easier for her friend than others, and mornings were often the worst part of the day—at least in regard to eating. She put a couple of the donuts into a bag in case Sarah decided she was hungry once they arrived at the apartment.

Soon they were all piling into the van.

Jim and Nancy took the front seats, which reminded Becca of their first trip in the van when they had come to the island together. That now seemed like an eternity ago.

Becca and Sarah sat in the second row, and Alton and Simon climbed into the very back. They claimed to like the back area where they could sleep if need be, but they had a rather comical time getting back there—hunching down and nearly tripping over their own feet. Everyone's spirits were high, and Becca turned around to see Charlie in his truck behind them.

She briefly wished that Joshua were coming as well, but he was working on framing the third house. He hadn't been able to make any progress on it the day before, and he was eager to get as much done as possible. She strained her neck to catch a glimpse of him, but they were already moving away from the houses and down the road.

"No worries, Becca. He won't forget you while you're gone." Alton sat back, a bemused expression on his face.

She would have liked to tease him in return, but his relationship with Sarah seemed to have changed into something like big brother–little sister. Besides, she didn't want to make things awkward for her friend. Instead, she settled for giving him a pointed look and turning around in her seat.

"Seems you've embarrassed her," Simon said.

"Do you think so?"

"I do. Her cheeks turned a nice rosy color."

"So she was embarrassed? I thought she was sunburned."

Becca pulled out her notebook and wrote a few notes for her mother, ignoring the banter behind her. They were driving toward the ferry, reversing the route they had taken that first day. Now she noticed different things driving through the downtown area of Port A. Construction on the new museum had begun. Several of the restaurants—still housed in FEMA trailers—had sandwich boards on the sidewalk displaying their lunch menu. The town seemed to be bustling with progress and optimism.

As soon as Jim had driven onto the ferry, Becca and Sarah jumped out of the van.

"I brought you two donuts for later."

"Let's give one to the birds."

They hurried to the back of the ferry, crumbling the cake donut in the bag and holding up small pieces as the ferry pulled away from the dock. The seagulls chattered and dove, causing Sarah and Becca to laugh and jump back—straight into Alton and Simon.

"Looks as if they're afraid of birds," Simon said.

"No wonder. A large seagull could carry either one of them off." Alton caught the piece of donut that Sarah threw at him and held it up to the birds.

When they had offered all of the donut, they moved to the middle of the boat. From there, Sarah and Alton decided they needed to go purchase a soda from the vending machines located inside the ferry. Becca thought that Sarah seemed happy, and when her mood was good her natural appetite returned.

"You turned serious all of a sudden," Simon said.

"Did I?" She glanced first left and then right. From where they stood, they could see both the island and the mainland.

"This has been a great experience." Becca glanced sideways and studied Simon. He was a genuinely nice guy. She was going to miss him.

"Are you glad you came?"

"Of course."

"Listen, Becca. We head out tomorrow, so I need to say this if I'm going to."

She felt her eyes widen but only nodded, afraid to speak at all, suddenly nervous about what he was about to tell her.

"No need to look like a doe caught in a hunter's scope."

"Huh?"

"Never mind. What I wanted to say is that I can tell there's something special between you and Joshua, and I wish you both the best."

"*Danki.*"

"But if that doesn't work out, and you decide you miss Texas, I'd love to see you again."

"You would?"

"Yes." He pulled a slip of paper from his pocket and handed it to her. "That's my cell phone number, email address, and street address in case you ever want to talk."

"Oh."

"And if you decide to come on another mission trip, be sure to let me know. Whether we're just friends or…or more, I'd like to see you again."

"You are a *gut* friend, Simon. I don't know exactly what Joshua and I are to each other. But thank you for this—" she held up the slip of paper and then tucked it into the pocket of her dress. "It's nice to know I have friends outside of Cody's Creek."

Alton and Sarah chose that moment to join them, each carrying a Coke and a candy bar.

"Wow. You two are going to be energized." Becca laughed. "You'll be like two rambunctious toddlers with all of that sugar in your system."

"We're hardly toddlers," Sarah said.

"No matter. You'll have lots of energy, which is a *gut* thing." Simon rubbed his chin as if he was thinking deeply, and then added, "Becca and I can sit back and watch you and Alton do the bulk of the work."

But once they were at the apartment, a dismal place located behind a retail complex, everyone worked. Fortunately, the apartment was downstairs. Simon, Alton, and Jim immediately began loading furniture into the truck that Alice had rented. Sarah and Becca carried boxes from the kitchen and bedrooms.

The apartment was small—only one bedroom with twin beds where the children slept. Alice apparently slept on the couch. How long had they been there? Becca counted back to when Orion had landed in October. And now it was May. Seven months? It was a long time to sleep on a couch. Yet Alice had managed to add small touches to the apartment—colorful curtains in the children's room, a reading corner in the living room, and plants scattered here and there.

Nancy helped Alice finish up the last bit of packing.

They worked as a team, and by the time they took a break for lunch, Becca looked up to see the truck half full. "It's going faster than I thought it would."

"I'll be surprised if we fill up the entire thing." Alice was wearing an old ball cap. She pulled her hair, fastened with a ponytail holder, more tightly through the back of the cap. "All we took with us, when we evacuated, were pictures, legal papers, and clothes. What furniture we have I found in garage sales or charity auctions where most things went for under ten dollars."

"It must be terrible to lose all of your things."

"It is…it was…but it bothers me less than I thought it would. I'm so grateful that the children were unhurt, and now…" She gave Becca a dazzling smile. "Now we have a new home. Some days I have to pinch myself. It seems too good to be true."

"We're so happy for you," Becca said.

"And we can't wait to see C.J. and Shelley settled in," Sarah added. "Will they come over this afternoon?"

"I couldn't keep them away if I tried. They'll be out of school at three."

"Which means we need to finish up this pizza and get the rest of your boxes loaded," Jim said.

Alton and Simon moved a little more slowly, but soon they were all back at it, and by two in the afternoon there was little left to do but clean the apartment.

"I can come back and do that tomorrow," Alice said.

"Nonsense. You'll be unpacking tomorrow. We'll take care of this for you."

Simon offered to drive them back in the van. Jim, Alton, and Alice left in the moving truck.

It took another two hours. Alice was a good housekeeper, but some things were hard to see until a room was completely empty. By the time they were finished, Becca and Sarah were ready to take a nap in the back of the van.

"You might want to stay awake," Simon said, his eyes twinkling as they met Becca's in the rearview mirror.

"Why would we want to do that?"

"Simon's taking us home a different way." Nancy fastened her seatbelt. "I think you girls will enjoy it."

Simon explained that the lines for the ferry could be quite long on a Friday afternoon. Instead, they were going to drive around via the bridge. "It's a little farther, but this way I can pick up some building supplies Jim ordered. We'll save him a trip next week."

Fighting the urge to put her head back and rest, Becca watched out the window. They stopped at a builder's supply store, and Sarah drifted off to sleep, basking in the afternoon sunshine. Soon the supplies were loaded in the back and they were on their way again. When Becca saw the bridge rising in the distance, she nudged Sarah awake. She could see the crest of the bridge but not the other side. Sarah leaned over Becca, trying to get a better view.

"Officially, it's named the John F. Kennedy Memorial Causeway," Simon explained. "But some of the old-timers still call it Don's Bridge."

"Who was Don?" Nancy asked.

"The TXDOT engineer who was in charge of building the bridge."

"What does TXDOT stand for?" Becca kept her nose pressed against the window. It was amazing what she could see from the top of the bridge—water, houses, boats, and plenty of other vehicles below. Everything looked miniaturized. It was a view she'd never had from a buggy, not that they had such large bridges or bodies of water in their part of Oklahoma.

"Texas Department of Transportation. They built this bridge to replace the old swing/lift bridge—that bridge was a problem because there would be long waits for boats to get through."

"But now they just go under," Sarah said.

"Exactly. And currently the state has plans to build an even taller bridge on the other end—where the Harbor Bridge currently is. If that happens, then they'll be able to dock cruise ships out of this area."

"Cruise ships?" Sarah sat back, covering a yawn with her hand. "Maybe they will make an Amish cruise ship—one with no television or casinos, but lots of time for reading and sitting by the pool."

When Simon met Becca's eyes in the rearview mirror, she explained, "I think she learned about that in a book she's been reading."

Once they had crossed the bridge, most of the construction disappeared. They soon passed a sign that said "Mustang Island State Park" and then they were in a vicinity she recognized.

They were nearly back to their trailers when Becca asked, "Orion didn't harm the bridge?"

"No, it didn't. There were some who predicted the bridge wouldn't hold. Orion may have swept a path of destruction, but at least the bridge remained. It was useful in getting help in quickly once the hurricane passed through."

He'd pulled up in front of the houses they were working on. Alice's moving truck was already backed up onto the small driveway, and Alton and Joshua were unloading her items. Nancy and Sarah spilled out of the van and headed toward the house. Becca held back, standing beside the van and studying Simon. "You know a lot about this area."

"I guess I picked up stuff here and there. Happens when you visit as often as I do."

"How far is it to your home?"

"Seminole is about six hundred miles, give or take a little." When Becca glanced left and right, he turned her to face the northwest. "It's that way. Not too far from Lubbock."

"What's it like there?"

"Dry, dusty, hard to farm."

"And you like it?"

"I do, but I also like visiting the coast. It's a nice change of pace, and it's *wunderbaar* to see water and rain for a change."

Jim called out, asking Simon to grab the other end of the couch.

Becca hurried across the street to put up her backpack and use the restroom. While she was there, she took a moment to glance at herself in the mirror—something she rarely did at home. She saw a Plain girl, with rosy cheeks, a nose that was a little too large, and freckles sprinkled across her cheeks.

Becca felt sure she was the same person who had left Cody's Creek a little more than two weeks ago, but she also realized that she had changed. She was older—maybe not in years, but in her outlook. She didn't feel like a child anymore. And there was another thing. She realized she was less worried about who she was and who she would become. Maybe such thoughts came from too many hours alone, but her time in Texas had moved her perspective out and away from herself.

She couldn't imagine living in the dry land that Simon described, or driving down every few months—driving six hundred miles—to work on homes in Port Aransas. But she could imagine God using her in the future the way He had used her here. And whether it was with Joshua or not, she could certainly trust Him to direct their paths the way they were meant to turn—either together or apart.

CHAPTER 51

The next afternoon part of their group met to dedicate Alice's house. The Mennonite group had left at first light, headed back to Seminole, Texas. They had vowed to return in three months to continue the work. When they did, they would check in on Alice.

All of Alice's things had been moved in the day before. There were still a few boxes to unpack and curtains to be hung, but basically their work was done.

The other two groups of MDS volunteers had driven over to participate in the home dedication. It wasn't required—they could have spent their Saturday at the beach. But everyone understood what an important moment this was, and they wanted to share it with Alice and her grandchildren, even if they hadn't worked on that particular site.

The little house was brimming over with MDS volunteers.

Joshua peeled off from a group of men and walked across the kitchen to settle next to Becca. She stood in the front of the sink, her hands braced against the porcelain as she stared out the window.

She didn't turn toward him but said, "Joshua, I can just imagine the vegetable garden Alice will have out there in the fall."

"Partitioning off part of the side yard was a *gut* idea. I could tell Shelley was quite excited about the prospect."

"They're learning about plants and how things grow in her second grade class. She's a smart little girl."

Becca glanced up at Joshua, and it seemed that a contented look spread across her face. Together they both returned their attention to the small plot of land outside the window. The garden consisted of a five-foot-by-five-foot raised bed bordered with landscape timbers. Earlier that day, Joshua had peered over the edge of the roof while he was checking on the house next door. They didn't work on Saturdays, but he usually walked through and noted what things had been done and what still awaited their attention. Jim had suggested he would make a good site coordinator, but Joshua didn't take that idea seriously. He was a farmer, through and through, though he'd learned some things about construction that he planned to speak to his father about. Their place could do with a bit of a remodel.

When he'd glanced over the fence, he'd seen Becca working in the dirt with the little girl, planting seeds. He'd realized at that moment what a good mother she would be. And he had admitted to himself—not for the first time—that he was in love with Becca Troyer.

She seemed to sense the serious direction his thoughts had taken and turned to study him. "I heard you boys are bringing pizza to the celebration tonight."

"*Ya*, and we heard you girls are grilling hot dogs."

Becca laughed. "I'm not sure how much help I'll be with an outside grill, but it will be nice to enjoy a cookout on the beach, even if our group is smaller."

"Do you miss Simon already?" The thought had caused Joshua to toss through much of the night. Did Becca care about Simon? Had he missed his chance to win her affections?

"Of course I do." She smiled up at him, and a part of his heart melted like ice cream spilled on a hot sidewalk. "We're good friends."

She emphasized the last word and then motioned with her head toward the group that had left the kitchen. It was their final pass through of the home. Alice lived here now. It was no longer an MDS worksite.

They moved slowly to catch up, and Joshua was glad for the chance to speak with Becca alone. Each day he'd looked forward to the little moments they found to be together, and he realized, with a start, that he would miss her quite a bit once they returned to Cody's Creek.

Breaking into those thoughts, she said, "From what Jim told us, there's an empty FEMA trailer, one near the beach. MDS keeps it in case they have extra volunteers, and they also use it for gatherings."

"Like tonight's."

"Exactly. The plan is to cook hot dogs outside, maybe walk the beach or go for a swim, that sort of thing—"

"Will you miss the ocean when we're back in Cody's Creek?"

She smiled a bit wistfully. "I will, but I have my bag of shells."

"And your notebook."

"Yes. And my notebook."

They caught up with the rest of the folks walking through the home. The other MDS groups, plus Alton, Sarah, Nancy, and Jim, were present. And of course there was Charlie, Quitz, Alice, and her two grandkids. They all barely fit into the combined living/dining room, but it seemed right to Joshua that everyone should be there. He didn't think he would ever forget the last few weeks. They had changed something deep inside of him—helped him to find a way out of his own self-preoccupation. Together they had done good work, and he looked forward to participating in such a project again.

"Pizza and hot dogs sound good, and a walk on the beach would be nice." He hesitated before lowering his voice and adding, "Though I'm not sure I have the energy for a late night."

"Oh, really?"

"*Ya.* I'm no spring chicken, you know."

"I didn't."

"Nearly twenty-eight. Do you think that's old, Becca?"

She blinked several times, as if she was unsure what he'd asked her. "*Nein.* Of course not. Too old for what exactly? Joshua Kline, I think you're teasing me."

"Maybe." He scratched at the sunburn on his face. "Maybe not. When all the groups get together we eat for hours."

"Hours, huh?"

"And then there's the bonfire."

"I could tell last time that you hated that part. We had to practically drag you away from the guy singing those cowboy songs."

"I heard one of the workers say he's bringing a volleyball and net. Ack! All of this fun is too exhausting. We might need to save our energy for church tomorrow and then one more week of work."

"Are you saying you're too old to hang out with us?"

"You are old, *bruder*." Alton was standing next to Sarah, shoulder to shoulder with her.

Joshua wondered about their relationship. He'd seen them the evening before, walking off together toward the end of the street to catch the bus. Alton had said they had gone to town for dessert and then walked the streets, looking at new construction by various groups. Joshua had been surprised that Alton wasn't surfing, but his brother had only shrugged. "Spider has a girlfriend now, so he doesn't go as often. We'll catch some waves tomorrow night, though."

One night with a girl, the next night surfing. His brother was a busy man. Though he'd been teasing Becca, he actually wouldn't mind a long afternoon nap.

"No one else is tired?" Joshua asked, bending forward and moving one hand to his back the way he'd seen old men do.

"You were framing a house yesterday." Sarah nudged him. "We only helped carry in boxes."

"We also unpacked a few," Becca reminded her.

"True, but I doubt it was anywhere near as exhausting as putting up a house."

"I offered to help when we got back from Alice's apartment," Becca said. Then she laughed. "If only you could have heard Jim's response to that. Ever since I nailed my sleeve to the wall two days ago, he's been keeping me away from the power tools."

Joshua glanced across the room at Jim and then back at Becca. "Jim turned down help?"

"He...um...gently reminded me that Alice wanted our help inside the house."

"I didn't mind getting an easy pass," Sarah said. "Someone needed to help her unpack, and I'm still sore from the work we did the day before."

"And the day before that. An easier day wasn't such a bad idea."

"You might have wanted to help with framing, but climbing the ladder in your dress would have been a problem—" Joshua stopped midsentence.

Charlie had moved to the end of the room and everyone fell silent. Alice was standing beside him, and next to her were the two grandkids—Shelley and C.J. Quitz stood close by, as always.

Charlie cleared his throat, looked around, and then addressed the group.

"We want to thank you all once again. Jim assures me that isn't necessary, but the way I was raised—well, it is. It's important to appreciate the people who have traveled a rough road with you. Alice, C.J., Shelley, and I thank the Lord for each and every one of you." He paused and took off his ball cap, staring at it as if he hadn't seen it before.

"You all know that my wife and I had just moved to the island in 1970, the year Celia hit." His hand came out, and he motioned toward something outside the window. "I told you this before, when I shared my testimony, but some things bear repeating."

He set the ball cap back on his head and continued. "My life was changed with that storm, and Madelyn's was too. We saw our neighbors in a new way. Through the aftermath of that horrific event, we carried each other's burdens—even if that burden was a stack of shingles headed up to the roof."

Laughter sprinkled throughout the room.

"Before she passed, Madelyn would sometimes remind me that the world had moved on. I know it's hard to imagine, but I'd become a bit cynical by then."

Joshua exchanged glances with Becca. They were standing very close to one another, and all eyes were on Charlie. Joshua couldn't resist. He reached over and laced his fingers with hers.

"Madelyn was right. Things have changed, but in spite of those changes you folks have reminded me that there is still a lot of good left in the world." He swiped at his eyes and laughed at himself. "You're fine folks, and we thank God that you came, you saw our need, and you helped."

Everyone clapped, and Shelley apparently asked Charlie to pick her up. When he did, a look of satisfaction crossed his face that brought a lump to Joshua's throat.

Alice held up a hand to quiet them. "I knew there was still good in the world because I care for these precious children every day. They remind me of all that is beautiful and true and honest. And Charlie—he's helped us since day one, since I first started serving him coffee."

Now there was outright laughter. Everyone knew how much Charlie loved his coffee.

"But he knew us." Alice's voice dropped lower, grew softer, and yet Joshua had no trouble hearing her. The group had gone completely quiet. "You didn't. We were strangers to you, but you gave us drink. You invited us in. You clothed us and you looked after us."

Alice's reference to Christ's words in Matthew stirred something deep in Joshua's heart.

"To me, those were just words from the Bible before, words maybe written for someone else. But now they're the reality of my life. I'm standing in my home because you have been the hands and feet of Christ to me. I am overwhelmed by your kindness, and I vow…I vow I will find a way to pass that kindness on to someone else."

When she'd finished, Jim stepped forward. "I invite you all to join with me in the dedication of this home."

CHAPTER 52

im had met with their group before leaving the day before, and he asked each person if they would like to participate in the blessing of Alice's home.

Of course they had all said yes.

Joshua stepped forward now, and read from the slip of paper Jim had given him. The verses were from the Book of First Peter. "'Above all, love each other deeply, because love covers over a multitude of sins. Offer hospitality to one another without grumbling...'" as he finished the passage, Alton stepped forward and read from his slip of paper.

"We dedicate this home to love and understanding..."

"We dedicate this home to work and leisure," the group responded.

The words splashed over them, sanctifying the home, the work they had done, and all of those involved in its building. In ten minutes it was done, but as Jim closed with a final prayer—a final blessing—Joshua realized that Alice's life in her new home was just beginning. As he bowed his head, he prayed that the years ahead would be filled with joy for her and the children.

When the prayer was ended, Sarah, Becca, and Nancy stepped closer together and sang "Surely Goodness and Mercy." Joshua had heard the hymn dozens of times, but still he found himself humbled by the words of the psalmist.

The gift-giving came next. Jim gave Alice a copy of the book, *The Hammer Rings Hope*. One of the other work crews stepped forward and offered her a quilt made in a log cabin pattern. Joshua recognized the pattern because it was so similar to the one on his own mother's bed. Lastly, Alice was given an envelope which contained money to help her get started—mainly it was one, five, and ten dollar bills, but everyone had donated something.

Alice was speechless, but C.J. wasn't. He tugged on her arm until she knelt down and whatever he whispered to her caused a smile to replace her tears. She nodded and said, "C.J. wants to know if it's time to play basketball."

Everyone began talking at once then. Several of the volunteers, men and women, followed C.J. outside, and soon Joshua heard the sound of a basketball on concrete.

Becca and Sarah had moved to the front of the room and were speaking with Alice and with little Shelley.

Joshua realized that he felt very close to these people, all of them, even his brother.

"It's been a *gut* trip. *Ya*?" Alton leaned against the wall, and though he was talking to Joshua, his eyes were on Sarah.

"It has. I'm glad we came."

"Me too."

"Sarah seems like a special girl."

"She is. No doubt, she is."

But he didn't elaborate, and before Joshua could respond he turned and walked out of the house. Still, at that moment Joshua had hope for his brother, more than he'd had in a long time. If he could fall in love with the right girl, perhaps he would settle down.

Fifteen minutes later, he wasn't so sure. Sarah was cutting cake and serving it with ice cream. She had saved back a piece for Alton. "See if you can find him, will you? Otherwise the ice cream will melt."

So Joshua had walked around the outside of the house, and indeed he had found Alton, standing with his back against the garage and smoking a cigarette.

He shook his head and reminded himself not to judge his brother. Had he actually thought that all of his behavior would change right away?

Alton studied him, as if waiting. But Joshua resisted the urge to lecture and instead set the paper plate on top of the hood of Alice's car.

"Sarah wanted you to have that."

"*Danki*. I was—" The chime of a cell phone interrupted him. Alton pulled his phone from his back pocket, read something, and then answered quickly, typing with his thumbs. "Surfing is on for tonight. Sure you don't want to come? Could be your last chance."

"*Nein*. I know nothing of surfboards."

"You're not as ancient and decrepit as you were pretending to be a few minutes ago. You could learn."

"I could—"

Their conversation may have turned into an argument, but C.J. had darted around the corner of the garage.

"There you are." He stopped short, staring at the cigarette in Alton's hand. "Nana says she used to smoke, but she gave it up."

"Smart woman," Alton continued to type on his phone.

"Are you gonna play with us?"

"Sure. Give me a minute."

C.J. rolled his eyes and walked away.

"That kid looks up to you."

"Uh-huh."

"Don't you want to be a *gut* example?"

"I'm not his father, Joshua. I won't even be here a week from now, and he'll forget me a week from that."

"I doubt it."

"Well, I have to live my life, and I think C.J. will be fine in spite of my rebellious ways."

"What's wrong with you, Alton? No. Don't even think of arguing with me. Since the police incident, you've been calmer, more like your old self. Now all of a sudden you're back to smoking, phones, and rudeness."

"I didn't mean to be rude." Alton dropped the cigarette to the ground and ground it out with his foot. "And I'm stopping those as soon as we start home. I just wanted to use up my last pack."

Joshua nodded, wanting to believe him. "So you're surfing with Spider?"

"Nah. He can't make it. Has a last-minute thing with his girlfriend."

"Then who—"

"Dax and Zach, and before you say anything, I spoke with Zach and he's completely innocent. He thinks somebody framed him. Someone who doesn't like him, obviously."

"Framed him?"

"Yeah. The police didn't find anything at his house, and they couldn't arrest him for something that wasn't in his possession. None of his fingerprints were on the stuff, either."

"He could have worn gloves."

"Or he could be innocent." Alton stuck his phone in his pocket, picked up the paper plate with the cake and melted ice cream, and walked toward the front of the house.

Joshua followed in his wake and rounded the corner of the garage as Jim was leaving.

"I'll come back for you two around six o'clock if that will work. Someone from the other group is going to pick up the ladies a bit earlier. Will that give you enough time to finish your game and clean up?"

"We'll be ready," Joshua said.

"Awesome. I can use your help picking up the pizza. I ordered quite a few."

But instead of going across the street with him to their FEMA trailer, Alton stopped outside to shoot some baskets with C.J. There was something in the way that boy looked at Alton that bothered Joshua. He stared at him with a sort of hero worship. He supposed that was normal enough in one so young, but he wasn't sure if his brother was quite ready for that level of adoration.

Joshua shook that thought from his mind. He needed to focus on tonight. He needed to think about how he was going to tell Becca about his feelings. He was going to tell her. They had one more week of work ahead, and he didn't want to spend a minute of it worrying about their future.

CHAPTER 53

*B*ecca enjoyed the evening at the beach. The sizzling hot dogs smelled and tasted delicious. The guys brought pizza and gallons of ice cream. Nicole from the other work group covered a table with all sorts of chips, sodas, and cookies. It was a lot of junk food and a ton of calories, but Becca finally understood that no one was watching her fill her plate.

She certainly hadn't lost any weight since coming to the island, but she had learned to accept who she was. For the first time she'd grown comfortable in her own skin. She no longer felt the need to count calories or berate herself for eating an entire hot dog.

She did groan after they had played a game of volleyball and Nicole set out fixings for ice cream sundaes.

"That looks so good, but I can't possibly eat anything else."

"Maybe you need another game of volleyball," C.J. said.

The child seemed to have limitless energy. Becca flopped back in her chair and pretended to sleep, which caused C.J. to laugh before leaving in search of better prey. Shelley and Alice had stayed at the house. The little girl was enamored with her bedroom and claimed she needed to put all her dolls in their special place. Charlie had agreed to bring C.J. and take him home early enough for his bedtime.

"If you're not actually asleep, a walk down the beach might energize you. Maybe even stir up an appetite."

She hadn't heard Joshua walk up behind her. His voice caused a flutter deep in her stomach, but it also made her inexplicably happy. Was that love? When being near someone, hearing them speak, caused a spark of joy deep inside?

"Are you asking me to go for a walk with you, Joshua Kline?"

"I am."

"Then I accept." Though the days were quite warm at Port A, the evening breeze over the water held a chill. "Let me find my shawl."

They were walking down the beach a few minutes later. The sun was nearly at the horizon, but there was still light to see by—enough to avoid the jellyfish that had washed up on the beach.

Becca smiled ruefully and said, "There's one thing I won't miss when we go home. Guess what it is."

"Jellyfish?"

"*Ya*. We've none of those in Oklahoma."

"Are you ready to go home, Becca?"

She hesitated before answering. Was she ready? She certainly missed her parents, but a part of her had enjoyed the full days of doing things she'd never tried before.

"I am, but I'll miss the work," she answered truthfully.

"Life on an Amish farm isn't busy enough for you?" His tone was light, but he reached over and snagged her hand.

"It is. Of course it is. There's always laundry to do or chickens to feed or produce to sell at our little stand."

"But…"

"I don't know. I was needed here, and that was nice. You know what I mean?"

"I do."

"It's very satisfying to help someone like Alice and her grandkids. People who desperately want and need our assistance."

"So you're saying you'd like to participate in another mission trip?"

"Yes! I'd love to." The thought lightened her heart. In truth, she was rather dreading the return to her mundane life. Or was it just that she'd no longer be seeing Joshua every day? Which was ridiculous. He lived down the road from her.

Joshua motioned to beach chairs that had been placed a few yards from the surf. Becca nodded, but she was surprised when she sat down and he picked up his chair, turning it to face her.

"Don't you want to watch the waves?"

"I'm looking at you, Becca. You're more beautiful than the Gulf of Mexico."

Heat soared into her cheeks, but she didn't respond. What was a girl supposed to say to something like that?

The silence stretched until she finally said, "Back home you're so…well, quiet. I don't know what to think when you say things like that."

"Maybe the salt in the air has given me courage."

He wiggled his eyebrows, and she laughed, grateful that he had lightened the moment. But her heart continued to beat rapidly as Joshua studied her in the fading light.

"Do you want to know what I'll miss most after we leave Texas?"

She nodded.

He reached forward and claimed her hand. "Seeing you each morning and each night. Sharing lunch with you. Watching you attempt to play volleyball."

"I'm not that bad."

"Hearing your laughter and knowing you're in the room with me. It's as if all of my senses are heightened when you're around, Becca. Everything seems more vivid. The colors are brighter." He shook his head, as if he had trouble believing what he was saying. "When you leave…well, I feel as if the world fades to black-and-white."

Becca wanted to say she felt exactly the same. She wanted to smooth the worried look off his face. But she sat mute, frozen, unable to move with her heart beating so fast she had to pull in a ragged breath.

Then Joshua did what she'd been hoping for since the night he'd kissed her in their trailer's kitchen. He leaned forward, cupped her face in his hands, and kissed her gently on the lips.

"I need you in my life, Becca. I want you in my life. When I think of us together, I find myself excited about the next day, month, years." He released her face and took her hand, rubbing his thumb over its palm. "When I hear Charlie talk about Madelyn, the love and adoration he had for her is still so strong. And that's what I feel for you, Becca. Do you... is it possible you could feel the same?"

"I do!" The words slipped from her mouth like the breeze sliding across her skin.

Darkness had fallen, and she couldn't see Joshua's expression clearly. But then he was standing, pulling her into his arms, and all of the worries about her future fell away. She didn't know exactly what lay ahead for them, but suddenly the details were not important. What mattered was that they had realized how much they cared for and needed one another. Funny that they hadn't done that back in their small hometown. Instead, it had taken traveling nearly seven hundred miles to help people they had never met.

They had found their love for one another amid Orion's wreckage.

CHAPTER 54

Charlie woke to Quitz's barking and someone banging on his trailer door. At first he thought he was back in his house, the one he had built for Madelyn. Then reality crashed in on him, as it often did upon waking. He remembered Orion, the destruction, and finally the FEMA trailer he was sleeping in.

Same location, different building, he thought.

Throwing on some clothes, he hurried to the front door. He flipped on the light as he pulled open the door. Standing on his step in a late-night drizzle was Alice.

"Is C.J. here, Charlie? Please tell me he's here."

"What...no."

All of the color drained from her face, and he thought she might collapse right there on his doorstep.

"Come in. You look as if you're cold. Tell me what's wrong. Something about C.J.? Have you checked his room and—"

"I've checked everywhere!" Alice's shoulders shook with sobs.

Charlie guided her to a chair at the table. Then he pulled a throw blanket off the couch and wrapped it around her shoulders. Before sitting down, he poured her a glass of water. "Drink this. Take slow, deep breaths, and then tell me what happened."

Quitz settled at Alice's feet, panting and looking worriedly from Charlie to Alice.

She nodded, closed her eyes, and attempted to sip the water, though her hands were shaking so badly that she spilled some of it onto the table.

"Don't worry about it." He mopped up the water with a dish towel. Sitting down next to her, he took her hands in his. "Now look at me, Alice. Slow and easy. What happened? The last I remember, we talked on the phone and you agreed C.J. could ride home with Joshua and Alton."

Alice nodded. "That's what he promised he would do. He wanted to stay a little later than you—"

"I came home earlier because Quitz's hip was bothering her."

"He wanted to stay and play a little more volleyball. But he promised, Charlie." Alice's gaze darted around the small kitchen, as if she might find C.J. if she only looked hard enough. "He promised he would come home with the boys, so I didn't worry."

"And he didn't?"

"No. By then I was watching out the front window, ready to ground him the minute I saw him. The clock inched past ten, and then nearly to eleven. A few minutes ago I heard Jim pull up in the van and then drive away again. I expected C.J. to come running into the house. I was so angry with him, but another part of me realized he's just a boy. He was excited about the house and you know how he looks up to—" A sob caught in her throat, and she pulled the blanket tighter around her shoulders. "He cares about both Alton and Joshua."

"What did Joshua say?"

"He said C.J. told him he was going to stay the night with you."

Charlie was finding his keys, jacket, and cell phone. "What about Alton? Did Alton know anything about where the boy is?"

"He didn't come home with Joshua. He had plans to meet some friends and go surfing."

"Night surfing?" Charlie glanced out the window even as he asked the question. The full moon confirmed his fears. No doubt Alton had fallen in with another reckless group of boys. Some of the young men who worked down on the docks thought they were impervious to danger. They were into extreme sports—including night surfing. Their age and foolishness were a terrible combination, but he said none of this to Alice.

"Who's with Shelley?"

"Nancy's staying with her. I hated to wake her up, but I didn't know what else to do."

"I'm sure she didn't mind."

"We've checked the house, Jim's van, and Joshua's house."

"All right. Let's go back to where we had dinner tonight. I want to check out the FEMA trailer on the beach. I'll drive. Call Jim and ask him to pick up Joshua. We'll need whatever help we can get to comb the beach."

"Should I call the police?"

"Yes. Tell them the boy has been missing..." He glanced at the clock over his kitchen sink. It was eleven thirty. "He's been missing three hours because I saw him right before I left at eight thirty. They may not start an official search yet, but they'll alert any officers on patrol to keep an eye out."

"Charlie, I can't lose C.J." Alice's voice had been shaky, but now it took on a steely resolve. "I won't lose him. Not after all we've been through. Not now, when things are finally starting to come together for us."

"Listen to me." He'd turned toward the front door, but now he stopped and put both hands on her shoulders. "Do not doubt for a minute that God is watching over that boy. I can't believe He saved C.J. from Orion only to take him from us now. We're going to find him, Alice."

She nodded, though she didn't appear convinced. That was all right with Charlie. The important thing was that a little ray of hope had come back into her eyes and the shaking had stopped. He opened up the hall closet and grabbed an extra coat that he insisted she wear. Then Quitz was following them out to his truck, and they were headed toward the last place he had seen the boy.

Alice insisted she could drive and might need her car, so she followed him to the beach.

By the time they pulled up to the FEMA trailer where they'd had dinner, Alice had made the necessary phone calls. "Jim is picking up Joshua and meeting us here. Nancy assured me that Shelley is still sleeping, and the police said they will inform all of their officers who are on duty. No set amount of time has to pass before they declare a child…missing."

Charlie reached over and squeezed her hand. "We'll find him."

Alice nodded and reached down to pat Quitz, who waited at her feet. "I know we will. They asked us to be in contact with everyone he's seen in the last twelve hours and then update them. If no one's seen him, they'll begin a full-scale search immediately."

CHAPTER 55

*B*ecca was not asleep when a car pulled up outside. She'd been lying in bed, playing the conversation with Joshua over and over in her mind. Savoring each moment of it. Dreaming, with her eyes wide open and staring up at the ceiling. Dreaming of their life together.

Then she heard the van.

When no one knocked on the door, she walked into the living room and looked out the window. She could just make out Jim talking on his phone, but then he started across the street toward their homes, and she could hear his footsteps on the stairs as he headed up to the boys' trailer. It was nearly midnight. She couldn't imagine why he had returned, but she knew it couldn't be good.

That was when she saw the note on the table from Nancy, saying that she was staying at Alice's, watching Shelley.

She hurried back to their bedroom and shook Sarah awake. "Something's wrong. Better get dressed."

Throwing on her clothes, her *kapp*, and a sweater, Becca hurried outside and up the stairs.

When she knocked on the boys' door, Jim opened it. "C.J.'s missing. Joshua is going with us to search. He's getting dressed."

"I'll go too."

She expected him to argue, but he nodded his thanks and said, "We'll need to tell Sarah where everyone's gone."

"She's dressing now."

"Good. The police want us to question everyone who was at the beach with C.J. tonight."

"What about Alice and Shelley?"

"Alice and Charlie are already at the beach. Nancy is staying with Shelley."

"Oh, yes. I read her note." Becca felt her thoughts were scattered like so many leaves in a storm. She ran back downstairs.

Sarah was fully dressed and pinning on her *kapp*. As she helped Becca straighten hers, she asked, "What's going on?"

"I'm not sure, but Jim needs us to go to the beach."

"The beach?" Sarah's gaze met Becca's in the mirror.

Becca thought they perfectly reflected each other's look of confusion.

"*Ya*. C.J. is missing. We're all going to search."

Sarah's eyes widened, but instead of asking questions she finished pinning on Becca's *kapp* and grabbed her shawl. They hurried outside, where Jim and Joshua were already waiting next to the van. Joshua caught her hand, squeezed it once, and then opened the back door and helped her and Sarah in. Jim started the van, and they sped off into the darkness.

"Alice thought C.J. was coming home with you and Alton." Jim glanced over at Joshua, who shook his head.

"He told me Charlie was coming back to get him. I thought that sounded a little odd at the time, because we were there and our trailer is right across the street from their home, but..." Joshua stared out the window, and then he seemed to shake himself, pulling his attention back to the people in the van. "I know the boy is close to Charlie, so I let it slide."

"Charlie hasn't seen him," Jim said. "He left early with Quitz and had never agreed to go back out for C.J. The boy told Charlie he was going home when you and Alton left and not to worry."

"Where's Alton?" Sarah asked.

"He said something about night surfing." Joshua scrubbed at his face.

Becca could see his expression in the light of oncoming traffic. He looked tired—weary actually. He also looked scared.

"Do you know who with?" Jim asked.

"Dax and Zach."

"I thought Zach was in jail."

"No. They didn't have enough evidence to hold him on the drug charges. After we ate dinner on the beach, I saw Alton answering a text. When I asked what it was about, he laughed and said not to worry, that they were meeting around eleven once the full moon was high in the sky."

Jim gave one quick nod. It all seemed inconceivably reckless to Becca. She didn't like the idea of catching waves in the daylight, let alone at night. She'd found the courage to wade in the surf up to her knees, but that was as far as she'd managed to go.

They lapsed into silence for the last few miles.

When they reached the FEMA trailer on the beach, Charlie's truck and Alice's car were both out front. Lights blazed from the trailer as well as the outdoor patio. A newer pickup was parked off to the side. Becca had never seen it before.

As they all tumbled from the van, Charlie and Alice rushed toward them.

"We don't have any new information," Jim said. "But everyone wants to help look."

"When did you last see him, Joshua?"

Becca turned to stare at Joshua. He rubbed his right hand up and down his jaw, and then he said, "A few hours ago."

Alice had a blanket wrapped around her shoulders. Though the moon had been shining brightly when Becca had gone to bed, and then a small rain shower had passed through. Now the moon was shining again. Alice's clothes looked damp to Becca. It could be that was why she was shaking, or maybe it was from fear.

"Was that Chevy truck here then?" Jim asked.

"*Nein.*"

Sarah worried her *kapp* strings. "I heard C.J. talking to Alton. C.J. wanted to go with him."

"Surfing?" Alice asked, her voice incredulous.

"*Ya*, but Alton said no, that maybe he could when he was a few years older." Sarah looked as if she didn't want to continue, but finally said, "C.J. insisted he was old enough, but Alton said you'd have both their hides. He told C.J. to hurry to the van before he missed his ride, and then he walked away."

No one said anything for the space of a few breaths as they considered their next move.

Sarah stepped closer to Alice and said, "Alton was preoccupied and not actually giving the boy his attention. I could tell it hurt C.J.'s feelings. I suppose he wanted to be included as one of the grown-ups. It was quite obvious how badly he wanted to go with Alton."

Tears streamed down Alice's face. "Where do you think he went?"

"I'm not sure, but if he's like my *bruders*, he probably tagged along behind Alton without his knowing it."

Jim checked the time on his phone. "All right. It's just after midnight now. Alice, I want you to call the police and update them. Then you wait here. More than likely, C.J. will find his way back to the trailer. Sarah, come with me and we'll head north. Joshua, you and Becca search south. Everyone meet back here in one hour. Charlie, head toward the road with Quitz and look for any signs that C.J. decided to walk home on his own."

Jim walked over to the MDS van to remove a backpack from the luggage area at the back. From that he pulled out flashlights and whistles for each of them. "If you find him, call me on your cell phone and I'll alert the others. If you don't have cell service or don't have a phone, blow the whistle."

Charlie had been quiet up to that point, but now he squared his shoulders and cleared his throat. Finally he held up a hand, as if to stop them all in their tracks. "As we search, we need to pray. God will protect C.J. I'm sure of that. Alice and I will check around this area in case the boy curled up and fell asleep somewhere. Then I'll head to the road."

They all solemnly considered his words for a moment, and then the teams scattered in different directions. Moonlight bounced off the water. The air smelled clean after the light rain shower that had passed through, and the sand was actually easier to walk on because it was packed down.

Becca and Joshua walked close enough that their shoulders were practically touching. Becca said, "The look of fear on Alice's face…it was heartbreaking."

"She's been through a lot," Joshua reminded her. "She's a good grandparent—good parent—to those kids."

They had only walked for a few minutes when Becca made out a group of men walking their way. At first she thought it might be teenagers, on the beach late at night. But then she felt Joshua tense beside her. He'd recognized Alton before she did. From the rigid expression on his face, Becca feared that the night was about to take another turn for the worse.

CHAPTER 56

*J*oshua saw Alton, laughing and joking with his buddies, walking carefree across the sand and carrying his *Englisch* surfboard. Anger flashed through his body, temporarily clouding his vision. He clutched his hands at his side and forced his temper down. He reminded himself of his revelation the week before.

Delight to show mercy.

Even now? Even when a child was missing?

Alton must have realized who was walking toward him, because he stopped in his tracks and the joke he was telling died on his lips.

"What's wrong?" he asked.

"C.J. is missing."

"What? That's not possible—"

"He was last seen talking to you."

Alton dropped the board in the sand and looked left and then right, as if C.J. might pop up out of the surf.

Finally he said, "That was hours ago."

"We know that. What we don't know is where he is now."

"Well, I don't know where he is. He's supposed to be home in bed."

"He's supposed to be, but he's not. Sarah heard him talking to you, begging to come along."

"And I told him no." Alton's voice rose to match his brother's.

"But did you watch him? Did you see where he went next? Did you make sure he didn't follow you?"

312

"The boy isn't my responsibility—"

"He *is*, Alton. We are responsible for one another, or have you forgotten that? Have your *friends* and *fun* blinded you to that?"

Alton shook his head as if to clear it, but Joshua could tell that his words had hit their mark. "We'll look. We'll all look."

"I wish I could help, man, but I have to go." This from Zach, who was sniffling and wearing a shark tooth necklace. He reached down and picked up the board Alton had been using. "I'll take this back to the truck for you."

"Yeah, we have to be at the docks in three hours," Dax said. "We'd help if we could, but—"

Both of Alton's *friends* peeled away.

"Tell me where you've been and what you've been doing."

"Surfing. That's all."

Joshua wanted to accuse him of drinking, wanted to find some reason to yell at his brother, but in fact he seemed sober and appropriately upset at the thought of C.J. missing. Still, he couldn't find it in his heart to soften his tone or attitude toward Alton.

"We'd better go back and tell Alice."

"She's waiting at the trailer," Becca explained. "If no one's found him, she's to call the police and they'll start a formal search."

Instead of defending himself any further, Alton rushed ahead of them toward the trailer. His two friends were already piling into the truck, but Alton stopped them, ran to the back, and climbed up into it, searching frantically.

"Joshua, bring your flashlight, please."

Joshua and Becca hurried to where he was standing in the bed of the truck. By this point, Alice was walking toward them, her arms clutched around her middle, forming a protective barrier against any bad news.

"It's not here," Alton murmured, moving back toward the cab of the truck and looking between each surfboard inside. He stopped long enough to holler at the guys in the truck. "Dax, come out here!"

"What are you looking for, dude?" Dax sounded groggy, as if he was already half asleep. He'd been about to start the truck, but now he got out and joined Alton.

Joshua moved toward the driver's side of the truck, reached in, and pulled out the keys. He didn't want this group leaving until the police had arrived. Perhaps they knew something, something they weren't sharing. He didn't think they would have hurt C.J., but they may have seen more than they had so far admitted.

"The boogie board," Alton said. "It was here when we left."

"Was it?" Dax scratched at the back of his neck.

"Yes, it was." Alton turned to Joshua, Becca, and Alice, who were all now standing beside the truck. "C.J. did ask to go with me, Alice. I told him no, that you would be expecting him at home, and he said he was old enough to stay out later."

Alton shook his head, a look of pure grief covering his features. "You were right, Joshua. I should have walked him to the van. I...I was in a hurry. I was worried I'd miss the best part of the waves."

When he glanced up at Alice again, a resolve had settled over his features. "He probably took the boogie board and walked down the beach. We'll find him."

"Hey, man. I have to—" Zach stopped midsentence when Alton turned on him.

"We'll find him. We'll all look. With *everyone* searching."

"He's been gone for hours," Joshua reminded him. Becca reached out and touched his arm, nodding her head toward Alice, who had slid down onto the ground and was leaning against the truck.

"Alice, are you all right?"

"Just...couldn't..." She gulped and tried again. "My legs just gave out. What if...what if he took that board out into the ocean? What if C.J. is out there in the waves, in the darkness?"

Alton jumped out of the truck and knelt down in front of Alice. "He wouldn't do anything that reckless. C.J. is smarter than that. He may be stubborn, and he was certainly angry with me, but he wouldn't do anything as foolish as to try and night surf alone. We will find him, Alice."

Zach and Dax had climbed back into the truck, but Alton literally pulled them out, giving them directions, telling them to look in the sand for small footprints and the trail of a boogie board being drug beside a small boy.

They had just begun to set out, when the night was split by a shrill whistle, coming from the direction that Jim and Sarah had gone. For one moment they all stared at one another, and then they began to run.

CHAPTER 57

Charlie had walked several yards down the road and turned back when he heard one of Jim's whistles pierce the night.

Quitz barked and began to prance about.

"That's coming from the north," he said to the dog. "We'd best see what they found."

Instead of fearing the worst, envisioning the worst, he prayed as they hurried toward the sound. Though it was still quite dark, he saw the light from flashlights bouncing from the direction of the FEMA trailer. Toward the north he could now make out the dying embers of a bonfire. As he drew closer to what he thought was Jim and Sarah, he saw a tight circle of people, more than he would have ever guessed to be up at such an hour.

Quitz broke from his side with a yelp and dove into the middle of the group of folks. Charlie peered into the shadows and caught sight of Alice, her eyes wide with hope. When Quitz reached the middle of the group, Charlie heard a sound that brought pure delight to his heart—the sound of C.J.'s voice.

"Hey, girl. I'm okay. I'm okay now."

Someone had thrown another piece of driftwood on the fire and it blazed high, lighting the small group in its glow. Jim stepped back, a smile spreading across his face. "Quitz must have been every bit as worried as we were. She's acting as if she hasn't seen C.J. in a month."

The group loosened up, and Alice walked through it to her grandson, knelt in the sand, and pulled him into her arms. The boy's face was streaked with tears, and Charlie noticed that his swim trunks were wet. He was shivering in the coolness of the evening. Someone had draped an old beach towel around his shoulders. Lying on the sand next to him was a boogie board.

Alice didn't say anything. She didn't admonish him or tell him how worried everyone was. She didn't ask where he'd been or what he'd been thinking. She simply put her arms around him and allowed her tears to flow.

One of the young men pulled away from the group, tugging a girl by the hand and walking toward Charlie. "Evening, Mr. Everman."

Recognition dawned on Charlie—the boy was Spider Nix, who always sat at the back of his senior English class, flirting with girls or sleeping whenever he thought he could get away with it. Not a bad kid—just a kid who didn't understand what Shakespeare had to do with his life.

"Is the boy your grandson?" Spider asked.

Alice and C.J. glanced up, and Charlie nodded. "You could say that."

Spider pulled Charlie back away from the group. "He's a little cold and a little scared. Other than that, I think he's fine."

And then Spider tugged on the hand of the dark-skinned girl, pulling her close to his side. "Janice, meet Charlie Everman, the best teacher I had in high school."

"Pleased to meet you..." Charlie said.

"Janice. Janice Cooper."

She held out a slim brown hand to shake his, and Charlie was struck by a long-lost memory from what seemed like a hundred years ago. He and Madelyn were taking their first evening walk on the beach. They were reveling in a new life together, a life beginning in a strange and beautiful place.

"We heard the boy in the waves," Spider explained. "He wasn't out too far, but he'd become disoriented and was paddling the wrong direction. Somehow, he must have then seen our bonfire, and he started to holler for help."

"Spider went in and hauled him out," Janice said.

"You did that?" Joshua had been watching Spider, and now he walked over to where they stood. "You went in and saved him?"

"It wasn't that big of a deal."

"It was. It is." Joshua stared up at the sky and then down at the ground. Finally, he held out his hand. "I misjudged you when I shouldn't have judged you at all. I'm sorry."

Spider shook and said, "No problem."

"You two know each other?"

"You could say that. I've been trying to teach his brother to surf."

"And tonight?" Joshua asked.

"No. I don't do the night surfing..." He glanced over at Alton and started to say something else, but he seemed to changed his mind. "After we'd brought him in, the boy was cold and scared and didn't want to tell us his name. We had a feeling that maybe he was in trouble."

"I suppose he was," Charlie said. "But now Alice is so happy to see him she'll probably make him his favorite meal."

"Can't hurt to feed and spoil him a little," Jim said, walking up to them and shaking hands with Spider and Janice. "I don't think C.J. will be trying another stunt like that for quite a while."

Charlie tried to remain focused on what Jim and Spider and Janice were saying, but instead his attention followed the four Amish kids—adults, really—who had separated from the group and were walking back toward the FEMA trailer. Joshua and both girls were walking together. Alton maintained a few feet of distance between them, and when one of the girls—Becca, if he could make her out correctly—called to him, Alton only shook his head and waved them on.

Was Alton blaming himself for what had happened?

C.J. was not his responsibility, but Charlie realized that the Amish took their obligation to family and friends seriously. Alton had never struck him as a bad kid, only an immature one. It seemed to Charlie, as he walked with Alice and C.J. and Quitz and Jim back toward their vehicles, that sometimes a dire event could mature a person overnight. Other times the person fled back into their childhood.

Which way would Alton go?

Because they were leaving the next week, Charlie might never know. But he could pray. That was one thing he'd learned over the years. Even during situations where he wouldn't likely learn the results of a certain thing, he could still pray. He could entrust that young man to God, even as he walked alone down the beach in the darkness of the night. In the same way he had entrusted C.J. to God, he could also leave Alton in His care.

Charlie realized in that moment that faith was not something you had or didn't have, like brown eyes or curly hair. Faith was something you chose—an outlook on life, a way of dealing with each day's joys and disasters. He vowed then that before he went to sleep, he would get down on his old creaky knees and thank the Lord for another day, for a ten-year-old boy who was safe in his home, and for his Amish friends—that they might find the path God had chosen for them.

CHAPTER 58

*B*ecca felt as if the next week passed in a blur.

They nearly finished work on the second house.

Alice and the kids were completely settled in, and C.J. was no worse for his mishap at the beach.

Jim invited them all back to work on future projects.

Joshua and Sarah both confessed to missing home at the same time that they hated to leave.

As for Alton, he seemed to have sunk deep into his own thoughts. At one time or another, they had each gone to him and assured him that what had happened wasn't his fault. But Alton was carrying the burden of C.J.'s disappearance on his shoulders, or perhaps he was carrying the weight of all his poor decisions there.

Becca was worried about him. She'd never had a younger brother, but it seemed as though Alton was just that. It hurt her to see him struggling.

Charlie reminded them to pray, and Joshua assured her that eventually everything would be fine. But even as he said it she saw the doubt in his eyes.

Their mood was subdued as they rode in the van, crossed over the water on the ferry, and then climbed onto the bus that would take them home. Only Nancy seemed the same, a port in the storm for sure and for certain.

She rounded everyone up under her wings, intent on seeing that they were safely on the bus back to Cody's Creek.

Alton slept most of the way... or pretended to.

Joshua studied a copy of the *Budget* Nancy had somehow found.

Becca tried to read. She was surprised she hadn't finished the book Rebecca Byler had given her. When had it ever taken three weeks for her to read a single book? She glanced again at the title, and then she tucked it into her bag. No doubt the story would make for good reading once she was home and back in her old routine.

When they traded buses in Dallas, Alton didn't even look at the street vendors. He walked straight to the new bus, found a seat, and pulled his ball cap down over his eyes.

"Is he sulking?" she asked.

"He's polite enough, but I think he's having trouble sleeping." Joshua handed her a soda and a hot dog, same as the last time they had stopped in Dallas. "He stayed up most of last night, sitting out on the patio."

"Still worried about C.J.?" Sarah asked. She'd opted for an ice cream cone and nothing more.

"I'm not sure. I think... I think maybe he's reassessing a few things. When I try to talk to him, he only shakes his head and walks away. I'm learning that sometime my *bruder* needs to work things out on his own." He reached for Becca's hand as they climbed aboard the bus.

By nightfall they would be home.

She felt incredibly eager to see her parents. She was amazed at how much she had missed them.

Becca waited until the bus had pulled out of the Dallas area, until the traffic was behind them and it seemed that Joshua and Alton were asleep. Then she turned to Sarah.

"I want you to promise me that if you have any trouble at home, anything at all, you will tell me."

"But what—"

"I don't know what I could do. I honestly don't know what anyone can do, but I do know that you aren't going to endure your situation alone any longer. We're *freinden* now. Right?"

Sarah nodded, wound her arm through Becca's, and stared out the window. It was the closest thing Becca was going to get to a promise, but it was enough. After living together for three weeks, a bond had developed between them now. Becca didn't know how to solve any of the problems Sarah would face, but she heard Charlie's voice softly reminding her to pray.

The trip home passed faster than she could have imagined, the miles unwinding until they were once again crossing over into Oklahoma, passing McAlester, and driving through familiar terrain.

When they reached Cody's Creek, a small group of folks were waiting at the bus stop.

Becca practically flew into her parents' arms.

She heard them telling her about a new foal and asking if she was ready to build a new addition to her father's workshop. She heard all these things and smiled at their teasing, but her attention was on her friends.

Alton and Joshua were greeted by their father, who clapped both of them on the back as they walked toward their buggy. Joshua said something to his father, and then hurried back in Becca's direction.

When he stopped in front of her and her parents, he took off his hat and fidgeted with it in his hands. Then he looked her father in the eye and said, "I'd like to take Becca to the singing Sunday if that's all right with you."

Becca wanted to melt into the ground. She also wanted to throw her arms around Joshua's neck.

Instead, she stood there, unable to say a word as her father shook Joshua's hand and assured him that would be fine, provided she felt up to going after their long trip and that she wanted to accompany him to the Sunday evening social.

"*Ya*. I do." She couldn't help smiling as Joshua walked back toward his family.

But as she climbed into her parents' buggy, it was Sarah that Becca watched. Sarah's mother seemed to be talking animatedly about something, and several young boys clung to her skirts asking her questions.

Her dad wasn't there, but perhaps he was busy in the fields. Though it was sunset, a farmer's day often extended into the early evening hours.

Sarah glanced her way once, and Becca waved.

When Sarah waved in return, Becca felt a certainty that her new friend would remain her friend regardless of what their futures held.

CHAPTER 59

Four weeks later

*J*oshua snagged Becca's hand as they walked through corn grown
waist high in his father's southern field. The Oklahoma sun was
setting slowly and a light breeze helped to dissipate the summer heat.

"I had a letter from Alice today." Becca stopped to pull a wildflower
from between two rows of corn. "C.J. has enrolled in a lifeguard class."

"Isn't he a bit young?"

"He turned eleven last week." Becca twirled the yellow-and-red
bloom—an Indian blanket flower—in her fingers. "Alice seems
happy about it."

"I'm sure she is, and I'm glad he's not afraid of the ocean after his
ordeal. That would have been a hard thing, considering they live on
an island."

"He told Alice he wants to *understand* the ocean."

Joshua nodded. "He's a smart one. I wouldn't be surprised if he
chose a profession where he works near or in the ocean."

"He's also going to a summer camp on marine conservation."

"And how is Shelley?"

"*Gut*. Fewer nightmares about the storm."

They walked for a few moments without talking, each lost in their
thoughts of friends on the Texas coast.

"Oh. I almost forgot." Becca tucked a stray hair into her *kapp*. "Charlie has decided to purchase the lot next to Alice and build a house there. He says he's too old to be living on the beach, but Alice thinks he wants to be near the kids."

"And close to her. Alice is like the daughter Charlie never had."

"I wonder if he regrets that."

"Not having children?" Joshua pulled off his hat and then resettled it on his head. "I suppose he and his wife tried. Charlie seems to be good at accepting the circumstances God gave him."

"Yeah. I miss him." Becca laughed. "I never thought I'd say that about an *Englischer*. I never thought I'd feel so close to someone who is so different from us."

"I'm not sure Charlie is so different from us. If there's one thing that I learned on our mission trip, it's that people are basically the same." When Becca looked at him quizzically, he pulled her over to the picnic table, the one where Levi had first spoken to him about going on the mission trip. The idea had seemed so ludicrous to him at the time. Why was that?

Joshua shook his head and laced his fingers with Becca's. "Don't you agree? That we're all basically the same?"

"But our lives are so different. Some days it seems as if those weeks at the coast are something from a dream."

"*Ya*. South Texas is certainly quite different from Oklahoma." Joshua stared out over the crops, the sun setting in a riotous display of color, and finally at the beautiful woman sitting next to him. "But people are born and die, they laugh and love, they cry and mourn the same. Whether we're Amish or Methodist or Presbyterian, we experience the same things. I'm not sure how much denomination or location matters to *Gotte*."

"Don't let some of our elders hear you say that, Joshua Kline. They'll think you need to attend the new member class again."

Joshua laughed. "Indeed. Your parents though, they understand."

"As do yours."

Silence fell around them like an old jacket worn on a summer night. His life felt so right and so good. All except for his brother, whose future resembled a giant question mark without an answer.

"Has Alton made any decisions?"

"Not that he's shared with me. He's quieter now. Changed after what happened with C.J. I think he realizes that the child could have died out there, and though it wouldn't have technically been his fault, he would have felt as if it was."

"It could have happened, but it didn't," Becca insisted. "He should move on. Before he was too carefree. Now it seems as if he's carrying the weight of the world on his shoulders. I worry about him."

Joshua marveled that Becca was able to put his own emotions into words. She knew him that well, and she was certainly better at expressing herself. "I worry too, but Levi says to give him time."

"*Daddi* has the patience of a saint."

He stood, pulled Becca to her feet, and allowed himself one fleeting kiss. She tasted like strawberries and sunshine. She tasted like the love of his life.

As they started back toward the house, Becca said, "We began sewing my wedding dress today."

"Did you now?"

"Only two more weeks and we'll be wed, Joshua. Everything keeps changing so fast that I can't seem to keep up. If our lives were written into the pages of a book, I'd say it was impossible to believe. Life can't change that quickly."

"And yet it has."

"*Ya.*"

"And I, for one, am grateful."

Instead of answering, Becca walked even closer, until they were shoulder to shoulder, hand in hand. In the fading light, Joshua could see the outline of their house. They had begun framing it. There was still much work to do, but it would be ready when they needed it. If not the day they were married, then soon after.

He didn't know what winter would bring. Whether they would need to again change the crops. Whether he could support a family as a farmer. He tried not to dwell on such things. *Gotte* knew what the future held. Joshua suddenly recalled a Scripture Levi had quoted on Sunday, something about God opening the floodgates of heaven and pouring out an abundance of blessings. As they walked toward his parents' home, toward their future, Joshua had no trouble believing that whatever lay ahead, they could face it together.

EPILOGUE

Seven months later

Watching the January wind blow across the prairie.

Walking from a country road to a small-town bus station.

Riding seven hundred miles south.

Looking for the MDS van and then boarding the ferry.

Enjoying the short trip across the bay.

Charlie could envision each leg of Alton's trip, and he prayed for the boy as he worked laying sod around his new house. It was a small house and a small yard, but he wanted Shelley and C.J. to have the extra place to play—children needed a yard to enjoy. Because his house was next door to Alice's, the kids had twice the space.

Quitz lay in the sun watching him and waiting. The old girl had trouble rising to her feet now, but she remained faithful in spite of the fact that her body was wearing out. Charlie told himself it was a natural thing. He and Madelyn had named her Quitz because she was to be the last one, but he had his eye on a medium-sized pup down at the animal shelter. C.J. and Shelley had suffered enough loss. He wanted to prepare them for Quitz's eventual passing, and a new pup might be just the ticket. Not to mention there was a possibility that it would perk up Quitz. Nothing like being around the young to encourage the old.

The MDS van pulled into his driveway, and Charlie stood and

dusted his hands off on his jeans. Alton popped out of the van, wearing a huge grin and his traditional Amish clothing. There were pats on the back and exclamations over Charlie's home, and then Charlie promised they would make it to Jim's for dinner. It was the beginning of a new mission week. They would be joining with Mennonites from Ohio and Amish from Pennsylvania. Working alongside the Methodists and Baptists, it looked as if they might be able to finish another three houses in the next few weeks.

Alton squatted beside Quitz. He turned a worried gaze to Charlie.

"She's all right. She just has a little trouble standing." He moved behind the dog and helped her to her feet. "Once she's up she can move pretty good, and we're starting new meds from the vet that should help with the hip dysplasia."

"Still thinking about the pup?"

"I am. Thought we might go by and see it tomorrow afternoon if you have any energy left after framing a house all day."

Alton nodded, and Charlie thought he detected a degree of satisfaction in his attitude.

"Your house looks good."

"It's pretty much the same floor plan as Rodney and Jalynn's. I thought single story was a good idea, given my age."

"MDS built it?"

"They did. I wanted to hire builders, but I couldn't find any. Workers are in high demand around here. The only construction firms that would even talk to me said it would be eighteen months before they could get to it."

Alton let out a long whistle. "Another year and a half in a FEMA Urban Disaster Trailer? Did you tell them no thanks?"

"I did. Then I talked to Jim. We came up with a compromise. I paid for supplies and made a large donation to MDS to cover the labor. One of his crews put my house together in no time."

Alton squinted at the home. "It looks like they did a fine job."

"Want to walk down the street? I can show you the other sites."

"Can Quitz make it that far?"

"Sure she can. In fact, walking is good for her."

Quitz nuzzled his hand and the three set off toward the end of the street.

"The neighborhood is coming together nicely." Alton glanced back over his shoulder. "I particularly like the attic windows on your place."

"It's mostly storage space, but I finished a portion of the east side so the kids could play up there on rainy days."

"They are lucky to have you, Charlie."

"I'm lucky to have them. I didn't realize that until Orion came through and turned our lives upside down."

They walked the rest of the way in silence. When they finally stopped in front of three slabs of concrete, Alton took off his hat and scratched his head. "Foundation looks *gut*."

"Poured last week."

"I worried you might be done rebuilding before I could make it back."

"Nope. In fact, Jim says we have enough projects and funds to last at least another two years."

Alton studied him a minute, and then he nodded toward the foundations. "Who are these homes for?"

"This one is for a couple in their thirties—no kids yet. As you know, MDS selects the most critical needs first. So I suppose we're on tier two now—folks who contribute to the infrastructure of the island but don't have young ones or older parents to care for. Helping them is important, but they could continue commuting from the mainland as long as they need to."

"So how do Mr. and Mrs.—" Alton stepped back and read the number painted on the curb. "Six Forty-Five Sea Side contribute to the island?"

"Teachers." Charlie sighed. "We've had quite the teacher shortage the last year. Enrollment is down more than twenty percent, but even so there are not enough teachers. Some moved on. The ones who stayed take more time off than they have—without pay—so they can work on their home. We'll be providing the Tuckers a real service."

"And those two?" Alton studied the other two foundations.

"Gabby and Sam Story. She is a waitress who works with Alice. Her husband, Sam, works on the grounds crew out at the state park."

They continued down the street until they reached the last foundation. "This home is for Michelle Baker. She works at the animal shelter. Nice lady in her thirties. I'm surprised she's staying, but she says she loves the island and loves her job."

"All good people."

"Yes, and all in need of our help."

They turned and walked back toward Charlie's. By the time they had reached his place, Alice had pulled up into her driveway. C.J. tumbled out of the car and launched himself at Alton. Shelley walked over to check on Quitz. Once she was sure the old dog was doing fine, she ran to Alton and threw her arms around his neck.

"I've missed that young man," Alice said.

"That makes two of us."

The kids finally went inside to work on their homework, but only after they had been assured Alton wasn't going anywhere. Charlie took Alton inside his home and showed him the spare bedroom where he'd be staying.

"This is a little nicer than a FEMA trailer," Alton said.

"I'm glad you think so."

Charlie made sure Quitz had food and water before he settled her in her crate. Though she still followed Charlie throughout the day, he made sure she was bedded down early in the evening.

It wasn't until they were in Charlie's truck that Alton opened up and began talking about his time at home—telling of the farmwork, his family, and the questions he'd been battling.

"We were worried you might be blaming yourself for C.J.'s accident."

"But I was to blame."

"No. I don't think so. C.J. has a stubborn streak wider than Mustang Island, and he needs to learn to control that."

Alton seemed to consider his words, something he hadn't been in the habit of doing on his first visit. Back then, Alton would smile at you, and you knew—were absolutely certain—that he was politely waiting for you to finish so he could go ahead and do what he had planned.

But something had changed. Perhaps he'd matured during the Oklahoma winter. Maybe he'd learned that he didn't have all the answers. Charlie knew from experience that the moment you realized that, a whole new world of possibilities opened up.

Charlie pulled to a stop in front of Jim's FEMA trailer, but Alton made no move to leave the vehicle. Instead, he stared out the windshield at the light rain that had begun to fall.

"I didn't want to come, you know. Last May, when Joshua told me about his plan, I had to fight the urge to scream at him and everyone else. I wanted to tell them it was my life and I could do what I wanted with it. I wanted to tell them if I chose to waste my life, it was my business, not theirs."

Charlie didn't interrupt. He'd counseled enough teens to recognize an important moment when he saw one. Alton wasn't so much explaining his decisions to Charlie as he was to himself.

"I was Joshua's mission, not…this." He waved toward Jim's home. "He'd never even considered doing something with MDS before. He did it because he thought it would save me. He thought it would turn my life around."

"And did it?"

Alton ran his right hand up and down his jaw. "It almost didn't. Even when I was here, when I saw the destruction and the need, I didn't see how it related to me personally. I could help for a few weeks, but what difference would it make in the long run? Another storm could come along tomorrow and blow it all away again."

"Yes, it could." The same thought passed through Charlie's mind at least once a day.

"It was the night with C.J. that changed everything. The way he looked up to me was kind of embarrassing and kind of flattering, but I didn't take it seriously. When he almost…when he almost drowned,

I understood that I have a responsibility to him even if we aren't related. I have a responsibility to him because *Gotte* has brought us into each other's life."

"So you had an epiphany."

Alton shrugged, and when he turned to look at Charlie, his expression was a combination of the old fun-loving, carefree Alton and the newer, more serious young man. "I don't know. Maybe. I do understand now that life is a gift."

Charlie nodded. "Some people never realize that."

Alton reached for the door handle. They walked up to Jim's trailer, not minding the mist that dampened their hair and clothes. Charlie took a deep breath full of air straight from the Gulf of Mexico. He could hear the waves from where they stood. He could practically taste the salt on his skin.

The amount of loss he'd endured in his life…Some days it felt as if he could fill the ocean with his tears and hurt and grief. But most days now he had the same thought that Alton did, that life was a gift.

DISCUSSION QUESTIONS

1. In chapter one we meet Charlie Everman. Charlie's wife warned him that "the world doesn't stand still, and you wouldn't want it to." Charlie thinks that perhaps he would like for it to. When we're in a place of profound grief, what specific Scripture verses can comfort us?

2. In chapter eight, Becca and her mother discuss the differences in Amish communities. Suzie says, "We read the same Bible and share the same faith, but the details we perceive vary." What differences are you aware of that exist between Amish communities? What differences exist between your church and other churches in your town? How can believers work together to be the body of Christ in spite of these differences?

3. As Hurricane Orion bears down on Port Aransas, Charlie stops to help several different families. Is this wise or foolish? Read Matthew 25:31-46. How can we minister to "the least of these" on a daily basis?

4. Alton's parents are scared and worried, but they don't seem particularly angry. Daniel tells Joshua that "We all have those days of questioning. For your brother, those days came a little later and lasted a bit longer." What do you think of this compassionate attitude? Is it biblical? Why or why not?

5. Becca's Aunt Nancy regularly volunteers with MDS. She tells Becca that "even when we have limited resources to contribute, we can donate our time and our talents." Do you agree with that? Why or why not? List types of mission work that someone could do in your area, even if they had limited financial resources.

6. When Charlie gives his testimony to the group of volunteers, he begins by quoting the third chapter of Ecclesiastes. Open your Bible to this passage and read it. Then discuss how the sentiment expressed there applies to us today. Is it still relevant to our life and our faith or simply beautiful words written a long time ago?

7. Joshua experiences God's call on his heart when the group attends Jim's church. He believes that God is calling him to "delight to show mercy." He understands that he has not shown Christian love toward his brother. When we have a situation which causes us to withhold mercy from one another, what things can we do to "make it right?"

8. After C.J. is found, Alton blames himself. Charlie believes "sometimes a dire event could mature a person overnight. Other times the person fled back into their childhood." Has this ever happened to you? Has God used difficult circumstances to bring you to a new level of maturity in Christ?

9. Joshua makes the decision to not worry about the future. He is certain that God knows our future, and He has blessings planned for us. What areas of your life do you worry about the most? What could help you release that worry and trust that God will care for you?

10. Alton finally realizes that he was Joshua's mission, not the work for MDS. What does the Bible tell us about caring for one another? What are some practical ways that we can support one another?

AUTHOR'S NOTE

Mustang Island has not experienced a major hurricane since 1970. The book *1919: The Storm: A Narrative and Photographic History* by Murphy Givens and Jim Moloney provides a thorough history of the island, as does *Images of America: Port Aransas* by J. Guthrie Ford and Mark Creighton. The Port Aransas Museum is also a treasure trove of information and can be accessed at http://portaransasmuseum.org.

Information about Mennonite Disaster Service can be found at http://mds.mennonite.net/home. Their stated mission is as follows: "Mennonite Disaster Service is a volunteer network of Anabaptist churches that responds in Christian love to those affected by disasters in Canada and the United States." You can donate to MDS at https://mds.mennonite.net/donate.

FEMA trailers provided in the aftermath of Hurricane Katrina and Hurricane Rita were purportedly plagued with problems, most especially the presence of formaldehyde. The Urban Disaster Trailers described in this book are a prototype that has been tested in New York City. At the time of this writing, they have not yet been used in a major disaster.

The town of Cody's Creek does not exist in Oklahoma. The place I visited and researched was Chouteau, which was originally called Cody's Creek when it became a stop on the Katy Railroad in 1871. The Amish community in Chouteau does allow the use of tractors, both in the fields and in town. They still use the horse and buggy when traveling to church, weddings, or funerals.

GLOSSARY

Aenti—aunt
Bruder—brother
Daddi—grandfather
Dat—father
Danki—thank you
Englischer—non-Amish person
Freinden—friends
Gotte's wille—God's will
Grandkinner—grandchildren
Gudemariye—good morning
Gut—good
Kapp—prayer covering
Kind—child
Kinner—children
Mamm—mom
Mammi—grandmother
Nein—no
Ordnung—the unwritten set of rules and regulations that guide everyday Amish life.
Rumspringa—running around; time before an Amish young person has officially joined the church, provides a bridge between childhood and adulthood.
Schweschder—sister
Wunderbaar—wonderful
Ya—yes
Youngies—young adults

ABOUT THE AUTHOR

 **Vannetta Chapman** writes inspirational fiction full of grace. She has published more than one hundred articles in Christian family magazines, receiving more than two dozen awards from Romance Writers of America chapter groups. She discovered her love for the Amish while researching her grandfather's birthplace of Albion, Pennsylvania. Her novel *Falling to Pieces* was a 2012 ACFW Carol Award winner. *A Promise for Miriam* earned a spot on the June 2012 Christian Retailing Top Ten Fiction list. Vannetta was a teacher for 15 years and currently writes full time. She lives in the Texas hill country with her husband. For more information, visit her at www.VannettaChapman.com

Fall in Love with the Amish of Pebble Creek!

A Promise for Miriam, A Home for Lydia, and *A Wedding for Julia* introduce the Amish community of Pebble Creek, Wisconsin, and the kind, caring people there. As they face challenges to their community from the English world, they come together to reach out to their non-Amish neighbors while still preserving their cherished Plain ways.

Enjoy These *Free* Short Story E-Romances
Download Them Today from Your Favorite Digital Retailer!

These two short story e-romances are an exclusive bonus from the Pebble Creek Amish by Vannetta Chapman. Fans of the series will enjoy this chance to briefly revisit Pebble Creek, and new readers will be introduced to an Amish community that is more deeply explored in the three full novels.

To learn more about Harvest House books and
to read sample chapters, visit our website:

www.harvesthousepublishers.com

HARVEST HOUSE PUBLISHERS
EUGENE, OREGON

2/16